D1607876

The Good Lawyer

A Novel

by

Thomas Benigno

Inspired By A True Story

Landview Books

Published by Landview Books Second Edition, January 2013

ISBN: 1463604815
ISBN 13: 9781463604813 (paperback)

Cover design by Nathan Wampler

Also by Thomas Benigno

The Criminal Lawyer
&
The Criminal Mind

For Angie

"long after…"

"If there were no bad people, there would be no good lawyers."

Charles Dickens

This novel is inspired by a true story.

ACKNOWLEDGEMENTS

I have much to be grateful for and many to be grateful to. This is a first novel. In many respects it is a product of all who have influenced me, good and bad. It is sometimes autobiographical, but if you ask me in person, I will seldom admit it. I have a beautiful mother, like Nick Mannino. To no one more do I owe the sense of decency that guides me, though precariously at times, and for better or worse through this grand scheme of life. Also, there would be no lawyer in me if not for the encouragement (urging) of my stepfather (father), John Benigno (d.1976). I wish I patiently appreciated him more back when. To my children, who drive me crazy from time to time, and I them for sure (does it surprise anyone that one who works on a book for many years is somewhat out of the norm): you are my pure prizes—intelligent, tough, and soft of heart. Thanks for putting up with me. I love you madly and deeply.

To James and Kathleen Gurrieri, for a lifetime of friendship, and encouragement and support. To my old friend, Gil Clancy, I will always miss you. To Ron and Sue Ross, for their constant encouragement. To the Benigno and Vasquez families, one and all. To my rediscovered Castagna Family in and around Syracuse, New York. How wonderful to have found you. Your kindness and love have been a cleansing. To the true characters that helped mold the pages of this book and enhance the story line with their integrity and high ideals: the Honorable Alice Schlesinger, the Honorable Joel Blumenfeld, Barry Scheck, all the attorneys of Complex C (1979-1984). To my content editors Mike Shain and Jeff Kellogg, and to my newly ordained copy editor, Jonathan Baker: the novel would read nothing like it does if not for your skill and support. For the affection and encouragement of all my family, friends and clients. You know who you are—my heartfelt thanks.

And finally, to my wife, Angie, my partner through every page and the thousands lost in countless drafts. You made this possible through your patience, devotion and love. This novel you well know is from a heart—that was and will be—always yours.

Long Island, New York
January 2, 2013

CONTENTS

In the end it was her virginity that would do her in.
Late afternoon, December 24, 1981.

A verdict was reached a mere thirty minutes after deliberations had begun. Were Christmas not less than a day away, I would have figured it for a courthouse record.

Just two-and-a-half years out of law school, this was my seventh trial and, I was hoping, my seventh victory. As I waited in the lingering quiet of the courtroom, a virulent chill penetrated the bleak walnut paneled walls, and my eyes locked on the man sitting next to me. Like the bust of a philistine, head held high, his smug expression never wavered, even when he refused probation and sixty days in jail to face trial and a mandatory eight-and-a-third years in state prison. His folded hands rested firmly on the defense table not far from mine. Our flesh tones nearly identical, I was reminded, once again, that we were both Italian American.

Angelo Bonagura made a dashing figure in his brown disco suit and white lapel shirt as he picked up Dina Rios outside a party in the Pelham section of The Bronx. A local boy, his Travolta look was hampered only by a thick mustache that made him look older than his twenty-one years. His ride—a shiny new Trans Am. Dina had just turned eighteen. She accepted this stranger's offer to take her home.

When he started to drink in sloppy gulps from a pint bottle of rye, she asked him to pull over. He ignored her and pulled behind a trailer in the deserted parking lot of an A&P. After popping down the front passenger bucket seat, he turned Dina on her stomach, yanked down her jeans, and raped her.

When she took the stand to testify, I reassessed the jury I had carefully selected with the limited peremptory challenges at my disposal. Three were Italian-American. One, a heavyset elderly woman with a cheerful smile and thin shadow of a mustache, couldn't stop smiling at me while she and the other jurors filed in.

As the panel of four women and eight men struggled to get comfortable in their seats, the Assistant District Attorney, his head rigid, eyes staring straight ahead, ignored their entrance. This was his third felony trial. The fingers of his right hand unmasked his nervousness as they fiddled with an evidence bag containing the victim's panties. "Let's Party" was emblazoned in silver script across the backside. An adjacent manila folder contained the police reports with the entry: "The complainant suffered no discernible physical injuries." There were no cuts, no bruises, and no blood, though Dina Rios testified that she was a virgin when she was raped. She failed to add that she had lost her cherry years earlier in a car accident. That she refused to tell her parents or report the rape to the police for over a week didn't further her cause.

Her parents, natives of Puerto Rico, sat vigilantly behind the railed balustrade in the second row of the courtroom, clutching their daughter seated between them. Years of working in the hot sun were scalded into every deep line on her father's chiseled complexion. Her mother's skin was a creamy white. At forty-five years she was even more beautiful than her daughter, and the daughter was quite beautiful. When the judge addressed the jury, I peeked at the young girl's anxious eyes one last time.

The foreman, a tall man in his fifties, with cropped gray hair and a forehead gleaming with perspiration, loudly read the verdict: "On all counts . . . not guilty."

The defendant lunged out of his chair, hands high in victory. The judge promptly ordered him to be seated. Muffled sobs emanated from the mother and daughter. I dared not look back, and quickly moved to have the record sealed.

The clerk, a Bronx Courthouse elder seated at a desk beside a wall of dingy oversized casement windows, stamped the court papers with callous ease. I reflexively stiffened as my guilty client hugged me. When he let go my entire body shuddered as the young girl burst forth with an agonizing wail: "He raped me! Rot in hell! Rot in hell, you bastard!" She was writhing on the courtroom floor, punching and kicking the dingy parquet wildly. The jury stood agape as she then jumped up, hurdled the balustrade, and raced past me.

I grabbed my client while his mother hunkered nearby, crying and *hiding her face in her hands. I jostled them both toward the courtroom doors until they slammed into me and the mother's thick heel tore into my shoe. I threw my head back and shut my eyes as a stabbing pain coursed through me. But Dina Rios had already scaled the clerk's hardwood desk and without so much as a momentary pause, a glimmer of consideration, jerked open the nearest casement window and leapt into a blistering snow-fall three stories high.*

She landed head first on the hood of a parked New York City police car. When her broken body finally lay still, she was face up on the sidewalk, arms outstretched, legs straight—a perverse crucifix image of suffering and forgiveness in a blanket of white and red.

Outside the courthouse, at the bottom of the sloping stone steps that led from the Supreme Court doors, my client was full of thanks and praise. I weakly shook his hand. His mother kissed me, said something in Italian I didn't understand, then caressed my face with a small, clammy hand. Snowflakes settled on my shoulders and hair. The murmuring of a gathering crowd and the squawking of several police car radios could be heard a half-block away as an ambulance screeched past us, splattering the slush on 161st Street in all directions.

One hour later, alone in my office, with the wind howling outside and the snow continuing to fall, I could still hear the young girl's screams.

I wept quietly into my hands.

Chapter 1

Two months after the suicide of Dina Rios, I was on my way to my first night arraignment since the trial. I thought I had finally put it all behind me. But I was young, and I was wrong.

The Bronx Criminal Courthouse, a four-story concrete block building, occupied the entire block along 161st Street between Sherman and Sheridan Avenues in the apoplectic heart of the South Bronx. Across Sheridan, murky brown two-story mixed-use buildings lined the block. Their burnt red brick belied their busy retail storefronts with overhead apartments converted to office space, occupied almost entirely by criminal defense lawyers—private practitioners on court-appointed lists anxiously awaiting the court clerk's call, or a walk-in with a wad of cash and an ATM card with easy access to next month's rent.

On the other side of the Courthouse, across Sherman, was a parking lot reserved for municipal employees. Judges and Assistant District Attorneys parked in a secured lot under the building.

Across 161st Street, a vacant lot leveled by the winter's dead weeds encompassed an entire city block. On its corner sat the wreckage of an abandoned diner, its metallic shine lost to decades of urban blight and indifference, its interior only partly visible through twisted metal net shutters.

Inside the Courthouse, a cold hard floor led to a short set of descending stairs. Straight ahead, were two standard department store escalators—the "up" and "down" just a handshake away in the center of a coal-colored marble floor.

I squeezed past fifty or sixty people gathered outside the locked courtroom doors of AR 1 and hurried into the clerk's office. Mine was a familiar face and no one questioned my passage. After stepping through a maze of desks, filing cabinets and court personnel, I pushed through the back door and entered the rear left corner of the courtroom.

Three Legal Aid attorneys were assigned to each arraignment session. Day sessions ran from 9:30 A.M. to 5:00 P.M. The evening shift began at 6:00 P.M. and usually lasted until one in the morning. All those arrested and charged with crimes committed in Bronx County (including those charged with felonies yet to be indicted by a grand jury) appeared in front of a judge for the first time at their arraignment in the Bronx Criminal Court.

Eddie, the steadfast Legal Aid clerk, was seated up front, facing the judge's bench, stapling complaints, arrest records and Pre-Trial Services bail evaluations to file folders.

In his early thirties, Eddie Lopez easily wore twenty more pounds than his five foot ten inch build comfortably allowed. With a neatly cropped beard and mustache, his bushy black hair dangled over his forehead, but not low enough to cover his eyes, which were fixed on his hands as they pieced together the court papers.

Eddie looked up from behind a file folder as I approached.

"Eddie, what's that stink?"

"One of the defendants must have thrown up in detention. The court officer went to get some ammonia."

"You sure it's not you? Your mama's spicy cooking maybe?"

He smirked. "I haven't been eating my mother's cooking for years, but you're gonna want to run home to yours after you see what's in the basket."

The arraignment basket held the finished case files ready for attorney review prior to entering detention, where criminal defendants waited in jail cells to meet their lawyers.

"What makes you think I'm going to take what's *in* the basket?"

"Don't you take all the sicko sex cases?"

My voice rose a few octaves. "No, I don't, but maybe if another Legal Aid lawyer would pick even just one up, I wouldn't have to. And, by the way, one of us might actually get a defendant who's innocent."

Eddie winced. I picked up the file that he had referred to earlier, looked at the complaint, then the defendant's arrest record.

"See, here's a guy twenty-four years old, charged with kidnapping and molesting three boys. Never been arrested before in his life. Doesn't it make you wonder when suddenly at the age of twenty-four, a man decides to molest three boys?" On the middle of Eddie's desk, I spotted the blaring cover of the *New York Post*...

SCHOOL AIDE FINGERED FOR SEX ATTACK ON 3 KIDS

I tucked the file under my arm, and headed for the holding cells.

Chapter 2

I was accosted with the stench of puke and piss and immediately became nauseous. Even with fifty or so arraignment sessions under my belt, I still hadn't gotten used to it.

I was standing in a prison vestibule, a locked cell gate before me.

"On the door!" I yelled.

In his mid-fifties, Correction Officer Hurtado shuffled up to the gate with the placid regularity of a parking attendant, and spoke in kind.

"Hey Nick! Who ya got?" Hurtado keyed open the barred door. Corrections usually had the scoop on the numbers being processed through central booking that were "in the system" and likely candidates for an evening's appearance in AR 1.

"Guevara," I said.

"Yeah, got him in this morning. The D.A. told us to push him through. What'd this guy do that's so special?"

"I hope it's what he didn't do."

"Whatever," Hurtado muttered, as he locked the heavy iron gate behind me. "He's here, and he's been asking for a lawyer for the last hour-and-a-half."

A female correction officer sat behind a desk, hunched over a logbook and a telephone at the end of a narrow cinder block hallway. Off to the left, past two small cells reserved for segregated prisoners, was the interview area. Three tables stood in a row against a concrete wall. Chairs were scattered about. I took a seat at the middle table facing the corridor where Guevara, the first defendant I would interview for the night, would turn down to meet me.

He appeared less than a minute later dressed in a red and white shirt and blue corduroy pants, seeming quite clean and neat for a guy who's been in jail all day. No messy hair. No five o'clock shadow. With a nervous manner, he stuck out his hand.

I shook it. And it was dead calm.

I always believed you could tell something about a man, his mood, his attitude, from his handshake. But Guevara was indiscernible. In the brief moment our hands met, I felt as if mine had been swallowed by a baseball mitt. Not a catcher's, fat and warm. But a first baseman's glove, long fingered and absent the stuffing necessary to prevent you from receiving a good sting when the ball slapped into your palm.

I placed my card on the table between us as he sat down. "My name is Nick Mannino. I'm an attorney with the Legal Aid Society. I'll be representing you at your arraignment tonight."

Guevara spoke quickly, calmer now than he first appeared. "I didn't do this. I love kids. I work with them every day. I've taken them to the Bronx Zoo on field trips. Parents trust me with their children." His voice got louder as he began to ramble. "I don't know why they're saying these things about me! One of the kid's mothers is crazy! She's a drug addict! A lunatic!"

I explained the charges: several B felonies, including kidnapping and physically sodomizing three boys—Rafael Rodriguez, Carlos Rodriguez, and Jose Chavez—no more than nine and ten years old.

"Rafael and Carlos are brothers," Guevara interrupted. "They've been to my apartment many times. I've got video games and pinball machines for them to play. Their mother was grateful I got them off the street. The other boy, Jose, came to my apartment only once. He's a wild kid, always getting into trouble. His mother has all kinds of boyfriends." He shook his head then looked up again. Our eyes met. His darted back down.

"Peter. These boys say you tied them up." His brow furrowed. I paused to change direction, but didn't. "It's my job to read these charges to you. So bear with me. They also say you sodomized them—anally and orally."

"That's crazy! I would never do such a thing! Jose's mother, that crazy bitch, is behind this! When the kid came to my apartment he wouldn't behave himself. I took him home and told him not to come back." Guevara ran his fingers roughly through his hair. "Speak to the teachers at P.S. 92. They'll tell you. I'm great with children. I have letters in my file from mothers who have written to the principal about me." He took three deep breaths and appeared to be on the verge of hyperventilating. "Speak to Shula Hirsch. She's in charge of Special Education. I work closely with her." He spoke with a strained calm. Teardrops formed in the corners of his eyes. "Can you get me out of here? Will I be going home tonight?"

I flipped through the court papers. "I'll do my best. You've never been arrested before. Do you think anyone is out there in court for you?"

"No. I have no family. Maybe someone from work—from P.S. 92. I go to Bronx Community College at night. I've been taking courses in education for the past two years. I'm supposed to finish up in the fall." A tear ran in a straight line off the side of his nose.

"I need you to tell me the whole truth Peter. Whether you're innocent or guilty, I took an oath to defend you to the best of my ability. Anything you tell me is strictly confidential. I can't tell anyone not hired to assist in your defense a damn thing. If I did, I could lose my license to practice law. Besides, the information could never be used against you in court. It's called attorney-client privilege, and it is the strongest privilege under the law." His eyes were riveted on me. I went on. "The more I know, the better prepared I'll be to defend you. If the D.A. knows something I don't, that I'm not ready to deal with, you're the one who's going to pay for it, not me. Even if you're dead guilty, it's my job to defend you, and see you get out of here. The only way you can help me help you is by answering my questions honestly and completely."

The tears dried as Guevara spoke of his childhood and relayed a disturbing case history.

His mother, a drug addict, had abandoned him at the age of two. The city Welfare System placed him in a string of orphanages and foster homes but failed to place him permanently. Adoptive parents, even foster parents, didn't want older children. A teenage boy—no less a Hispanic teenage boy—hadn't a chance in hell of finding a family.

I took copious notes as he went on to describe his early adolescent years—orphanage life—a loosely run military barracks, episodes of harsh but erratic discipline, crimes between juveniles so unspeakable that they would be easily termed evil if committed by adults. His deadpan manner surprised me.

He referred to himself as a bright child, a loner, full of hopes and dreams—and nightmares. He spoke of three years at St. Joseph's Orphanage in the Catskills, remarking how he admired the priests there, their devotion to the children, their unselfishness, their kindness. Something he had not experienced in other placements before. "The orphanage though, wasn't without its demons," he remarked.

Even though the priests would sleep in the same quarters with the younger and weaker boys for their protection, they could not monitor the boys twenty-four hours a day, everywhere on the grounds. In a break period before lunch, the boys would take turns going to the lavatory in groups of five or six, to wash up after the morning's exercise, and go to the bathroom as needed. These lavatory periods were largely unsupervised.

One December morning, an eleven-year old Guevara was cornered by four older boys who grabbed his arms, bent him over a sink and stuffed half a roll of toilet paper in his mouth.

They raked down his pants and underwear and were seconds away from sodomizing him, when a young priest burst through the door and pulled them away.

The priest, who was just twenty-one years old at the time and had been assigned to the orphanage only weeks before, was almost as shaken by the occurrence as young Guevara.

The two often spoke about it afterwards. The priest seemed genuinely concerned that Guevara not be emotionally scarred by the attack.

"We're still friends to this day," Guevara said. Then without pause, he declared himself to be a Roman Catholic, nodding at me as if seeking some common ground.

Aside from the family wedding or funeral, I hadn't attended mass since early high school. I had done my time: eight straight years of Sunday mass, Tuesday novenas, and weekly confessions at Saint Francis of Assisi, Brooklyn, New York—grades one through eight. Besides, Mom prayed enough for the two of us.

Guevara stated that he had no girlfriend "at the time," but dated frequently. And although this would have been the perfect time to end the interview, I let him talk himself out, which I never let a defendant do, having learned early on the judicious practice of poor man's counsel—spend only the time necessary to do your best job under the circumstances, and not a minute more.

Guevara though, had struck a chord.

Chapter 3

I had daydreamed about a case like this maybe a hundred times before, and the daydream was almost always the same: I'm the most famous criminal defense lawyer this country has ever known, brilliant beyond my years, unbeatable in any courtroom. I'm entering a courthouse (probably in some small Southern town) to deliver the final summation in a grueling trial. I've turned the tide of public opinion that from the start was squarely bent on hanging my client. The charge is murder in the first degree. My client, of course, is innocent. I alone believe in him. I alone can save him from an almost certain conviction and execution. With the world watching, I deliver the summation of my life. The jury quickly finds my client "not guilty." Soon after the verdict, the real murderer is caught and confesses. Nick Mannino is a national hero. Little children all over the country want to become criminal defense lawyers. There's talk of naming a candy bar after me. And then I float, with gratifying gentleness, back down to earth, and the implacable strains of reality grip me whole.

I was Mary's son, the product of a gutsy first generation Italian-American who, with no money and an unfaithful husband whose idea of romance was two brutish minutes in the sack, did what few women dared in 1956—she divorced the louse.

My biological father was never heard from again.

When we moved into three small rooms in a two-story walk-up on New York Avenue in Flatbush, Mom worked in the dry cleaner below, fended off the married owner's advances, and paid the rent. We ate a lot of oatmeal.

When Mom's younger brother, Rocco, a soldier and hit man rising up the ranks of Brooklyn's organized crime, offered to help, she refused. Her son would not be fed, clothed or sheltered from the ill-gotten gains of criminal activity.

Mom's righteousness was not lost on me.

Three years later, she would marry John Mannino, a divorcee also, and strong-willed son of Sicilian immigrants whose lungs had been badly scarred by tuberculosis contracted when he was twenty-one. When he and Mom finally tied the knot, he went from being called Uncle John to Dad, and the Dad stuck, and deservedly so, forever.

Put simply—he saved our lives.

I do believe in those wonder years from childhood through my teens, John Mannino and I argued over every conceivable subject: playtime, the food I ate, my mother, music, bell bottom pants, the length of my hair, the time I spent in the bathroom, the time I spent sleeping, Archie Bunker, politics, and even the meaning of "making love."

Back then, I thought he was picking on me mostly. Years later, Mom, swearing me to secrecy, revealed his pride in my rhetorical skills. She said, for what it was worth to me then (I actually shrugged it off at the time), that he thought I was brilliant.

He loved me. And although I never told him—I loved him too.

When I was nineteen, I legally changed my last name to Mannino. I didn't do it out of love or affection, I'm now ashamed to admit. I did it out of gratitude and loyalty.

After being bedridden for weeks with the flu (with his limited lung capacity, the common cold was debilitating), at home, with an oxygen tank and respirator at his side, the only father I ever knew died in his sleep at the age of fifty-eight. He never saw me graduate college with honors, or law school three years later.

Using funds from a lump sum civil servant's death benefit, I got through an arduous three years at Cardozo Law. Mom had no idea that prior to his death, John Mannino opted for the widow's pension. That's one that pays out more to your beneficiaries if you die, than to you and your family if you survive to retire.

John Mannino was the reason I became a lawyer.

Almost everyone in the crowded courtroom—mostly Hispanics with some blacks and fewer whites—was there to witness Guevara's arraignment. Aside from a few probing glances from the throng of reporters that lined the back wall, they all ignored my entrance.

A sharp pain like an electric shock shot into my left temple—the beginnings of a monster headache. I made a beeline for my briefcase and a bottle of Extra-Strength Excedrin stuffed in a corner next to the Tums. There wasn't a trial lawyer I knew who didn't carry around in his pocket or briefcase something for his head, as well as something for his stomach. I popped the last two aspirin and dry- swallowed them. Their sour taste crept down my throat, scratching it ever so slowly along the way.

I hunched over the defense table, my elbows on my thighs, thumbs on my temples, my eyes barely open, wanting to believe the throbbing in my head had begun to dissipate. But in the half-light of my cupped hands, another headline off a crinkled copy of *Newsday* on Eddie's desk glared up at me.

SPIDERMAN RAPIST STILL ON THE LOOSE
By V. Repolla

He climbs in windows. He strikes under the cover of night shimmying down the sides of buildings—a single woman's worst nightmare. At 3:00 A.M. this morning, he raped a 23 year-old nurse in her apartment at 2170 Walton Avenue in the Kingsbridge section of the Bronx, leaving as he came on a knotted line of rope draped from the rooftop—his calling card. According to the detectives investigating the case, this serial rapist, who claimed his third victim in twenty-seven days and who comes and goes like Spiderman, is expected to strike again, and soon. A task force devoted to investigating the case has yet to be formed...

"Looks like you need this more than I do." The voice came from behind me. It was Tom Miller. He handed me a bottle of mineral water. I took a few gulps to rid my mouth of the aspirin's aftertaste.

As senior attorney, it was Tom's ultimate responsibility to oversee arraignments, and if things got crazy, he, like the chief resident in an emergency room, would have to step in and take over. The client came first, and the client was represented not by Nick Mannino, but by the Legal Aid Society, which was, incidentally, the biggest law firm in the City and State of New York.

With four years' experience on me, Tom had tried twenty-one cases to date, all jury trials, and with great success. Almost six feet tall, thin (a strict vegetarian), with short blonde hair and a light, almost pale complexion, Miller had been raised in Nebraska, and the homespun Midwest was woven through every syllable he uttered. Due to its attendant publicity, Tom should have taken the Guevara case, but it was more than my early arrival and completed interview that secured it for me, if only for the night arraignment. Tom, under no circumstances, would represent an alleged child molester. Not that night. Not ever.

In addition to my own seven trials and seven acquittals, I had won six out of seven hearings to suppress evidence, and had seven out of eight felony cases where my client, at great risk, testified before a grand jury, dismissed.

Most criminal defense lawyers go their entire career steadfast in the belief that a client should never waive his or her right against self-incrimination—only to be subject, early on, to cross-examination by a prosecutor at the grand jury stage. These dismissals by grand jury vote were probably the greatest accomplishment of my young career.

Had the Excedrins not begun to kick in, the decibel level in the packed courtroom would have been unbearable.

The last time I saw a Bronx courtroom so overflowing, I was about to cross-examine "Crazy Joe," a renegade cop who had his own unwritten manual on police procedure in the South Bronx. This included beating every suspect mercilessly, and then planting, as was necessary, a gun or a vial of crack to cover his tracks. Only this time, in addition to the mob of Bronx natives stuffing the courtroom pews, dozens of standing-room only reporters packed the center and rear aisles, salivating for a juicy headline.

The crowd was startled into silence when the rear courtroom doors swung open, and Court Officer Jose Figueroa jostled his way through the crowd.

Figueroa and I had made courthouse history together about six months earlier when he was threatened with contempt—a posturing subterfuge by a judge named Leon Fanghetti.

All it took was a sweltering August day (the kind that makes municipal air conditioning a nonentity), a voluminous court calendar, and a judge who hadn't the acumen or temperament to deal with any of it. So when Figueroa, married with three kids and living paycheck to paycheck like the rest of the South Bronx (including many of its lawyers), was about to lose his job (and fast) on false charges, I stepped forward as his sole supporting witness. In a venture that could have been more than mildly hazardous to my otherwise blossoming Bronx Courthouse career, this Bronx Legal Aid Warrior, this valiant defender of the underdog, this foolish young boy from Long Island, vouched for the good Court Officer's mild manner in the face of Fanghetti's ill temperament and low-ball racist tactics.

Fortunately for me and Figueroa, Ernie Krenwinkle, the Administrative Judge and a streetwise Bronx native, believed me, and when all was made right, Figueroa was nuts about paying me back. The favor I planned to ask of him on the Guevara case would, I thought, more or less, make us even.

Chapter 4

F iguerora joined me at the far side of the courtroom where we slipped
into a rear corridor reserved for court personnel.

"Jose, I have to get rid of this crowd. Once the judge sees the press and
the packed courtroom, he'll surely set a high bail or remand my client."

"You picked up the school teacher who molested those kids?"

"Yes, but he's only a school aide, not a teacher. He's twenty-four years
old and never been arrested. For Christ's sake he's an orphan. He's made a
life for himself and even goes to Bronx Community at night."

A sneaky grin appeared on Figueroa's face. "Christ Nick. You want me
to help you put an accused child molester back on the streets?"

"You got it, buddy."

We re-entered AR-1 together.

Returning to the defense side of the courtroom, I was distracted by
the presence of Rick Edelstein, the third Legal Aid attorney working arraignments. His short brown hair, peppered with premature gray made
him appear older than his thirty-two years, as did his five o'clock shadow
and wrinkly pinstriped suit. Like me, he had worked the entire day, and
looked it.

Figueroa took his position at the bridge man's table and announced:
"The arraignment of Peter Guevara will be postponed until tomorrow
morning at 10:30."

Amid the audience stir, an unkempt male reporter shouted, "We were
told it would be tonight!"

"This is between the defense attorney, the prosecutor, and the judge,"
Figueroa shot back. "I'm only a messenger."

Minutes later, amid grumbling complaints and creaking pews, the onlookers dwindled to about two dozen, almost all of whom moved into the first three rows—all except for a young man in a red parka, who sat in the last row on the defense side of the courtroom.

Figueroa returned to the bridge area, cool as a cucumber.

I ambled over. "Do you think anyone is hanging around outside?"

"I doubt it. Court Officer Velasquez is out there."

"Okay, but what if the reporters sit on the phones, and an Assistant D.A. comes down and blows the whistle on us?"

"Got it covered. Velasquez taped 'Out of Order' signs on all the booths. I did the same thing in the lower lobby."

Assistant District Attorney Jimmy Ryan carried himself with a dispassionate air of authority and privilege. A tall, well-built Irishman, he sauntered into the courtroom, lugging a storage box packed with files.

"How are you this evening, Mr. Assistant District Attorney?" I figured he'd warm to the respectful salutation, however pretentious.

"If it isn't Nickel Ass Mannino," he said with a counterfeit grin. I hated being called Nicholas, no less Nickel Ass, last borne from the imagination of some forgotten second-grader.

"I got this case tonight, but I don't know if you'll be handling it," I answered.

"What's the name?"

"Guevara."

"Why wouldn't I be handling it?" His fingers picked through his files, and then yanked out a folder. "Seems this upstanding citizen likes to play with little boys." I wasn't sure if he was talking to me or himself. "How about we agree to dispense with all this due process shit, take this guy up to the roof, and toss him off, head first?"

I remained expressionless.

Although thicker than most (there were, after all, three complainants), the folder on Guevara comprised a mere seven or eight pages. I imagined a couple of overloaded storage boxes by the start of trial.

"These kids seem pretty credible," he blurted. "All three say the same thing. As to the third one, Chavez, Guevara got a bit rougher with him. And lookie here, the defendant made a statement. '*I'm innocent. They came to my apartment to play video games.*'"

I closed my eyes for a moment and quietly sighed.

"That it, counselor?" Ryan slapped the file shut and began slipping it back into the storage box.

"Any medical evidence?" I nervously bit my lower lip.

Ryan reopened the file, turned a few pages and said: "Yep. The third boy, Chavez, had a hairline laceration to his anus."

Chapter 5

Figueroa gave me a nod. Guevara's court papers were tabled up front, the first to be called. Over a dozen felony yellow-backs and more than two dozen blue-backed misdemeanors followed in line. It was 9:00 P.M. exactly. What remained of the spectators in the courtroom, although noticeably restless, were well-behaved.

Rick and Tom were still seated, file folders on their laps—ready for arraignment. I grabbed the Guevara file and remained standing.

"All rise!" Figueroa shouted. "Bronx County Criminal Court AR-1 is now in session, the Honorable Arnold Benton presiding! Everyone please be seated and remain quiet! First case: People v. Pedro Guevara, docket numbers 2X0105481, 2X0105482 and 2X0105483!"

Arnold Benton was far from my first choice for a judge this evening, not that there was a choice to be had. Though a lifelong member of the Bronx Democratic Club, his leanings were most definitively pro-prosecution. Save the pitch for sympathy or compassion, save the histrionics. It'll only piss him off.

Guevara was soon positioned at my side, two police officers squarely behind him.

"Does defense counsel waive a reading of the rights and charges?" Figueroa asked.

As always, I answered in the affirmative.

Figueroa slapped the court papers down before Benton. The judge scrutinized the complaints. His mouth twisted with disgust.

I turned toward Guevara and whispered, "No matter what the D.A. or judge says, just remain silent. Don't react."

He nodded.

Benton had yet to flip to Guevara's rap sheet and the caption *No Prior Record,* when he looked down at the assistant prosecutor and asked: "Do you want to be heard on bail, Mr. Ryan?"

This was not a good sign.

"Yes, your honor." Ryan answered.

With his massive build and arms like tree trunks, Guevara certainly didn't fit *my* profile of a child molester. I hoped that gruesome image would be as difficult for a jury to conjure, as it was for me. Aside from a slight overbite and a little extra vocal emphasis on his "Ss" and "Ts", Guevara was the picture of physical masculinity.

After a few kiss-ass salutations to Judge Benton, Ryan upped the volume and continued: "Judge, this defendant is charged with not one, not two, but three unspeakable crimes." Unfortunately for Guevara, they would soon become speak-able. "This man, your honor"—that made three "your honors"—"tied up, on three different occasions, on two different dates, three boys, nine and ten years of age. Then... anally and orally sodomized them."

A woman's gasp ignited a grumbling behind me as Guevara moaned, "Oh my God." He seemed as shocked as the onlookers.

I turned around and stared down the audience. The man in the red parka was still sitting in the last row. Head down, he appeared to be writing. Benton flipped to Guevara's rap sheet. No convictions. No arrests. He looked up and shuffled his shoulders uncomfortably. Ryan wasn't finished though.

"As advocate for the people"—I hated when prosecutors said this, as if in opposition stood my client, an alien creature or some odd form of organic life—"I wish to point out that this defendant is not recommended for release on his own recognizance by Pre-Trial Services. And I now, pursuant to Section 710.30(1)(a) of the Criminal Procedure Law, give notice of the people's intention to introduce at trial the following statement made by this defendant." Ryan looked down and read from his file: "*They came to my apartment to play video games.*"

The "I'm innocent" part was conveniently omitted.

Guevara blurted: "I'm innocent, judge! I told the police that! I've worked with children my whole life!"

I grabbed his arm—it was rock solid—and whispered, "Shut up Peter."

"Mr. Mannino," Benton snapped, "another outburst like that and your client can spend the night in jail, and if he's lucky, get arraigned in the morning."

"Your honor, I apologize for my client. It won't happen again."

"I'm sorry too, judge." Guevara's voice sounded composed, almost rehearsed.

"Mr. Ryan, have you anything else?" Benton calmly asked. Guevara's outburst appeared to have gotten to him a little.

"Yes, your honor," Ryan shouted, as if about to divulge proof positive of Guevara's guilt. "A medical examination of the boy Chavez at Lincoln Hospital revealed an anal laceration."

A few spectators groaned.

Ryan asked for seventy-five thousand dollars bail.

Guevara looked horrified.

All that remained was the defendant's mandatory opportunity to be heard—a masquerade of due process. As more often than not, it fell upon deaf judicial ears.

"Mr. Mannino," Benton said, leaning so far back in his chair that only his head was visible.

Feeling like I had been steamrolled, I began with Guevara the orphan and foster child, and ended with Guevara the teacher's aide of emotionally handicapped students, about to earn an associate's degree in education—a mere semester away.

"Do you think, Judge, the person who committed these crimes could work every day with emotionally handicapped kids without some past incident; some circumstance developing that would give rise to an allegation the likes of which he is charged with today? Maybe just one time in the last few years?" I paused for several seconds, desirous of driving home the illogical connection of Peter Guevara to the crimes charged. "It is also my understanding that Mrs. Shula Hirsch, his supervisor, will be providing written testimonials to his character from the principal, parents, and other teachers."

Benton was smiling coyly, letting me know I was getting somewhere. My confidence doubled.

"I would be finished, Your Honor, except Mr. Ryan made a few comments I must address in all fairness to my client. Mr. Ryan says my client's statement to police was: 'They came to my apartment to play video games.' But Mr. Ryan omitted two key words that my client wants this court, and this entire community, to hear. They are: 'I'm innocent!' I trust this omission was completely inadvertent."

I paused to let Ryan squirm, if only just a little. At a trial, he was legally bound to introduce the whole statement, or none at all.

"Then there's the reddest of all herrings in the prosecution's case—the anal laceration, which isn't a laceration at all, as we laymen understand it. Mr. Ryan, whether it was again inadvertent, or another move toward his becoming 'Prosecutor of the Month,' left out a most descriptive medical term, which when disclosed, denigrates this evidence to proof of absolutely nothing; that is the word *hairline*. The exact medical diagnosis, and Mr. Ryan can correct me if I'm wrong, is *hairline anal laceration*."

"I wish to strenuously object to Mr. Mannino's characterization of me Your Honor!"

"Tell the whole truth and I won't have to characterize you at all!"

"Gentlemen, please!" Benton scolded. "Mr. Ryan, is it true this laceration was hairline?"

"Yes, well that's the exact medical description, for what it's worth." Ryan spoke like a spoiled child.

Benton scowled. "I'll decide what it's worth. And Mr. Mannino, in the future, please direct your comments only to this court. Now finish up, please!"

I continued. "There is no way anal sodomy could have occurred between an adult male and a nine year old boy without serious determinable physical injury to the child." I hated drawing this mental picture, but had no choice. "A hairline? That borders on irritation. Diaper rash could result in more than a hairline tear of the skin. And why don't the other boys have anything medically and physically wrong with them? How is that possible?" I paused, but only for a second or two.

"Mr. Guevara has lived in the Bronx his entire adult life. His work is here. His college is here. His friends are here. I beg this court, in view of his background, in light of this questionable case, to release my client on his own recognizance. Or, if Your Honor is inclined to set bail, to please do so reasonably, so his friends and co-workers might help free him pending the final outcome of this case."

"Bail will be set at fifteen-thousand dollars, cash or bond," Benton said. "That's five-thousand dollars on each docket." Guevara looked like he was about to vomit.

It was a reasonable bail under the circumstances. "We can work with this," I said quietly into Guevara's ear. "I can make a motion for reduction in Supreme."

"I've got one thousand dollars in the bank," Guevara whispered. "Could you maybe get it down to that?"

"I'll do what I can. As for now, the case will be adjourned to Tuesday. If there's no indictment by then, you'll get released—that's by Tuesday, 5:00 P.M."

"Really?"

"Yeah, but don't count on it."

"Does the defendant wish to testify in the grand jury?" Ryan was back on his pulpit. "The case will be presented in the morning."

I looked up at Benton. "No he does not, your honor."

The Grand Jury is a one-sided affair. Make no mistake about it. You're on the prosecution's turf. Outside the presence of the judge, the grand jurors sit, watch, and listen to the Assistant D.A. call witnesses and introduce evidence. When he is done, all the grand jury has to determine is if there's reasonable cause to believe that the defendant committed the crimes charged. If so, they vote to indict.

Twenty-three people are impaneled. Sixteen must be present to have a voting quorum. Twelve must agree to indict. When they do,

21

which is almost always, the case is sent to Supreme Court just two blocks away, and the defendant is arraigned all over again on the felony indictment.

The three kids were expected to testify in the Guevara case; probably their mothers too. Plus, there was the medical evidence. And in the grand jury there's no opportunity to defend yourself. Cross-examination, challenging the evidence—doesn't exist. Though a defendant may testify, and bring his attorney, the lawyer is forbidden to speak.

Under such circumstances, Guevara didn't stand a chance.

Benton examined his calendar. "The case is adjourned to AP-6 March 2nd. Call the next case!"

I escorted Guevara back toward detention, the two police officers corralling us forward and marking our every move. Guevara would be sleeping that night (and those to come) in either the Bronx House of Detention or the Men's Prison at Riker's Island in Elmhurst, Queens.

He said, choking on his words, that he would have his supervisor, Mrs. Hirsch, call me. I mustered some lame words of encouragement, and then saw that fear I had seen hundreds of times before—of protracted imprisonment—in my client's eyes.

I told him not to talk to anyone about the case and to call me tomorrow afternoon.

He nodded dejectedly and followed the officers through the steel frame doorway into detention, beyond the gated bars.

Figueroa and Benton were on to new business.

As for me, I was ready for home and a warm bed. Felt I deserved it. But there were at least three hours left in the evening, and I had arraigned only one case.

Though pleased with the fifteen thousand dollars bail, I wondered what I might have done differently. A different judge and maybe, just maybe, Guevara might have walked.

As I chatted with the mother of one of my new prospective clients, the man in red got up to leave. Since he'd appeared to be writing during

Guevara's arraignment, his sudden departure piqued my curiosity. I concluded my conversation and rushed to catch him.

He was about my age, maybe younger, white, with a dusky complexion that suggested Italian or Spanish descent.

"I saw you writing before," I said. "Are you a law student?"

He flashed a broad smile. "A crime reporter for *Newsday*. I cover Manhattan, Brooklyn and the Bronx."

"Isn't *Newsday* a Long Island paper?"

"We're trying to break into the city. With just *The Post* and *The Daily News* here, there really isn't a quality paper to choose from other than *The Times*."

"How come you hung around so late?" What I really wanted to know was why the hell he'd still been there after Figueroa told the spectators and the press to leave.

He explained how he overheard Figueroa in the Clerk's Office asking for help clearing the courtroom, and then spied him pinning "Out of Order" signs on the otherwise in-order telephone booths. "But I'll tell you what. I'll keep my suppositions to myself, report just the arraignment as I saw it, if *you* do something for me."

"I'm listening."

"Take my calls—about this case and maybe some others. Give me something to report, and maybe, just maybe, I could help you out too."

"Listen, I hate surprises and what you call 'help,' may not be. And as for favors, forget it. I'll take your calls, but one cheap shot, and this source is history." With the Guevara case, I could use all the friends in the press I could get.

My new reporter friend was all smiles. "You got it, Counselor." We shook hands. It felt honest and comfortable. "See ya' round."

As he darted toward the escalator, I shouted, "What the hell's your name anyway?"

"Vinny Repolla!"

I reentered the courtroom and did the four arraignments Tom gave me, and six more after that. These were the regular run-of-Legal Aid cases:

robbery, burglary, car-theft, assault. Nothing especially horrible. I was glad, thrilled even, to be done with Guevara for the evening.

My '66 Chevy Malibu was parked just outside the revolving front entrance doors. Despite how often I walked outside the Criminal Court Building during the day, at the end of a night arraignment, I never forgot where I was, when I belonged here, and when I didn't. At one in the morning, with or without a full moon, the South Bronx could be a dangerous place. I started my car, locked the doors, and headed for Long Island.

The closer I got to Merrick, the greater the sensation of peace and serenity.

After turning onto Central Parkway, whose name belied this quiet street, I drove under a trellis of bare tree branches until reaching my driveway and pulling in. Sitting in the quiet darkness, I stared at the small five-room house I had lived in since turning thirteen. The living room lamp glowed behind a drawn shade. It was on a timer and would shut off automatically in the morning.

I grabbed the briefcase I had thrown onto the front seat just thirty minutes earlier, and stepped back out into the cold.

Chapter 6

E leanor Wellington Vernou came from a long line of filthy rich Southern aristocrats: her father a direct descendant of Napoleon's Imperial Guard who fled France in 1815, only to hide in a thinly settled region outside Atlanta, his coffers stuffed with the fallen empire's fortunes; her mother, a direct descendant of the very General Wellington who led the British army to the crushing defeat of those Imperial troops at Waterloo.

We met on May 11, 1979, at a '50s dance in lower Manhattan's Cardozo Law School, and danced to Mancini's *Moon River*.

She was about to graduate NYU Law and had been offered, but had yet to accept, a position as an Assistant District Attorney in Manhattan, one of the city's top career appointments in criminal law. My heart jumped at the prospect of her staying in New York after graduation, but then dropped (along with my stomach) as I realized come June, I might never see her again.

We said goodbye that night on a cold and gusty corner of Fifth Avenue and Twelfth Street. Eleanor hailed a cab, wrote her number on my palm, then jumped in. We met once again before graduation—for dinner on Long Island. She drove out to meet me. Afterward, we got in my Malibu, and headed to Jones Beach, where we strolled along the shoreline and talked for hours.

Like starry-eyed children, we cataloged our hopes and dreams to one another—young magnanimous fools.

At one point, I caught her looking at me intensely. The moonlight on her hair traced a shadow across her mouth and neck. The moment was perfect for a kiss, a first kiss. I moved my lips closer to hers.

Her hand gently covered my mouth. "We can't, Nick. I'm engaged."

I felt as if I'd been punched in the chest. She grabbed my hand, patted it, then pulled me close.

We hugged.

An invisible ship's horn cut through the night sky.

I have no idea how long we stood there. All I remember is we barely spoke from stepping off the beach to parting back at the restaurant.

In June, we graduated law school; Eleanor from N.Y.U., and I from Cardozo. She left for Georgia the next day. I went home to Long Island.

We didn't see each other again until late August, in that summer of '79, when (over her parents' protestations) she accepted the position of Assistant District Attorney in Lower Manhattan.

Law school behind me, my best friend Joey, the fireworks king of Marine Park, basted me with a one thousand dollar graduation gift. Having been hired in May by Legal Aid, the only wrinkle—and prerequisite to my continued employment—was passing, as the personnel director's letter put it, "that little quiz in late July." I chose the cheapest bar review course available in the metropolitan area and went through the motions of reading the materials and watching lectures on video on the myriad areas of New York Law. All I had to do was pass.

On the last weekend in July, just a few days before my twenty-fifth birthday, I took the bar exam. By mid-September, I was working in the Bronx—thrown head first into the fray, in court every day, and loving it.

Legal Aid lawyers and Assistant District Attorneys waiting for the bar results, were permitted to practice law under a special Appellate Division Student Practice Order, applicable only to the lower Criminal Court. The honor and prestige attached to representing indicted felons would have to wait, and although I wasn't patient by nature, I made the best of it. I was young. It was my first full-time job. And it was all new to me. I treated each case as though it was my first, and my last. I loved the challenge, the responsibility, the overload of Legal Aid cases, the daily rout of arguments, pleas, and victories. And I got more cases dismissed (or so I thought), or adjourned in contemplation of dismissal, than any of my Legal Aid colleagues. But I couldn't wait to get my hands on those felony cases.

On November 23, 1979, I received a letter from the State Board of Law Examiners. I flunked the bar.

Eleanor called the next day from Georgia, tentative and sympathetic. When she'd contacted the Appellate Division to check on her own results, she also inquired about mine—said I was her husband. Eleanor had passed, and I was genuinely pleased to hear it. I told her she ought to be celebrating with her friends and family— even her fiancé. Not consoling yours truly.

Two weeks later, she enrolled me in the best and most expensive bar review course available, and she paid the tuition, in full and up front, so there was no backing out. I could pay her back in dinners when I passed, she said.

And pass I did, later that May.

When I broke the news to Mom, she grabbed me in her arms and together we did the tarantella around the dining room table, into the living room, down the back steps, and into the yard. The Clancys next door thought we were nuts.

A few months later, Eleanor broke off her engagement, and the following weekend we went out on our first "real date." It was under Broadway's glittering *Grease* marquee that we kissed for the first time.

And I had never felt more in love.

Chapter 7

After the double shift the day before, I didn't get into the office until 10:00 A.M. Brenda, from the secretarial pool, who acted like I was her sole responsibility, promptly put a call through from Eleanor.

"If I didn't know you better," Eleanor said, "you might give a girl cause to wonder. What is it with you and these sex cases? Robbers, burglars, car thieves, murderers: they don't appeal to you?"

"Legal Aid doesn't take murder cases."

"Don't be a smart-ass."

"I wasn't going to take any more, except"—I took a long deep breath—"this guy's never been arrested before. He'll get convicted on the publicity alone. And I don't know why, but…I actually think he may be innocent. Besides, he at least deserves a good lawyer."

"Of course he does. But why does it have to be you?"

"Just got lucky, I guess." I promised to call later.

There was a gentle knock on my office door. Brenda stuck her head in. "Sheila and Doug are waiting, and it ain't good, Nick."

"Give me a minute."

Brenda rolled her eyes.

As secretaries went, Brenda was more than I could have ever hoped for. This was no Park Avenue law firm, and I wasn't exactly the crème de la crème of Harvard or Yale's elitist Law Review. The Legal Aid Society was a nonprofit organization. As such, it was a training ground for lawyers and unionized support staff. Newly hired attorneys were lucky to get their choice of borough, let alone a secretary. When some lower level administrative pundit decided that Brenda should sit at the desk outside my office, we both got lucky. Brenda and I got along great.

Brenda was my age and black; dark black. As tall as me at five foot nine, she had a girth that gave her a matronly, almost motherly appearance. Brenda looked after me—and for one wet-behind-the-ears lawyer—she was a true find.

Brenda had no man in her life, but she had a daughter, seven years old. Her name was Jasmine. And she had leukemia.

Although Jasmine would have her bad days (and nights), aging Brenda in multiples as her long term prognosis dimmed, at the time, she was attending school regularly, her white blood cell count was in check, and amid hope and prayer, little Jasmine was holding her own.

Since a grilling was on the menu this morning, I was in no hurry to throw myself on the fire. I sent Brenda into Sheila's office to stall. My daily tribulations were Brenda's welcome distractions. Besides, it would give me some time to think.

I slowly looked around the room.

On the walls hung three movie posters covered in plastic and backed by cardboard: *Casablanca*, *Gone with the Wind*, and *Rebel Without a Cause*. Each I had carefully selected for reasons at the time not entirely clear to me.

In the quiet I detected the scampering of a mouse across the top of the ceiling tiles. A heavier succession of rat paws followed, quicker and louder. As I got up to leave there was a faint squeal. The sound of singular helplessness sickened me. I grabbed my coffee cup, added some milk from the tiny refrigerator by Brenda's desk, and headed for Sheila's office.

The Criminal Defense Division of the Legal Aid Society in the Bronx occupied four floors in a building known as Executive Towers, located on the corner of 165th Street and the Grand Concourse, only six blocks from Yankee Stadium. Four complexes of attorneys were housed therein, each comprising about fifteen lawyers, and each headed by a supervisor and an assistant supervisor.

My office, which I shared with no one (an only child's dream come true), was considered the worst in all of Bronx Legal Aid. Located on the fourth floor, it was right beside the borough chief's, and right down the hall from the watchful eyes of both of my complex supervisors.

Sheila Schoenfeld, under five feet and pushing forty, was head of Complex C. She had a bent Streisand nose and an equally charming smile. Intensely dedicated to getting the best results possible for every client of every lawyer in her charge, it wasn't long before I realized that I was damn blessed to be one of those lawyers.

Sheila was the best of the best of us.

New York City Legal Aid attorneys were the only unionized attorneys in the country. Consequently, it was almost impossible to fire one, once they'd made it through the one-year probation period. Thus, some lawyers became "dead wood," devoid of desire, creativity, and the requisite concern to do the job well. Unwilling or unable to find work elsewhere, these lawyers became The Legal Aid Society's permanent and antiquated fixtures.

Despite my early arrogance and prevailing egotism, Sheila liked me, and had been mentoring me from the start.

"It's not enough to be smart, even brilliant," she'd once told me. "Quick, clever, and tough retorts are fine, but if you don't know the law, the cases, the principles, and aren't able to argue both sides of every issue, every time, you have no business calling yourself a trial lawyer. These are not civil money cases or the petty squabbles of matrimonial law over who gets the pots and pans. People's liberty is at stake here, and many— given the opportunities we've had, and maybe the second chance you give them—can turn their lives around. You can do some good here. You have the talent. Just set aside that ego of yours, and get crackin'."

Sheila was a straight shooter, and I valued her counsel immensely.

Douglas Krackow, the assistant supervisor and second in charge of Complex C, lived by the motto: "No matter what, the end justifies the means!" Krackow smiled slightly as I entered Sheila's office. The smile told me that although he wasn't with me, he wasn't against me either.

"Your court-clearing scheme was a hoax on the Court, and everyone else for that matter," Sheila said, in a tone a hundred times gentler than I expected. "The president of a neighborhood watchdog group you also sent packing, called me first thing this morning. He was angry as hell over missing the arraignment of this, and I quote 'atrocity committed by a school employee.'"

"That's exactly why I wanted him and the rest of the mob out of there. One reporter did stay and covered the arraignment though."

"Vinny Repolla?" asked Krackow.

I nodded.

"Well, he spelled your name right," Krackow said. "Says in this *Newsday* article you argued 'valiantly'—he made quote marks with his fingers—'for your client.' Fortunately, it doesn't mention anything about the courtroom being cleared."

A wave of relief swept over me.

Krackow went on. "The fact that it did get reported, if only by a Long Island paper, takes *some* of the heat off you."

"From now on," Sheila said, "no more screwing with the press without first consulting with me."

"You got it."

"You did okay on the arraignment," Sheila admitted offhandedly.

"Then I can keep the case?"

"For now. We'll talk more before he gets arraigned in Supreme."

"Good enough." I tried to contain my exuberance.

"Now go be a good lawyer. I've got work to do too. And here." She handed me a phone message slip. It was from Shula Hirsch, Guevara's supervisor at P.S. 92. *Call late this afternoon.*

As Krackow and I left Sheila's office, he put out his palm for a low-five and I complied as we parted.

I spent the remainder of the morning sizing up my calendar for the week and outlining two discovery motions for misdemeanor cases I wasn't sure would wind up in a plea before motion time expired—the odds in favor of a guilty plea to a lesser offense being greater than a hundred-to-one on misdemeanor charges in Criminal Court. Most lawyers in the office wouldn't waste their time with such paperwork. But I'd vowed early on to take no chances, so my case files were often replete with motion papers—that ended up nowhere.

Then I turned to the Guevara case.

Were these three kids really lying? And if so, why? Why did three boys, nine and ten years-old, suddenly get together and conspire, of all things, acts of sodomy; and worse, against a teacher's aide who was kind enough to take them on class trips and invite them to his apartment to play video games?

I hated the sound of that: *play video games in his apartment.* It seemed like a ruse, but the truth was, Peter Guevara had worked with kids his entire adult life. He loved kids. Nevertheless, the double entendre made me squeamish. It wasn't long before the attorneys in my complex would quip: "Maybe he loved kids just a liiiiiiittle too much."

Was an adult behind the boys' fabrications? I made a note to dispatch our best investigator to interview Jose Chavez's mother, Sandra, who Guevara claimed was a "drug addict," and a "lunatic," with all kinds of boyfriends. If someone goaded the boys into lying, she was the most likely suspect.

I ordered lunch in and grabbed a discarded *New York Post. The Spiderman Rapist* had again made headlines.

Chapter 8

"They're closing in on this Spiderman guy," Vinny Repolla gasped. I had just downed a burger and fries when he phoned. "He raped a forty-year old nurse just two nights ago. Hooked a rope onto the roof and scaled down into her window. That's his M.O. What the police can't figure is how he knows where to strike. All four victims are women living alone, except the second one. She has a twelve-year old girl. When he found them together, he gave the woman a choice: her or her daughter. Then he locked the kid in a closet, and raped the mom. He then kept his word."

"Did he hurt any of the victims?"

"You mean besides raping them?"

"Of course I mean besides raping them."

"No. He just ties them up, puts duct tape over their eyes and mouth, and then rapes them. He even calls himself 'The Spiderman.' Real smug about it too. Afterward, he thanks the women, apologizes for any roughness, and climbs back up the rope to the roof. One time as many as four floors."

"A regular Charles Atlas," I said.

"Anyway," Vinny continued, "his latest victim got a good look at him before he taped her eyes shut. He's black, medium skin tone, and completely bald; about five foot ten with a pencil mustache like Clark Gable. Hey, when this guy gets arrested maybe you could take the case, and you know, get me an exclusive. After all, I did right by you in today's paper. No mention of that court officer emptying the courtroom."

"OK, Repolla. I owe you one." And why not? He was true to his word and he wrote like he spoke—with enthusiasm in every sentence. Besides, I was starting to like this guy. His story on the Guevara arraignment jumped off the page. And when did anyone ever read about a Legal Aid lawyer in a positive light in a widely circulated newspaper?

I said I'd see what I could do, if or when this Spiderman guy got arrested. I made no promises.

I thought about the Spiderman's ability to target his victims. "Say Repolla, what did the comic strip Spiderman do for a living when he wasn't scaling tall buildings?"

"Holy shit! Yeah! I can't believe the cops didn't check this out. If this pans out, Nick, dinner's on me. I'll bring the girls."

"I've got my own, thanks."

"You married or something?"

"No."

"Then like I said, I'll bring the girls." He hung up before I could say another word.

I called Shula Hirsch a few minutes later. You know you've become a hardened criminal defense lawyer when you can discuss the macabre modus operandi of a rapist who drops from the rooftops in the dead of night to methodically ravage his victims, then close the conversation with laughter and dinner talk. Many years later, you think about these things and wonder. At the time, you take another sip of Coke, and plod on.

In my limited experience, witnesses who want to nail your client upside down to a cross may call the District Attorney, the press, or even your client with a few real or veiled threats. But they don't call the defense attorney. Not usually, anyway.

So I assumed Shula Hirsch would be supportive. However, charges like child molestation—in three separate instances and to three separate children—could sour even the best of friends and closest of relatives, no less a teacher of emotionally handicapped children. I'd settle for a credible and impartial character witness. Besides, after a conviction, lawsuits would pour into the Board of Education, and all those connected by some duty of care to the children, directly or indirectly, would be sued. Mrs. Hirsch was his direct supervisor. I did not expect Miss Congeniality. And I didn't get her, either.

Only after holding for five minutes and twice assuring her that I was indeed Guevara's attorney, did she set terms. She would not speak over the phone. She would see me privately the following day at 4:00 P.M., and only in her classroom at P.S. 92. I told her I'd be there. The entire conversation took thirty seconds.

I was sprinting down the hall, headed home, when Brenda called out to me. Eleanor was on the phone.

Justice had prevailed in Manhattan's Supreme Court. She had won all the preliminary suppression hearings at the start of her robbery trial. Both the defendant's confession and the gun he had used in the robbery would be introduced into evidence. A conviction was a lock. She expected a plea to a lesser C felony in the morning. Divorcing myself from an ever-constant defense posture, I congratulated her.

We made a date for Saturday night—dinner on Long Island. (The Island was my choice.) I could tell she wanted to talk, but at the risk of hurting her feelings, I cut the call short. After a full day, and a double shift the day before, I was exhausted.

During the drive home, I couldn't stop thinking about Guevara—the day's revelations, the battle the night before. Three little boys.

As I slowed the car to pay the toll at the Throgs Neck Bridge, like the bell signaling the next round of fighting, I heard the ringing squeak of the brake pads. Soon I would be exiting the Bronx. I tossed seventy-five cents into the wire-mesh basket.

Pressing down hard on the accelerator, I squeezed the steering wheel until my hands ached, and I prayed, secretly, that I would never have to see the Bronx again. But I knew, come the next morning, no one and nothing would be able to keep me away.

Chapter 9

Eleanor called me at 7:30, shaking me from a dead sleep—my punishment for cutting our call short. She demanded to know what was wrong.

I told her about my flash of burnout the day before. She shot back that I was "working too damn hard," and questioned the wisdom of my keeping the Guevara case.

Mom reiterated the same sentiment over breakfast. "These hours you keep sometimes. You look terrible!"

"I feel fine."

"Maybe Rocco could get you a job with one of those firms in the city that keeps normal business hours." She turned up her palms to qualify herself. "Nothing crooked. Your Uncle Rocco knows plenty of honest business people."

"Forget it, Mom."

Mom was the twelfth of thirteen children. Only her brother Rocco was younger by three years. Their mother died in 1930 when Mom was seven. Rocco had just turned four. They were the only children still living at home.

My grandfather was ill-prepared to assume the dual roles of both father and mother; so he abandoned the matter of parenting completely and became a hardened taskmaster instead.

Mom became the only mother Rocco knew. She would see to it that he did his work, and ate properly. When he goofed off, she covered for him. Otherwise, Rocco would have to answer to my grandfather's barber strap.

On a weeknight in December, when the temperature in East New York dropped to a record low six degrees, while shoveling coal into the furnace like he had done a thousand times before, my grandfather died.

Mom found him the next morning on his back, his eyes open, his hand on his heart, a look of resolve on his face. After the funeral, Mom went to live with her married sister, Gina. Rocco, at age eleven, was left behind. No one wanted him.

Several of the surviving brothers and sisters chipped in part of their inheritance and raised over a thousand dollars. They offered it to their brother-in-law, Vito, an unemployed drunk who beat their sister Julia regularly, if only he would take Rocco in. Vito jumped at the offer.

When Rocco awoke one night to find his sister on the kitchen floor—her jaw broken—two front teeth dangling in her mouth—four men could barely pull him off what remained of Vito after he pummeled him, first with his fists, then with a cast iron frying pan. Rocco was only fourteen when he was sent to Holbrook Juvenile Detention Farm, just outside Cooperstown, New York. He would remain there until his eighteenth birthday.

Mom was the only one who showed up for his sentencing.

By the end of 1972, Rocco became underboss to Carmine Capezzi, head of the most powerful crime family in the country, and was running the rackets in all of Brooklyn. Uncle or not, he was both a scary and powerful figure in this young boy's life. Consequently, the older I got, the more we drifted apart. Whether this distance was my saving grace, or my penance, I would never know.

I had kept Rocco, and his biography, from Eleanor, and not just because she was an assistant District Attorney. It was who she was—the Vernou name, the dispassionate old money—that I feared would drive her away from me.

Chapter 10

An extra helping of Aunt Jemima's buttermilk pancakes and I was running late. Grabbing my coat and briefcase full of the morning's cases I shouted a good-bye to Mom and ran out the front door. I had forty minutes to get to the Bronx.

With Cousin Brucie on the radio and music filling my '66 Malibu via four corner speakers, my thoughts drifted…to Eleanor…the cool smell of the beach…the perfume in her hair.

Exiting the Cross Bronx Expressway, I drove up the Grand Concourse to 165th Street, then made a right at the corner, where a ramp led to a secure indoor parking garage. Not bothering to check in at the office, I walked briskly past Legal Aid's entrance doors and back down the Concourse toward the Bronx Criminal Court.

The temperature was much colder than the Long Island morning I'd left behind, and wind added a chill to my every step.

I had cases on in AP-2, 3 and 6.

After parking my briefcase and coat in AP-2, I scoured the respective courtrooms and third floor lobby for my clients, half of which I feared I wouldn't recognize.

It was 9:45 A.M. The courtrooms were overflowing with people. I hurried over to AP-3 and called the names of my three defendants scheduled to appear there. All were present.

One was an anorexic-looking prostitute named Wanda. At her arraignment, Judge Schneider insisted on jail time. It was Wanda's tenth arrest. Her pimp paid her bail of five hundred dollars. Greely, a haggard-faced old jurist, now sitting in AP-3, would go along with the Assistant D.A.'s recommendation of a two-hundred-fifty dollar fine or five days in jail.

The case was disposed of in a matter of minutes—a career prostitute's guilty plea—my hundredth in the last two-and-a-half years.

Exiting the courtroom's swinging doors, I smacked flush into a woman. My files went flying. Court papers, subpoenas, notes and motions scattered across the lobby floor. I fell to my knees in a frantic attempt to restore all manner of paperwork to their respective folders. So did she.

I managed to grab three files, papers protruding, but intact. She got together another, and a police officer I first thought was unselfishly coming to my aid, retrieved the other two. He wanted a closer look—at her.

Ocean-blue eyes searing through her straight blond hair alternated between my own glances and the fumbling files in my hands. She wore a cream-colored waist length jacket and matching skirt, under which long silk-stocking legs curved onto a shapely dancer's body. A gold crucifix dangled from her neck. It was a wonder there were not more accidents in her wake.

"I'm really sorry," she said. "I wasn't looking where I was going. Have you got all your files?" The dark shadows under her eyes were impeccably covered by foundation make-up.

I poked the police officer with my elbow and thanked him. He apologized and stepped back.

"It's all right," I said. "No harm done." It was easy being gracious to her.

She squeezed my hand, said "thank you," and entered AP-3.

The police officer grinned.

My hand tingled from the gentle clasp of her fingers as I walked over to AP-6.

* * *

Administrative Judge Ernie Krenwinkle was on the bench. Circus clown, stand-up comedian, traffic cop, court calendar clean-up wizard—never was there a more outrageous character to rule the Bronx Criminal Court.

Running through the court calendar while taking felony pleas as an acting Supreme Court Judge in the Criminal Court, he gave new meaning to the term "speedy justice." And in the process, created his own special intermediate appellate tribunal.

Whenever and wherever a particular case was calendared in his courthouse, if you could convince Krenwinkle your client was getting a real screwing before a particular judge, he would order the case pulled, and brought to him in AP-6.

And no ADA or judge would dare attempt to stop him.

Where handguns bounced only once on the streets of the South Bronx, and drugs plagued every facet of society there, Krenwinkle knew the limits of the law he spent the greater part of his life enforcing, and dispensed justice accordingly.

As I walked into his courtroom—and it was *his* courtroom, make no mistake about it—he waved me into chambers.

Chambers in AP courtrooms were makeshift windowless rooms with a single desk, a chair for the judge, and a phone. Ernie's, though, had guest accommodations: solid-armed mahogany chairs with seats that formed to your butt. He also had a sofa, where it was not unusual to find five or six lawyers, mostly defense counsel, shooting the shit with Ernie on calendar breaks or before and after a day's daily dread.

"So who's the blonde?" Krenwinkle asked.

"What blonde?" I responded innocently.

"The gorgeous one who came in here early this morning asking for you. The Bridgeman nearly ate his mustache as she walked out."

"One did help me pick up some files I dropped in the lobby."

"Aren't you seeing some Assistant D.A. in Manhattan, some rich girl from Virginia?" Krenwinkle seemed intent on pursuing new romantic courthouse gossip. Starting such a rumor would have made his day.

"She's from Georgia. Is there anything you don't know?"

"That blonde was a beauty. I just told her to look around for Al Pacino."

"No wonder she couldn't find me."

Sounding more like a mobster than a judge, Krenwinkle asked: "So what's with this guy Guevara? Did he do it?"

My eyes widened. I was annoyed at the question, and curious as hell at his reason for asking it. "Judge, if you're worried about the press coverage—"

"Oh, I don't give a shit about the press. If I did, I'd be on the Court of Appeals by now, instead of playing bullshit referee in this asylum." He huffed. "Will those kids stick to their stories?"

"We'll know when they testify. Judge, if you don't mind my asking, what's your interest in this case?"

He took a long breath. "My wife is helping raise bail for this schnook."

I tried to seem only slightly surprised.

"And Judge Meyer in Supreme—his wife too." Now I was thoroughly confused. "Judge Meyer's wife and my wife are teachers at P.S. 92. They both think the charges against your boy are a load of crap. Evidently they're not alone. They've raised close to two thousand dollars already."

Chapter 11

Evidently someone cared a great deal about P.S. 92, for it looked like no other city school in the Bronx, and nothing like I imagined it would: no cracked and broken windows, no bubbled and bent gating, no garbage strewn hallways, no kids hanging out in the doorways or sitting on the sidewalk and—most shocking of all—no graffiti. So out of place and time was this two-story brick building in the Kingsbridge section of the Bronx that I stepped inside, then out again, to survey the neighborhood before I entered.

Across the street, a no-name gas station abutted a no-name factory that employed illegal immigrants and others willing to accept less than minimum wage. On the south side, a short strip of stores lined the block, half of which were either vacant or abandoned, except for the bodega. But the most unsettling view came from the vantage of the second floor windows, on my way to Mrs. Hirsch's classroom.

Across a narrow street, and beyond the huge schoolyard below, loomed a sprawling junkyard encompassing an entire city block.

A rusted chain link fence ran around it, leaning at angles that belied any appearance of sturdiness, or threat of security. Truck bodies, bumpers, mountains of tires, metal and chrome body parts were piled so high and deep, I could not see beyond the hills of twisted steel to the streets that lay beyond.

When I arrived at the door to Mrs. Hirsch's classroom, she greeted me with a youthful smile and a petite but certain handshake.

"I'm sorry if I sounded on the phone like death had passed over me," she said as she reached for a wooden cane with thin bamboo reeds wrapped around its handle. "I wasn't feeling very well." There was a touch of despair in her voice, as if recalling a bout of seething physical pain. "My legs are getting worse. M.S. Had it since childhood. Thought I'd be a goner by now. This cane is like a best friend." She regarded it pensively, then gazed up at me and smiled. "That is, when Peter's not around. He won't let me use it. Insists on my leaning on him—his shoulder, his arm." She waved a hand, gesturing casually as she spoke. "Says there's healing power in the human touch. I don't know about that. But damn if I don't feel better when he's around."

She eased back into a sunken leather chair beside her desk. Despite her sixty-plus years, barely a wrinkle lined her pale skin. But it did not have to. Her age, and her history, was evident in her every movement. She reached down and lifted one metal-braced leg, then the other onto a wooden footstool.

"So what can I do for you, Mr. Mannino?" Mrs. Hirsch smiled. "Better still, how can I help my friend, Peter?"

Ordinarily, a lady like Shula Hirsch does not unabashedly side with a Peter Guevara—accused child molester. She could not possibly know if he was guilty or innocent; yet she wanted to help, merely because she was fond of him. An older, hard-bitten warhorse of a trial lawyer would have understood this from her simple request to see me.

I vowed to myself then, that in the defense of Peter Guevara, I would not allow anything to surprise me again. There was, after all, no percentage in advertising how green I actually was when it came to handling the "big case."

Mrs. Hirsch knew, though. It was in her smile and in that warm twinkle in her eyes. And she didn't care.

"Only two of the three boys were in Special Ed classes," she said. "One of the Rodriguez brothers, Carlos, and the boy, Jose Chavez."

"Can you tell me a little about them?"

"I can tell you a lot about them. Jose and Carlos that is. I've had little or no contact with Rafael. He's in regular classes and I understand is a good student. As for Jose, he was in my classes for almost three years, on and off. On and off, that is, between suspensions. Even though I'm head of Special Education in this district, I also teach. School Administration tells me I don't have to. But I want to. I used to teach three classes a day. Now it's only one." Her pride was overlaid with disappointment as she lifted herself inches off the chair, the legs in braces remaining on the stool. While she adjusted herself, I struggled to hide my astonishment at the exhibition of strength in this elder teacher's arms.

"What God took from my legs," she said, "he gave me in my arms." She took a moment to catch her breath.

Over the next twenty minutes, she told about Jose Chavez, summarizing the volumes of paper generated by teachers, paraprofessional school aides, psychologists, social workers, the principal and herself—documenting the litany of antisocial behavior of this deeply troubled ten-year old, whom School District 10's Committee on the Handicapped classified "… emotionally disturbed, placement recommended, not public school appropriate." And this just six months before Guevara's arrest.

Hirsch also described young Jose as a pathological liar. Despite student, teacher and paraprofessional witnesses to his assaultive conduct, abusive and obscene language and thievery, he would steadfastly deny all guilt. He had been suspended more than a dozen times.

Each time, his mother was asked to come in for a consultation. But only once did she do so. Glassy-eyed, visibly stoned, she unleashed complaint after complaint at Hirsch, the principal, the entire city school system and even the mayor for their inability to educate her child. Sandra Chavez was unmarried and on welfare, and Jose would often complain to Mrs. Hirsch of a number of "mean and nasty" boyfriends who would "come and go" and intermittently make his life miserable. He would stay out all hours of the night to avoid them, then be late for school, or sometimes not show up at all. Mrs. Hirsch would have thought Jose was lying about this too, had it not been for the Bureau of Child Welfare reports, and the bruises.

Repeatedly, the District Chief Administrator's Office rejected Jose for Special Education classes and any other schooling alternatives short of full-time residential placement and daily structured therapeutic counseling. Each time, Mrs. Hirsch ignored them, and kept Jose in school. She moved him at monthly intervals in and out of different classes so that no one group would suffer more than another from his disruptive conduct. She had worked with kids like Jose before and had her success stories. But Jose, she said regretfully, was not one of them.

Prior to Guevara's arrest, he began to verbalize and act out, in startling bursts, a sexual proclivity that was both perverse and violent. Twice he openly fondled a girl's breasts in class. When he pulled up a second girl's skirt, and rubbed his erect penis against her backside, he was expelled permanently.

Then, almost as an afterthought, she added that a notice of claim was served on the Board of Education "this morning," naming Sandra Chavez, "as mother and lawful guardian of one Jose Chavez," demanding two million dollars in damages for the kidnapping and sodomy by their lawful employee under their direct supervision, one Pedro Guevara.

What I had suggested to A.D.A. Jimmy Ryan prior to Guevara's arraignment had come to pass. Sandra Chavez was looking for her lotto payday, and in kind, may have provided one for Peter Guevara earmarked, "not guilty."

A defense was born, and the central figure in my case was no longer the unblemished, law-abiding, hardworking Peter Guevara, but the drug-addicted, conniving, and money-grubbing Sandra Chavez.

A no-show at her son's mandatory school counseling sessions, Sandra was *numero uno* when it came to slapping the city with a two million dollar lawsuit. She probably would have sold little Jose to Central American slave traders for the right price. And so I would argue to a jury, and not sound the least bit incredible.

Hirsch shifted uncomfortably in her chair. With the faint affection of a mother attempting to conceal her bitterness and disappointment, she reflected on young Carlos Rodriguez. And it soon became clear to me that Carlos occupied a very special place in her heart.

"He is a strikingly handsome boy," she began. "Beautiful even, with those large deep blue eyes, he could have been a child actor—if not for his behavior." Her face dropped in sadness, as if she believed that she alone could have made a difference in Carlos' life, but had failed to do so.

45

"Carlos' behavior?" I asked politely with eyebrows raised.

"Oh, yes…well, Carlos' mother was quite supportive. On welfare too, with no husband, she worked off the books in the Korean fruit store around the corner. She practically ran the place for old Mrs. Ho."

"Did Mrs. Rodriguez come to school often?"

"Always. And when Carlos got in trouble, she'd race right in."

"What about Carlos? What was his problem? Why the so-called bad behavior?"

"I had my suspicions. It seemed Carlos would get depressed first, then act out. So one day I called Mrs. Rodriguez in and grilled her but good." The corners of Hirsch's mouth turned down. She took a deep breath then spoke quickly. "Carlos, it seems, was his father's favorite toy. That is, until Mrs. Rodriguez caught the creep having oral sex with his son, and kicked him out. She told him she'd have him thrown in jail if he came back."

"How did Carlos deal with this?" I asked.

"Not well. The boy blamed himself, and worse his mother, for his father leaving. I think he'll realize as he gets older why she had to kick him out, unless of course, he blocks the abuse out of his mind. I've seen that happen. Then he has a problem that never goes away. Once I overheard him describe his father to another boy. And do you know whom he described to a 'T'? John F. Kennedy." Hirsch chuckled.

I stared at her, faking a smile. A boy without a father did not exactly tickle my funny bone, and making another one up, was sadder still.

Hirsch stood up, joints crackling, and said wistfully but with a hint of anger, "If only we had the resources we should to properly counsel Carlos psychologically. But that's, well…that's a pipe dream, isn't it."

I called my office from the second floor teacher's lounge. Looming in the distance, just a hundred yards away, was the junkyard.

As I waited for Brenda to pick up, I thought about Carlos Rodriguez. Shula Hirsch had painted a vivid picture in my mind: bright wide-eyed little boy face, deep blue eyes. Eyes that are hard to forget. Fatherless. Lost. Little boy eyes.

"Nick? Nick are you there?" The receiver blared in my ear.

"Yes Brenda," I said somewhat startled. "That new client of mine, Guevara—did he call?"

"Not since I've been here," —she chuckled— "and I've been here all day."

When I hung up the phone, my eyes were transfixed on the gates to the junkyard—its chain links on each side that bowed out and down at the middle—its perimeter piping in tandem, winding round.

And as I stared out the window I saw an image form from the skeletal remains of rusted gate. It had the clarity and color of some horrific cartoon.

It was a wicked sinister smile.

Chapter 12

Little Italy in the heart of the South Bronx exists as a splendid anachronism along one long block of Arthur Avenue between 187th and 189th Streets. In the center, among a half-dozen Italian restaurants, homemade ravioli retailers, butcher shops and Italian delis, is Mario's. There is no more famous place to dine Italian in the borough.

As the rest of the neighborhood deteriorated, rebuilt itself, gentrified, regentrified, and then deteriorated again, Mario's and this one rock-solid Italian block held on. Whether the forces which acted upon it were legitimate or not would be left to pundits like Repolla when the occasion was right for an off-beat human interest story, or a real estate bit on cultural diversity, or maybe some local political news, or even a piece on organized crime.

Murder, money, mystery and making love was in the air in this old-world restaurant. It was in the food, the aroma of the tomato sauce, the gold-rimmed dishes, the red and white tablecloth, the house wine, beside the mirrored bar, and settling inside you with the attending passion of Enrico Caruso, Mario Lanza, the faint strings of a mandolin—a piano solo of *Speak Softly Love*.

I was sitting opposite Vinny Repolla, tearing apart garlic bread and curious as hell about his sudden lunch invitation: "An offer," he mimicked in a bad Sicilian accent that I "cannot refuse."

"So what did I do to deserve this generosity?"

"You didn't do anything yet," answered Repolla. "I've been thinking about what you said the other day about the Spiderman."

"I'm starting to think you're a little nuts. My job is to put the criminals back on the street, remember."

"Don't flatter yourself. It's not like I'm asking you to assist in his capture. It's just that my friend on the force thinks there may be something to tracking this guy through the comic book."

"Except the comic book hero didn't rape women," I answered.

"But the comic book hero," Vinny remarked with a proud gleam in his eyes, "when he wasn't donning his Spiderman suit, was a freelance photographer. I got the inside word that the detectives working the case are checking out every camera jockey that's ever done work for a city paper. They've started in the Bronx, of course."

"Any results?"

"Well," Vinny whispered, and then bent so far forward that the end of his tie was buttering his garlic bread. "I'm not supposed to say, but they're watching a guy who works for *The News* very closely."

"It still doesn't explain how the Spiderman knows what apartment to hit, and how he targets women who live alone. This guy's no amateur. He's calm, collected. This is a very strong grown man, who can climb up and down tall buildings like an Olympian."

Vinny took on the look of someone thinking hard, and getting a headache in the process. "Well, we've got a good idea what he looks like."

"The uncontrollable urge to rape repeatedly doesn't just surface in someone's psyche in their mid-twenties. This guy's got a history. Have the police checked out all the sex offenders recently released from prison?"

"Came up empty. This guy though…He knows the Bronx. He talked to one of the women he raped as if he'd lived here his whole life."

"Maybe he's changed his appearance. Maybe he wasn't bald and muscle-bound in prison."

"Doubtful." Vinny seemed annoyed at himself for being a step behind me. He flipped open the menu, welcoming the change of subject.

Chapter 13

Angling my Malibu into a parking spot in front of the building, I gauged the wisdom of leaving it out in the street merely to avoid the short walk from the Executive Towers garage. I double-pumped the door handle to make sure it was locked.

Jose Torres, one of Legal Aid's day clerks, was walking toward me, coming from the direction of the courthouses.

"Mannino!" he shouted. "Krenwinkle signed your subpoenas. They're in your mailbox." Before I could thank him he was upon me, and added in a half whisper: "By the way, a gorgeous blonde was here asking for you. I told her you were probably out to lunch. She must have been waiting for over an hour because she was still here when I got back from court. She looked kind of nervous or something." He got wide-eyed as if acknowledging some shared secret.

The waiting area was empty. I asked Frances, the receptionist, for the blonde's name, but when asked, she had refused to leave it.

Torres caught up to me as I entered the elevator. "I forgot to tell you," he said, panting and out of breath, "while the blonde was here asking for you, your D.A. girlfriend stopped by." He winked and gave me a conspiratorial grin.

* * *

Reception rang a call directly into my office. Brenda had left work early. Her little girl was sick again; something to do with her cell count.

"So who's the blonde you're screwing when you're not screwing me?"

I should have known better. Between men and women, there is no due process. And since decorum had been tossed out the window, I answered Eleanor in kind.

"She's a hooker, and a damn good one at that. Got arrested in a high-class sting operation in the Country Club Estates section. Was so pleased with my courtroom savvy, she offered me a freebie."

Eleanor ignored my remark. I told her it was probably the same blonde that I ran into outside AP-3—and that, I too, was curious as hell as to why she needed to speak to me again.

"Did you give her your name?"

"No. That's the funny part." I thought of the cop who helped pick up my papers. "Maybe she wanted to talk in private, found out who I was, and went to the office."

"But why didn't she leave her name?"

I huffed. "You'll have to ask her. Is this why you called?"

"Carolyn was in a fender bender; nothing serious."

I knew it wasn't serious. I knew Carolyn.

I did not think it was possible for two people to look so much alike, and one be so beautiful and the other so plain and hard looking. After graduating with a B.A. from Harvard and a Master's in English Literature from Columbia, by the age of twenty-five, Carolyn had authored a collection of short stories—all featuring women as central characters—all fighting for respect and recognition in, of course, a male dominated world.

Eleanor referred to Carolyn as her "absolutely best friend," but it was only in the past month that I came to know the whole truth about Carolyn.

Her not-so-secret "secret" was that she was a lesbian. So all things considered, she scared the shit out of me.

Before Eleanor and I hung up, we agreed to get together Saturday night. She insisted on meeting at my house.

Mom would be disappointed at missing Eleanor. Friday night was poker night—a nickel ante with a ten-cent raise cap. Saturday was Bingo with the girls. Mom was as religious about her Bingo and her poker as she was about her daily mass and Tuesday novenas.

Midnight approached and as Friday turned into Saturday and Johnny Carson introduced his first guest, *Baretta's* Robert Blake, the phone rang.

"Nick? I hope I didn't wake you? It's Ernie Krenwinkle."

"Why, hi Judge." I tried to mask the surprise in my voice.

"Sorry to call so late. Well, not really. That blonde that came in my courtroom the other day looking for you...The police found her on the front lawn of the Riverdale Towers. Dead. Seems she jumped. Thirty stories."

"My God...Who is she?"

"That's the funny part. No purse, no ID at all. Police are asking anyone who knows anything to come forward. Maybe you should call, Nick."

I thought for a few seconds. "Judge, I'd only add to the confusion. I haven't a clue who she is." I then imagined what her body must have looked like after falling thirty stories. "You sure it's the same woman?"

Krenwinkle sighed. "There's a picture of her in the evening *Post*, face up in the grass, crucifix around her neck, beige jacket and miniskirt. I'm positive it's her. Dead and all, she's still beautiful."

Chapter 14

At 4:00 A.M. an irrepressible exhaustion finally took over, and I fell asleep.

And the nightmares began.

I was inside a small battered wood shed. My eyes scanned about like flashlights. I tossed aside rusted rakes and sickles and hardened bags of fertilizer and mulch, as pins of light pierced through wallboard cracks and nail holes. There was something hidden in the darkness.

A patch of white, no bigger than a postage stamp appeared inches above a dirt floor. I reached for it. My fingers wormed their way inside two hard cylinders, smooth as ivory. I drew the object closer. I was holding a child's skull.

Attached to it was the torso of a fully dressed baby doll in cleats and Yankee pinstripes. I could feel my heart pounding and my body convulse in a silent scream.

I awoke. It was dawn.

I pulled myself free of tangled sheets and blankets. Struggling at first to keep my balance, I walked to the kitchen and opened the refrigerator door. The cascading light startled me.

I poured myself a glass of ice-cold milk and looked out the rear window over the sink. The sun was giving new life to the day. Behind my backyard and beyond a neighbor's fence were two adjoining baseball fields that belonged to the Birch Elementary School. The grass there would soon be green with spring, but for now it strained to glisten a tarnished gold in mid-March's early morning sun.

I wished Krenwinkle hadn't called. I could have used a good night's sleep.

Refusing to ponder my dreams for some meaning or interpretation, I went back to bed, and if I dreamed again, I did not remember it.

Chapter 15

I wanted the night to be perfect, considering the week I'd had. I hadn't seen Eleanor since the weekend, and it scared me how much I missed her.

A brand new BMW pulled into the driveway and came to an abrupt stop. The driver's side door swung open and Eleanor stepped out. She was wearing a black mini-dress that clung to her every curve. She wore heels and white pearls, and her hair was twirled up in a bun with two thin locks hanging down alongside diamond-studded earrings. She never looked more beautiful, and walked toward me with a sexiness that riveted me to her every move.

We kissed in front of the porch light, casting giant shadows across the lawn.

I tugged her gently into the house and locked the door behind us.

We made love in my eight-by-twelve bedroom for hours, then laughed and struggled to catch our breath. My eyes moved to the alarm clock on my night table. It was 8:00 P.M. I grabbed the phone.

"Who are you calling?" she asked.

"Dario's. We're going to be late, and there are only twelve tables in the whole restaurant."

Eleanor looked scared, like a child about to admit something awful. "Nick…"

In a pause that brought my world crashing down, I imagined her a black widow. We had made love; now she was going to kill me. Not with a knife or a gun, but slowly—by leaving me. She was going back to Atlanta to marry some rich guy; or…maybe just to get away from the likes of me. We were getting too serious. Her father hadn't raised this perfect young woman to marry some greaseball from Long Island. If she were my daughter, I'd have pulled the plug on this romance too; never mind Uncle Rocco.

"I understand Eleanor. Maybe we are going too fast." The inflection in my voice revealed my own uncertainty.

She looked confused and even more frightened. "Too fast? Do *you* think we're going too fast?"

I caved easily. "Is this something we have control over?"

"I guess not." She smiled weakly as I cradled her in my arms. She then said softly: "I love you, Nick."

With heartfelt meaning in every word, I said what I had never said before to anyone, ever: "I love you, too."

Life would never feel as good, nor have more wonder, magic, and exhilaration. I was frightened before she spoke, and more frightened after, for I knew then I could never survive losing her.

We kissed, Dario's all but forgotten, until we fell asleep. I awoke with a jolt half-an-hour later.

The thought of Mom coming home and finding Eleanor post-coitus sent me vaulting out of bed.

She searched the covers for her bra and panties. "Nick, what if you got your own place?"

"It's been me and Mom my whole life. We respect each other."

She pulled me close and laughed like a schoolgirl into my chest and neck. "Such a good son."

Later that night, I drove us to Jones Beach in Eleanor's BMW. We arrived at exactly midnight. The temperature had dropped below forty so we grabbed a quilt, wrapped ourselves in it, and walked along the boardwalk of Field 6. It was desolate—I knew it would be.

Eleanor questioned the wisdom of such a brazen confrontation with the cold and the wind colder still, rushing at us from the ocean's blackness.

"The quilt will keep us warm if we stay close," I said.

She smiled and cuddled under it as we walked along the rail.

A city block of darkened beach lay between us and the shoreline, where the sound of cresting waves rushed at us and dissolved away. We paused by a boardwalk lamp and gazed into endless blackness.

What could be more horrifying, I thought, than to be dropped in the middle of that darkness and left to die, or drown in a panic, or float as prey for whatever horrible creatures roamed the ocean's depth where the darkest secrets lie.

I was trembling. My thoughts shifted to the junkyard behind P.S. 92— its heaping debris piled higher than its dilapidated fences. Secrets were there too, contrived and stirring, like a spreading contagion.

Eleanor pulled me closer, and with one sweet smile, she drove away these pawing, meandering thoughts.

But they would soon return, and when they did, she would not be present to save me from them.

Chapter 16

The Bronx Supreme Court is a classic courthouse structure. Towering columns hold up an ancient Greco-Roman architectural design. Over fifty wide stone steps lead up to the entrances in front and back and on the Grand Concourse side of the building. Midway up these steps, I heard someone call out to me in a loud hoarse voice. It was my uncle, Rocco Alonzo.

I cringed.

A black limousine sat at the curb on 161st Street, just off the corner. Uncle Rocco, in black suit, white shirt (top button opened), and black patent leather shoes, began to scale the stone steps with two younger Italians in overcoats a few feet behind.

"That's my nephew, Nickie." The two henchmen looked at me blankly. "He's a lawyer with Legal Aid."

A broad smile never left Rocco's face as he kissed me on the cheek.

"What are you handling, a murder case in here or what?" he asked, pinching the sides of my face. "You know my nephew here never lost a trial." The two overcoats were now standing beside us. The youngest smirked contemptuously. Fortunately for him, Uncle Rocco didn't see it. He was busy covering my eyes with his hands as a flash camera went off in our faces. The two young Italians reflexively reached inside their overcoats then casually drew their arms out empty handed as a reporter sped away. "No need for you to be photographed with us, Nickie," Rocco said apologetically.

I figured, at worst, the flash caught the back of my head. "No problem, Uncle Roc."

There was a glimmer of sadness in his eyes.

We walked past the huge columns and into the courthouse. An elevator was waiting. All four of us got in. Rocco and his boys were headed for the third floor. I was on my way to the all-purpose Supreme Court Parts on the fourth. When the elevator opened on three, Rocco asked me to step off so we could "talk." He motioned for the overcoats to wait as we walked down the hallway.

There was a coarse edge to his voice that softened as he began to speak.

"Your mother called me. Says you're workin' too hard. Everything all right, Nick?"

I patted his shoulder in a not-to-worry fashion. "Just a tough case. Nothing I can't handle. Don't worry. Really."

"You know I only want the best for you. Not, not this." He nodded at the young Italians so I would understand he was referring to their life—to his life.

"I know, Uncle Rocco."

He was getting emotional and it didn't suit him, not the Rocco I knew. I wanted to change the subject.

"So what brings you to the Bronx?" I asked.

He took a long deep breath. "One of my boys, a neighborhood kid"— he revised his words, but not their import— "got into trouble. So I came to help out the mother. You know how it is."

"I'm sure she appreciates it."

He smiled, knowing I would ask no more questions. We walked back toward the elevator.

He pressed the "up" button for me and kept his arm on my shoulder until the doors opened. Normally, this display of affection would have made me feel awkward, but with Rocco it made me feel protected, secure, even at the age of twenty-seven. After the death of John Mannino, he was the closest thing I had to a father. Nevertheless, when the elevator arrived and I kissed him on the cheek, I was grateful no one was around to see.

Brushing the back of my lapel, he said: "We're all real proud of you, Nickie… Your mom and me. Your dad would've been too." There was love in his eyes.

I wondered when the time came whether he would rightfully succeed Carmine Capezzi or be passed over. The ramifications of either alternative saddened me deeply.

Chapter 17

Although no more than fifty-five years old, Judge Joseph Graham had the reputation of being an unpredictable and caustic geezer. That's a polite description—because I liked him. Many thought he was crazy—mostly Assistant D.A.'s, few of whom he liked.

Known in courthouse circles as Three-Gun Graham, he took the bench with three pearl handled revolvers: two shoulder-holstered, and one behind his back in Peter Gunn fashion. He also had a fourth revolver holstered at his right ankle. It is believed he added this additional artillery sometime after the name "Three-Gun" was permanently attached.

Although he was smart as hell, and therefore, receptive to a good legal argument—researching carefully his decisions and quite generous to the defense in plea-bargaining—he was much too discordant as a rule. With his sloppy appearance, and a reputation for eccentricity, he often had to fight for the judicial respect afforded other judges. In the process, he made enemies—on both sides of the bar.

As I stood before him to take a plea in the *People v. Raymond Jackson*, his honor was in an unusually jocular mood—unusual for Graham, especially on a Monday morning.

The cold weather had fogged up the courtroom's windows, while radiators beneath them hissed and clanged as a hard rain fell outside. Three out of six overhead globe lights were out. When thunder started to roll out over the building, and the day darkened and lightning cracked the sky, the atmosphere inside the courtroom became surreal.

With my client standing at my side, Graham ordered the Assistant D.A. and me to approach the bench. He told us that my client had written him a letter; congenial, courteous and respectful as it was, pleading for leniency.

Evidently, Graham was moved by it. Unfortunately, it would do Raymond Jackson no good.

Jackson was a predicate felon caught with a loaded revolver (the case now before Graham) while attempting to beat a subway fare by jumping a turnstile. Less than ten years earlier, he'd been arrested and convicted for robbing a Bronx bodega with two others. Jackson was merely the lookout. His court-appointed lawyer took an open plea, which meant, within sentencing guidelines, his fate was totally up to the judge.

In my entire career as a criminal defense lawyer—and I'm sure this is true of many able-minded attorneys—I never took an open plea in state court. It's just not done. You either make a deal you're satisfied with, or go to trial—the risk of leaving sentencing to the broad discretion of the judge, an unwise gamble.

Jackson's open plea was entered only one month after his arrest—at his first appearance in Bronx Supreme Court, moments after his arraignment on the indictment. His attorney had been Charlie Farkas, known otherwise around the Bronx Criminal Courts as "bleed 'em and plead 'em" Farkas.

I had always heard of ambulance chasers in personal injury cases. But I never saw a courthouse shyster work a hallway like Farkas. Working out of a storefront office on Sheridan Avenue, directly across from the Bronx Criminal Court, for just a hundred dollars or two, he'd take a case. Then, commanding thousands, he'd collect whatever he could, and when the money ran out, so would his effort (as limited as it was to begin with). A guilty plea was sure to follow.

And he got away with it, time and again.

Raymond Jackson did not deserve to go to jail for jumping a turnstile, loaded gun or not, for no less than two, and no more than four years—the mandatory minimum for a predicate felon in 1982.

Three witnesses saw Jackson scale that turnstile: the token booth clerk, a retired postal worker on his way across town to do volunteer hospital work, and one of New York's finest. When searched, a .32 caliber pistol was found in Jackson's waistband, along with a phony Toys 'R Us police badge and whistle. Jackson was a wannabe cop, who, because of his prior felony conviction, was ineligible to join the force. He had jumped that turnstile after receiving a 911 beep from his girlfriend, signaling she was in labor and about to give birth to their second child. But that wasn't all there was to Raymond Jackson's story.

On weekends, Jackson, along with half-a-dozen other volunteers, patrolled his neighborhood in the Soundview section of the Bronx. Their primary goal was to ward off street crime, particularly the corner-drug trafficking trade endemic to almost every South Bronx neighborhood.

Raymond Jackson was doing his part, and more, to make his world, and the world of his neighbors, friends and family, a better place. And *I* couldn't do a damn thing to help him.

In a political climate of one-year mandatory jail time for first offense loaded gun possession, for a predicate felon like Jackson, the gun charge would stand. And as a predicate felon, he could only plea down to an E felony with a minimum indeterminate sentence of two-to-four years.

I wanted to strangle Charlie Farkas.

Raymond Jackson, two heads taller than me and black as a moonless night, took the plea that Monday, amid the objection of thunder and lightning, in one cold and drafty courtroom.

Although it was unheard of to let a predicate felon walk out of Bronx Supreme Court facing a certain two to four, Graham allowed Jackson to remain free, pending sentencing six weeks later.

But that's why I liked Joseph Graham.

The Assistant D.A. had a shit fit—for appearance's sake. And I did believe Graham secretly hoped Jackson would skip, live a happy life somewhere else with his common law wife and children. I know I did. Sadly, if Jackson *had* chosen to skip, he would have done so with only his firstborn. The baby his girlfriend delivered while he was under arrest was stillborn.

On the way back to Executive Towers, I stopped by Farkas' storefront office, took a deep breath, and let the expletives fly. When I was done, to my shock and dismay, his son stormed out of a rear storage room and tore across the office like an uncaged lion.

I had forgotten about Charlie Junior. I had also forgotten that before he started law school, he was an all-city running back at Fordham U.

As I braced myself to sail through the plate glass window behind me, the bell atop the storefront door rang and the huge shadow of Raymond Jackson cast its way into the office.

"Hold it right there," Jackson shouted. Charlie Junior froze in mid-stride behind his still-seated iceberg of a father. I expected the fear on Junior's face would soon melt into a yellow puddle at his feet, for his knees shook as his eyes fixed in horror on the sight of the colossal Raymond Jackson.

"I'll do my time, and make the best of it." Jackson said. "And in the end, I'll be all right, but you…you will always be a leech lawyer, feeding on people's misfortunes. I pray your young one there learns a better way."

"You finished?" Charlie Sr. asked with brazen disdain. "Now don't let the door hit you two in the ass on the way out."

I looked up at Jackson, who, with a sardonic grin, turned and held the door open as I walked under his extended arm and into the street.

Among the sounds of the Sheridan Avenue traffic, a bus hissing to a stop, and the chatter of passersby, Jackson just smiled, and said "See ya."

As he walked away, I gave him one last look of apology—or perhaps it was a request for forgiveness.

Chapter 18

B renda handed me a stack of phone messages.

   "Nick, please give me any typing you have. I'm leaving at four. Jasmine has tests."

In heels, even half-heels, Brenda was an imposing figure, and she was noticeably losing weight with each passing week. What was always a healthy cherubic face had grown tired and older, and darker lines, darker than her dark black skin, hung like half-moons under her eyes. I patted her on the shoulder and handed her a Hershey bar.

   "Here. Give this to that pretty little girl of yours after she leaves the hospital. When I was a kid, my mom would always give me one after I got a shot."

   "Well then you'd better buy a whole bag full because she's a pin cushion already."

   I looked over my phone messages.

   Brutus Washington's wife called: *Wants to know why after two months her husband is still in jail.* Maybe it had something to do with Brutus trying to kill his next-door neighbor with a hatchet, and his caring Mrs. (now phoning his lawyer), squandering the bail money his mother gave her on a VCR and some smack. I set her message aside.

   Eleanor had called too: *Love and kisses and call me back.*

   There was a message from a Father Karras from Saint Nicholas of Tolentine: *Please call me re Peter Guevara.*

   Father Karras? I thought to myself. Where had I heard that name before? Was this the priest Guevara talked about? The priest that saved him from being gang raped in the orphanage as a boy? Guevara had never mentioned his name. Then it struck me: Damien Karras was the priest in *The Exorcist*.

I immediately dialed his number.

An elderly man answered and curtly asked me to hold. I heard the receiver quickly pass hands.

"Father Karras?"

A much younger but dispassionate voice said, "It's Kerres, K-E-R-R-E-S. Not Karras, like the priest in that awful movie."

"I actually thought the movie was pretty good."

"If you're a movie critic it was. If you're a priest, the subject matter, and the ending especially, were quite disturbing. Particularly if you're a priest with a similar sounding name, and, like the character in the film, a psychiatrist as well."

"You're giving me the creeps," I said jokingly, "although a part of me is disappointed. I could use a good exorcism."

I figured by the sound of his voice and by calculating his age via Guevara's encounter with him as an adolescent orphan, he must have been in his early-to-mid thirties. So I expected the young priest to joke back, and throw a witty retort my way. But none came.

And as time passed, I came to realize that this was a man who either had no sense of humor, or had lost it somewhere. I'd met people like this before, and almost always disliked them. Self-righteous, self-serving, self-pitying souls who had little excuse for their malcontent other than the selfish, unsatisfying lives they chose for themselves. But as a Roman Catholic myself, how could I feel this way about a priest?

To a child attending grades one through eight at Brooklyn's Saint Francis of Assisi, there was no one else on earth closer to God. It didn't have to be taught. It was understood. It was the priest who put *the body of Christ* in our mouths. *Amen.* Wild bandits on horseback may burn, rape, pillage and plunder, but in the end, spare the priest, whose life was its own sanctuary. Nuns were special—pure, good, trustworthy. But priests were God-like. I revered them—and feared them.

"You called me about Peter Guevara," I said.

He didn't react.

"Have you known him long?"

"A dozen or so years."

"Then you must have met him while he was an orphan at Saint Joseph's?"

"Yes. That's right."

A slew of follow-up questions raced through my mind, all concerning the attempted gang rape of Guevara, and Kerres' nick-of-time rescue. But asking them would have been too much, too soon, and Kerres seemed far from pleased with the course of our conversation.

"You've obviously gained Peter's trust, and rather quickly. You must be a very good lawyer."

There was a purpose to Kerres' flattery, but it got past me. Why did Kerres care about what I knew?

"Thank you, but it's hard work that rarely bears fruit. If we could meet in person I would really appreciate it."

Kerres offered to stop by and see me later in the week. My office was on his way to Yankee Stadium. It was his turn to pick up season tickets he shared with three other priests. Since we had a common love for baseball (not necessarily the Yankees, though), I was hopeful we would get along; if not famously, at least enough to be allies in the defense of Peter Guevara.

I could use all the allies I could get.

I called Eleanor. Her secretary, Jo, answered. Before I could utter a sound, she rattled on about how wonderful it was that Eleanor and I could get away from "all this court crap and have a great weekend." I was dumbstruck when she mentioned the Garden City Hotel where Eleanor and I spent Saturday night, but was relieved that she had the impression it was my treat. It wasn't. Not at two hundred a night. I could barely afford Dario's on my Legal Aid salary.

After Eleanor got on the line and teased me about getting my own place, she relayed some news via Peachtree Heights, Georgia. Her baby brother was getting married. The wedding would be held in Atlanta on the last Saturday in April, just six weeks away.

"Where they going to elope?" I asked. "How do you plan a wedding in six weeks?"

"It's been planned for over six months. I'm in the wedding party."

"Great. When were you going to tell me?"

"Listen. You know about what's-his-name?" She was referring to her ex-fiancé. I suspect she was alternately relieved and bothered that I never asked about him.

"Now that you mention it, no. I don't even know what what's-his-name's name is. And I don't care. Don't tell me you were going to the wedding with him?"

"Not since I broke off the engagement, of course not." She took a breath. "I can see you're getting the wrong idea. I wanted you to be happy about this, not angry."

"I'm not angry, just confused."

"Then come over for dinner tonight, and I'll unconfuse you."

"I'll be there at seven."

"Fine." She then whispered: "I love you, stupid."

As I hung up, Tom Miller popped into my office, bouncing a Nerf basketball on the front and back of his right hand. I hadn't seen him since the Guevara arraignment, and I wanted to know if he got any supervisory flack over my taking the case.

"If you get good results, most of the time the bosses will leave you alone," he cracked, bouncing the Nerf ball higher and higher. "C'mon let's shoot some hoops."

Through a narrow maze of corridors, we arrived at Tom's office where a small plastic basketball hoop hung atop the inside of his door. Acting like awkward fools (dribbling optional) we took turns shooting the Nerf from all angles until we broke a sweat and stopped.

And for those few minutes, as my adrenaline pumped and I struggled to catch my breath, I felt like a kid again, lost in innocent play—oblivious to evil's frenetic pace in the world.

Chapter 19

The FDR Drive moved at a crawl as I headed south on my way to Sutton Place. It was just after 6:00 P.M. and the heart of rush hour. After listening to about a half dozen tunes on the radio, I exited on East 58th Street and faced the greatest challenge of my life since leaving the office—finding a parking space on the East Side of Midtown Manhattan.

Twenty-minutes later, the search ended and with briefcase in hand I began a four-block trek to Eleanor's building. A grand Bulova clock atop a nearby billboard flashed the temperature and time. It was thirty degrees, and windy to a howl.

My ears were hard and numb and I was convinced I had frostbite; yet in the streets, crowds of pedestrian commuters seemed unfazed by the freezing cold.

I passed under the canopied entrance to Eleanor's building and the concierge buzzed me in.

I took the elevator to the seventh floor and hit the pop-in bell on apartment 7C.

"It's open!" Eleanor sung out.

Annoyed, I entered to find Eleanor in her bare feet by the stove, peach blouse un-tucked and hanging over a brown skirt. She stepped around a counter that separated the kitchen from the dinette and living room. We hugged. I was still holding my briefcase at my side. The two top buttons on her blouse were open and I could feel the swell of her breasts against my chest. We gave each other a few short kisses, each a bit longer than the last.

"It's hamburgers, fries and Coca-Cola. I'm doing a fifties thing."

I set my briefcase down next to the couch at the edge of a red tasseled area rug. "You know, if you really loved me you'd make sauce."

She smiled and walked into the kitchen. "Because I love you I won't make sauce. Trust me. I'd poison you." She headed for the bedroom. "Give me a minute."

"Eleanor, what's with the unlocked door? This is New York City for God's sake!" I took my jacket and tie off and draped them over the sofa arm.

"I know! I work here!" she yelled back. "Freddie buzzed me that you were coming up. I won't live in fear, Nick!"

"Just promise me you won't do that again. I don't care who you're expecting."

She emerged from the bedroom wearing jeans and a Harvard sweatshirt. "I promise."

She had gone to Brown, then N.Y.U. Law. *What's with the Harvard sweatshirt?*

Perceptive as always, she said, "I got this a few years ago in Boston. My father insisted I attend a meeting with him at Fidelity Investments regarding some trust money."

Relief poured over me. At least it wasn't the ex-fiancé's, who probably had a background, educational and otherwise, that made mine pale by comparison. And I wanted no reminders.

Eleanor grabbed a tray of burgers, fries and two eight-ounce bottles of Coke, and brought them to a small table by a window with a view of the river. I sat down and poured soda into two glasses packed with ice. Eleanor went back into the kitchen and returned with a bottle of Heinz ketchup, and sat down across from me. "Nick, we have to talk."

In the time it took me to clean my plate and finish my Coke and some of hers too, she told me everything she wanted me to know about the ex-fiancé, their relationship, and their break-up.

I gave her my undivided attention, while trying to conceal the knot in my stomach as she told me about their high school sweetheart days and relationship through college, even though she had gone to Brown, and he Georgetown. They got engaged during her first year at NYU Law, right after he was appointed vice president of his father's publishing company, the second largest in the country. They planned to marry after she graduated. Hating New York City, he'd visited her only once, and was incensed when she took the job as an Assistant District Attorney. Their parents counseled them in the hope of keeping them together.

They broke up anyway.

"Aside from a *Moon River* dance with a really nice guy I met at Cardozo Law, I never cheated on him, or wanted to." She tilted her head, and smiled that smile—the one that had just the right dose of reassuring love and attention I needed at that moment.

"And when I took the job downtown, I ended it. He readily agreed, and I suppose that hurt a bit. But then again, there was this new friend of mine; a little cocky, a bit conceited, who looked at me like no one ever has. But then you flunked the bar and I thought for sure you would turn into this horrible person." Eleanor caressed my knee with her hand. "But you didn't." She looked out at the river. "And, of course, there was the bar-hopping with Pal Joey. So I asked myself: is this a man who could be faithful? But when you asked me out and kissed me for the first time, I figured you'd turned out all right."

"Just all right, huh?"

"More than all right. I love you, Nick, more than I have ever have or will love. So don't give me any crap over why I didn't invite you to my brother's wedding sooner." She reached for my hand, squeezed it, and asked tenderly: "Do you feel better now?"

"Yeah I do."

We kissed…then fell onto the floor—Eleanor, chair, and me. Entwined, we rolled over and over on the rug, wrestling each other's clothes off.

"Nick? I think I'm catching a cold."

We were completely naked, the tender curves of her body pulsing against mine. "It doesn't matter." I said. "It doesn't matter."

Just after the eleven o'clock news I saw Eleanor to bed with two aspirins and a cup of tea. Then I did something this mama's boy had never done before—I washed all the dinner dishes, glasses and pans. I used Brillo on everything. Afterward, I borrowed her Harvard sweatshirt and a scarf, bundled up, and headed home.

Soaring along the Long Island Expressway, her words of love softly repeated in my head, along with visions of sailing the open seas with her—and never returning.

Chapter 20

A s I left for work, late as usual, the headline in *Newsday*, wrapped in a thin plastic bag on the porch steps, caught my eye. *Spiderman Rapist Kills #5 In Bronx.*

When I arrived at Executive Towers, Vinny was chatting with Frances at reception, who was sitting at her desk like a bank teller behind a bulletproof partition. She was goo-goo-eyed, as Vinny, in a wide collar shirt, sports jacket, and dress pants, made the dashing figure. With his Casanova look and American style, I was sure he'd abandon the free press and land in network news by the time he was thirty. He followed me into the elevator, and waited until we were behind the closed door of my office before revealing the purpose of his visit.

"They caught him!"

"The Spiderman?"

"He's a janitor in the same building where victim number five lived. And this time he murdered!"

"But why?"

"She put up one hell of a struggle. The police figure he couldn't get it up. So after he tied her hands behind her back, he strangled her." I shook my head in disgust. "It gets worse. She's the ex-wife of a Brooklyn cop—Italian guy, lives in Sheepshead Bay. Every paper and TV station across the country is expected to pick up the story."

"This janitor had better be guilty. He's going to hang on even the flimsiest evidence." I envisioned the hordes of press and camera crews mobbing the arraignment, along with thousands of cops thirsting for vengeance.

"My detective buddy in the 50th says there was a baby—a girl, ten months old—in a crib next to the bed. He made me swear not to tell. I'm the only reporter who knows so far." Vinny paused. He was breathing hard. "The bastard suffocated her with her own pillow." His face flushed red. "The father had to be restrained when he found out." Vinny sat down. I felt the blood rush to my feet as I leaned back on my desk.

I folded my arms across my belly, forcing my eyes not to close, even to blink, for fear I would never rid my mind of the mental picture of a dead baby. "Can they connect the janitor to the other rapes?"

Vinny got to his feet. "His prints are all over the apartment—even the crib."

"But he was the janitor there. And why were no prints found in the apartments where the other rapes took place?" The idea of slam-dunking this guy just didn't sit well with me.

"There's more. He's black, in his mid-twenties, muscular, and bald. But he wears a wig. Said he caught some childhood disease from eating bad bananas and lost his hair."

"OK, so he's bald," I answered, disconcertedly. "Why climb down from the roof like the Spiderman? As the janitor, couldn't he just go in the front door?"

"They'd know it was him," Vinny half-whispered, as if he alone had figured this out. "Victims two and three lived in the same housing complex five blocks away. He is one of seven custodians there also!" Vinny's eyes brightened.

"Does he have a record of sex crimes?"

"No," he said slightly disappointed. "No record at all. But he was seen in the building around the time of the murders, and get this: a search of his apartment uncovered a twenty-four karat gold locket belonging to the baby."

I didn't hide my astonishment. "What about rope and gloves and duct tape?"

"None of those things were found." Vinny's impatience was evident. "I wouldn't bet my life that this is the guy, but I'd damn well bet a year's salary. And if you take the case, like you promised, you can widen all the potholes of proof to your heart's content."

"I never promised to take the case." He put his hands on his hips as if betrayed. "If I can get the arraignment, I will, and that's it. Then it'll be assigned counsel or a Major Offense Bureau attorney at Legal Aid. If he's charged with murder right out of the box, there's no way my supervisors will let me touch it; and that's if the judge doesn't appoint counsel at the arraignment. And I'm playing no games this time. I mean it!"

Vinny turned obstinately and walked out. I felt like shit.

I caught up to him at the elevator. "If they don't charge him with the murders right away, I'll take the case, somehow, some way. Alright?"

"Alright," Vinny said quietly to the unopened elevator door, and I could see that my young reporter friend would not be happy unless I gave him an unconditional guarantee.

"You know there's no way I can take it if he hires private counsel."

Vinny arched his shoulders and said, "He's a janitor, for Christ's sake," then disappeared down the stairwell.

And it struck me: not only did I have to arraign the alleged Spiderman, but I also had to stay with the case long enough to get Vinny his exclusive—the real return favor.

The way the case was breaking, I figured that wouldn't take long.

Chapter 21

K renwinkle ignored me as I entered. It was Peter Guevara's adjourn date. Only corrections had no record of him.

I hurried into the clerk's office where a liver-spotted courthouse relic named Gilbert O'Toole peered at me over thin bifocals. When I asked about Guevara, he stepped to the rear of the clerk's office, made a phone call, then returned and said, "Pedro Guevara made bail the evening after he was arraigned. Fifteen-thousand cash."

I took a seat in the first row of the courtroom, feeling as if I had just been told Guevara had been beaten to death. I hadn't heard a word from him since his teary-eyed entrance into detention.

At any moment, I expected him to walk in with private counsel and not a drop of gratitude for what I'd done thus far. Regardless, it would be tough as hell justifying to Sheila why a Legal Aid lawyer should keep a case where a defendant had come up with fifteen grand cash to buy his release. Damn that I had already begun an investigation. My work would only wind up enhancing some private defense counsel's file.

Legal Aid's plead-em-out deadwood lawyers would laugh at my early jump on the case. Regardless, I wasn't going to wait around only to get bumped by some three-piece suit with a five-figure retainer. He could call me at the office if he wanted to review my file. I rose to leave.

Krenwinkle called out to me. "Mannino! Don't disappear! Your client was here looking for you!"

"Sure," I called back, my voice full of sarcasm. My *client* probably wanted to introduce me to his new attorney.

As I passed through the exit doors, I saw Guevara approaching. He was holding a small brown paper bag, crumpled at the top. Wearing a gray suit, white shirt, polished black shoes and a matching gray designer tie, he looked better groomed than any lawyer in sight.

"Nick!" he exclaimed like an old friend who had dearly missed me. I looked around for his new attorney. "I didn't see you in the courtroom so I went across the street to get some coffee." He pulled a Styrofoam cup secured by a shiny white plastic lid out of the bag. "Here, I got you one too. It's a regular."

"Thank you. But we'll have to drink them out here."

I grabbed the lid and pulled it off my regular to cool. He tossed his in a nearby garbage can and sipped piping hot black coffee without hesitation. "I can't thank you enough, Nick. An officer in detention told me I got lucky when I got you. You were really great in court last time, and that D.A. was a real crumb, and you made the judge see that."

I realized then that, for better or worse, Guevara had every intention of taking his chances with me.

When the case was called, Krenwinkle didn't seem the least bit surprised to see my client free on bail. With his wife at the helm, P.S. 92 had raised two-thousand-five-hundred dollars of Guevara's bail. Guevara himself came up with the thousand he had in the bank. An employer, I knew nothing about, a real estate broker in a part-time job Guevara had renting apartments on weekends and weeknights, staked another twenty-five hundred. And to cap off this pot of generosity, a doctor friend, who lived in the affluent Country Club Estates section of the Bronx, put up the balance—nine-thousand big ones. Guevara handed me the M.D.'s number and asked me to give him a call—at the doctor's request.

Assistant D.A. Jimmy Ryan had sauntered in minutes earlier. Since he was out of rotation in AP-6, it was apparent he was intent on seeing this case through. When he saw Guevara in suit and tie, he became visibly incensed. "Your honor. Yesterday the grand jury voted to indict this man on all counts, regarding all three child complainants."

A few deliberate "yeahs" came from a small group behind us—part of the neighborhood watchdog committee, no doubt still bitter from missing the arraignment. Krenwinkle waved them quiet.

"I move the bail be increased to fifty thousand dollars," Ryan said indignantly.

Krenwinkle stared down at the prosecutor. Guevara stiffened. No doubt Krenwinkle was concerned I would then respond, and appropriately so, by stating the source of all the bail money, including his wife's part in raising it.

"Judge," I said, "over two dozen friends and co-workers helped raise this man's bail. They believe in him enough to stake their hard-earned money on his returning time and again to face these charges. And they did so the very day after his arraignment. My client has been free for six full days knowing, as Mr. Ryan assured us all at arraignment, he would show up to hear he had been indicted. As a result, there have been no changed circumstances that would justify disturbing the bail set by Judge Benton."

"Application denied," Krenwinkle said. "Mr. Ryan, you may renew your request in Supreme Court before Judge Graham, Part 30, April 6th. Case adjourned for arraignment on the indictment."

Ryan slammed his folder shut and shoved it under his arm as if part of a military drill. "See you in Supreme, Mannino." He brushed past Guevara and myself and left the courtroom, the smell of his cheap cologne filling the air.

Outside in the lobby, Guevara gave me a pat on the back and a hug, all with the comfortable camaraderie of an old football buddy. I was amazed at how quickly his emotions changed, depending on the circumstances in or out of the courtroom. But I thought it healthy that he was able to express himself so easily in view of the terrible stress he was under.

To my relief and surprise, he hurried away, telling me he'd call in a couple of days.

When I returned to AP-6, Krenwinkle, no doubt relieved he and his wife weren't the afternoon *Post's* front-page news, had called a ten-minute recess.

I found him sitting behind his desk in his makeshift chambers beside the courtroom. A *Daily News* was draped on his lap. The headline was simpler than *Newsday's,* but announced in equally horrifying terms: *Spiderman Kills.*

"I figured you'd be back," Krenwinkle said, as he pushed the news-paper aside. Of course, he had no way of knowing a suspect-janitor was already in custody. "I've got news for you on that blonde," he blurted.

"I thought you might." Knew was more like it. If the Administrative Judge wanted to know the status of an active investigation in his county, he merely had to pick up a phone. Krenwinkle had lived and worked in the Bronx his whole life; he'd get whatever information he wanted, and from reliable sources too.

"That was no suicide," he said. "She was tossed off that roof and put up one hell of a fight. The cops think she hung from the edge until her assailant stomped on her fingers. Evidently, she also tried to cling to the side of the building as she fell. Her palms and fingertips were scraped to the bone from contact with the brick facade."

"So they can't take her fingerprints?"

"They can take them, but it ain't gonna do much good. They're trying to piece together her identity from partial prints. Don't hold your breath."

"Jesus. And no one's come forward looking for her."

"You got it, *paisan'*. You might be of help too, if you can shake some screws loose and figure out why she wanted to see you."

Chapter 22

I left the Bronx Criminal Court in a blur of suits, briefcases, and blue uniforms. By the time my head cleared I had walked over two blocks up the lightly traveled Sheridan Avenue, instead of along the busy Grand Concourse on my way back to the office.

The further I walked along the side streets and outside the imaginary zone around the Criminal Court within which lawyers, civil servants, court officers, and police regularly trafficked, the more I invited a confrontation with the worst of the local element—the poor, the desperate and even the drug-crazed.

I scaled the curb on the corner of 164th with my head bouncing pugnaciously toward 165th, defiance in every step—come and get me.

A small garbage-filled lot flanked my left side. Car parts, cans, bottles, and tattered newspapers lay in the dirt and weeds. The carcass of a dead cat covered with flies lay crumpled against a pile of egg white stones.

A row of abandoned buildings with boarded and cinder-blocked windows and doors followed. Concrete stoops, faded and cracked, stood as a relic to the families who long ago struggled and commiserated there, on its landing, on its steps, while their children played—shared lives lost to politicians, businessmen, landlords, gentrification, neighborhood fear, street fear, fear of the unknown.

In the middle of this block, on this same side of the street, there stood a two-story brownstone. It was the only visibly inhabited building on either side. Two wooden doors with beveled glass panes separated the South Bronx Street from those who dwelled within. Standing behind one of the doors, in the pale light of the vestibule, was a shirtless Hispanic boy, nine or ten years old. Dark-skinned, with straight black hair, oval eyes and full lips, he watched as I walked, then stared as I stopped on the sidewalk at the bottom of the steps that led to his front door. He pointed his finger at me contemptuously.

I looked down, then back up at the door. The boy was still standing there. Only this time he was black. I winced then looked at him again, and he was laughing, like he hated me, relishing my confusion. My heart was pounding, but I wouldn't look away.

I watched as the boy disappeared into the murky vestibule, then I continued walking toward 165th Street—quickly.

I called Vinny Repolla from my windowless office. With a reporter's resources at his disposal, he was in a good position to learn the identity of the dead blonde. Once I knew who she was, I would know why she wanted to see me.

Vinny called midway through a meeting that Sheila Schoenfeld, Douglas Krackow, and all fifteen Complex C attorneys attended for the sole purpose of setting next month's arraignment schedule. I handed my choice of dates, good and bad, to Tom Miller, and took the call at my desk.

Vinny was intent on talking about the Spiderman. The accused janitor was headed for central booking. He would be arraigned in the morning. But not for double murder. And not for rape either. For burglary—for taking the dead baby's locket.

The D.A.'s Office might as well have held a press conference to announce they had problems—big problems connecting the defendant to the murders of the mother and child, no less the sexual assaults on the other four victims.

"Wonderful," I said incredulously. "I suppose you'll want me to do both arraignments; one for the burglary, then the follow-up for the rapes and murders." I was disgusted at getting sandbagged in a way even Vinny hadn't intended.

"Just do what you can," Vinny said with a sudden complacency. "I'll be happy just to get one inside story on this. I don't care when it comes."

"You may just get your story," I answered bitterly. "A team from my complex is on arraignments tomorrow. It shouldn't be hard for me to do a switch."

"I knew you'd come through."

This was a handshake deal, one I could easily get out of, and he knew it. I wondered if he'd practiced that look of betrayal he leveled me with last time, just to sucker me in.

"But I need you to help me out on something else," I said.

I described the blonde I'd run into at the courthouse, and how she'd shown up later at my office. When I told him she was found dead, and that the police were unable to identify her and suspected a homicide, I asked him to speak to his friends on the force to see what they could find out. He swore he'd clear all information with me before anything went to press. I thanked him. My treat at Mario's next time.

Switching into arraignments for the next day was easier than I thought. Of the three lawyers scheduled, I picked the one who looked the weariest as he left the complex meeting. As I expected, my tired associate was thrilled to give me the following full day in court in exchange for one of my day arraignments two months hence.

I passed Tom Miller in the hallway and thanked him for securing a good mix of dates for me. In return, he wanted to go another round of Nerf ball.

I still had to knock off an investigation request on Sandra Chavez, and with the dead blonde on my mind and thoughts of the circus that awaited me at the Spiderman arraignment the next morning, I could barely keep my eyes open. The look on my face was all the answer Miller needed. He waved back and said, "Tomorrow then," and disappeared down the hall.

Tomorrow. Sure. I sat down in my office and cupped my eyes in my hands. And in the blackness I imagined a hurricane, stirring, picking up speed slowly, dangerously, with the Bronx Criminal Courts and Executive Towers directly in its path.

I called Eleanor at the Manhattan D.A.'s office and reminded her again to lock her apartment door no matter who she was expecting. My tone was patronizing—a result of the mood I was in. I realized this afterward when she responded that she would, with no note of appreciation for my concern. Then again, it wasn't concern I was speaking from. Eleanor was now something else I had to worry about. I was sure I sounded cold. And she responded in kind.

She mentioned that Carolyn would be spending a weekend with her sometime next month. Great. I started to cut the conversation short.

"By the way," she said. "I put in for a transfer—to Rackets."

I felt my stomach drop. "Rackets?"

"Yeah, Rackets, organized crime. You know."

"Why would you want to transfer to Rackets?"

"Don't worry. The mob doesn't kill assistant D.A.s. It's bad for business." She paused then said sternly, "Lord knows I don't tell *you* what cases to handle."

"I'll make a deal with you. After this week, I promise I will not take another remotely sex related case, if you stay out of Rackets."

"What is your problem with Rackets? It's not like I'm going to take on Carmine Capezzi himself." She thought again. "Oh, I get it. This is some Italian thing that I could never understand. Right?"

The thought of Eleanor discovering that my own mother's brother and Carmine Capezzi's most senior underboss were one and the same, terrified me. I was certain my uncle's identity, which I had been concealing from her since law school, would end it for us, no matter how much she loved me.

I backed off a little. "It's just that it's a dirty business, El. One I hate to see you involved in. Just think it over, ok?"

"Fine. But if I do decide on Rackets, I don't want any more guff from you; just support, like you're supposed to give."

"All right," I said weakly.

It could have been worse, I thought. But not much worse. She could have been an A.D.A in Brooklyn—Rocco's stomping ground. What a cruel twist of fate that would have been. Rocco would have had to come first, if merely out of simple family loyalty, however perverse or misguided. It *must* be in the blood. Maybe Eleanor was right. Maybe it was an "Italian thing." Or maybe it was just a sign we never belonged together from the start.

Chapter 23

Before I left the office, I slid an order marked "RUSH" under the door of Legal Aid Investigations on the third floor. On it was a request to interview Sandra Chavez, little Jose's mother. I expected her to talk it up and good, and wanted a full recitation of her version of the facts before and after Guevara's arrest. She was the one who'd called the police and brought the Rodriguez boys into the case. I wanted her probed for a motive to lie, or better yet, a reason to press charges she knew to be false. Money, I figured, was at the top of the list.

I knew from Shula Hirsch at P.S. 92 that Sandra Chavez had wasted no time hiring a lawyer. This was to be expected from a parent whose child had been victimized by a city worker. But the ink had barely dried on the criminal complaint. So how distraught could she have been?

I also needed to know whether she'd spent any time alone with the Rodriguez boys. Had one of her sleazy boyfriends been present? Had one or both of them coerced the boys into lying?

I specified that my request go to Gene Raines. Sheila used him exclusively on all her cases, and although I would on occasion use him also as the rotation of assignments allowed, on this case I wanted and needed the best—especially if I was going to succeed in putting Sandra Chavez on trial along with Peter Guevara. Aside from the charges against Guevara, her pedigree of parental neglect and drug abuse would provide a stark contrast to Guevara's hard working background and college education.

Gene had a keen sense of when to talk and when to listen, when to be aggressive, when to be charming, and even when to be rude in order to elicit an answer from a suspecting or unsuspecting witness. Unlike most of the investigators at Legal Aid, he'd never been a street cop and had no detective experience. When he retired as a state trooper, his wife, who worked in personnel at Legal Aid's Park Row headquarters, got him the job. At fifty-five, he had been with Legal Aid for over ten years.

I expected Gene to come through for me. On the big cases he always did. He also always suggested the defendant take a lie detector test. "It helps," he'd say, "to know whether your client is lying to you."

Gene knew as well as anyone that almost all our clients were guilty; and almost all our clients denied guilt, especially when it came to sex crimes. Gene seemed to think you represent an innocent man one way, a guilty man another. I felt differently.

I ordered the lie detector test anyway.

Arthur Cantwell, president of the National Association of Polygraph Examiners, was considered one of the best in the business. He had an office in Midtown and I had used him five times in the previous six months. Since each examination cost the Legal Aid Society four hundred and fifty dollars, I needed Sheila's approval first. She gave it easily. I also needed Guevara's.

After my assurance that it was strictly a confidential procedure, Guevara voiced what I viewed to be a natural reluctance, but then complied. He insisted though, regardless of the outcome—which he was optimistic about—that he was most definitely an innocent man. It was important, he said, that I believed this.

Chapter 24

M om cooked and served dinner, then quickly cleared the table, all the while humming Sinatra. An evening ahead of poker with the girls had lightened her mood. I followed her as she hurried out the door. I figured a stroll around the Little League fields behind our backyard would relax me. Lord knows, I needed relaxing.

"Leave the dishes," she said. "I'll do them later."

"I don't mind Mom, really."

She asked if everything was going okay with Eleanor. When I assured her that we were doing fine, she wanted to know why I looked so worried during dinner. I blamed work, and told her she mistook worried for tired.

She stopped at the top of the porch steps. Not tall myself, I was still a head taller than her and like a little boy in tow, I paused and stood alongside her. She suddenly seemed to want to talk some more. I suppose I did too.

"I heard you ran into Uncle Rocco the other day." She looked at me for confirmation.

"Outside Supreme Court."

"He said you looked like such a handsome lawyer. Said you had a big case on."

"It was just a gun charge, but you know Uncle Rocco. Sometimes he sees just what he wants to see."

She turned to face me and her soft manner became instantaneously stern. "He sees *you*, Nickie. Better than you think." She poked my forehead with her index finger. "And he's a better man than you think he is."

Right. The gangster with the heart of gold. I looked down at my watch.

She sighed and led me back into the house. "There is much you don't know, and probably don't need to know," she said. "But you being a grown man and a lawyer now too, I suppose it's better you hear it from me."

We sat down on the living room sofa and faced each other.

Mom gave me a melancholy smile, then began...

Holbrook Juvenile Detention Facility was located just outside Cooperstown, New York. In December of 1941, Rocco was sentenced to remain there until his eighteenth birthday for the murder of his brother-in-law, Vito.

Three days later, he was fighting for his life against the worst Holbrook had to offer, and his three attackers quickly discovered how terribly they had misjudged their mark. He had broken bones in their arms, hands, and faces. And their leader, Paulie Rago, would never see clearly out of his left eye again. He vowed revenge.

For over two years, the Rago gang had terrorized Holbrook—robbing inmates at will, and raping the younger, weaker boys. One stormy night Rocco jumped Paulie, dragged him behind one of the outhouses, and killed him. Paulie's body was never found.

Thereafter, Rocco would rule a safer and more disciplined inmate population, to whom the mystery of Paulie Rago's disappearance...was no mystery at all.

Sexual attacks ceased. Baseball and basketball teams were formed. Boxing became the favorite form of recreation for the worst of Holbrook's juvenile offenders. Rocco became heavyweight champ, while also attending school and doing surprisingly well in most subjects.

He became a model detainee, and accumulated a following—forty-two boys, all Italian, all from Brooklyn, all under his direct leadership. He had created his own gang. He called it—*The Pigtown Boys*.

One month after the bombing of Hiroshima and Nagasaki and the end of World War II, Rocco, at age eighteen, was released from Holbrook. He hopped on a bus down to Westchester, through the Bronx, and into the city. And as Rocco's Brooklyn-born inner circle was released from Holbrook, the *Pigtown Boys* of Flatbush and East New York grew in number, with Rocco as their leader.

Sallie Gurrieri was small for his age, even for the son of native-born Sicilians. At sixteen, he'd been arrested for a string of burglaries committed with an older boy in Marine Park, Brooklyn. The older boy got away. Sallie didn't.

Upset that Sallie's accomplice escaped, and with the goods too, the police proceeded to beat the ever-living daylights out of him. He refused to give up his partner. Sallie was still limping when the judge sentenced him to eighteen months at Holbrook. Sallie was tailor-made for Rocco's crew.

What began as a means to keep the as yet uncivilized Pigtown Boys of Holbrook in line, soon became a profitable criminal enterprise, and it was not long before Rocco's growing notoriety and success could no longer remain a neighborhood matter.

When Rocco met Brooklyn's *capo*, Carmine Capezzi, it was a match of the young worthy upstart and the older self-made *Mafioso*. Both were from the streets, and each shared a similar perspective on life, their world of crime, and what it took to sustain it. The meeting took place in the basement office of the Portelli Ravioli Shop on Thirteenth Avenue and Seventieth Street, in Bay Ridge, Brooklyn.

Rocco knew Capezzi's reputation, and how things worked. He could be fed, warmed with attention and kissed on both cheeks—only to be shot in the temple after dessert without so much as a clearing of Capezzi's throat. Sallie, armed and ready, waited in a car out front.

Carmine Capezzi looked younger than Rocco imagined, and with the slow upturned hand of a pontiff, he gestured for Rocco to sit. By hour's end, they were lining small coffee cups with lime peels, sipping piping hot demitasse, and sampling pastries Rocco brought. They'd quickly struck a deal.

Rocco would work all of Brooklyn, not just Flatbush, while Capezzi provided the police protection. Half the precinct captains were on his payroll and there wasn't a Brooklyn judge he couldn't get to. For this he would get twenty-five percent of the gross. It would be up to Rocco to run his operation at a profit.

Other than Rocco, only Sallie, Rocco's right arm and most trusted soldier, got a guaranteed share of the take.

As time passed and business flourished, Rocco made more for Capezzi than the Brooklyn *capo* ever expected. As a result, Capezzi cut Rocco a better deal. He knew Rocco was a find; a true old- world mobster with brains, guts, and steel hard loyalty, and Rocco had a keen sense of the politics of crime—the fast and hard nature of the business.

Rocco got rich. Capezzi got richer.

In the underworld of crime, Rocco's reputation grew as a no nonsense *capo* who managed a tightly run operation. His word was granite, the loyalty he gave and demanded unquestionable. Cross him and die. There were no warnings.

With the reins of power, however relatively and temporarily secured, money poured in—in truckloads. As a result, Rocco began to funnel his newfound wealth into real estate: dozens of two-, three- and four-family houses scattered throughout Brooklyn, all owned by shell corporations, and all managed by Rocco and his crew. Rent was not hard to collect.

Come 1954, however, with the increasing enormity of Rocco's operation, even real estate could not cover the growing cash profits. Rocco needed a steady business and an easy constant vehicle for laundering money.

At Rocco's direction (and with his recipe), on my birthday, July 29th, 1954, Sallie opened up their first pizzeria on the corner of Parkside Avenue and Nostrand. Come 1958, Rocco had ten pizzerias scattered throughout Brooklyn. Add laundered mob money, and no single store, pizza place, or restaurant chain in the state declared more on the book's income.

Three months after the first pizzeria was opened, I was baptized.

Out of love for her brother and to ensure my ultimate safety and survival in a way few mothers could, Mom made Rocco my godfather over the privately adamant, but publicly quiet objection of my biological father.

Rocco arrived at my christening in a sharkskin suit, and to Mom's surprise, with a date. A catered affair at the Parkside Lanes was but one of two gifts from the godfather himself. The other: two hundred shares of AT&T stock, and in my name only.

Mom had never seen Rocco happier.

But there was more.

Rocco Alonzo, for the first time in his life, was in love.

I slapped down hard on my knees. "How come I never heard this?"

Mom glanced at the clock on the TV and grabbed her coat. "I'm late for poker. Some other time, maybe."

"Oh, no you don't. And what do you mean, maybe?"

She kissed me on the cheek and rushed out the front door. I ran after her.

She paused by the driver's side door. I was a few steps behind. "Your uncle loves you, Nick. Whatever happens, you remember that." She started her Corolla and rolled down the window. "I love you too, Nick."

I watched her turn up Kirkwood Avenue until she made a left and disappeared.

"And I love you, Ma," I whispered.

I went back inside and prepared my own special tranquilizer of chocolate ice cream and Coca-Cola, then went to bed.

Out of my night table drawer I pulled a paperback copy of *The Great Gatsby*. I had kept it there since taking an English Lit class in college. I read the first page, relishing the poetry of its beginning: *"In my younger and more vulnerable years..."*

Then, my thoughts wandering, I flipped to the end. *"...So we beat on, boats against the current, borne back ceaselessly into the past."*

I drifted off to sleep.

Chapter 25

Rain pounded the Bronx Criminal Courthouse. Television crews armed with cameras propped on their shoulders like bazookas covered in plastic scrambled on the sidewalks and curbs, rushing to secure a spot outside AR-1 where Oscar Jefferson, the prime suspect in the Spiderman rapes and murders, was about to be arraigned.

I parked in a garage a block away and raced, umbrella in hand, briefcase in the other, to the Sheridan Avenue entrance. The doors were locked. They were never locked before.

I trotted to 161st Street, hugging the building, turned the corner and headed for the main entrance. News vans and broadcast trucks crammed every inch of curb, and there were more police cars double- and triple-parked than were needed to quell the worst inner city riot. Traffic was at a standstill. Inside the courthouse, barricades had been set up just a few feet from the escalators leading to and from the second floor. Tables stationed beside three short makeshift aisles were used as a security canvas. Every civilian was frisked before being allowed to enter. A court officer I knew noticed me at one of the checkpoints and motioned me through after a cursory check of my briefcase. He said that Krenwinkle had called for the heightened security.

After the murder of the Brooklyn cop's ex-wife and baby, every newspaper characterized the Spiderman with a different printable expletive. *The Daily News* declared the killer of the infant "the most hated man in New York." And no group wanted him dead more than the New York City police force.

In the rain, the rush, and the rigors of courthouse security that morning, the paradox of fate had come full circle: hundreds of cops with holstered guns at their sides, and hatred in their hearts, passed through checkpoints undisturbed.

The lobby outside AR-1 was packed like Times Square on New Year's Eve. Cameramen were assisted by crewmen with overhead lights on long silver poles. TV reporters, several of whom I recognized from the evening news, congregated near the closed courtroom doors, and it was hard to tell who was more blood thirsty: the public, the media, or the blanket of uniformed cops gathered in the rear of the lobby.

I ducked into the hidden corridor that ran behind the courtrooms and entered the rear of AR-1. Robert Cantor, a Legal Aid Major Offense Bureau attorney working out of Complex C, had the Oscar Jefferson file in his hand. I still had my coat on and my hands were soaked from holding my umbrella. Cantor must have owed someone in our Complex big time to be working arraignments. As a Major Offense lawyer, he handled only the most serious of cases, and one of the perquisites he enjoyed was the elimination of all arraignment duties.

He caught my look of concern. "What's the matter, Mannino? You want the Spiderman?"

"I think I got this guy on another case," I said unconvincingly.

"Bullshit. This guy's got no priors. If you want to arraign the case, just say so. I'll probably wind up with it anyway."

"I want the case," I said, and with a flip of the wrist he handed it over. I thanked him.

"No problem, hot shot. You need any help, let me know."

Chapter 26

O scar Jefferson sat like an obedient little boy behind a table in the back of the interview area of pre-arraignment detention.

"I knew I never should have taken that locket," he said while looking down.

Believing I was about to hear more incriminating statements, I took a seat across from him and signaled him to keep his voice down.

"Why do you say that?" I asked.

"You my lawyer right?" He was staring at the business card I had placed on the table between us. "You're no D.A., cop or detective tryin' to trick me?"

"I'm your lawyer," I said emphatically. "The courtroom is out there and you're about to be arraigned on a burglary charge."

"Burglary? I went into that apartment to put up window guards 'cause of her baby. I'm the custodian. When I was moving the crib to get to the window, the locket was on the floor so I picked it up. Grace was in the kitchen feedin' the baby."

I braced myself for the gory details to come.

"So Grace says I should keep it, as a tip. It was a cheap gift from her no-account husband, she says. It was pretty and all, but I really didn't want it. A couple of bucks woulda' been better."

"Did you tell this to the police?"

"Sure I did. For twelve fuckin' hours! And the more I repeated it, the more they hit me in the head with a fuckin' phone book. They punched me in the kidneys too. One crazy fucker kicked me in the balls. I thought they were gonna kill me. They wanted me to say I killed Grace and her baby."

"Are you all right now?" I asked, even though he looked fine—his lack of hair and beard compensating for that grungy, tired look I'm used to seeing on defendants after days of pre-arraignment detention.

"I'm okay. Just wanna get outta here."

"I can understand that, but I don't want you making any more statements to anyone, especially the police. Anything you say, they'll use against you if they can."

Jefferson listened like a nervous pupil. With the fluorescent light fixtures beaming down on his smooth head, his complexion seemed lighter than it actually was. His small straight nose led me to believe there was some Caucasian in his background. I looked at his hands. They were not large by any means. Veins lined his muscular biceps and forearms. I asked him to take his shirt off so I could see for myself if the cops had left any bruises. This was only partly true. I wanted to check his physical condition. The Spiderman had to be built like a gymnast with lean, cut muscles. Jefferson was built exactly that way. And he had no bruises.

Vinny Repolla's police sources had told him that Jefferson always wore a wig to cover his bald head, and that his prints were found all over the apartment.

"Do you shave your head?" I asked, pretending not to know the answer.

"No. I lost all my hair at the age of ten," he said as if repeating this for the thousandth time.

"How'd that happen?"

"Bananas. I was livin' with my father on a chicken farm outside Macon, Georgia. One day, I ate about a dozen bananas and got real sick. A few weeks later my hair fell out. The doctor said it would grow back, but it never did."

He looked down and told me about the teasing he endured from other children, until he moved to Jamaica, Queens at the age of fifteen, where all the kids at school thought he looked cool.

An only child, his mom died of pneumonia when he was six. I asked about his father, and he told me that he passed on a year ago after a long bout with cancer.

As we spoke, Jefferson never stopped drumming the table top with his fingers and bouncing his knee. He looked at me and grimaced. My subtle search into his background for something, anything that could have created a maniac killer, was evidently not appreciated. He demanded, in kind, to know about my own family.

"My father is dead, too," I said, meaning my stepfather. (I had no idea where the sperm donor, as I often called him, was.) "And I don't have any brothers or sisters either."

Jefferson stood. "We both know I'm not here for some burglary. I didn't get hit with a phone book and beat to shit for no burglary."

"Oscar, I'm here to help you, if I can. You'll just have to trust me on that. Now I can buy what you told me about the locket, but why were your prints all over the apartment?"

"They're not all over the apartment. They're probably on the night table next to her bed, the headboard…" He put his hand to his head as he thought, and I leaned back, astonished by his candor. "Some of the kid's toys, a toy chest. Yeah, definitely the toy chest." His eyes widened as his face lit, not in shock or horror, but in remembrance and satisfaction. I was growing nervous at the ease of his recollection and his lack of remorse. "Some chairs, a small kitchen table…I can't think of anythin' else." He sat down and nodded, as if marking an accomplishment—pleased to have re-membered so much. I expected nothing short of a full confession to follow.

"How did your prints get on all those things?"

"Because I touched them."

I demanded to know why. He calmly told me that he had helped Grace unload a van filled with these items one week before the murders. She had been living in the building for about a month and gave him twenty bucks afterward.

"Did anyone see you moving her stuff in?" I was trying to test the au-thenticity of a near perfect explanation for the prints, assuming of course the lady in residence had not cleaned or waxed her furniture in a week.

"A cop. Musta been her ex-husband. She was real cold toward him. He brought her the baby. I was just puttin' some stuff down in the kitchen when he walked in."

"He had a key?"

"No. The door was open."

"What did he say? What did he do?"

"He didn't do nothin', just gave Grace the baby and looked at me real weird."

"And, what did *you* do?"

"Nothin'. I just finished puttin' some boxes against the wall where she told me to and stood there waitin' for my money. I felt funny being there. They were talkin' about when he would see the baby next, you know, like they were doin' business or somethin'. Then he looked at me like who the fuck *are* you? And Grace, you know, saw this and got me my twenty. Then I left."

"Did you ever see this cop again?"

"Nope."

"Did you ever see Grace again?"

"I saw her by the mailboxes about two days before…you know…what happened."

"Did she say anything to you?"

"Just hi… 'Hi Oscar'. That's right. That's what she said. I remember exactly because I thought it was nice she called me by name; friendly like. She seemed like an alright person."

"Was the baby with her?"

"In a little stroller…a little carriage. I held the door for her."

"What was the baby like?" I was probing his feelings for the victims, hoping he would not pick up on it. Beads of sweat tingled on my forehead and I asked myself what it was I feared most: that I was sitting across from a diabolical killer. Or that I wasn't, and if so, that he deserved a much better lawyer than me—especially since he was about to become the number one target of prosecution and the subject of the most torrential negative publicity the Bronx had seen in decades.

A headache was beginning in my eyes.

Jefferson still seemed to be searching for words to describe the infant girl. "She was cute…tiny…wrapped in white blankets. She wasn't big enough to walk. Like she was just a few months old."

"Was she crying when you saw her?" Maybe that's why he killed her that night. A baby's cries could sound like a siren to someone not used to them, no less a maniacal rapist.

"I never heard her cry. She was just goo-goo-in', stuff like that."

"What about Grace? What was she like?"

"I told you. Nice."

"What did she look like?"

"Pretty. Very pretty. Looked pretty good too for just havin' a baby."

"Did you ever think maybe, you know, since she was so nice, you... stood a chance with her?"

"You mean like as a boyfriend or somethin'?"

"Yeah."

"You kiddin'? I'm a janitor. I live in the basement next to the boiler room. She's a cop's ex-wife. I'm black. She's white. Besides, I wasn't interested."

"Because she was white?"

"No." Oscar frowned with displeasure.

I figured he was on to me. I didn't want a calculated answer so I pressed him again. "Why? Why weren't you interested in her?"

He looked at me as if I just missed a solar eclipse on a cloudless day. "Because I'm gay."

I was stunned. "You mean you're homosexual?"

"No. I'm just a very happy fuckin' guy. Yeah, I'm a homosexual."

"So you're gay...gay?" I repeated this a few more times as I absorbed the ramifications of this simple revelation. "Have you ever been with a woman? How long have you been gay?" I was rambling—grateful Oscar wasn't the most worldly of men, because I must have sounded idiotic.

"Always, I suppose. I mean, I liked girls—they were nice and all—but they never, you know, excited me."

"Have you ever tried to have sex with a woman?"

"When I was fifteen but... she was fifteen too and neither of us really wanted to. I was kind of relieved."

"So you've never had sex with a woman?"

"Never."

I sat back in my chair and studied Oscar for a bit, then sprung my next question.

"Would you take a lie detector test?"

"Sure. I'll take it today! Will they let me out when I pass it?" He seemed so thrilled at the prospect, that I braced myself for an awkward hug that didn't come.

"I'll set it up. The Administrative Judge will have to sign the order while you're still detained." A glow remained on his face. "Listen, Oscar. Even though you're only charged with burglary, the police and the D.A. believe you're the Spiderman rapist, and killer of Grace and her baby. I'm sure the prosecutor will mention this in court. This will mean you won't be going home today." His expression soured and his teeth clenched. "Also, don't expect a big show from me this morning. You're not being released, no matter what I say. Even though there's only a burglary charge against you, the judge will set a bail neither of us could ever make. Now we both have to play it cool and not get upset, no matter what happens out there. Okay?"

"Are you goin' to tell everyone out there I'm gay?"

"I don't think it would do much good today, Oscar."

Chapter 27

The steel door slammed shut behind me—in prejudgment, like an ominous prevaricator, and I wasn't sure what smelled worse: the courtroom or the detention area.

Almost everyone in attendance was still damp from the morning's downpour, me included. A restless mix of reporters, court personnel, and pedestrians packed the courtroom pews, but what bothered me most was the blank stare from every police officer in the room.

When several court officers entered from the clerk's office, the courtroom became conspicuously quiet and the traffic on Sherman Avenue could be heard two floors below. It was an "adults only" crowd. Attorneys in attendance were talking in whispers.

I sat down on the defense side of the courtroom and considered the squall of hostility soon to be unleashed at my client. I thought about the interview with Oscar Jefferson and his exuberance over the prospect of taking a polygraph.

Repolla was sitting in the second row on the right side of the courtroom (the defense side), scribbling notes in a tiny pad. He looked up and smirked at me. I winked back nervously as the Bridgman (the Court Officer who calls the calendar of cases), with court papers in hand, yelled, "All rise!" and Judge Preston Shefflin strutted out of chambers and up to the bench.

The audience rose and then sat back down like dutiful churchgoers.

I stood before the court, and in seconds Jefferson was stationed beside me, three officers in triangular formation behind him. For the first time, I felt uncomfortable with my back to the crowd.

Preston Shefflin had been a criminal defense lawyer for over twenty-five years before taking the bench on a mayoral appointment to fill a slot vacated by a retiring judge from Queens Supreme. Shefflin had long been a member of the Queens County Democratic Club. One would think all those years on the defense side would have imbued him with at least some defense-oriented judicial perspective. Not so. If the first twenty-five years had been for the defense, the next twenty-five would be for the prosecution.

He peered down at me over reading glasses, his gaunt face and sunken eyes giving him an almost skeletal appearance.

I waived the perfunctory reading of the rights and charges, as I always had, and noticed the assistant prosecutor was none other than Paul Ventura, Chief Assistant D.A. of the Supreme Court Bureau and one hell of a trial man. This was a clear message to the court, the crowd, and the legions of police watching and waiting, that when a cop's kid is killed, the Bronx D.A. will send in his best man to seek swift and certain justice. Never mind that the only charge was a mere burglary.

Robert Cantor was sitting by the defense tables. His eyes offered what little support they could. Repolla's presence, two rows back, served as a constant reminder of why I had taken this case. I now felt ashamed it was only to return a favor.

"How do you plead, Mr. Jefferson?" Shefflin asked, sounding like a Roman emperor offering a condemned man a moment to beg for mercy before the lions were let loose to tear him limb from limb.

"Don't say a word," I whispered quickly in Jefferson's ear.

This was just a grandstand play to the press. In Criminal Court, it was completely unnecessary to enter a plea. All defendants at arraignment were presumed to plead not guilty. If a plea agreement were reached in advance, then and only then would a guilty plea be entered. Otherwise, a defendant remained silent. I had not prepared my client for this. A more experienced lawyer would have.

"My client pleads not guilty to this single burglary charge," I said, "the only charge before the court at this time, and to any charge the District Attorney's Office may or may not bring in the future." The breathless silence in the room made my voice seem garish. Perspiration was building under my arms and across my chest. The room was starting to feel like a furnace.

Ventura, out of the crowd's line of sight, shot a wry smile my way.

Only forty years old, Ventura tailored a trim figure under a four-hundred dollar Armani suit—an unusual touch of class for an assistant D.A. from the Bronx. His small eyes and nose made him look more Waspy than Italian. Add a light olive complexion, and you had a look of universal appeal, which no doubt contributed greatly to his success as a trial lawyer.

Shefflin sneered at the not guilty plea. I was certain he would have loved to get Oscar talking with a little Q and A that would have made one great headline: *"No Nonsense Judge Lashes Into Baby Killer."*

"Let's hear you on bail, Mr. Ventura," Shefflin ordered.

I started to feel like I was in that small Southern town I often daydreamed about, where the politics of small minds and big bats governed. The court officer to my left was looking more and more like Sheriff Buford Pusser.

Ventura kept his application short. Years of experience had no doubt taught him the less said the better, particularly when you're riding the crest of a monster wave. Keeping Jefferson in jail long enough for the police and his investigators to make a case for the grand jury on the rape and murders wouldn't be difficult under the circumstances.

"The locket found in the defendant's apartment seals shut any hope for acquittal," he said with a level professional air. "The investigation into the horrendous murders that took place in the same apartment that had been burglarized, and the defendant's suspect status in the Spiderman rape cases that have been terrorizing the citizens of Bronx County in recent months cannot be ignored."

I had to give Ventura credit. Without saying one word more than he had to, he'd all but secured an order of remand without bail. Since Shefflin's mind was made up when he read the morning paper, this left me with the forlorn task of merely making a record.

Before ordering my response, Shefflin asked Ventura for his bail demand.

When Ventura didn't answer right away, it hit me. He had such little faith in a case against Jefferson for the rape and murders, he was hoping not to have to make a record at all.

99

I glanced at my nemesis. He looked uncomfortable in his tailor-made suit.

"The People ask for fifty-thousand dollars bail, unless the court sees fit to remand the defendant."

Ventura had too much integrity to play to the crowd on a mere burglary charge, so he simply asked for a bail he knew Jefferson could not make. It was then up to Shefflin, as a torrential rain continued to fall unmercifully on the South Bronx, to be the one to call for a remand.

"Do you have anything to say in response, Mr. Mannino?" Shefflin asked impatiently.

"I most certainly do have something to say, Your Honor." I felt my shoulders stiffen, then relax. "All that is before this court today is a burglary charge. My client has been in custody for a day-and-a-half, being questioned for crimes he did not commit, at the hands of police officers whose tactics included punches to his kidneys and blows to the back of his head with a telephone book. My client has no prior record for sexual assaults, no history or the kind of background that could remotely lead one to conclude he is capable of committing the crimes for which he is being investigated. He stands before you today not for stealing a locket. He's the janitor. He has the key to the apartment. For there to be a burglary, he would have had to enter the apartment with the intent to commit a crime. Does anyone in their right mind believe the janitor went in to steal a ten-dollar locket and yet left behind cash, jewelry and other more valuable items, like a television set, stereo and VCR? And then to beat all, he kept the locket on his night table in his basement apartment in the same building. The absurdity is irrefutable. And the locket case, at worst, is a misdemeanor petit larceny."

Shefflin twisted in his chair and scowled. He had heard enough.

"Defendant's remanded. Call the next case."

"Remanded!" I shouted. "The D.A. didn't even ask for a remand! This Court's obviously out to make Bronx Criminal Court history! You just remanded a man for a petit larceny, and a bogus one at that!"

"This case is about more than petit larceny!" Shefflin shouted back.

"Then why hasn't my client been charged with more?"

The three officers had begun ushering Jefferson back into detention. His hands were trembling and a look of desperation was on his face. I don't think my tirade was making him feel any better. Robert Cantor rose, took a few steps in my direction, and then stepped aside while Jefferson and the officers passed.

I was not through with Shefflin.

"Proof? Evidence? All the things a case resulting in a remand is supposed to be about are absent here!"

"That's enough, Mr. Mannino!" Shefflin was beet red.

"No it's not; not as long as I can bring a writ of habeas corpus for unlawful detention!"

Cantor grabbed my left arm. Jefferson was gone from the courtroom. The steel detention room door slammed shut in a courtroom dead silent, except for the banter of an irate judge and an attorney who was on the brink of being held in contempt.

"That's enough," Cantor whispered in a harsh tone. "You did good; the best you could. Now shut up and sit down."

Grateful for the interruption, I took a deep breath and calmed as Cantor's fingers dug into my forearm. Shefflin would get the last word.

"One more peep out of you, Mr. Mannino, and you'll follow your client right through that door."

The courtroom broke into applause. Cantor gripped me tighter.

"Let go of me, damn it," I whispered back. "I'm done."

I glared at Shefflin as Cantor let go, my heart still racing. Shefflin called a ten-minute recess and left the courtroom.

Ventura walked over to me. "You all right?"

I wasn't surprised by his concern. "Yeah. Thanks."

"I'll be calling you," he said quietly, and then left as he came—through the corridor behind the courtroom, avoiding the press.

A court officer passed me a note. It was from Repolla: *Great work, Pacino. Don't bug out on me now! Call you later.*

I caught my breath as the courtroom emptied. Then I went back into detention to see Jefferson. The sole occupant of one of the smaller cells, he sat against the wall, his head down, his thumb and index finger pressing the corners of his eyes. Tears rolled down his cheeks.

"Oscar," I said gently.

He looked up at me, but made no move to rise. "I ain't never been so scared in my whole life."

"You should be scared." My voice was hoarse and I sounded colder than I intended.

He stood and approached the bars. Our faces were inches apart. "When can you get me that lie detector test?"

"I'll have the Administrative Judge sign the order this afternoon and try to set up an appointment for tomorrow."

"OK." He returned to the corner of the cell and sat down.

It was cold in detention. Jefferson held himself and shivered.

"Hang in there. If you're innocent, I'll get you out. I promise."

"I *am* innocent. Don't you believe me?"

"That's not important."

"It is to me."

I didn't answer, but only half waved a goodbye as I walked down the cinder block corridor to the exit gate, the pain on Jefferson's face etched in my mind.

Chapter 28

I skipped lunch and ran back to the office to prepare the polygraph order. Brenda was about to leave but offered to stay and type it. As I hovered over her, I couldn't help but notice how much weight she'd lost.

She was headed for the Children's Ward at Lincoln Hospital to spend her lunch break with her daughter. She had been sleeping there too, so Jasmine, who had taken a turn for the worse, wouldn't be alone. Massive doses of chemotherapy were being tried as a last ditch effort.

I watched Brenda type, and felt guilty as hell.

The back corridors of the Criminal Court Building provided the quickest route to Judge Krenwinkle's chambers. When I saw Charlie Farkas, Jr. approaching from the opposite direction, I tucked the polygraph order under my jacket. The last time I'd seen Junior, his threatening grimace had been fixed on me as I exited his shyster father's law office.

He had the broad build of a Peter Guevara and was about as tall. I hadn't the slightest desire to tussle with him. I tried to sidestep him in the narrow hallway. He grabbed my arm.

"You made an ass of yourself in front of Shefflin this morning." Saliva was pasted in the corner of his mouth. "The good judge should have thrown you in jail along with that scum you were representing."

"Let go of my fucking arm."

A buddy of Figueroa's shouted, "Hey Nick!" It was the court officer who had worked the lobby on the night of Guevara's arraignment

"Next time," Farkas said then walked off with a scowl on in his face.

I continued onto AP-6.

The polygraph order was *ex parte* and *in camera*. That meant it was one-sided and did not need the D.A.'s consent or response. A secret for the moment anyway, I asked Krenwinkle, the *mench* that he was, to keep it that way. When I got back to AR-1, I telephoned Jose Torres at the office and asked him to run the order over to Arthur Cantwell in Midtown Manhattan. I added a note requesting that Cantwell do the test himself, ASAP or by tomorrow 5:00 P.M. at the latest, and to call if he had a problem. I was tempted to ask if he had done the test on Guevara yet, but didn't.

A few minutes later, I thumbed through the morning's messages Torres had brought me. Eleanor had called to confirm dinner at her place. The last message was from Paul Ventura. I called him from the clerk's phone inside the courtroom.

Ventura was going to make a motion to have Jefferson produced in his office for blood and hair samples. Would I object? Thinking to myself that I should probably object to anything the D.A.'s office wanted to do in furtherance of Jefferson's prosecution, I stalled by saying that I was still in arraignments and would have to check with my supervisors. I wanted the polygraph results first and feared Jefferson's production for blood and hair samples—*good luck with the hair*—would jeopardize his immediate availability for Cantwell's exam. Besides, if Jefferson flunked the lie detector, I didn't want investigators from the D.A.'s office running into Cantwell and his polygraph machine over at Riker's Island.

Chapter 29

I left arraignments at 4:00 P.M. sharp. I had done more than my fair share of cases by then and desperately needed to get back to the office. After the Jefferson arraignment, Shefflin and I had kept each other at arm's length, though that didn't stop him from setting a higher bail than was justified for all the other defendants I represented that night.

A stack of phone messages that comprised a veritable "Who's Who of Network News" was waiting for me at the office. ABC and NBC News had called, along with the Associated Press, United Press International and *The Today Show*. At the bottom of the pile was a note for me to call Repolla at *Newsday*. Since I had refused to leave the courtroom to be interviewed after Jefferson's arraignment, I had no intention of returning phone calls from the media. There was no advantage in it. But I did return Repolla's call.

"Nice show this morning, counselor."

"Shefflin really pissed me off."

"The D.A.'s going to put your boy in a lineup to see if the other victims can identify him, right?"

I wondered where Repolla got his energy. Every time we spoke, he sounded like he was ready to sprint fifty laps.

"Vinny, I know you've got a job to do, but when I'm talking to you, I want to know I'm talking to a friend first and a reporter second. So unless the terrain has changed, I'm assuming all our conversations are off the record."

"Absolutely, buddy."

"O.K. then. Ventura asked if I'd consent to have Jefferson produced for blood and hair samples."

"I should have guessed. But no mention of any lineups?"

"Not yet. And no reporting the blood and hair sample stuff. He didn't call and ask my consent so that I could blab it to the press. I've got a feeling his heart's not in this one, but I'm not exactly sure why."

"I'll see what I can find out. I gave a detective buddy fifty-yard line seats to the Giants last season. He owes me. But I've got to protect my source, Nick, and I mean to the grave."

"I live this job pretending I don't know what I know and selectively forgetting where I got it from."

Repolla laughed. "The people's lawyer! Now if you could get me in to witness a lineup, they'd make me editor-in-chief."

"I may have something better." I paused just long enough to make Repolla antsy. "Give me a day or so to work it out."

"You're killing me, Nick."

"Stop talking about killing and graves. My nightmares are bad enough."

As I hung up, the red light started blinking on my phone. Brenda had still not returned from lunch. I answered the phone, angry with myself for forgetting to ask Repolla if his detective friend had come up with anything on the dead blonde.

It was Shula Hirsch. I hadn't spoken to her since my visit to P.S. 92. The afternoon edition of *The Post* had come out and there was a story on the Jefferson arraignment. My name was mentioned. Mrs. Hirsch congratulated me on my notoriety. I told her to save her congratulations for when I won the case. Then she told me that she had received a notice from the District Office that Peter Guevara had been suspended without pay.

"The suspension was to be expected, Mrs. Hirsch. When he's acquitted, the Board of Education will have to reinstate him at his current salary level, including reimbursement for back pay." I had no idea why I was sounding so optimistic about Guevara's prospects.

Hirsch asked if I had received any school and psychological records on the boys. I told her it sometimes took several weeks for a response to subpoenas, particularly from city agencies. She huffed in acknowledgment, saying something about the frustrations of "red tape".

She asked me if I had spoken to Sandra Chavez. I told her since Mrs.

Chavez was the mother of one of the three boys and an important witness for the prosecution and maybe even the defense, it was best if an investigator spoke to her so an independent record could be made of her statements. I expected to hear from Gene Raines in a day or two.

Just before we hung up, she asked about the bail contributed by those from the school. She was concerned that it not fall into the wrong hands at the end of the case. I asked her if she knew who brought the money to the clerk's office. She said she did, and that she gave her name with the school's address to the Clerk of the Court. I assured her that if Guevara faithfully appeared in court, no matter what the result, the bail she posted would be refunded. She wished me luck with both Guevara and Jefferson then added, "Inasmuch as they are both innocent."

Chapter 30

B renda's chair was still empty. Motion papers in a blueback cover were hanging half off her desk. Typing paper was scattered under a pen, a bottle of Wite-Out, and a stapler. Brenda's work area was always meticulous. It was unusual to see her desk in even slight disarray.

I began to prepare a letter, at Sheila's request, explaining how a defendant like Guevara could come up with fifteen-thousand dollars bail and still be eligible for Legal Aid representation. Legal Aid policy required such. At the beginning of the letter, which had turned into a memo, I wrote that Guevara had been suspended from his job without pay. I omitted any mention of his moonlighting in the real estate office where his broker-boss posted two-thousand five hundred dollars of his bail. I asked myself again why Guevara had not told me about the boss, or the job. It would only have enhanced his resume to the court. I then detailed the other sources of bail and when I came to the largest, the nine-thousand dollars posted by a doctor friend, I remembered Guevara had asked me to give this altruistic M.D. a call. To make such a generous showing of faith and trust, he must have believed in Guevara's innocence also.

Dr. Norris Terkel, Daisy Place, Bronx, N.Y. I checked the map. Daisy Place was in Throgs Neck, in the Country Club Estates section. And on the water. I dialed his number.

After one ring a man answered.

I introduced myself and told him I was Peter Guevara's attorney.

"Oh yes, Mr. Mannino. I've been expecting your call. Peter speaks very highly of you. When I heard he had such an excellent lawyer, how could I refuse the chance to be a benefactor of his bail? What do you think his chances are?"

Terkel seemed more amused than concerned. But he had put up nine-thousand dollars, so I couldn't just brush him off.

"It's a tough case with three children saying basically the same thing," I answered, "though I don't think it takes much to get a child to lie." I thought of Sandra Chavez and her million-dollar lawsuit. "I believe a civil case with a large money judgment is the true motive."

"Ah yes, a great deal of money." I remained quiet, not wishing to feed a conversation I was hoping would soon come to a close. Terkel continued. "Money, money, money. It can buy you your freedom. And it can cost you your freedom. Am I right, Mr. Mannino?" He sounded jubilant, like he had just discovered some hidden cure for rheumatoid arthritis. The musing of an old eccentric I figured, but I didn't want to risk offending him.

"Absolutely, Dr. Terkel." I had no idea what I was confirming so emphatically and wondered how well he was reading me over the phone.

"You seem like a fine young man, Nicholas Mannino. I hope I get the opportunity to meet you."

I asked if he would testify as a character witness. He apologized and declined, citing his ill health.

"Maybe by the trial date you'll feel better," I said.

"If you're in my neighborhood anytime before, please stop in to see me. I'm home almost all the time."

"It'll be my pleasure." Perhaps I could convince him in person.

After we said our good-byes, I realized I knew no more about this doctor and how he befriended Guevara, than before I had called.

One thing was for certain though: without Terkel's money, Guevara still would have been in jail. So what did it matter how they'd become acquainted?

Chapter 31

T he workday was nearly over when Sheila called me into her office with an uncharacteristic bark of my name.

Peter Krackow was standing beside her desk, looking like a disheveled Che Guevara and, as always, like he was ready to kick the shit out of someone. And most of the time I was convinced that was exactly what he wanted to do.

At first, I had thought our political and social differences would put me on the receiving end of his otherwise contained hostility. I was wrong. That I had working class roots and was moderately liberal by his socialist standards was good enough for him. And when he saw how amoral I was in advocacy of the poor criminals of the Bronx, I was his kind of lawyer.

"Nick, first Guevara, now the Spiderman," Sheila said. "Cantor was in the courtroom at the time of the arraignment, but you took the case! Why?"

"It was a burglary, first arrest, and I can always give the case to Cantor if I have to. Arthur Cantwell is going to test Jefferson tomorrow. I'll bet my paycheck he passes."

"You're supposed to get supervisory approval on all polygraph testing before Legal Aid eats another four-hundred-fifty dollars on one of your clients."

Krackow chimed in. "Nick mentioned it to me in passing. I told him to just get the order signed, that it shouldn't be a problem."

Sheila smelled the bullshit but had no choice but to play along. "OK. But while you're handling the case, you are to report to Peter, and Peter only. He will be directly responsible as much as you are."

"No problem," I said, though Krackow seemed less than thrilled.

"And Nick, what's with all these publicity cases? If you're looking to pave your way into private practice, you're going about it all wrong. Poor clients are only going to recommend more poor clients, and you're only going to get negative publicity on the Jefferson case and others like it. And don't expect to be praised for any brilliant defense work by the press. It doesn't sell papers. Have lunch with your uncle. I'm sure he could recommend a ton of clients for you."

Even Krackow looked appalled at Sheila's reference to Rocco. Until then I had assumed my secret was safe, though I was naïve to believe I could keep it forever. I thought of Eleanor, and took a long deep breath as embarrassment turned to resentment.

"Even my uncle and those he would recommend would want an experienced lawyer, which I haven't the gray hair or the years under my belt to fake." I took a breath and tried to rein in my anger. Sheila was only being honest; it was not like her to be intentionally antagonistic. Regardless, I wanted no more talk about mafia uncles, and I told her so. I gave her a no-harm-done smile as I left her office. She nodded back.

Krackow stopped me in the hallway.

"Listen, just clear any major moves on the Jefferson case with me or Sheila. We both know you're in over your head, but I know plenty of lawyers with twenty years of experience who would be too with a case like this. All things considered, you might just do this Jefferson some good. Just know your limits, okay, and get help when you need it."

I nodded.

"And that thing about your uncle…If who he was mattered to Sheila, she wouldn't have mentioned it."

"How did you guys know?"

"She saw you hugging this very Italian, very dangerous looking older man on the courthouse steps a week or so ago. She reads the paper, looks at the pictures too, and your mom's maiden name is in your bio with personnel. It wasn't hard to figure out."

"Eleanor…she doesn't know a thing about Rocco."

I had never gotten personal like this with Krackow before, but I knew he could keep a confidence. I was on my way to Eleanor's and the truth about Rocco was eating at me worse than ever.

"You know, you ought to tell her. She's an A.D.A. She's going to find out sooner or later."

I patted him on the back as we turned to walk in opposite directions.

"By the way," Krackow blurted. "I thought you should know—old shyster Charlie Farkas dropped dead about an hour ago in the Criminal Court Building. A cool twenty was still in his hand when the paramedics threw a sheet over him."

As I drove to Eleanor's for dinner, I actually felt sorry for the crooked bastard. I shuddered to think how his son, the pugnacious Charlie Jr., felt about me now.

Chapter 32

Eleanor had prepared two sirloin steaks with baked potatoes and creamed spinach. I promised her I would do the dishes.

When dinner was over, we moved over to the couch, she with a mug of tea and me with a cup of coffee. I sat quietly, mustering the courage to tell her about Rocco.

"I've been wanting to talk to you about something," I said.

She kissed me softly on the lips. "You know you can tell me anything, darling." *Darling?* There was a trace of Georgia in her voice I had never heard before. "But first there's something that I want to tell you. Promise me you won't get mad." She headed for the hall closet, looking and sounding like a teenager in her jeans and white T-shirt, her hair hanging long and straight down her back. She opened the closet door, and pulled out a black tuxedo.

"I bought this for you today on my lunch hour."

"Eleanor, I can't let you pay for this."

"You can, and you will." She tossed the suit over a chair and sat down next to me. "I love you Nick, and I'm very proud of you."

On the coffee table next to us were copies of the local papers. The evening editions had write-ups on the Jefferson arraignment. My name was in every one of them.

"Don't get me wrong, I love the tuxedo, but I could never afford something like that."

She put her arms around my neck. "In Atlanta, at my brother's wedding, I want everyone to see you as the decent, special, wonderful man you are." As she hugged me I sensed something I never had before—her awareness of the differences between us.

The wedding would be an elaborate reception on the back lawn of her parents' estate. Eleanor was in the wedding party. I would sit with Carolyn, who had promised to be nice to me.

Finally, Eleanor asked me what it was I had wanted to talk about. I lied and told her offhandedly that we'd already covered it.

She kissed my cheek and ran her fingertips up and down my arm. I pulled back, just enough to look into her complacent blue eyes, and thought: *No man will ever love her as much as I do.*

Chapter 33

Memo: To all Supervisors, Attorneys and Support Staff
*   Just a few minutes past midnight, this day, March 20, 1982,*
Brenda Harrison's daughter, Jasmine passed away.
*   Services will be held at the Southern Baptist Church on 170th Street*
and Jerome Avenue, tomorrow at 10 a.m. All wishing to express their con-
dolences may attend.
*   Arlene Panzarella*
*   Support Staff Supervisor*

I couldn't stop imagining little Jasmine lying in a hospital bed, tubes running from her nose and arms, machines monitoring her heart, flashing green digital pulses, and Brenda holding her hand or laying beside her during the final moments. Brenda, a single mother, now left alone.

I thought of calling her, but couldn't imagine what to say over the phone. I would see her at the service the next day. Oddly, I was anxious to express my sorrow in person.

I called Mom. She was on her way to church and said she would light a candle and say a prayer for Jasmine.

* * *

I went down to the Investigators' Unit on the third floor to see how Gene Raines was coming along with the Chavez interview.

I took a seat while he jotted some notes on a legal pad. After he stabbed down a period he said, "I've got some information for you, counselor. Gimme another twenty minutes to write it all up."

"OK, but is there anything you have to tell me I may not want written down?"

"No," he responded casually, "But I can give you an oral report now if you like."

"Lay it on me."

According to Raines, Sandra Chavez was unquestionably the one who had pushed for Guevara's arrest. She made that quite clear to him. She seemed more concerned that Raines should know who she was and the part she had played in the arrest, than in telling him about the crimes committed against her son.

Raines had interviewed Sandra Chavez in her apartment, though she seemed at first perfectly content to talk in the hallway, no matter who may be listening.

During the interview, he had asked to use the bathroom, but what he really wanted was to check the medicine cabinet for evidence of drug use and, on the way, eyeball more of the apartment.

In the only bedroom he noticed two beds, one a full size, the other a single twin. They were in opposite corners and it was not a big room. Evidently both mother and son slept there, which left one question unanswered: where did Jose sleep when Sandra had one of her boyfriends over?

Raines found nothing illegal or unusual in the medicine cabinet or anywhere else in the tiny bathroom. When he came out, Sandra was sipping orange soda from a Mickey Mouse cup at the kitchen table. She didn't look much like the drug user Shula Hirsch and Guevara had described, at least not that day. She was thin though and chain-smoked Marlboros during the entire interview. She seemed jittery when *she* spoke, but relaxed when Raines spoke and she listened.

"If she was a drug user," he explained, "it was behind her."

"Any tracks on her arms?" I asked.

"Long sleeves. Got her date of birth though. You can run her NYSID. But I know what you're going to find." He took a slow breath. "Last week she got sentenced on a plea of guilty to attempted robbery in the second degree. She's doing five years' probation. She also has prior misdemeanor convictions for trespass and petit larceny."

Jackpot! The accuser with the biggest mouth was a predicate felon. I wondered if the D.A.'s Office had even run her criminal record.

But as I listened to Raines repeat Sandra Chavez' version of the circumstances that led to Guevara's arrest, I got an irrepressibly uneasy feeling. Her story had that ring of truth I had so often heard prosecutors talk about in jury summations. Sandra Chavez told a good tale.

In the coarsest terms, she described how Jose came running home screaming that Peter had touched him "with his dick." Guevara, she said, had bound the boy's hands with a belt and pushed his face into a pillow. While Jose continued to resist, Guevara pulled Jose's pants down and rubbed his erect penis against the boy's backside.

"Did he penetrate the boy? Did he say Guevara came?"

Raines' expression soured as I shot questions at him. "She said your client touched the boy's anus with his penis, but didn't really penetrate it."

"Touching it is enough for first degree sodomy," I said to myself. "But did she say if Guevara came?"

Raines was probably the most hard-boiled investigator at Legal Aid, but like everyone, there was a line he just wouldn't cross. He had never worked on a child molestation case before and had refused this one as well, until Sheila coaxed him into taking it by emphasizing my belief, however shaky, that Guevara could very well be innocent.

"Nick…" Raines was starting to sound like the impatient father who had just been asked his last childish question. "Just listening to her made me sick. And the boy kept walking in and out of the apartment as we were talking. I couldn't ask such a question. Besides, a defendant doesn't have to climax for it to be a rape or sodomy."

"I know. But if the boy says he did, I could argue that the police should have lab tested the boy's pants, or the bed covers, or even Guevara's clothes. Their failure to do so points to a sloppy investigation. And you don't get convictions from sloppy investigations. Anyway, sounds like you did a terrific job. Did you get a chance to speak to Jose?"

"She wouldn't let me."

"Did she mention the million-dollar lawsuit?"

"Her attorney told her not to talk about it, but she did say she expects to get paid."

"Get paid? What does that mean?"

"Get a lot of money. 'Get over.' It's a street expression. You never heard it?"

"It's not exactly one of the expressions we bandied about growing up on Long Island."

"You've got to get out more."

"I'll take that under advisement. Did you speak to the Rodriguez boys?"

"To their mother. Nice woman, reserved, hard-working, a single mother. She was reluctant to speak to me. Said she works three jobs, was tired, and didn't want to discuss the case. I think she's embarrassed by the whole thing. Don't be surprised if she doesn't want her two sons testifying at trial." Raines gazed out the window. "Damn if I would want mine to. I'd kill the bastard first. Anyway, while we're chatting at the apartment door, little Carlos comes over and asks me how Peter is. Can you believe that?"

"What did you say?"

"Nothing. His mother nudged him away. When I asked again if I could speak to one of her sons, she said they don't remember much about what happened. Those were her exact words." Raines jabbed at a piece of loose-leaf with his pen. "I wrote them down."

"Did she say whether she was suing the city also?"

"She said a hard-working woman doesn't have time for such things. Then she closed the door."

Back in my windowless office, I made notes to subpoena Sandra Chavez's criminal record and order the court transcript of her arraignment, plea and sentence on the robbery charge, as well as a copy of all the court papers on the case. I planned to grill her good on every aspect of it during cross-examination. In the end, if I had done my job, her own crimes would loom so large in the jury's mind, they would overshadow the allegations of three confused and disturbed children.

Raines' written report would be typed and on my desk the next morning. I was more than pleased with his handling of the interviews. Going to the bathroom to snoop around and eyeball the apartment I thought was especially clever. Opening the medicine cabinet was downright unscrupulous, but no less than any good detective would have done investigating a crime. Look first. Explain later.

Chapter 34

S heila was in the library eating something that looked Chinese out of a Tupperware container. I filled her in on the investigation results.

She cued right in on the two beds in the only bedroom of the Chavez apartment, and suggested we investigate Sandra's boyfriend and also the codefendant in her robbery case. Maybe one or both had a record of sex crimes. If so, Sandra Chavez would be better advised to stick to playing Lotto, because she won't be making any money on this case.

As an afterthought, Sheila mentioned that Guevara had called her first thing that morning, expressing concerns about my availability to diligently work on his defense. He had seen my name in the papers as attorney for Oscar Jefferson.

"What did you tell him?"

"I told him that you are not overworked and probably would not be keeping the Jefferson case anyway."

"Well thanks, and no thanks."

"Nick, your fragile ego notwithstanding, you are not keeping the Jefferson case if he gets charged with murder. That is final. We're a non-profit organization for Christ's sake. Let the court appoint counsel. Let the state foot the bill."

It was unlike Sheila to shun a case because of publicity or politics. And since when had Sheila cared who paid for what? It was always the client's best interests that mattered to her. Then it occurred to me: this was one client she wanted no part of.

"What if he's innocent?" I asked. "You would let an innocent man roll the dice with the barrel pick of appointed counsel? If we had capital punishment, you'd be signing his death warrant."

Sheila bit her fork, and I could tell she was choosing her words carefully. "If it makes you feel any better, I'll personally ask the Administrative Judge to see to it that that Spiderman rapist of yours gets an effective court appointed attorney." Her manner lightened. "And what makes you think he might be innocent?"

"A lot of things. But most of all, the polygraph results I expect to get at any moment."

Sheila looked amused. She could accept my belief in my client's innocence, but with less than three years experience, I had no business taking a case that generated such widespread publicity. And a double murder besides.

Sheila's secretary, Louisa, yelled into the conference room. Arthur Cantwell was on the phone. Sheila and I looked at one another.

I bolted from the room.

"Mr. Oscar Jefferson is totally and completely innocent of any rapes or murders," Cantwell blurted as I got on the line.

"Arthur, I love you!" I said. "But are you sure?"

"I've never been so sure. I tested him for an hour-and-a-half. No way he beat my machine. He seems like a decent guy, Nick. Not too bright. But a decent human being. I hope this helps."

"Thank you, Arthur."

I was both relieved and afraid—relieved that I had gotten the answer I wanted, but afraid all the more for my innocent client. I ran back to the library. "The son-of-a-bitch is innocent!"

Sheila smiled. "Maybe you can convince the prosecutor to hold off on any further indictments. You might want to consent to the blood and hair sample testing."

"How did you know about that?"

"I do get paid to review your cases after arraignment, remember."

"Nick! Telephone!" It was Louisa again.

"Take a message, please!" I was desperate for Sheila's input.

Louisa yelled back. "It's Cantwell again!"

I ran to the phone. "Yes, Arthur."

"You know Nick, despite the *in camera* order, it's hard to keep secret a polygraph test at Rikers Island, especially when I have to take my machine through four checkpoints before I even get to the prisoner."

"So Corrections knows. What's the difference? He passed."

"Yeah, but I don't usually tell the defendant the results either way, particularly if he's imprisoned. This way, no cop, detective or snitch in Corrections can figure them out. Since I don't tell if someone fails, I don't tell if they pass either. In this case, though your excitement, the publicity, and Jefferson being nothing what I suspected..."

"Arthur, I have no problem with you telling him."

"But I think he's in danger."

"From whom?"

"The guards. I don't have to tell you that they can easily get him alone, unguarded and unseen. It's my business to read people. And these guys scared the shit out of me."

Chapter 35

Krenwinkle's clerk said he'd left for the day. I asked him to transfer me to Arnold Benton's chambers. I had neither seen nor spoken to Benton since the Guevara arraignment. He picked up the phone before I even heard the ring.

I explained Cantwell's concerns without revealing the test results. He suggested I order a suicide watch as the quickest and easiest way to keep Jefferson segregated from the rest of the inmate population. He'd make the call right away. I thanked him, hung up, and called Vinny Repolla. He'd owe me and big-time on this one.

He was out in the field. I left him an urgent message to call me.

At 2:00 P.M. I ran to Supreme for a sentencing. Repolla still hadn't called. I was crazed with anticipation over telling him the news, and fully expected it to land on the front page of every edition of *Newsday* the next morning. When I hadn't heard from him by 5:00 P.M., I left him another message and headed home.

After dinner, I called him a third time and then hung up in a huff. I gazed in frustration out the rear kitchen window. The sun was hovering low in the sky like a ball of orange flame, half under the horizon. Gray and blue clouds poured from it like pretty poison. I jerked as the phone rang.

It was Vinny.

"Where the hell have you been? I beeped you three or four times."

"Sorry, Nick. I was at the mayor's office—another stab at city corruption. Seems half the waterfront leases in all five boroughs are connected to mob run corporations."

I thought of Uncle Rocco. "Vinny, Oscar Jefferson—"

"I heard. I'm sorry."

"Sorry? He passed with flying colors!"

"Nick…Jefferson was found dead about two hours ago. The AP wire says he removed the window bars from the fourth floor lavatory at Rikers, then jumped. Did you know he was on a suicide watch?"

I froze, stupefied, as if my brain were no longer connected to my body; the receiver in my hand, the receiver at my waist. I could hear Repolla faintly calling my name as I stared blankly at the flowery kitchen wallpaper.

Then, with animal ferocity, I smashed the receiver down until the base of the phone went crashing to the floor—pieces of plastic, wire, and metal everywhere.

Chapter 36

Almost all of Complex C turned out for the funeral service of Brenda's daughter. Sheila and Peter came together in one car. I drove alone in my Malibu.

The morning papers headlined Jefferson's death. All but *Newsday* called it a suicide. Under the headline, *"But He Passed A Lie Detector,"* Repolla noted the "coincidental" lack of supervision that permitted such a tragedy in a case sorely lacking in evidence, anticipating, with appropriate sarcasm, nothing short of a full investigation into the incident and a continued search for the real Spiderman rapist-killer.

Before I'd left for the funeral, I had drafted a consent-order (more in the language of a demand) to have samples of Jefferson's blood and hair preserved for testing.

I wanted Jefferson exonerated, postmortem or not, even more than I wanted the real killer found. I was on my way to a child's funeral, yet all I could think about was the death of an accused rapist and murderer who'd been *my* ultimate responsibility from the moment I'd taken on his representation, however warped my reason for doing so. With no family or friends left behind, I was the only voice he had left—his last chance to be heard.

* * *

Legal Aid's lawyers, secretaries and clerks sat in the middle of the church. Brenda's family and friends, none of whom I knew or recognized, sat in the first three rows. They numbered about forty. Several empty wooden pews separated the two groups, allowing those Brenda worked with to give deference to those truly close to the child, who shared a deeper, more intimate grief.

Thoughts of Oscar Jefferson left me the moment I saw the open casket at the foot of the altar. Jasmine rested there like a pristine offering, between a huge golden crucifix candelabra and a cherry-wood pulpit, and I wondered if anyone realized that this was the first day of spring.

The reverend's voice echoed harmoniously off the walls and wood beam cathedral ceiling. It was a voice that spoke little of loss and sorrow, and more of joy and celebration. He was a large man and wore a purple robe that hung down to his knees in front and back. He was dark black, and his bright eyes and beaming smile flashed like a beacon over his portly frame. At first, I thought this Bible Belt preacher would phony up the solemn occasion with blazing rhetoric and preachy storytelling. But when he called Brenda by name, and spoke of the suffering of both mother and daughter, it was clear he had been there to witness and comfort in those last awful moments.

Toward the end, he walked over to Brenda and held out his outstretched arms. Brenda was sitting low in her pew and crying into a lace handkerchief while an older woman in a blue bonnet hat held her.

But upon gripping the reverend's hands, Brenda stood up as if mesmerized, and her crying stopped.

When their prayer concluded, the reverend told Brenda and all those in attendance that her beautiful daughter was with God in a place more wonderful than any of us could imagine. Then he released Brenda's hands, and she sat back down with amazing grace and composure.

Those in the first three rows—family and friends—formed a single line and passed the coffin, stopping for a prayer, a touch, a final kiss.

Then those of us at Legal Aid, who weren't uncomfortable with the religious custom of the open casket, drifted up. The sound of crying got louder the closer I got to the altar and the coffin.

The last time I'd seen Jasmine, she was in pigtails and smiling a "thank you" for two Hershey kisses I put in her hands. My eyes got watery as I knelt on a red cushion beside the casket.

Jasmine's head was wrapped in a pure white kerchief—her hair lost to intensive chemotherapy. She wore a white satin dress, her ankles and neck covered with ruffles and creamy lace. On her feet were shiny white shoes with gold buckles. I marveled at how the sunlight streamed through the stained glass windows and glinted off those buckles, sending beams of light bouncing in all directions.

I said a Hail Mary to myself, made the sign of the cross, then looked at Jasmine's face and returned to my seat, imagining wonderfully, foolishly, that I had kissed her cheek and brought her back to sweet life.

When everyone had settled back in their pews, two deacons rolled the coffin directly in front of Brenda for one last parting moment between mother and child.

As the coffin's casters came to a stop, Brenda let go an agonizing wail.

Flailing her hands and arms in the air, still holding the handkerchief, stomping her feet on the church floor, she screamed and cried, "Why!" until collapsing into the arms of the woman seated next to her.

Friends and family surrounded her, as the rest of us sat there, helpless witnesses, agape in stunned silence.

I had never felt so close to someone else's pain and sorrow. I prayed that I would never have to feel that way again.

I envisioned the young Puerto Rican girl from my December trial dead on the Bronx sidewalk, her parents helpless to stop her rage and despair. I thought too of Oscar Jefferson, and felt not only a peculiar sadness, but more—the dangerous mix of anger and frustration.

Brenda and Jasmine had taught me something I should have known instinctively—that it is the worst thing, the absolutely very worst thing, to lose your child to suffering and death.

Having never been to a child's funeral, I thought my despondency would disappear upon my return to the case files that littered my desk. But no sooner did I pick up one, then another, and my workday pace resumed. And I was lost again, in a momentum that would take me everywhere, and nowhere.

Chapter 37

I dialed Father Kerres' number. A few weeks had passed since he'd promised to stop by the office on his way to Yankee Stadium.

He reluctantly agreed to meet me at 1:00 P.M. outside the stadium ticket office.

It was a warm day for March, by New York standards, and I walked in the sunlight to help counter the cool Grand Concourse winds.

Kerres was waiting when I arrived.

Tall and slim, Kerres didn't look a day under forty-five, yet he'd been only ten years older than the eleven-year old Guevara when he rescued him from the gang rape in the orphanage lavatory. That made Kerres an ill-preserved thirty-five.

According to Guevara, Kerres was a friend "to this day." Some friend.

When Kerres first called me, I had assumed he would offer his support and assistance, and would stand behind Guevara in his time of need. Instead, the priest's manner seemed more the product of banal curiosity. Charges of sexual abuse on children can sour even the closest relative. But a priest? Kerres acted more obliged than willing to meet me.

As I approached, I could see the discontent growing on his face. Maybe he just didn't like lawyers. If so, I didn't plan on changing his opinion.

"So Father, what can I can do for you?" I followed him as he began walking toward the stadium parking lot.

"I'm sorry?" There was smugness in his voice.

"It was you who initially called me a couple of weeks ago. So why did you call me?"

"I heard about Peter's arrest and thought you could shed some light on it."

"What would you like to know?"

We were now well inside the parking lot. He picked up the pace and was straining my capacity for courtesy.

"Father Kerres?"

"I later found out all I needed to"—he corrected himself—"all I wanted to know from Mrs. Hirsch at P.S. 92."

"When did you speak to her?" I was practically trotting to keep up with him.

"A few days after you and I first spoke on the phone."

"Well then, I'm confused. Why didn't you ask me what you wanted to know when we spoke?" I was almost jogging now. We were both visibly sweating. "Are you late for an appointment or something?" I asked between short, hard breaths.

No answer.

"Father. Would you slow down please?"

He stopped cold. I unbuttoned my overcoat in an attempt to cool down, and hunched over, my hands on my thighs, catching my breath.

"What's with you, Father?"

Kerres regarded me with the stone face of a scientist watching a lab experiment gone awry.

"Nick!" a voice shouted out from across the parking lot.

I turned toward the ticket office. Vinny Repolla was running toward us, his red parka billowing like a cape. His shoes scraped the asphalt as he came to stop.

"You and the Father going for an afternoon stroll?" he asked between breaths.

I introduced the two men. Kerres stared blankly at Repolla.

Vinny smiled broadly and shook the priest's hand. Kerres complied weakly.

Vinny, aware a chill was in the air, directed the conversation my way. "My buddy on the force got a lead on the identity of that blonde. She was wearing a blouse with a tag on it from a clothing store chain called Bailey's."

I shrugged. "Never heard of it." With the sun at our backs, I saw the shadow of the priest's head turn toward Vinny, and then disappear as Kerres slipped away without saying a word.

"That's because you've never been to Danbury, Connecticut," Vinny answered. "It's a family-owned business."

"So our blonde's from Danbury?"

"Maybe. The FBI is now involved. This case has really got my detective friend's goat. He swears he won't give up until he finds out who she is."

Kerres sped by us in an old Saab with a worn muffler.

"That guy looks like death warmed over," Vinny said. "Last rites must be his specialty."

"He's hiding something and I can't figure the why or what of it."

"Demons in his past," Vinny said jokingly as he slapped my back.

We walked toward Gerard Avenue.

"Just so they're not in his present—or mine."

"I'm sorry I had to be the one to tell you about Jefferson," Vinny said.

"I would have been damn angry if you'd known and hadn't." Vinny's black Corvette was parked at the curb. His press ID was on the dashboard.

"You gonna be OK? Sounded over the phone like you went nuts last night."

"This morning I went to the funeral of a ten-year old girl. Last night my client got murdered in jail. No, I'm not OK." We climbed into the car.

"Hey, be nice." Vinny responded. "After that Jefferson arraignment I might be one of very few friends you have left in this city."

Chapter 38

The Carroll Avenue Hunt and Fish Club had little to do with hunting or fishing, aside from the hunting down of those who crossed the Capezzi Crime Family, and the ensuing fishing out of the bloated egg white corpses from the East River.

No trophies the National Rifle Association would recognize and no mounted heads from any taxidermist adorned the walls inside. And civilians were rarely allowed. Exceptions were made of course—like for the Brooklyn boss' nephew and godson.

As I pressed the bell on the front door, a faint ringing could be heard inside the club. I gave my name in response to a "yeah," the "yeah" coming from Fat Julee, who opened the door and greeted me with a kiss. Once inside, he bolted one door, then another behind us.

Outside, the place looked like the remains of a dingy social club, long since closed. But inside, behind two solid oak doors and steel plated walls that faced the street, was the daily meeting place of Rocco Alonzo and *La Cosa Nostra* that ran the Brooklyn rackets.

Upon entering, a mahogany bar, always fully stocked, jackknifed into a corner that housed a cappuccino machine and two espresso coffee makers. Italian oil paintings hung on dark walls against which older members played cards, drank past their limit, sipped espresso out of lime-rimmed cups, and chatted like family who had never left the old country.

Younger soldiers came and went, but rarely stayed for more than a drink or cup of coffee, and only if asked; otherwise, they were there to receive orders, and execute them.

The dining and meeting room seated approximately eighty men and contained four large mahogany tables, but no tablecloths to prevent scuffs and scratches. No Italian-American housewife would tolerate the abuse these tables took. But then they didn't have to. No women were permitted inside.

The rear of the club contained the kitchen, and a huge dining room table. To the side of the table was a doorway leading to the basement. I lost count, long ago, how often I had eaten at this table; always with my uncle, and almost always with Sallie present. I wondered if they still had the wooden booster seat Sallie had built for me when I was four years old and refused to sit in a high chair. He threw two coats of shellac on it so I wouldn't "get splinters in my ass."

When I entered the bar area, three retired soldiers were sitting at a corner table playing Brisk and sipping espresso. They nodded as I passed. The strong smell of Italian coffee filled the air and reminded me that the last time I'd been anywhere near the club was the summer before law school. I weakly waved back as I brushed past a large man who opened the dining room door for me.

Sitting behind a large table in a polo shirt pulled tight over his ballooning middle, was Sallie. Now fifty-three years old, he looked twice as heavy as I remembered.

"Nickie! Look at you! Briefcase and all! A real live lawyer! Come give your Uncle Sallie a kiss!" I hugged him around his huge chest until he grabbed my face in two pudgy hands and kissed me twice on the cheek.

He pulled a chair close to him for me to sit in, and immediately began reminiscing about Flatbush; how he and Uncle Rocco used to pick me up from school in Rocco's Caddy and buy me an ice cream soda at Nick and Joe's on Midwood Street and New York Avenue. When they took me home, Mom would scold them for spoiling my appetite. Sometimes they'd even play stickball in the street with my friends and me. It was hard back then not to love these guys.

Regardless, when I graduated law school, I swore I would never enter the Carroll Avenue Club again. But I realized as I sat across from Sallie, and the scent of Old Spice filled the air, that I was, in some respect, home again. And like every child who returns home after a long absence, I did so because I needed something.

When I heard the grumbling of hoarse voices and deferential salutations, I knew my uncle was near.

With a smile as warm and charismatic as Sinatra's, he burst through the door. Approaching fifty-five, my uncle had taken such good care of himself that he looked more like an older brother, than a man old enough to be my father.

He reached over and hugged me so hard I nearly lost my breath. After kissing me on both cheeks, he pulled up a chair and asked how I'd been. I responded with "working hard," but saw in his eyes that he knew there was more.

A tall, clean-shaven, young Italian in an out-of-season trench coat stood inside the closed dining room door, watching us. He had followed Rocco in. This was one of the overcoats who was with him at Bronx Supreme Court. Bay Ridge's answer to the Secret Service, he stared at me with guarded eyes and a blank expression. Rocco asked him to wait outside by the bar.

Though he kept the conversation casual, I could tell Rocco was keeping mental notes. Later he'd probe deeper if he had to, not letting up until he learned the true reason for my visit.

Sallie just leaned back in his chair and listened. My uncle's second in charge, Sallie was counselor on all matters concerning the Brooklyn *Cosa Nostra*. Rocco never gave direct orders to anyone. Every command went through Sallie, whose loyalty, dating back almost forty years, was unquestionable. They were as close as brothers, and inseparable.

Sallie's looks though, could be deceiving. This warm, round, bear of a man was capable, in the course of Family business, of the most horrific executions. How he was able to separate that part of himself from that which emanated genuine affection, I could never understand.

Rocco's temperament, normally even-keeled, included a well-contained anger that manifested itself in orders of brutality expeditiously enforced. He had an aura of strength, the likes of which I had never seen before or since.

Such an awareness should have made me shudder. But it didn't. I'd never felt safer or more protected.

Our cook for the night was Fat Julee. The aroma of sauce, which had been simmering for hours on the cast iron stove in the kitchen, was arousing my appetite. Sallie had yelled to Julee to add some extra sugar. I affectionately squeezed Sallie's arm in thanks for remembering how I liked my sauce.

Minutes later, a pan of oven-hot baked ziti was placed on a serving board in the middle of the table. And as soon as it touched down, all conversation ceased, and we began eating heartily, like family.

When a huge bowl of sausages and meatballs arrived, with a serving tureen of extra sauce and a pitcher of red wine, my uncle demonstrated the innate perceptiveness that both kept him alive, and thrust him to power.

"So what can I do for you, Nick?" he asked. "And don't feel sorry that this is why you came. I don't expect you to come here just to see Sallie and me. You're a grown man now." He reached across the table and grabbed my hand like it was a child's, and I felt ashamed at how well he saw through me. "I'm just so goddamn happy to see you. But I know something is wrong." His face soured. "So tell me. You never asked me for anything. What'd'ya need?"

I looked in my uncle's loving eyes, and then at Sallie. In a moment's flash I was thrust back in time, propelled by the divergence of emotions passing through me: strength, love, discipline, anger, frustration and even hate—stirring inside Rocco, like the whirlpools that churned inscrutably beneath *The Hell Gate Bridge*...

I was just a baby then, merely a few weeks old, when the story of Rocco and Dorothy began. I remember none of it, of course, and have pieced it together from accounts told to me by Mom mostly, with a little help from Sallie, and even Rocco.

I had always known that Rocco, at the age of fifteen, had killed my Aunt Julia's husband, Vito. It was an incident personal to the family, unlike the rest of Rocco's nefarious life. But Holbrook, Paulie Rago, and the methods by which Rocco rose to power—these were mysteries to me, until Mom took me aside, and told me all she knew.

When Mom arrived home later the same evening, she had started her story of Rocco. I had a pot of decaf ready on the stove. The girls usually quit playing poker about eleven. This time though, they ran a little late, which only served to heighten my anxiety and enthusiasm to hear more. Mom had barely gotten her coat off when I insisted she pick up where she left off, and tell me about Rocco and Dorothy.

By the time she sat down, I had a cup of coffee waiting, along with a slice of her favorite pound cake. She needed no further prompting.

With auburn hair, round green eyes and creamy white skin, Dorothy Neal, at the age of twenty-two, stood in sharp contrast to Rocco's dark, hard look. If not for her healthy breasts, her slight frame would have been completely lost in his arms as they fawned over me at my baptism party held at Brooklyn's Parkside Lanes.

Mom watched as they considered each other with tenderness and respect, and realized then how her marriage to Tony Pacifico was beyond saving.

In the spring of 1955, after six months of dating, Rocco presented Dorothy with the biggest diamond ring anyone in the neighborhood had ever seen. They planned a September wedding.

Dorothy lived in an apartment in Astoria, Queens, and taught first grade at the very private Bennington School on the North Shore of Long Island. Her mother and father lived in Brooklyn, just a few blocks from the Parkside Avenue pizzeria run by Rocco and his men. She was visiting her parents when, along with her younger sister, she came into the pizzeria.

Seconds after they left, they were mugged by two teenage boys, and their purses stolen.

Rocco ran out when he heard their screams and ordered Sallie and three of his men to give chase.

Dorothy's fifteen-year old sister lay on the ground crying, her knees badly scraped, their pizza pie upside down on the sidewalk. The faces of both girls were wet with tears. Rocco escorted them back into the pizzeria, then gently washed the fifteen-year olds' knees and bandaged her cuts.

Within minutes, Sallie returned with his men, and handed the two purses back to the girls.

Rocco insisted on walking them home. The next night, Rocco and Dorothy had dinner in Sheepshead Bay, and then strolled along the dock filled with moored fishing boats. When he brought her home, he asked permission for a good night kiss. Afterward, she accepted another date for the following evening.

Dorothy's parents, both of whom had some college education, did not approve of the match. Her father was half-English, half-Scottish; her mother, first-generation Italian.

Besides regularly sending her parents food from the pizzeria, Rocco brought flowers for Dorothy, her sister, and her mother each time he visited. When they announced their engagement, her parents were reluctantly resigned to the pairing—a graduate of the revered Barnard College for women, and their daughter ends up with a pizza man and mobster.

Mom had pinched her nose and winced, a sign the story was about to turn, and to a part only Mom could tell. There was no way Rocco would talk about, no less utter, the name of Ernest Leskey.

How much Mom had embellished I will never know, but with what Rocco had later told me, and from that which I came to learn from other sources, it seems that she filled in the blanks quite well.

Ernest Leskey was a champion swimmer and the picture (as Mom had described) of Ivy League handsomeness. He was also rich—old money rich. By 1953, the family had a chain of department stores across the entire East Coast that bore the Leskey name.

It was in his senior year at Columbia University—the all-male counterpart to neighboring Barnard College—that he fixed his sights on the beautiful Dorothy.

At first, he was a gentleman. But on their third date, in the back of his father's chauffeured limousine, Dorothy barely escaped with her virtue by the mere strength of the elastic on her garter strap. Her parents were devastated when she broke it off.

Leskey was furious.

Though Dorothy and her parents were forced to change their telephone numbers, the letters and telegrams kept coming. Campus security at Barnard, and Columbia, were put on notice.

Finally, after grabbing his crotch and threatening Dorothy with penile impalement in full view of several dozen Barnard students, Leskey was suspended from Columbia University. He never returned.

A few months after Dorothy graduated, she began dating Rocco. But unbeknownst to her, Leskey had taken an apartment in Astoria just two blocks from her own. And he was watching her every move, and planning.

After their engagement, Rocco and Dorothy were inseparable. And although Rocco became increasingly desirous of her, and she of him, Dorothy wanted to marry as a virgin. And Rocco respected her wish. It was 1955.

Brooklyn's Fourth of July celebration that year was especially raucous. The inordinate amount of exploding fireworks caused Rocco to be especially mindful of his surroundings, and he soon discovered that he was being followed.

The following Friday night, when Rocco left Dorothy's building, Rocco noticed a man standing in almost complete darkness against a telephone pole. Rocco cued Sallie who was waiting nearby with two button men in an old Chevy. In an instant, all four tackled the man then threw him in the trunk of the car. Surprisingly, the man gave little resistance. Rocco jumped in the front passenger seat as they sped away.

Under a nearby train bridge, about a hundred feet from the rat-infested rocks that lined the shore of the East River, they stopped. Several dark figures, drunk and tired hobos that made their home near the water's edge, scurried off in the darkness.

The two button men opened the trunk and pulled the man out. He was tall and thin, with chiseled good looks. They pinned him against the car.

Rocco grabbed the man's head and slammed it into the car's chrome bumper. The man's body stiffened, then collapsed, and a wig he was wearing fell to the ground. His true hair was short and blonde. Rocco demanded his name.

"Go fuck yourself," the man responded. "You're nothing but garbage!"

To a trumpeted groan that echoed between the concrete bridge pilings, Rocco buried his fist in the man's testicles.

Yanking him back by his hair, Rocco gripped the man's Adam's apple, squeezed it and demanded, once again, the man's name.

"Ernest Leskey," the blonde man grumbled, "and if I'm found dead, my father will see you all fry."

"Why are you following me?" Rocco leveled a smack across Leskey's face.

"Because, you dumb greaseball, she's mine." Leskey looked Rocco dead in the eye. "I should have fucked her back in college when I had the chance."

Rocco wrenched Sallie's pistol from its shoulder holster and put it to Leskey's temple.

"Roc, no!" Sallie yelled.

Rocco kicked Leskey in the groin, and the underbelly of the bridge was consumed by a deafening howl.

Rocco ordered the men back into the car, and they drove off, leaving Leskey rolling in the dirt, the rusted girders of the train bridge that connected Astoria with Randall's Island and the Bronx looming overhead. Beyond the water's edge, treacherous whirlpools created by the intersection of the East River, Harlem River and Little Neck Bay spun incessantly. Many a ship that had passed there during and before the great wars had been swallowed and sunk in its wake. As a result, the bridge had been given a haunting nickname that stuck for all time.

Sallie asked whether Rocco planned to tell Capezzi about Leskey. Rocco waved him off.

Charlie the driver then confirmed Leskey's identity. He'd been in the Leskey stores where a portrait of the whole family hung over every exit.

Rocco panicked and ordered the men to rush back to the bridge.

In less than a minute, the car skidded to a stop between the two towering concrete buttresses of the train-bridge. Sallie snapped off the headlights. All four men jumped out of the car as dark human figures disappeared into the descending blackness of the water's edge.

Rocco, Sallie and the two men rushed to the spot where Leskey had been left curled and howling. But he was gone. Rocco looked around for the wig that fell off Leskey's head. It too was gone. Rocco ordered the men to spread out.

Sallie had searched Leskey and come up empty. No weapons. No ID. The men drew their guns anyway. Rocco had taken Sallie's revolver, but knew his friend had another. Sallie always kept a small pistol taped to one ankle, and a thin serrated hunting knife to the other.

Rocco walked toward the water and behind the bridge's monstrous concrete foundation. More dark figures sped away, and lost themselves in the dirt and slime that crested down toward the rocks and the river, where rats could be heard scattering and squealing.

Beyond the treacherous whirlpools lay Randall's Island. Beyond Randall's Island, on the other side of the river, was The *Bronx*.

Rocco raced back to the car yelling for Sallie and the others.

With the doors still open and everyone barely inside, Rocco floored the accelerator. Running every red light in his path, he reached Astoria Boulevard.

When they arrived at Dorothy's building, the sidewalk, covered by a long green canopy extending from the building's doors to the curb, was blocked with two black and white police cars. Rocco lunged out of the car and vaulted over the hood of one of the black and whites. Sallie ran after him. The two button men followed.

Rocco scaled the steps until he reached the third floor. Two uniformed officers were standing in the hall outside Dorothy's door. Rocco was dripping sweat. One officer reached for his gun. Another was from Flatbush, recognized Rocco, and pleaded with him to remain in the hall.

Rocco howled Dorothy's name then charged the door. Sallie vaulted onto Rocco's back and hung there until the button men and officers wrestled Rocco to the floor. Rocco kicked and punched wildly until pinned into submission. The officer who had reached for his gun, now reached for his cuffs. The cop from Flatbush told him to put them away.

Rocco sat pressed against a wall across from Dorothy's door, his head between his legs, wailing like a tormented child while Sallie held him.

Sallie got up and ordered the two button men to stay with Rocco.

The cop from Flatbush whispered something to Sallie then let him pass. An ambulance crew appeared with a stretcher and cautiously followed.

Rocco watched them all go in and yelled, "Bring her to me Sallie! Let me see her!"

In less than a minute, Sallie came out and walked over to Rocco. More police officers materialized at the top of the stairs. Some went into the apartment. Some didn't. A voice came from inside that cautioned others not to touch anything.

Sallie pulled Rocco to his feet. Rocco stared at Sallie like a lost child. With Rocco's arm over his shoulders, Sallie walked him down the narrow stairwell. Outside, the two button men helped Rocco into the car.

Sallie drove to Capezzi's place in Bay Ridge.

When they arrived, Capezzi and his men thought Rocco had been shot. One of Capezzi's bodyguards unlocked a heavy industrial door next to the storefront entrance of the ravioli shop. Rocco was taken upstairs to a fortified apartment whose walls were armed with steel sheeting. He was taken into a rear bedroom.

His shoes removed, he was laid on a bare mattress and covered with blankets.

After Sallie briefed the Brooklyn *capo,* Capezzi asked, "Why this? She was just a woman."

Sallie just replied, "To him, she was a dream."

Capezzi called his personal physician.

The doctor arrived and injected Rocco with a sedative. He did this every morning for three days. Mom visited each of those days, fed Rocco vitamins, and held his hand for hours as he slept. Rocco would have no memory of any of this—or so Mom thought.

On the fourth day Rocco began to come around. Before Capezzi sent a car to Flushing to pick Mom up, he telephoned, and told her to "bring the baby." Reluctantly, she complied.

At first (as Mom would tell it), I was a little frightened of the strange surroundings, but laughed and giggled when I saw my Uncle Rocco. I was only a year old, and walked like a tiny Frankenstein toward his bed.

"Roc, Roc, Roc," I said over and over until I reached him and slapped my hands on the bedcovers. Rocco looked down at me. Mom jumped nervously. Capezzi stood next to her and patted her arm as instruction not to worry.

Rocco picked me up and placed my face against his, and smiled, his eyes shut tight, a look of serene acceptance on his face. My tiny hands patted his head and nose and his smile widened. He placed me on the blanket next to him and handed me a tablespoon, which I promptly stuck in my mouth.

Mom ran and embraced him, then cried in his arms.

The next morning, for the first time in over a week, Rocco shaved and showered, and put on new clothes Capezzi had bought for him. Sallie had burned everything Rocco was wearing that night. The car was destroyed too. Since Leskey had been inside it, Capezzi wanted no links to Dorothy's murder.

Leskey had left his prints all over the apartment, and from the way he killed Dorothy, the police believed him to be insane and extremely dangerous. He was at the top of the City's most wanted list. Yet the newspapers seemed to ignore the story.

Leskey's family had big hooks in the press, not the least of which were the millions every year their chain of department stores spent on advertising.

Ten days had passed and no sign of Leskey. Sallie had put a twenty-thousand dollar price on Leskey's head, and had every shield on Capezzi's payroll reporting directly to him on the progress of the investigation. Rocco grew increasingly angry and despondent. Sallie consulted with Capezzi's physician and stayed close to Rocco at all times.

Although Capezzi was as fond of Rocco as he was of any loyal friend and soldier, if Rocco wasn't back in the swing of things and soon, he wanted Sallie to take over. Sallie assured Capezzi that this would not be necessary.

He failed to mention that Rocco had begun his own search for Leskey.

In the end, though he never referred to Leskey by name, Rocco told me exactly what happened the day his search ended. And I knew then that I was listening to a Rocco I had never known. He had kept so much bottled up for so long, it must have been a waterfall of sensory relief to simply, and finally, tell it all…

Darkness was about to fall. A light drizzle hit the windshield. It was a cool night. The wipers strummed rhythmically across the glass. Rocco parked a block from the bridge near a construction site.

He got out of the car and looked across the river to the Throgs Neck section of The Bronx. Houses were being constructed on the water's edge. That would be a fine neighborhood someday, he thought to himself. He and Dorothy could make a home there. Have a pool built in the backyard. She would teach the kids how to swim. Rocco had never in his life gone swimming.

He was not sorry Dorothy died a virgin. She was his Dorothy. Her end, however it happened, secured that for all eternity. They would have their time together. Some day. Somewhere.

He walked in the dirt that met the street. As he approached the area under the bridge, the street turned to cobblestone. The ground between the two concrete buttresses where he last saw Leskey looked different, slightly illuminated. The moon was full. He expected to see homeless men scatter as he got closer to the river. No one did. No one was there.

Pages of newspapers were strewn in the dirt. He could see a copy of *The Daily Mirror* folded and crunched against the bottom of a rusted dumpster. He crouched down and held the cover page to the moonlight to decipher the date: July 15, 1955, the day after Dorothy's murder. The newspaper was double-folded and had apparently been that way for some time. A small indentation had formed in the middle. Some bum must have used it for a pillow.

A swift kick hit the side of Rocco's face, and he tumbled onto his belly. He tasted dirt and the blood in his mouth, and could hear coarse laughter.

The shadow of a raised boot was cast over Rocco's head. Rocco rolled as the heel crashed down in the dirt, skimming his left ear. He gripped an ankle and took the body down to the ground. In an instant, he was pummeling a head with left and right hooks. Blood burst from the nose and mouth, spraying the dirt around him. Rocco did not stop until his attacker lay limp and lifeless.

He stood up and looked down. It was Leskey, the brown wig now hanging off his head. Rocco reached into his shoulder-holster. It was empty.

Leskey, his face a pulpy mess, looked up, and smiled. In his raised hand, cocked and pointed, was Rocco's gun.

Leskey slowly got to his feet and walked backward toward the water. Though he was unsteady, the gun's aim never appreciably wavered.

At the edge of the river, he smiled mockingly, and like an executioner in a firing squad, aimed the gun with renewed composure. Rocco, a dead-on target, spread his arms wide and prepared to die.

Leskey then fired, emptying the gun into the side of the dumpster. Cackling like a madman, he threw the gun at Rocco then turned and dove into the river.

Under the train-bridge, the swirling whirlpool currents spun dark rings in the water. Rocco picked up the gun, packed a fully loaded clip in its handle, and ran to the water's edge. He fired in and around the ripples, but saved one last round for when Leskey surfaced.

After repeatedly patrolling the shoreline of jagged rocks and debris, Rocco walked back to the construction site, and then to his car parked nearby.

He would press the search for Leskey no more. Rocco had killed dozens of men, and even beaten a few to death. He knew what to expect, and it wasn't the guffaws of a madman. Leskey could not be found unless he wanted to be found. He was a beast for sure.

Rocco drove to Brooklyn, putting Leskey out of his mind the only way possible—he fantasized about a life with Dorothy. Three kids. Teaching his two boys to play baseball, Mommy's little girl playing shortstop. Green grass. Morning kisses. Sunday Mass as a family. Leaving the life of crime he'd grown so accustomed to behind. It was a recurring fantasy, he confessed—one that would sustain him for the balance of his life.

Sometimes though, without warning, and for no apparent reason, he would hear Leskey's sardonic laughs, and the name of that train-bridge stretching from Astoria through Randall's Island and into the Bronx, that loomed over the whirlpool waters of the East River, would echo like a haunting whisper in his head—*Hell Gate...The Hell Gate Bridge.*

Rocco never married, and never had children.

By the summer of 1965, the number of soldiers under Rocco's command exceeded all other factions of the Family combined. It was a tribute to Rocco's even-handed leadership and unselfish style. When Don Genafrio, the head of the five families, was deported after a ten-year federal investigation and conviction for income-tax evasion, Capezzi feared Rocco would ally with one of the other families for a bigger cut of the action and depose him as heir apparent. But Rocco remained loyal.

When Capezzi became reigning head of the entire New York Metropolitan operation of *La Cosa Nostra* and leader-apparent of all the Mafia families in the United States, Rocco was made Capezzi's underboss with full reign over Brooklyn, Queens and Long Island.

Except to Mom, and once to me, Rocco never talked about Dorothy or the details of her murder. And he never spoke of Ernest Leskey's disappearance to anyone.

What Sallie saw in that apartment that Friday night, in July 1955, he promised he would never tell, and out of respect for his close friend and underboss, he swore to himself back then, he would keep secret, forever.

As I sat there in the dining room of the Carroll Avenue Hunt and Fish Club, and Rocco's life of violence and tragedy passed through my consciousness like the sweet yet painful memory of a child lost and stolen, I knew then, that I loved this man.

I asked myself how different we were, how different would he have been. I looked at our hands. They had identical flesh tones. I remembered why I came.

"Oscar Jefferson's death," I blurted.

My uncle sat back in his chair, and gripped the edge of the table, which creaked as he applied pressure. "This is that Spiderman client of yours I heard about."

I nodded.

"Is it true what I read, that he passed a lie detector the same day?"

"Yes."

"So he got whacked in jail," Sallie said brashly. My uncle patted his arm—a signal not to sound so callous.

"That's right," I said.

"So what do you want us to do?" Sallie spoke more slowly than before, and just barely loud enough for me to hear.

Rocco's eyes never left me.

"This man was innocent." I said. "I want to know who murdered him."

Sallie pulled his heavy shoulders back.

"Then what?" Rocco asked.

"I don't know then what. I just have to know, that's all."

"And then...what?" Rocco was demanding an answer.

"Maybe I'll go to the D.A., maybe the press. I just can't leave it unresolved. It's eating me up. I feel I owe it to the guy."

Rocco and Sallie looked at each other. I wasn't sure whether I had gained or lost their respect by coming to them and letting on how much this mattered to me. Until two days ago, Oscar Jefferson had been a perfect stranger. Why would they waste their time, energy and resources in finding *his* killer? It never occurred to me that favors, valuable ones, might have to be used up, or money spent, and lots of it. I was positive that all legitimate channels would only turn up proof confirming the reported suicide. I knew that Rocco, particularly with Sallie's help, would get the truth. And I also knew I could trust them, with my life if necessary.

My uncle winced slightly. "I'll help you. But you promise me something. Whatever information I give you, you will do nothing without my permission."

"Fine," I said, much too quickly.

"You can live with that?"

"If I have to."

"I don't want you ending up like your client."

Chapter 39

For a Saturday morning at Kennedy Airport, the Pan Am departure terminal was practically deserted. Eleanor had her bags checked with an hour to spare before her flight left for Atlanta. She was flying first class.

It was one full month before her brother's wedding and her parents insisted she show up for rehearsal. As we sat in a coffee shop overlooking the airfield, I wondered, with her being a bridesmaid, who would be her partner. I was hoping for a bucktoothed cousin, twice removed, with pimples.

"It's only a week or so. I'll miss you." Eleanor sounded like a little girl. I suppose thoughts of returning to the bosom of her family's estate made this come easy.

"And what makes you think I'll miss you? Joey, me, and his Olds '98 will be hitting all the clubs along Hempstead Turnpike. Just like the old days."

Eleanor was looking at me with pretend piercing eyes. "You know my family has enough money to have you killed." She popped another bite of coffee cake in her mouth, still grinning. "You're worried about my going home. Aren't you?"

I hated that she saw right through me. "No," I said emphatically.

She pulled her hands away and slapped them down on her lap. "You'll survive Atlanta. Trust me. I wasn't left on a doorstep, you know. My family is nice. They'll like you."

But it wasn't her family I was thinking about. I was starting to sweat. I needed to change the subject.

"Where will I sleep when I go down for the wedding?"

"The house has eight bedrooms. When I get there, I'll lay claim to the guest bedroom next to mine." Her eyes widened over a Cheshire grin.

"I take two showers a day, you know; one when I get up, and another before I go to bed."

"I'm sure my parents will appreciate your cleanliness. And Nick, while I'm away, get some sleep for God's sake."

We walked over to the boarding area. When the last call came we kissed, long and hard, like two leads in an old movie, letting go of each other slowly. I watched as she drifted down the accordion tunnel, and disappeared from sight.

Chapter 40

"I have Carlos Rodriguez with me!" It was Peter Guevara. He was on a pay phone and shouting over the morning's rush hour traffic.

"What did you say?" My grip tightened on the receiver until my fingers ached, and I imagined Guevara being led into the Criminal Courthouse in handcuffs and shackles. "You're not supposed to be anywhere near him. You could get charged with tampering with a witness if the D.A. finds out."

"*He* came over to me."

"Why isn't he in school?"

"You'll have to ask him. But listen. He says everything he told the grand jury is a lie. He admits I never touched him. He says Jose's mother put him up to it."

"Put him on the phone," I demanded.

A cute voice said: "Hello?"

"Is this Carlos Rodriguez?" I was lamely attempting to sound friendly.

"Yeah."

I introduced myself and told him I was Peter's attorney. "Carlos, would you mind taking a drive over to my office?"

"I don't drive."

"I'll send someone to pick you up. His name is Mr. Raines."

"What kind of car does he have?" I was being repeatedly reminded I was talking to a ten-year old.

"I think it's a green Ford. But you can sit in the front. OK?"

"Okay."

"He's going to bring Peter and you to see me."

A voice recording interrupted our conversation. *"Five cents for two more minutes please."* I heard a coin drop into the telephone. Guevara was back on the line.

I got their location—a public phone booth on the corner of a *Gaseteria* one block east of P.S. 92. I ran down to Investigations and gave the directions to Gene Raines. I made a point of telling him to let Carlos sit up front and to put Guevara in the back.

Twenty minutes later, Raines phoned me from the third floor. Guevara and Carlos were with him.

Chapter 41

Guevara was sitting outside Investigations in a pass-through office occupied by Martha Fox, the secretary-receptionist for over a dozen Legal Aid investigators. This was Raines' doing.

Raines sat behind his desk, facing me. He appeared to be making comforting small talk with Carlos, who was sitting in a chair beside the desk, his little feet dangling inches above the floor. He was wearing what looked like a new pair of Pro-Keds.

Guevara's eyes were fixed on Raines and Carlos. He seemed to be straining to listen. Martha Fox, in her mid-sixties and hard of hearing, smiled sweetly. She was reading a Danielle Steele novel and appeared oblivious to the goings on around her. Guevara rose from his chair when he saw me. I shook his hand.

"Peter, I want you to go." An irritated expression shot my way which quickly morphed into a look of confusion. "I don't want you anywhere near this boy when I take his statement. Not even in the building. It's bad enough he came here with you. The D.A. will probably claim you coerced the boy somehow. Could this be even remotely true?"

"No way. He ran over to me, hugged me and said he was sorry he lied to the police."

"And you haven't seen or spoken to the boy since before your arrest?" I was cross-examining him, and felt perfectly justified in doing so.

"Correct. Nick, I'm telling you, the boy is speaking out now from a guilty conscience. I was good to this boy. He knows I didn't abuse him."

"Okay, then. Go home, go wherever you have to go, and let me speak to the him alone. Maybe I can get his brother in too."

"Thanks, Nick. Really." Guevara shook my hand, gave me a nod of understanding, and left down a nearby stairwell. I walked over to the little boy waiting for me.

"Carlos? I'm Nick Mannino." I put my hand out to shake his as he wiggled out of an open blue ski jacket. When he got his right arm free, he looked up at me, smiled and grabbed my hand. I shook the tiny fingers. Mrs. Hirsch was right. He was a beautiful boy. Only once before, on the now-dead blonde who confronted me outside AP-3, did I see such shining blue eyes. This kid had the looks of a child actor and, as I would soon discover, a sweet personality too.

Small for his age, he sat on his jacket, arms at his sides, and though I don't know why, he reminded me of a Christmas angel.

I asked Raines to get a tape recorder as I led Carlos by the hand out of the investigator's unit, a little-boy look of disappointment on his face. He seemed to have enjoyed listening and watching the other investigators at their desks, their NYPD-issued pistols visible in shoulder holsters. I was worried that he might feel uncomfortable or even frightened being alone with Raines. But he showed no sign of it.

He slid onto a chair in a nearby conference room, and Raines hit the REC button on the tape recorder.

I sat down and told Carlos exactly who I was, and thanked him for coming to my office. I motioned Raines with my finger to stop the tape. I wanted to hear Carlos' story *before* I made a permanent record of it. Though his presence alone was pure gold, should this meeting backfire, I didn't want to bolster the prosecution's case with a taped conversation substantiating the charges.

The advocate in me reflexively took over, and for better or worse, I started with a leading question, while Raines kept his poker face on.

"Peter says that you told him that the charges against him aren't true." *Charges* sounded awfully official, like something a little boy would have nothing to do with.

"That's right. It ain't true. I'm no faggot."

Raines and I glanced at each other. I gestured with my eyes for him to turn on the tape recorder. Carlos was looking up, and in whispers, started counting the suspended ceiling tiles.

I started by giving the date, time, and place, and persons in attendance. I had Carlos repeat his full name and smiled when he rattled off: "Carlos Luis Rodriguez Sanchez." Then I asked him his address. He answered precisely, emphasizing his apartment number.

"Carlos, is it true that Peter Guevara abused you?"

"No."

"Do you know what I mean when I ask if he abused you?"

"Yeah."

"What is that?"

"You know, like a faggot does."

"What is it that, as you say, 'a faggot does?'"

"You know. He touches you between your legs and on your butt."

"Did Peter ever touch you between your legs?"

"No."

"Did Peter ever touch you anywhere on your body with his penis?"

"No way. If he did, I would have punched him in the nose and run away."

"Thank you, Carlos." I leaned back in my chair. For all intents and purposes, the prosecution's case had begun to crumble.

"Did Peter ask you to tell me this?"

"No."

"Did Peter tell you to lie?"

"No. I'm not lying."

"Did Peter ever threaten to hurt you?"

"No. Never."

"Did anyone force you to come here and talk to me?"

"No. This man picked me up," he pointed to Raines, "and brought me here."

"Was that okay with you?"

"Yeah. It was okay with me."

"Why did you lie to the police?" Inasmuch as I wanted to quit while I was ahead, this was a question the Assistant D.A. would be sure to ask. I might as well hear the answer first.

"It was Jose's mother who made me. And my stepfather. He hits me when my mom isn't around. When the police came to our apartment, Jose's mother was with them."

"Sandra Chavez?"

"Yeah. She started talking to my stepfather. My mother was in the living room, but didn't say nothing. Then he called me and Rafael in, and started screaming that we should tell what Jose said to the police about Peter. Jose's mom then starts screaming and picks up a statue off the table and slams it down. My stepfather was standing there too, being very mean in his face. So I lied to the cops, so he wouldn't hit me."

"Will you tell all this to the Assistant District Attorney? His name is Mr. Ryan."

"Yes, but I'm afraid I'll get into trouble for lying." His naiveté was a welcome relief to the sadness in his eyes and his childish frustration.

"You won't get into trouble for telling the truth. You may have to tell it to the judge too." The case was in front of Three-Gun Graham, and he might want to talk to Carlos, and Rafael too if he joined his brother in recanting. Realizing the frightening figure a judge might present to a young boy, I added: "Don't worry. The judge is a nice guy. He'll be happy to hear you are now telling the truth."

"I only hope my stepfather doesn't find out."

"It will be our little secret, Carlos." I cringed. That's what child abusers say. "I'll tell Assistant District Attorney Ryan not to involve your stepfather in any of this."

"OK," he said.

"Do you think you can speak to Rafael, so he can come and talk to me also?"

"Sure. I'll also tell Rafael to do what I did first."

"What you did first? What is that?"

"I told Father Kerres in Bible class that I lied first."

"When was this?"

"Just last week."

"And what did he say to you when you told him?"

"Nothing. He didn't say nothing. He just told me to sit down."

"When exactly did you tell him this?"

"Last Saturday."

"The one that just passed?"

"No, the one before."

Guevara's reference to Kerres at the arraignment interview rang in my ears: "We're still friends to this day."

I asked Raines to drive Carlos to school and deliver him personally to Mrs. Hirsch. I also told Raines to tell her about his stepfather's beatings and that she shouldn't tell anyone about the boy's visit to my office.

Carlos agreed to contact me in a day or two, when and if Rafael was willing to talk. I gave Carlos two dollars in change just before he left. Knowing it would mostly go to candy and soda, I stuck a dime in his back pocket and made him promise that he would use it to call me, whatever the reason.

Later that day, I telephoned Paul Ventura and asked him if there was any progress on obtaining Oscar Jefferson's hair and blood samples. This time I added skin exemplars to the list. Whatever helped get to the truth, I wanted done.

I was angry but not surprised when Ventura told me that he was under orders to cease all further investigation into the Spiderman cases. With Jefferson's death, the District Attorney felt the resources of his office could be better served elsewhere. Ventura sounded sickened over his boss's position, and I remembered that at the arraignment Ventura's mind may have been in the prosecution of Jefferson, but his heart wasn't. I asked him outright why he was so uneasy then.

He took a long slow breath and told me that just prior to coming to court that morning, he'd received a call from victim number one, a high school teacher. She was dealing with the rape better than the other three survivors. Her name was Hazel Waters. She had given the most detailed description of her assailant. The first in a serial case can often be the best— not hampered or influenced by those that had come before.

Ms. Waters saw CBS's coverage of Jefferson's walk into central booking, a detective on each side of him, his hands cuffed behind his back. The camera was positioned so it caught Jefferson full-faced, then in profile. Her assailant, she said, was heavier, bigger, not as thin as Jefferson, not as young in the face, and with a wrinkly forehead. Jefferson hadn't a line or wrinkle anywhere.

I thanked Ventura. Twice.

Responses to my subpoena requests were dribbling in and, sure enough, the documents I received from P.S. 92 and Children's Village, where Jose Chavez and Carlos Rodriguez sought counseling, were several inches thick. And it was all as Shula Hirsch had said. Both boys had emotional difficulties that caused them at times to be disciplinary problems. The recommendation for Carlos was continued counseling and Special Ed classes. Jose's was much worse. Psychiatrists at Children's Village recommended full-time placement. This meant twenty-four hour attention that included intensive counseling, combined with prescription medication to curb his erratic and sometimes violent behavior. The Board of Education also had psychological records on both boys, which I had yet to receive.

The only records I asked for and received on Rafael, Carlos' younger brother by one year, were from P.S. 92: report cards that showed he was attending regular classes and doing quite well.

I waited anxiously to hear from Carlos regarding Rafael. I feared word of Carlos' visit had gotten back to his stepfather, and the boy had suffered some real harm as a result. By Friday morning I was tempted to contact Mrs. Hirsch to see if all was well with the two brothers, when I received a surprise call from Father Kerres. Rafael and Carlos were with him in the rectory of Saint Nicholas of Tolentine Church.

Chapter 42

Raines' thumb had yet to hit the rectory bell when the door opened. Father Kerres was standing there. I greeted Kerres with a "Hello Father," and without word or gesture, he led us through a jalousie-screened porch into the rectory proper.

We found Carlos, Rafael, and Guevara seated in what looked to be a back room reserved for prayer. A kneeling post faced a wall where a large crucifix hung over a small unlit candelabra.

Kerres took a seat beside the crucifix. The boys were facing him, sitting upright in red velvet chairs. Guevara sat by the doorway on the opposite side of the room. I sat next to Rafael on a folding-chair that didn't seem to belong. Raines remained standing. My attention quickly turned to Rafael.

I would have asked Guevara to leave, but the priest's presence was a major neutralizing factor. At least it would be considered as such by the D.A.'s office and a jury, if the case ever got that far. In truth, the priest wasn't a neutralizing factor at all. He appeared more the reluctant witness and seemed quite detached from the events that were about to unfold.

Guevara leaned forward, sending a look of hope in Rafael's direction. Raines clicked on his tape recorder and I began as I had with Carlos: stating the date, time, place, and listing those in attendance.

Rafael was smaller than his brother, a miniature Carlos. Although just one year younger, he was a head shorter than Carlos, but just as cute. Carlos sat next to him, fidgeting, unable to get comfortable. I led Rafael through the recantation. He seemed to be expecting me to.

I talked about Carlos' visit to my office, their stepfather's threats, Sandra Chavez's screams, the smashing down of the statue. Rafael confirmed everything, but without elaboration. A few times, he nodded and I had to ask him to verbalize his responses for the tape recorder. But by this point, I had gotten what I needed—what Guevara wanted—two out of three children had recanted. And Rafael's was the most important. Without the emotional and disciplinary problems of the other boys, Rafael would have been the D.A.'s best witness at trial.

"Did you ever speak to Jose Chavez about this case?"

"No," he answered, appearing confused by the question. He then continued on his own, as if I had asked another, different question. "I didn't want to go to the hospital after the police came to our apartment either. Neither did Jose. So when we got there, Jose's mother slapped him, and then she slapped me."

"Was there anyone around when she did this?"

"No. We were behind one of those curtains they pull around the bed."

"Did you tell anyone? Did you tell your mother?"

"I'm not allowed to tell my mother when my stepfather hits me. So I didn't tell her about Jose's mother, either."

I looked at Raines. Our eyes met. Guevara gave me a look as if to say: *Can you believe I got arrested for this?*

Father Kerres was looking out the window, a peculiar sight considering the red velvet shade was drawn down well over the sill. I thought about paying a visit to the boy's stepfather when the case was over—and bringing Sallie along.

On tape, the charges were shrinking away, along with the credibility of Sandra Chavez—melting into nothingness like the Wicked Witch at the end of *The Wizard of Oz.*

I then asked the *why* question. In court, in front of a jury, I would never, no matter how great cross-examination was going, ask the *why* question. But there was no jury here. I looked up at the crucifix on the wall—at least none that I could see.

"Why are you now telling the truth, Rafael?"

The little boy looked at Guevara, and then at Father Kerres, who was now staring up at the ceiling. "I didn't want Peter to lose his job for this. That wouldn't be right for something he didn't do."

"You're absolutely sure that Peter Guevara never showed you his penis and never touched you with it at all?" I was making my last and final record.

"Yes," Rafael said, straining emphasis. "If he did that, I would have punched him in the nose and run away."

A burn hit my stomach. I'd heard this before.

Kerres' eyes were fixed on Rafael.

"Did Peter ever touch you in your private parts with his hands?" I asked.

"No, never." He paused, looked at the priest, then added: "And Father Kerres told us at Bible lesson that we must all tell the truth before God."

Kerres bowed his head.

I thanked Rafael and Carlos, and with a decisive nod at Raines and Guevara, signaled an end to the interview. Father Kerres told the two boys to go straight home. It was a comforting sensation, however peculiar it felt to me at the time, to hear and see Kerres come to life.

Raines and I shook his hand, and I thanked him for letting us use the rectory.

He muttered something back that resembled "you're welcome."

After showing my appreciation, it seemed off the mark to ask him why he didn't tell me when we met at Yankee Stadium that Carlos had recanted to him—this priest—this friend of Guevara's. So I didn't.

The two boys were waiting by the curb on University Avenue. Carlos asked me for two dollars again. Rafael had started to walk down the block. I gave Carlos the money and asked him to split it with his little brother. Then I watched as he caught up to Rafael and gave the smaller boy one of the dollars.

"Bribing witnesses are we?" cracked Raines.

I smiled weakly and looked back at the rectory and the church dome behind it. A hearse covered with flowers was parked out front. A frail old man was being helped out of a limousine by its chauffeur and a young woman. Once standing, he pushed everyone aside, and with cane in hand, hobbled indignantly toward the church steps.

I thought of Dr. Terkel and turned toward Guevara, who was walking beside us, observing, listening intently, as if making mental notes.

"What's with this doctor friend of yours? He calls me up. I call him back. He sounds like he's old and dying, then comes back to life and says something weird about how someone can buy freedom and how I should come see him."

"He's not that old," Guevara remarked casually. "I don't even think he's sixty. He acts strange, but that's because he's losing his mind from AIDS."

"Jesus Christ, I had no idea."

"He's confined to his bed. A nurse cares for him. As much as I'd rather stay away, I'll have to go thank him in person when the case is over for posting all that bail."

"He must be very fond of you."

"He's been like an older brother to me for the past seven years. Fact is, that's what he was—a Foster Brother. When I was younger and in the program, Terkel and I would see each other every two weeks. Sometimes, if he wasn't too busy, even once a week."

I glanced back at the church. "When the case is over, we'll all have our thanks to make."

Back at the office, I thanked Raines for accompanying me. He was smart enough to know when to remain silent and had said very little in the rectory. His presence though, even if only to operate a tape recorder, was a crutch for me. Before I even asked, he said he would have both interviews transcribed and sent to me ASAP.

I phoned Jimmy Ryan.

"Bullshit! Absolute bullshit, Mannino! I spoke to those kids myself before they went into the grand jury." Ryan was bordering hysteria.

"Jimmy, I got it all on tape."

"Yeah and I want to hear those tapes."

"They're being transcribed as we speak."

"I want the originals." This was a textbook reaction from one arrogant son-of-a-bitch prosecutor, and it didn't surprise me in the least.

"You'll get the originals at trial, if there is one. By the way, I'm making a motion to dismiss all charges."

"The third boy—what's his name, Chavez—didn't recant too, did he?"

"No. But one never knows."

"Forget it, Mannino. His mother's rock solid on taking the case to trial."

"But the mother isn't exactly rock solid herself. Did you know she pled guilty to robbery, third-degree, two weeks ago, and got probation? She also has a prior misdemeanor conviction, not to mention her on-again, off-again drug problem."

"I know about the misdemeanor." Ryan had calmed, but was still seething. "You're kidding about the robbery, right?"

"No, I'm not. I've also got a shitload of school records on Jose Chavez, describing him as a pathological liar. Not only that—they're also replete with numerous verbalized sexual references, dozens of violent episodes, and even a sexual assault on a little girl in a clothes closet. I could go on in court for days about what's in those reports. His mother's credibility, and his credibility, will go right in the crapper at trial."

"Got any good news for me?"

"Yeah. Once I win my motion and get the charges brought by the Rodriguez brothers tossed, you can look like a stand up guy by giving my defendant a fair shake at testifying in the grand jury regarding the Chavez boy."

"Make your motion. Just make sure Three-Gun Graham doesn't execute your guy on the spot if he doesn't believe the recantations."

"He'll believe them. They're the truth."

I had been filling in Eleanor on the developments in the Guevara case in daily phone calls to and from Atlanta. She was happy for me, and I was happier still as each day brought me closer to seeing her again.

It was Friday night and the eleven o'clock news had just begun when she called. The lead story—a mob hit on Staten Island. The victim's name appeared under a photo of a torched Cadillac. It didn't ring any bells. I thumbed down the volume on the remote control, then switched channels to a rerun of *The Honeymooners.*

Eleanor was rambling on about her brother's wedding, reveling in the guest list—politicians, dignitaries, rich big shots. But the wedding was three weeks away, too soon for me to get anxious about. Besides, I was only half-listening. The sound of her voice was its own pleasant distraction. She seemed truly happy.

She repeated how much she missed me, and after we hung up, I tried to recount how many times she'd said it.

Lost in thought, my eyes traveled around the room until they landed on the fireplace mantel, and John Mannino's picture.

"Stepfather" is such an irreverent eulogy to the only father a kid ever had.

As I sat there, I imagined him looking down on me, reveling in another of my existential dilemmas as I wondered, in the smallness of my Merrick home, if I hadn't been a lawyer, would I have even stood a chance with Eleanor?

The nightmare I had exactly one month earlier repeated itself. The shed. The search in the dark. The doll in Yankee pinstripes. The skull without flesh and blood. Only this time, a door in the shed led to a dimly lit hallway that curved in and out of darkness. At the end of the hall, three hooded figures waited inside a cone of light. The three then merged into one. My heart was pounding. *Who the fuck are you?* I mouthed the words. No sound came out. Two eyes appeared in the blackness under the hood. They were human.

I awoke.

My eyes were burning in puddles of salty sweat. I wiped them with the bed sheet, only to be blinded by a crack of sunlight beaming through a curve in the window shade. I buried my head under the covers in a futile attempt to fall back asleep, but the sun was not to be ignored.

Chapter 43

I waited at a table by the window in the Villa Rosa restaurant on Merrick Road in Freeport, a two-minute drive from home. Uncle Rocco insisted I come alone. He had information on Oscar Jefferson's death.

The owner of the restaurant, a short, stocky man, pushing seventy, with a thick half-cigar in his mouth, showed Uncle Rocco to my table. At Rocco's insistence, we moved to the rear of the restaurant away from the window. Rocco sat with his back to the wall.

The waiter arrived to take our drink order, but Rocco sent him away with a tight shake of the head.

It was cold in the dining room, yet I watched Rocco wipe perspiration from his upper lip. I had never seen my uncle so ill at ease.

"So what's up, Uncle Roc?" I asked, attempting to lend a casual air to the otherwise serious mood.

He took a sip of water.

"Now listen, and listen carefully. Then...you forget everything. You hear me. I have no idea how much danger you'll be in if you don't. You've never asked me for anything. So I could not say no to you. But I should have."

I patted his arm reassuringly. "You're not making a mistake Uncle Roc. I keep confidences for a living. I appreciate what you're doing for me. Don't worry."

He leaned toward me and whispered, "It was a hit, from the inside."

"From the inside?" Since Rocco had never discussed his business with me, I needed clarification.

He nodded in assent.

"Brooklyn people?"

He shook his head. "From Aldo Leone's gang in the Bronx." He spoke so softly I could hardly hear him.

"But why?"

He put a finger to his lips.

I whispered: "Why would the mob want Jefferson killed? Where's the connection?"

"I don't know. I still have to find that out. Leone owes me a favor."

"But how will you explain why you want to know?"

"You know the cop—the one whose ex-wife and baby got killed? The one who walks the beat in Sheepshead Bay? He's been on our payroll since he was a rookie. He's my reason for asking."

"So you'll tell Leone that this cop's been loyal, and you owe it to the guy to find out."

Rocco smiled proudly. "Very good, Nickie. You sure you don't want to take over for me when I retire?"

I smiled weakly.

We spent the rest of our lunch in light conversation. I assured him all the house bills were getting paid out of my Legal Aid salary, and when he asked about my career plans, I told him that after Legal Aid, I hoped to get hired by a top criminal defense firm. He responded that he could be of assistance when the time came. I didn't brush him off as I might have years earlier.

Rocco picked up the check. There was no arguing with him so I didn't even try. Outside, he told me to take care and hugged me long and hard. I watched him drive away in his Mercedes until I lost sight of him beyond the Meadowbrook Parkway overpass.

Chapter 44

Monday morning and Gene Raines was in true form. On my desk were the original tapes of the recantations alongside two cassette copies. Underneath were two sets of written minutes. After listening to the tapes and checking the minutes for accuracy, I immediately dispatched Jose Torres over to Jimmy Ryan with a set of each.

Since my lunch with Rocco, I had been wondering exactly how Aldo Leone got to Oscar Jefferson. I wouldn't dare ask Rocco. Not that he would tell me if he knew. Then again, there must be a hundred ways to murder someone inside a prison, and at least half as many to make it look like an accident, or even a suicide.

But why the mob? Why *did* Aldo Leone order the hit? Cops out for revenge could easily do it themselves, especially inside a prison. Tossing an inmate out a window and calling it a suicide seemed easy enough. But it wasn't. It was actually a messy, and therefore, risky proposition. Too much could go wrong from too overt an act. And if a cop or guard wanted an inmate killed, all he had to do was put him in with the wrong crowd, and drop a shiv on the floor. And why would the cops, via the mob, be in such a rush to eliminate Jefferson?

So I asked myself: *Who had the greatest motive to kill Oscar Jefferson, and fast, before some young and ambitious defense attorney started uncovering evidence of his innocence?*

I came up with only one answer—*the real Spiderman.*

I shook off a chill as the diabolical nature of this unknown rapist and killer sunk in. Was he Mafia? Not if he was black. Could he have bought Leone's services?—pieces to an incomplete puzzle—all scattered at my feet.

I had put the dead blonde out of my mind since the Jefferson case began. But it occurred to me then that perhaps there was a connection between her desire to speak to me, and her getting thrown from the Riverdale Towers. I thought about calling Eleanor and telling her some or all of it. But there were too many unanswered questions, the ramifications of which were nothing short of frightening.

I came upon Court Officer Jose Figueroa before court reconvened for the afternoon session. He was working the Administrative Judge's courtroom, in Supreme Part 40, where felony cases got sent out to Trial Parts. As a result, the plea action was intense and the room was always packed.

Jose's pleasant face lit up when he saw me. It had been months since we'd crossed paths, but he greeted me as warmly as he did the night of Guevara's arraignment.

"Hey," he said, "what do you say we sneak out for a margarita?"

"I say—how come the supervisor's still working the bridge?"

"Because the son-of-a-bitch Administrative Judge asked me to. Says no one works the bridge like me. Thanks and no thanks. So when it gets real busy, I come over and kiss his ass." Figueroa waved a set of court papers at me. "You got a case on? I'll stick it near the front."

"Just a couple of adjournments down the hall. Figured one of my clients might be in here by mistake. But thanks anyway."

He extended his hands over the line of cases on the table. "Whatever I can do."

Figueroa went on policing the court calendar as lawyers approached him with requests that he place their cases on the bridge to be called. He complied stoically and without preferential treatment. He gazed back up at me as I was about to step away. "Hey, I heard about your bout with Judge Sheflin at the Spiderman arraignment."

"He wasn't the Spiderman. He passed a lie detector the day he died. It was in almost all the newspapers."

"I don't read the papers. Got enough here to fill my days, and my nights."

"Tell me about it," I turned to leave.

"Hey Nick. That blonde ever find you?"

I stopped dead. A shiver crept down my lower back. "What blonde are you taking about?"

"About a month back, a knock-out blonde was asking for you." He smirked then glanced toward the judge's chambers. "Evidently she was asking around until she stumbled on me."

"What exactly did she say?"

"At first I thought it was personal, like maybe a girlfriend. But when I saw how concerned she was, I figured it was business. Especially when I realized she had no idea what you looked like."

"But what did she say exactly?" My voice wavered in desperation.

"Christ Nick, it was a while back. I can't remember exactly."

"Try. Please."

"OK, I think it was something like, 'where can I find Nick Mannino? I need to speak to him today.' Yeah. She said 'today,' and that it was important."

My face must have shown my anxiety, because as I stared into space, Figueroa asked if I was all right.

I didn't answer.

"One other thing." He took a breath, checked the judge's chambers, and spoke quickly. "At first I thought she was with this guy. You see, we were in the fourth floor hallway, about a courtroom away from the elevators. This guy was standing about twenty feet from us. I saw him watching. He got closer as she spoke, close enough to hear. So I figured they were together."

My stomach wrenched in anticipation, and fear.

"Not that they looked like a match made in heaven. She was a white blue-eyed beauty, dressed to kill. And he was black, kind of big. Stocky. He was wearing a black cap and jeans. Can't remember much else. When she got in the elevator, he followed. As I walked past I could see them inside."

"And?"

"And nothing. He took off his cap is all."

"Did you see his hair?"

"His hair? No."

"Shit." I said in exasperation.

Figueroa looked at me curiously. "Ain't my fault the guy was bald."

Chapter 45

I spun through the revolving doors of the Supreme Court Building onto the Grand Concourse and found myself at the curb, not recalling how and when I had scaled the fifty-odd steps to get there.

Traffic moved in a quick and orderly fashion, the occasional horn a reminder of the ever-impetuous New York City driver. Lawyers in suits and uniformed police officers milled around the courthouse. Waiting to cross at 161st Street, I could smell the exhaust of a hundred cars. I lowered my head. I was standing over a sewer drain embedded in the asphalt, the bottom sludge a timeless mixture of unrecognizable garbage that had long lost its vile smell to the everyday. But the garbage was there nonetheless. Festering. Underground. Piling higher.

The sunny spring day, the seasonal ritual of rising spirits, was lost on me as I walked robotically back to the office.

That blonde had been trying to get me, to speak to me. Had the bald guy in the elevator been the Spiderman? Was she just another one of his victims? But there was no evidence of rape or even attempted rape. And why had none of her identification been found?

Because her killer must have taken it.

I stopped outside Executive Towers, and thought to myself: *but why?*

Because her very identity would provide some link—lead somehow to the identity of her murderer?

But why kill her to begin with? Did it have something to do with me? Was I a link in all this?

I felt like a fool as I realized the extent to which I was grasping at straws. Life is full of awful coincidences—random occurrences that create rippling effects.

That bald man did not have to be the Spiderman. And the Spiderman did not have to be her killer.

Tuesday. 10:00 A.M. I met Peter Guevara outside Part 60. He was in a blue vested pinstripe suit, and I blithely remarked how he looked more the lawyer than I did in my plain gray two-piece. He hugged me, bubbling over with thanks for my "swarm" on the Rodriguez brothers. *Swarm* was the word *he* used.

"We still have the Chavez boy and his mother to contend with, but the D.A.'s case has lost most of its strength." What I really wanted to say was: *We've got this case beat and at worst it will fall apart midtrial.* But that would have sounded like a guarantee, and in the business of law, there is none.

Upon Guevara's case being called, and without so much as an advance phone call, Jimmy Ryan moved to dismiss all counts of the indictment that had Carlos and Rafael Rodriguez as complaining witnesses. Guevara threw an arm around my back and squeezed.

"Great," he whispered.

Judge Graham, peering at Ryan over reading glasses that always seemed on the verge of falling off the end of his nose, said: "The grand jury deliberated and voted to indict this defendant on many very serious charges brought by your office with these Rodriguez boys as complainants. Would it be too much of me to ask why you now see fit to dismiss these charges?"

"Is your honor objecting to my dismissing these charges?" Ryan said defensively.

Graham stood up and threw his glasses down on the bench. "First of all, Mr. Ryan, *you* are not dismissing anything. The State of New York is, which your office and the District Attorney who employs you represent. I, sir, in case you haven't noticed my black robe, am the judge here. So before I accept dismissal of charges that have been voted on by a grand jury, I want to know why!"

"The judge doesn't want to dismiss the charges?" Guevara asked frantically.

"Don't worry," I whispered back. "Ryan just has to put on the record that the two Rodriguez brothers admitted they lied. If he doesn't, I will."

Ryan collected himself. Red-faced, but still the wise guy, he told the judge about the tapes and the minutes I sent him. "Father Kerres is a Roman Catholic priest. In his presence and mine, the two boys, in separate interviews, stated that they lied about the charges they made against this defendant."

"Very well," Graham said. "The court accepts dismissal of all charges concerning Carlos and Rafael Rodriguez as complainants. I trust you are proceeding with the charges brought by the Chavez boy?"

"Yes, Your Honor. Those charges stand," Ryan said with renewed bravado.

"I don't suppose you have any objection, Mr. Mannino, to what has just taken place?" Graham asked.

"Actually I do, your honor." Guevara stiffened. "I accept dismissal of most of the charges, but I strenuously object to the continued prosecution of any other charges voted on by this same grand jury. Any vote to indict on the Chavez charges had to be tainted by the perjured testimony of the Rodriquez brothers, who also allege that Sandra Chavez, mother of the third boy, suborned their perjury and even committed perjury herself."

"Do you have motion papers with you?" Graham asked.

"Yes, Judge. Returnable in ten days, if that's agreeable to all."

"Mr. Ryan?" Graham asked.

"The date is OK with me. The People will strenuously oppose the motion, however."

"Don't pull a muscle in the process, Mr. Ryan. All right. Let's arraign Mr. Guevara on the remaining charges." Graham then read the counts of the indictment concerning the Chavez boy. "There are two counts of sodomy in the first degree." One was for oral sex and the other for anal sex by forcible compulsion. "Two counts of sexual abuse in the first degree." These were lesser charges amounting to the same act, but characterized under the law by mere sexual contact as opposed to sexual entry. "How do you plead, Mr. Guevara?"

"Not guilty!" he shouted.

Graham gave us an adjourn date ten days hence. "Don't forget to give

Mr. Ryan a copy of your motion papers, Mr. Mannino. He just might want to serve a written response."

"Judge," I interrupted. "Over a dozen people have contributed to raising fifteen-thousand dollars bail. Now that eight of the twelve counts have been dismissed, I respectfully move that the defendant's bail be exonerated and that he remain released on his own recognizance."

Graham needed no time to think, nor did he ask Ryan if he wanted to be heard. "Bail is reduced to two-thousand-five-hundred dollars cash or bond. Twelve-thousand-five-hundred dollars of the fifteen-thousand is exonerated."

"Thank you, Judge."

"Yes, thank you, Judge!" Guevara shouted.

Graham eyed him curiously, then called for the next case.

"This mean it's all over?" Guevara asked me as we left the courtroom. His face was so close to mine I could smell his cologne. Aramis. My best friend Joey wore it all the time. It was damn expensive too.

"Not exactly," I was careful to say. "The most we can hope for on my motion is a dismissal with leave or permission for the D.A.'s office to re-present the Chavez charges to a new grand jury; one which hasn't heard the perjured testimony of the Rodriguez brothers."

"So we go to trial then on the Chavez charges," Guevara said.

"First, we might try a shot at the grand jury ourselves." I was sounding, and feeling, more daring.

"How's that?"

"Look at you in that suit. You're confidant, self-assured. I think you're now ready to testify."

"You mean to the grand jury?"

"Why not? We'll be up against Jose Chavez, the pathological liar, and his predicate felon drug-addicted mother. The odds just got a lot better."

Guevara seemed to be thinking hard. "You're my lawyer, Nick. Whatever you say, I'll do." He stepped into the empty elevator.

"Now get to that polygraph examiner. It wouldn't hurt to have the judge actually believe you're innocent. And don't wait for Cantwell to call you. Call *him*. All right?"

"You got it." He released the button, and the elevator doors jostled closed between us.

Later that day, Shula Hirsch called. Guevara had told her the good news. I was optimistic about getting a second crack at the grand jury with only the Chavez charges to contend with, and told her so. She offered to testify and I thanked her.

Grand juries are under no obligation to hear defense witnesses other than the defendant. Unless the prosecutor called her to testify, which was unlikely, or the grand jury specifically asked for her, she would not be heard.

It was Mrs. Hirsch, the perfect picture of the dedicated inner city schoolteacher, who could testify to the Chavez boy's proclivity to lie, to his outbursts, to the visible evidence of his severe psychological and emotional problems—problems that made teaching him in the public school system impossible. Evidence of assault, stealing, and deviant sexual activity would render his testimony against Guevara almost worthless.

Hirsch could also discredit Sandra Chavez. As awful as it was to capitalize on someone's affliction, Hirsch, with crutches and leg braces, would make one riveting, sympathetic witness, and she wouldn't have to fake a thing. I also had an idea or two about how she might explain away that anal laceration found on Jose the night of Guevara's arrest. Somehow I had to get her into that grand jury room.

Chapter 46

In a thick Irish brogue, the Bronx Supreme Court Clerk told me that all but the bail posted by Shula Hirsch, who had given her name as representative for those who contributed from P.S. 92, would be exonerated.

"Why's that?" I asked with overdone politeness.

He batted the air with his hand. "Why should I expect you to know any more than the rest of the ass-wipe lawyers around here?"

He held up the list of those who posted Guevara's bail and I noticed Guevara's name on top for one thousand dollars.

"My client was in jail. How could his name be on the top of the list?"

"Because someone else posted the bail for him and gave his name and address."

"Does it say who?"

"No. But my guess is it's the guy who's next in line." He put on his reading glasses which were dangling from a green cord around his neck. "*Vincent Tedeschi, Kingsbridge Road Realty.*"

This was the real estate broker who employed Guevara part-time. Guevara mentioned him to me after his release—the first I had learned of this footnote to Guevara's resume.

Taking on a glazed look, the clerk started chewing on one end of his glasses. "I remember this name," he said as if coming out of a trance. "Sophie!"

An obese middle-aged white woman with several unappealing beauty marks, looked up and over a desk cluttered with piles of thick manila folders.

"Vincent Tedeschi. Ain't he the one who called a couple times wanting his bail money back?"

"Yep. Real pissed off too. Said the defendant owed him money, and he wanted to take back the bail he posted. Called about a week ago, and again yesterday."

I asked the clerk, "How do these people get their money back now that most of the bail has been exonerated? Can you give me their checks? I'll be happy to deliver them."

Though I had no desire to see Dr. Terkel, the largest donor, I did want to speak to Tedeschi. I was curious why he was so upset, and did not want to lose him as a character witness should the case go to trial. Perhaps if I returned the bail money, I could coax him into burying any gripe he might have with Guevara.

"Counselor, do you think I've got a wire to some bank account where I can cut checks from my ten-by-twelve office back there on some push-button machine or somethin'? 'Cause if you know of such a contraption, tell me where I can find it, and I'll cut me a big one-way ticket the hell out of here!"

He did a one-hundred-eighty-degree spin, and then laughed along with Sophie. Upon quieting down, he explained that after a two percent fee was deducted, a check would be mailed to the respective benefactors in about ten days from the New York City Comptroller's Office, which in retrospect made perfect sense to me.

I called Dr. Terkel to inform him of the new developments in the case and the bail refund. A woman, who I guessed was his nurse, answered the phone with a deep Jamaican accent. I could hear Terkel in the background, disdainfully commenting on the mid-day news. She pleasantly asked him several times to pick up the phone.

"He gets preoccupied with the crime reportin' on the TV," she said. "Give 'im a little bit. He'll pick up."

I heard the receiver lift to the loud blare of a television commercial.

"Dr. Terkel? This is Nick Mannino."

"Yes, yes. How are you? When are you coming to visit me?" He shot the two questions at me in one breath. I was fumbling for an answer to the second.

"I'm fine. Either before or right after the case is over, I'll come visit you. I promise."

"Fine, fine." He sounded older and more debilitated than when we'd spoken weeks earlier.

I told him about the bail reduction and the recantations of the Rodriguez boys. To my surprise, he knew about both already.

"Peter was here last night," he said hoarsely, as if every word required the greatest effort. "I knew he was innocent. Smart boy. Smart boy. He's going to beat this case. I know it. They'll never convict him, never convict him at all." He was babbling on and I hadn't a clue how to stop him. I gave up all hope of ever using him as a character witness. He sounded too far-gone. "Never convict him. Killed a man. That's right. No trial. No conviction."

I thought I might have heard wrong so I asked him: "Who killed a man? Peter?"

"Peter!" he shrieked. "No, no, no. Me. I killed a man. Long time ago. Long time ago. Deserved it. Deserved it he did…"

"So it was self defense?" I asked, amazed at the turn in the conversation.

"Oh yeah. Killed him. Killed him. Killed him."

Whatever was physically wrong with Terkel had evidently affected his mind. The nurse, who I suspect had been absent from his room, picked up on another extension. "Please hold the phone, Mr. Mannino."

I could hear her thick rubber shoes squeaking across the floor. Terkel was mumbling on incessantly. I don't believe he knew who he was speaking to any more, or even if he was speaking at all. He kept repeating: "Killed him, killed him, killed him," over and over until I heard the nurse say something in Jamaican, followed by the smack the phone onto its hook.

She came back on the extension. "He fadin' fast," she said sadly. "Pay 'im no mind. He ramble on like this all day long. He dyin', you know. Very sad. Got that AIDS and won't let go. Hangs on like a battleship."

"He seemed all right when I spoke to him a few weeks ago."

"Some days he okay. But half the time, he like you heard. The news set 'im off."

I told her to tell him to expect his bail money back in about ten days.

"Sure, I'll tell 'im."

"Thank you. And I hope things go as well as they can for him." I had no idea how to close a conversation about a dying man. And it showed.

She responded with a simple, "All right then."

Chapter 47

Kingsbridge Road Realty was named, unimaginatively, for its location on Kingsbridge Road off Aqueduct Avenue, a location central to Saint Nicholas of Tolentine Church two blocks south, and P.S. 92 two blocks north. Guevara lived in a four-story walk-up on University Avenue, just half a block away.

I had called Vincent Tedeschi just before leaving Legal Aid. He said he was on his way out and spoke with a forced courtesy after I told him I was Guevara's attorney. Upon hearing I had news about his bail money and was headed right over, he agreed to wait.

After racing uptown in my Malibu, I rang the bell outside his storefront office. He buzzed me in.

Tedeschi, who seemed about thirty-five, had a handshake that was all salesman—like a man who shakes hands for a living and works on commission. He had a thin face and was about my height and general physical appearance—at least until he tossed off a powder blue sports jacket and displayed a toned chest under a fitted shirt. His hair fell constantly onto his forehead.

I took a seat in a private office in the back as he spoke on the phone to a seller about the benefits of the Multiple Listing Service and its broad subscription by hundreds of brokers in the Bronx and adjoining boroughs. He was quite the smooth talker as he pushed to secure the listing without sounding heavy-handed. He winked at me in victory when he set up an appointment to see the homeowner.

As he leaned over a desk calendar, I noticed that this young, personable yet obviously vain real estate broker was wearing one cheap and terribly unconvincing toupee.

Oddly, this display of both insecurity and bad taste made him somewhat likable. And I wondered if subconsciously he wore this chink in an otherwise well-kept armor to endear himself to his older more conservative middle-class clients. His discount department store pants and 100% polyester shirt rounded out his dime store wardrobe. No wonder he was screaming at the clerk's office for his bail money back.

I scanned his desktop for family photos. There were none.

"So, Mr. Mannino. What's the news on my bail money?" He spoke like a creditor inquiring about an overdue debt.

I explained the usual protocol of bail posting—how the money didn't get returned until the case was over and the accused had made all his appearances.

He nodded again as if he knew this already. His fingers tapped the desk impatiently.

"Since the bail you posted got exonerated, you should be getting a check from the Comptroller's Office in a week or two." I was surprised when he didn't brighten up with the news.

"The thing is," he said in a business-like manner, "I posted an additional thousand dollars in Guevara's name."

"I saw that on the list. But why in Guevara's name?"

"Because I'm an idiot, that's why." He stood up and looked through a glass partition. A young Hispanic woman neatly dressed in a skirt, blouse, and high heels was being buzzed in by one of the sales agents.

Tedeschi hit the intercom button. "Dolores, would you see to this young lady please?" A smartly dressed sales agent offered her hand to the young woman. "It's a rental," Tedeschi remarked. "Since Peter left, the other agents have been taking turns with them."

"Peter did the rentals?"

"Yeah, and he was damn good at it too. He was supposed to take his salesman's test and get his license to sell, but he never did. So I kept him on rentals. If an inspector came around and caught him showing apartments instead of houses, I was less likely to get in trouble."

"Well, that explains why Peter didn't tell me about his job here." I was quick to point this out in a veiled attempt to regain some of Guevara's favor with Tedeschi.

Tedeschi was unmoved, but seemed uneasy. He then told me about an apartment rental Peter had handled the Saturday before his arrest.

The prospective tenant had agreed to take it and was supposed to come by the office the following week to drop off a month's rent, a month's security, and the broker's fee. Then Guevara got arrested. When he called Tedeschi from Rikers Island and asked for help raising bail, Tedeschi agreed to post two-thousand-five-hundred dollars of his own money. With all contributors accounted for, this still left Guevara a thousand short. Since Tedeschi already owed him three-hundred dollars in previously earned commissions, and the Saturday rental meant another four hundred dollars' due Guevara, that left Tedeschi—upon posting an additional thousand dollars—in the hole for only three hundred. Guevara promised to make good on it immediately upon his release.

Guevara never kept his promise. When the prospective tenant for the second apartment never materialized, that left the real estate broker in the hole for a hefty seven hundred, and no sign of Guevara since he'd left Rikers Island.

I apologized for my client, and blamed it on the strain of the criminal charges. I also told Tedeschi about Guevara's suspension from P.S. 92, and that I would personally see to it that Guevara repaid him in full as soon as he was able.

"I'll believe it when I see it," Tedeschi said while rolling his eyes back. He took a deep breath and looked around the room. "Just tell him to forget about it, okay? And tell him I filled his position with a licensed sales agent, so I don't need him back either." He stood and extended his hand.

"I'm sure he'll repay you," I appealed.

Our hands met. He gave mine a quick conclusive shake then pointed toward the door. "Please, I've got work to do."

Chapter 48

I waited for Eleanor, one of an anxious group of onlookers, behind a rope a few feet from the bottom of a descending escalator that reminded me of the Bronx Criminal Court. A short black security guard stood watch nearby as a single file of passengers rode down, their eyes combing the crowd below.

Though it had been only ten days since I saw her last, she looked years younger. Wide-eyed, rested, relaxed, she had never appeared more beautiful to me than in those seconds before our eyes met. She smiled broadly and ran toward me.

Dropping her suitcase and shopping bag, she threw her arms around my neck and gave me a long, intense kiss. We hugged until the crowd had parted and the security guard left his post. We held each other as we walked to my car, Eleanor carrying her shopping bag, me carrying her suitcase.

"So, have I lost you to Atlanta?" I asked.

A cool wind whipped her hair back, and I was reminded again of the night we first met and the confusion I'd felt as we parted outside Cardozo Law amid the gusts of Fifth Avenue.

She looked down at the pavement. "I missed you terribly, Nick. I don't think we should be apart for this long again."

I opened the passenger door of the Malibu. She slid in and held her breath as tears formed in the corners of her eyes. I reached over and hugged her.

She futilely attempted to blow dry her eyes by waving her fingers in front of her face. When I started the car, the radio came on. *The Long and Winding Road* was playing with Paul McCartney's voice in the lead. I held her hand during the entire drive to Manhattan.

When we got to her apartment, she emptied the shopping bag. A tiny cherubic doll pushing a rust-tinted Coca-Cola crate was delicately placed on the coffee table. It commemorated the first sale of America's favorite soft drink out of a drug store on Atlanta's Peachtree Street in the late 1890s. She then draped across my knee a tie emblazoned with a picture of Rhett Butler playing cards in a black cape and white ruffled shirt.

Eleanor studied my reaction as I examined each gift. I told her I loved them both and kissed her twice in thanks, though I couldn't imagine where or when I'd ever wear the tie.

She then took a third gift from the bag—a porcelain, hand-painted bust of Saint John the Baptist so delicate, I was actually afraid to touch it. "I thought your mom would like this."

Eleanor had remembered that my stepfather's full name was Giovanni Baptiste Mannino.

She would gain a special place in Mom's heart with this one.

"I know you don't wear jewelry," she said handing me a small box. "But I thought of you when I saw this."

I opened the box and gaped at the Rolex inside. *This must have cost thousands.*

"Don't even think about saying that I shouldn't have. It's a gift, and I'm not taking it back. So just tell me you love me, and always will."

"I love you, and always will," I said, and meant it. I hoped my sincerity successfully masked my embarrassment. The last thing I wanted her family to think was that I was taking advantage of their daughter, or worse—was only interested in her money.

"Eleanor, don't misunderstand me, I love the watch. But this must have cost you a small fortune. The tux. Now this. What will your family think?"

"My family will love you and probably loves you already. I've spoken about you enough." She paused. "Now look closely at the watch."

Its numbers were in tiny gold numerals that glistened in the lamplight. I turned the watch over and read the engraving: *Nick Never forget I love you Eleanor.*

We made love on her living room couch—for hours.

The next day, I showed Mom the bust of Saint John the Baptist. She fought back tears as she held it up and rotated it in her hands. She called Eleanor at work and thanked her. After getting the statue blessed at Cure of Ars Church in Merrick, it took its proper place on top a doily on the chest of drawers in Mom's bedroom, next to the picture of the husband she had buried.

Chapter 49

It was a quiet Friday afternoon. I stood before Judge Graham in Bronx Supreme. Guevara was at my side. The ten-day adjournment on my motion to dismiss the remaining counts of the indictment containing the Chavez boy's accusations had passed and, as expected, Jimmy Ryan had not filed a written response. But with passion, some oratorical skill, and little logic, he argued against it.

"The grand jury would have indicted Mr. Guevara anyway, had they only heard the testimony of the Chavez boy."

"That's some crystal ball you've got there, Mr. Ryan," Graham said sharply.

"The Chavez family should not be denied their day in court merely because the People dismissed the two cases that the perjured testimony affected, Judge."

"You don't think the grand jurors who voted to indict on the Chavez case were influenced by the perjured testimony of the Rodriguez brothers?"

"There's no proof of that, Your Honor."

"And there's no proof it didn't. We're not expected to be mind readers, Mr. Ryan. The grand jury heard from two witnesses, the same age as the Chavez boy, who testified falsely to the same type of crime as the Chavez boy." Graham halted Ryan's approaching rebuttal with a raised hand. "This Court has heard enough. The remaining charges in the indictment are dismissed. The D.A.'s office *may* re-present only the charges concerning the third boy—the complainant Jose Chavez, and only within the next thirty days to a different grand jury panel."

"The D.A.'s Office will be re-presenting the case concerning the Chavez child next week," Ryan said. "Does the defendant wish to testify?"

To Graham and Ryan's surprise, I answered, "Absolutely, your honor."

"This matter is adjourned pending a grand jury determination," Graham bellowed. "Call the next case."

With my arm pressed against Guevara's back, I led him out of the courtroom. He wanted to talk, but held up when he saw me put my finger to my lips. Ryan was approaching. I told Guevara that we must start going over his testimony on Monday. He nodded, then hurried off in a businesslike manner.

"What's the rush?" I asked Ryan. "Do you have to go to re-present next week?" I wanted more time to prepare Guevara. There were others I also wanted make sure were ready to testify, like Mrs. Hirsch, and maybe a character witness or two.

"If not for that kid's nutty mother, I don't think we'd even re-present at all," Ryan said.

"Did you confirm that robbery conviction I told you about?"

"Yes, I did."

"And her drug use?"

"Yeah, but she's clean now. Besides, you wouldn't get that into evidence at trial anyway."

"Don't be so sure. And what about that two-million dollar lawsuit? Think that might cloud her sense of fair play just a little bit? A guilty verdict and her civil attorney gets one-third of a cool two million. You still go home with your shitty paycheck."

I looked down the corridor and saw Guevara standing at the far end, his eyes riveted on Ryan and me.

"Listen Nick, I'll give your man his chance to tell his story in full, without interruption. If you've got any material witnesses, bring them in, and I don't mean little old ladies who'll testify what a good guy he is when he's not sodomizing little boys."

"How about a witness who'll testify that Jose Chavez is a pathological liar?"

We approached a bank of elevators on the opposite side of the building. "I'll give your client the fairest opportunity I'll probably ever give a defendant in my entire career."

"If you're expecting me to genuflect, forget it. Your case is shit, Jimmy, and you know it. You don't want to try this case anymore than I do."

Ryan smirked at me.

We set a date and time. The following Friday, 10:00 A.M. I would be back from Atlanta and Eleanor's brother's wedding on Monday. This would give me the time I needed to prep Guevara, Mrs. Hirsch, and maybe a couple of character witnesses on the chance Ryan might let the latter bunch testify. But the trouble with a guy like Ryan was, even when you thought you could trust him, you couldn't. Especially when he had no cards to play, and nothing to lose.

Chapter 50

I slept nearly the entire flight to Atlanta. Screeching tires and a slight bounce of the plane woke me. My left hand was in Eleanor's, on her lap. My head was on her shoulder.

As we exited the aircraft, I watched her legs silhouetted in the sunlight under a semi-sheer granny dress. "Are we going to be able to control ourselves this weekend?" she asked.

I smiled slyly. "For my sake, I hope so."

Eleanor had warned me. Her parents were not medieval and did not need to be told that two adults in love and in their late twenties were having sex. But bedding down together under their roof was out of the question.

As soon as we retrieved our bags from the conveyor belt, a uniformed chauffeur appeared.

"Miss Vernou?" he asked, in an accent that had a lifetime of Metropolitan New York buried in every syllable. "I'll take your bags."

A paunchy man in his sixties, he limped through the exit doors to the black stretch limousine parked outside. Eleanor and I followed.

Within blocks of her home, Eleanor patted my arm and gave it a reassuring squeeze. "Everything will be fine."

I felt a headache coming on and rolled my eyes.

We turned onto Piedmont Road and I remembered Eleanor telling me she lived in a neighborhood called Buckhead. After driving several long blocks past large antebellum homes that resembled courthouses on plots of land as big as baseball fields, the limousine turned into a driveway inside an opening in an eight-foot high brick wall.

The house was set back an entire city block from the road. Two huge dogwoods, one with white flowers and the other with pink, were separated by over two hundred feet of meticulously manicured bluegrass. Apple and cherry blossom trees adorned each side of a circular drive.

I stared in wonder and awe at the eight white columns inside a shaded portico.

As the limo came to a smooth stop, I put on the jacket that I had carefully folded and draped over the seat next to me, and began to pluck tiny bits of lint off my pants.

A butler exited out an enormous oak door.

Eleanor whispered in my ear. "Inasmuch as I like to see my Bronx warrior vulnerable, you really have very little to fear this weekend."

"And why's that, my fair princess?"

"Because if my parents don't like you, they'll never show it."

Eleanor exited the limo first and greeted Charles the butler with a big hug. Charles directed the driver to follow him with our bags. I watched as they made their way through a prodigious center hall up an expansive staircase that widened as it rose toward the second floor. Paintings of Parisian street scenes hung on paneled walls under a huge bronze chandelier suspended a full story from a coffered ceiling.

Eleanor took my hand and led me through a library and into a dining room that had been cleared for the wedding. A table large enough to seat thirty was positioned against a far wall. A mural of a windswept sky had been painted on the sixteen-foot high ceiling.

We passed through a swinging cherry wood door into the kitchen. There, standing in front of three wooden tables with marble tops cluttered with dishes, glassware and serving platters, was Charlotte Vernou. A half-dozen men in full aprons scurried around her bouncing to her instructions. She greeted her daughter with a long hug and a kiss on the cheek.

Eleanor introduced me with a sweep of her hand. And to a drum roll in my head she said: "Mother—this is Nick."

Charlotte Vernou smiled warmly. And I was careful not to mistake warmth for style and grace, which seemed to emanate from her with a calculable ease. I hoped, early on, she would give me a chance, and not just feign interest.

She extended her hand and I shook it gently. I had intended to give her a respectful kiss on the cheek, but her extended arm made the distance I had to cover impossible to cross. She promptly commented on the weather. Said she hoped it would be as beautiful for the wedding tomorrow as it was that day. As she spoke, her reddish brown hair bounced lightly around delicate facial features that reminded me of finely cut crystal. I had to concentrate hard on her words for fear of showing my astonishment at how young and beautiful this woman of fifty appeared.

She suggested Eleanor show me to my room and that we "kids" enjoy what remained of this "heavenly day." Then added: "Nick, I'm sorry if we don't get to give you much attention this weekend, but I do hope we get some time to get to know you." She then threw her hands in the air, smiled like a teenager and said, "In the midst of all this chaos."

"Thank you," I replied. "I hope so too."

I had been politely dismissed.

Chapter 51

There were nine bedrooms in this twenty-room house. Since parting from Charlotte, I had been sleeping like the dead in one of them, flat on my back in a Chippendale canopy bed centered in a room the size of my entire house. Eleanor left me alone for two hours, then shook me awake. She said I was moaning. I joked and told I was having a sex dream, but it was the beginnings of another nightmare. Only this time, the shed was engulfed in flames, black smoke billowing into a night sky. I was running toward it, and the harder I ran, the farther the shed became. I felt Eleanor's hand on my face.

Sunlight beaming through sheer white curtains made me wince. A short nap and I had lost my bearings. I panicked. *What must her father be thinking of me*: this rude New Yorker who'd come into his home, said hello to his wife, and then retreated upstairs to sleep.

"El, what about your father?"

"He should be home in an hour. We'll all eat dinner then."

I shaved quickly in my own personal bathroom, while Eleanor unpacked my things. She treated my clothes as if they were a child of ours—carefully pointing down the collar on a shirt, gently smoothing out a sweater before placing it in a top drawer.

* * *

A large mahogany table covered with a cherry red tablecloth had been brought to the center of the dining room. On it was a bronze candelabra with candles burning. Its chairs had pinned burgundy upholstery that matched the silk wall fabric. George Vernou sat at the head of the table.

He was reading a page of newspaper, his eyes running down columns of closing stock prices. There was no clue in his expression whether the news was good or bad. On the table in front of him was the main section. I glimpsed down and caught the words **BRONX** and **RAPIST** in bold type above a fold in the paper.

Eleanor softly uttered, "Daddy."

George Vernou looked up. His smile widened as we approached. His eyes never left his daughter as she moved quickly toward him. Rising to a commanding six feet, he embraced and kissed her. His resemblance to Eleanor was uncanny. They had the same big blue eyes, curved cheekbones, and round nose.

"Daddy, this is Nick."

"How are you, Nick? I feel like I know you already." He shook my hand with a warmth that was both reservedly diplomatic and powerful. It told me I was welcome for the time being, and at the same time warned me that could change.

"I'm fine, sir. Thank you. It's nice to meet you. I hope I can live up to whatever good things Eleanor has said about me." Right off, I was talking too much, but he didn't seem to mind. This was exactly what he wanted me to do.

He gestured to an adjoining two chairs. "Please. Sit down."

I knocked into Eleanor as I pulled out the chair closest to her father for her to sit in.

I took the seat on her other side and looked down at the exquisite place setting in front of me.

George Vernou leaned back. He was wearing a blue blazer and white shirt, both perfectly tailored to fit his portly frame. "Eleanor tells me that you've been handling a couple of publicity cases up there in The Bronx."

"Yes sir. That's true. Although I didn't invite the publicity and in one case even tried to avoid it."

"I suppose the press can be a liability in your line of work."

"For the most part, yes."

"You think it could be an asset ever?"

"Rarely. I got some positive press once, but it's not usually the politically correct thing to side with a poor criminal's defense attorney, even when it's deserved."

"What made you pick criminal defense work?" He spoke with a tone of genuine interest, concern even, and my worst fear—that I would be ignored—passed.

I told him it was my stepfather's idea at first, and that he had raised me since I was five.

He nodded, though I wasn't sure if it was in acknowledgment of what he already knew, or in acceptance of my explanation.

"Anyway, he planted the seed. Criminal defense work seemed exciting to me as a kid, and that certainly has proved to be true. Whether I'll do this for the rest of my life, I can't say. I've been working hard lately, and I'm a bit tired. After I clear my calendar of some big cases I'm going to take a few weeks off and see how I feel. Legal Aid asks for a three-year commitment. That's up in September."

George Vernou never took his eyes off me as I spoke, not even to look at Eleanor. He seemed to be studying me intently, and yet with such surprising deference, that I actually felt myself relaxing—and inasmuch as that was possible under the circumstances. When Charlotte Vernou walked in, holding four bowls on a silver tray and announced "lobster bisque," George smiled, then said with such pleasant contentment that it made me jump inside for joy: "I just love lobster bisque."

The bisque was not too creamy, and the little chunks of lobster melted in my mouth. A Veal Marsala followed and then a delicious chocolate mousse. I caught Charlotte winking at Eleanor and realized the two had managed a culinary conspiracy of sorts, with me as their intended target.

George, as it turned out, was a diehard Braves fan with box seats just two rows behind Ted Turner's. Charlotte's guilty pleasure was inside a locked room on the second floor, where a collector's ransom of *Gone with the Wind* memorabilia was on display. George joked that not even he was allowed inside. She called it "The Tara Room."

As Charlotte fanned her piping hot coffee with her napkin she began talking about, of all things, Wayne Williams and the Atlanta serial murders. George Vernou's mouth turned down at the change in subject. Picking up the cue, Charlotte veered off course a bit and asked how I felt about capital punishment.

"I don't recall a time when I believed in capital punishment," I said easily, and without hesitation.

"George and I feel the same way, but not Eleanor. Right Eleanor, darlin'."

"Really?" I turned to look at the beautiful young woman seated next to me, whom I forgot, as I often had in social settings, was an Assistant District Attorney.

"Ted Bundy should not remain among the living. Nor should have Jack the Ripper, or Hitler, or those mobster hit men who kill between meals as casually as you hit the remote button on your television."

A burn hit my stomach as Eleanor summarily executed my uncle Rocco between sips of milk-cooled coffee.

George Vernou was staring again, and this time his eyes had an asphyxiating hold on me.

After dinner, the Vernous went upstairs to bed, protesting they would need all the sleep they could get before their home was invaded the following day. Eleanor led me into the library, and on a sofa in front of a fireplace, she taught me how to play backgammon, then beat me a dozen straight times.

Afterward, we kissed in front of a crackling fire. When the fire's glow had faded, we went upstairs and parted amid hugs and kisses to our separate bedrooms.

Chapter 52

The next morning's preparations swept through the house and grounds with the organized excitement of a movie set. Trucks had arrived at 7:00 A.M., bringing tables, chairs, floral arrangements of all sizes and shapes, wooden platforms for a twenty-piece orchestra, table linen, food for a whole neighborhood, barbecue pits, electric stoves, additional refrigerators, and enough wedding decorations to charm royalty.

I awoke that morning alone in my canopy bed. On my night table I found a note from Eleanor next to my Rolex. It informed me that I would be on my own until after the ceremony, which was scheduled to take place on the marble terrace overlooking the back lawn at 2:00 P.M. If I needed anything, I should see Charles. She asked me to look out for her friend, Carolyn, who was usually uncomfortable at these gaudy Southern affairs.

The note closed with: *I'll miss you 'til later. Love Always, Eleanor.*

I found a pad and pen in the night table drawer. Before I got out of bed, I scribbled down a few notes on Guevara's appearance before the grand jury.

Never Arrested Drug Addict Mom Teacher's Aide Liar Video-Games Community College Anal Laceration.

My mind was a jumble and for a moment I didn't know where Peter Guevara began and Jose Chavez ended. I ripped my notes into little pieces and flushed them down the toilet.

I could hear guests starting to arrive as I shaved, showered and blow-dried my hair with the care and attention of Travolta in *Saturday Night Fever*. My tux fit perfectly, as did my shoes. I checked myself in the mirror one last time, took a couple of calming breaths, and proceeded down the stairs and through the center hall. Walking past ceiling-high French doors, I stepped onto the parquet floors of a room so enormous it seemed ethereal.

Three crystal chandeliers hung from a hand-painted fresco ceiling that rose two stories. An orchestra played a string-led version of Patsy Cline's *Crazy*, while an array of tables adorned with flowers, ice sculptures and hot and cold appetizers had just been rolled into place. A crowd had begun to form by an inlaid mahogany bar with smoked mirrored shelves stocked with liquor. I then stepped through more French doors and into a six-acre lawn and garden paradise.

Standing on a marble terrace the length of the house and enclosed by a matching balustrade, I looked out over an Olympic-sized swimming pool and a patio the size of a tennis court, where a five-piece band played jazz and bartenders served drinks from sterling silver trays. Beyond the patio and the pool, luminous flower gardens encircled sparkling fountains and two white tents housed over fifty tables draped in pink lace linen.

The ceremony would take place inside a gazebo facing the house at the center of the marble terrace where folding chairs were set up in a triangular formation.

I had just made my way back inside when Charles pointed out a light-haired young woman in a pink dress standing on the far side of the pool. Her profile was Eleanor's. But it wasn't Eleanor; it was Carolyn, and she had never looked prettier. For one hard-core lesbian, Carolyn was looking exceedingly feminine.

I went back down the marble stairs and approached her by the cabana. She slyly turned toward me.

"Carolyn?"

"Yes, Nickie boy, it's me."

I put my hand on my heart. "Would it be piggish or chauvinistic of me if I told you how pretty you look?"

Her eyes narrowed and she smiled a crooked smile. With the gait of a tomboy, she walked toward me, and linked her arm in mine. We strolled toward one of the fountains.

"Listen, Italian boy from Long Island or Brooklyn or wherever. Eleanor made me promise to be nice to you. And since she talks you up so much every time I speak to her, I will keep my promise." Her head turned up at me. "So tell me, now that you've had your fun—what are your intentions with my best friend. And don't lie to me or this purse might just crack into that tool box of yours and you can bet your life you'll have to sit out the rest of this lavish David O. Selznick Production, and alone."

I felt the urge to laugh, but didn't dare. "Whatever happened to ice-breaking small talk?"

"Just answer the question, lawyer. And be forewarned, I have a rock-hard camera in this purse."

One minute with Carolyn and she'd put a gun to my head. I hadn't even broken in my new shoes. We were now circling the fountain, Carolyn's arm still in mine. I noticed two middle aged men admiring her as we passed.

"I don't know," I said. "I'm a bit shell-shocked from all this, you know."

"So what are you saying, she's too rich to marry?"

"No, but I have to admit I would feel funny asking. I mean—what can I offer her? A three-room apartment?"

"Fine. So you don't love her. Remind me to tell her to dump you, and fast."

I stopped and clutched Carolyn's arm.

"Of course I love her. I just wish she wasn't so goddamn rich."

Carolyn pulled me closer, entwining my arm in hers. We began walking toward the house. Half the chairs on the terrace were filled and the orchestra had set up outside.

"So you're a sexist pig," Carolyn said matter-of-factly.

"And how is that?"

"If you were rich, and she were poor, that would be all right with you. But since she's the rich one, it makes you feel inadequate. Like you can't provide for her."

I thought about it for a few seconds. "I suppose you're right."

"You'd call it pride. Perhaps it is to some extent." Carolyn pulled me to a stop. The orchestra had started playing *The Blue Danube* waltz.

"You know, Eleanor doesn't go for all this." Carolyn waved her hand in the direction of the house and marble terrace. "All she wants is a white picket fence and some babies and a dog to run around a real backyard, and you. And once in a while, to come visit Tara and let the kiddies go crazy back here."

I then noticed what Carolyn and Eleanor had most in common—a quiet beauty in their eyes. I led Carolyn up the marble steps. The ceremony was about to begin.

After a long kiss that seemed rehearsed, the ceremony ended. An hour later, Eleanor was freed from picture-taking prison and we joined for a dance. And it was to the same song we had first danced to when we met at Cardozo Law.

"Do you remember what I said to you when we last danced to this song?" I asked.

"You said that *Moon River* was a sad song." She sounded tired. I kissed her on the lips, and then the chin.

"Nick, there's something I want to ask you." Her voice cracked. I pulled her closer.

"What did Carolyn tell you?" I asked softly.

"She didn't tell me anything I didn't already know," Eleanor answered abruptly. "She has nothing to do with my question. And believe it or not, I think she likes you."

"And believe it or not, I think I like her too. She really cares about you."

She tossed back her head and squinted her eyes at me.

"So will you marry me, Nick?"

My eyes widened, but without the smile I believe she was hoping for. "El, you've got to know I want nothing more than to spend the rest of my life with you."

"There's a 'but' in this, isn't there?"

"No. There isn't. I just want us to be happy, and I know we won't be, no matter how much we might think so, unless we have your parents' blessing."

"They'll give it."

"But they won't mean it. Not when they just met me yesterday. And what about my mom? She's all but used up my father's lump-sum pension."

"We can support her."

"No. You can. I can't. And I have to be able to. And support myself as well."

"You won't take money from me?"

"Not enough to support my mother too, I won't. Now when I leave Legal Aid, with the right move, I could easily double my salary in a year or two."

"A year or two? Nick—"

"We don't have to wait a year or two. It will be enough when I know I've made the right move. If I'm lucky, it could be in a month, or two."

Eleanor sensed that I wasn't through. "Anything else on your mind?" Her fingers combed the back of my hair.

"Yes. I want a prenuptial agreement."

All color left her face as her hands dropped to my shoulders. She stopped dancing. I was looking at an Eleanor I had never seen. Her expression was frighteningly morbid—as if I had died in her arms.

"Either you get the lawyer or I will, but the agreement must say: if we divorce, for whatever reason, I get nothing. I walk out of the marriage with only what I brought into it."

"I will sign no such document," she said.

"You won't have to. I'll do it all myself. It's important to me that your parents and everyone else know I'm marrying you only because I love you."

Her lips tightened. "I don't give a good goddamn what everyone else thinks."

"Well, I do."

Her eyes did a double take on mine. "I don't know whether to hug you, or slap you. And what about our children?"

"You can buy them an island in the Bahamas for all I care."

She rested her head on my chest. I could feel the pounding of her heart against mine.

She wasn't through. "I can't believe it. We just had our very first fight and it comes seconds after we decide to get married." She looked up at me. "I still feel like hitting you."

"Oh. One more thing," I said casually.

"Christ Nick. Now what?"

"No hitting."

We told only Carolyn. She congratulated us, expressed both sympathy and understanding for my concerns, but dismissed them as easily resolvable.

When she embraced and kissed us both, I knew I had made a new friend.

Chapter 53

I experienced many firsts with the Guevara case, and yet another by preparing him *ad nauseam* to testify before the grand jury. But when his time came, despite the many office vigils during which I pored over every piece of paper in my file—every record, report, letter, court document and note I had made no matter how obscure or superfluous—I still felt that there was something I had overlooked. I attributed it to last-minute jitters. With the support of two P.S. 92 mothers willing to testify as character witnesses and the stalwart and charming Shula Hirsch ready to tell all about Jose Chavez, whatever it was I had forgotten, I told myself, could not be consequential.

It was Friday morning, 10:30 A.M. I had just left a chilly May wind along 161st Street to meet Guevara in the grand jury waiting area on the fourth floor of the Bronx Criminal Court Building. He had lost weight. Overhead fluorescent lights accentuated several premature lines of age on his face.

Clean-shaven and in a gray pinstripe suit, he looked more like a junior executive than a defendant about to testify before a grand jury. He carried a black leather attaché case, also identical to my own (a gift from Mom), but without the initialed inscription under the handle. And he never looked more serious as he thanked the women from P.S. 92 for coming, while politely kissing Mrs. Hirsch on the cheek. I admired his stoic resilience and grace under pressure.

Oddly, I felt uncomfortable in Guevara's presence as we waited for Jimmy Ryan to call us in; not because we were short of small talk, never having engaged in any, but because he acted like no other client I'd ever had. No nervousness. No bitterness. No need for reassurance or comfort. It was as if he knew he had to rise to the occasion, and was perfectly confident he could.

The grand jury was on a ten-minute break. They'd begun at 9:30 A.M. having heard the first witness, Jose Chavez. Sandra Chavez followed. Afterward, Jimmy Ryan motioned me over for a private one-on-one. Since the arraignment, Ryan had developed a small spare tire. With a blotchy red face and Nordic features, he was beginning to look like a bloated leprechaun, with the button on his suit jacket about to pop.

"I hate this fuckin' case. And you know why?"

"Enlighten me, Jimmy," I said in a ho-hum manner as I pictured myself punching his lights out in the grand jury room while he attempted to save his case through bitter cross-examination of Guevara.

"Because I think your client is dead fuckin' guilty and my a-hole boss wants me to lie down on this one, give your boy his head in the grand jury room, let him tell his bullshit story, lighten up on the cross, and save the taxpayers a trial he's convinced we'll lose." He cocked his shoulders as if to brace himself. "So when this piece of shit goes out and does it again, it's my head that'll roll. I'll be lucky to get a job selling hot dogs in the parking lot."

"You're forgetting that two children recanted," I said gamely.

"Yeah, right. What did you do, drug 'em?"

"Yeah. With truth serum."

Ryan huffed then yanked open the grand jury room door. He took a deep breath, composed himself, and walked in. Guevara and I followed.

When I turned to pull the door closed, Mrs. Hirsch gave me a reassuring smile. She had been standing with the help of a walker and leg braces, refusing to sit down for over twenty minutes.

Inside a room that looked more like a college lecture hall, Guevara and I planted ourselves in two armless metal chairs. I nodded in respectful salutation to the jurors facing us. The grand jury foreman, a man in his sixties, dressed in a vest sweater over a white shirt with a triangle knotted tie, sat at a heavy wooden table just left of Guevara. A female clerk sat next to him. A court stenographer—an attractive Hispanic girl in her early twenties—sat in front of the foreman, facing us.

Ryan took a deep breath. He had a waiver of immunity in his hands that Guevara had signed before entering.

Any witness who testifies before a grand jury in New York State has automatic immunity for all crimes which relate to the subject matter of his or her testimony. A defendant is allowed to testify in the grand jury only if he or she waives this right of immunity.

The grand jury foreman swore Guevara in. "Do you solemnly swear to tell the truth, the whole truth, and nothing but the truth, so help you God?"

Guevara calmly gazed out over the grand jurors' heads, and said: "I do."

Ryan approached with the waiver.

For five minutes, he questioned Guevara on the authenticity of Guevara's signature on it; that it was signed voluntarily, and with the advice of counsel. Ryan must have asked the same questions five or six different ways. It was the same every time I took a defendant into the grand jury to testify. And I was never sure if this drawn out series of questions was for the sole purpose of covering the D.A.'s ass, or some feeble tactic to get a defendant to change his mind about testifying.

I had prepared Guevara for this. Good student that he was, he answered each question with absolute certainty and did all but tell the grand jurors: *I'm here testifying, knowing that what I say could be used against me, completely aware of the danger, but willing to speak anyway.*

His forthright manner was already leaving an impression—and he hadn't even begun to discuss the case. He was all composure and credibility.

I thought about the impression the undisciplined Jose Chavez and his loudmouth mother must have made, and what a stark contrast Guevara must seem.

Even the court stenographer was listening intensely, and when her skirt rose up high on her thigh, as closely as I was watching the grand jurors' every reaction, I couldn't help taking a few furtive glances. But not Guevara. He was rigid with involvement.

After a brief pause, Ryan walked to the back of the room and asked Guevara if he wished to make a statement. Without answering, Guevara began to outline his entire life story: from abandonment by a drug-addicted mother, to adolescent life in a Catholic orphanage, to developing into a hardworking college student and full-time teacher's aide. He set forth,

201

chapter-and-verse, with a poise and directness that was nothing short of captivating.

He talked about the prospect of post-graduate study in education and his dream of becoming a teacher. I had organized this short biography for him and gave him the word *dream* to use. Everyone dreams. It is instinctively American to do so. It's the kind of word that touches jurors where they store their heartfelt sympathy.

He again neglected to mention the part-time job in the real estate office, which didn't naturally fit into his background and goals anyway.

He told the jurors about Jose's psychological problems, and how Mrs. Hirsch had tried against all odds to help. He spoke deftly but with empathy about the child's horrible home life, Sandra Chavez's abusive boyfriends, her-on-and-off-again romance with heroin, and her failure to attend over a half dozen appointments with school officials to discuss her son's disturbing behavior. His voice soured with each detail of Jose's life, as if his own sadness deepened with each comparative recollection.

Guevara had moved beyond the what-to-say and the how-to-say-it of my preparation and coaxing. He was reliving with every word the events as they happened. Had I any doubt about his innocence, it was wiped away then and there.

He did not believe his job as a school aide ended with the three o'clock bell, especially when working with Special Ed students like Jose. But Jose never stayed after school, despite Guevara's urging and Jose's need for help in every subject. So Guevara invited him to his apartment for tutoring, as he did with many other students. As a reward, when the lessons were over, he'd let the kids play video games on his TV. Jose, however, only came over to play. On his last visit, when Guevara insisted that he participate in the lessons or leave, Jose responded by kicking a hole in the plaster wall next to the apartment door and running out. Later the same day the police arrived with Sandra Chavez—the stink of liquor on her breath and screams of "Arrest him!" He choked up with emotion. It was the worst day of Peter Guevara's life.

Although I had thoroughly prepared him and rehearsed the ending to this soliloquy over and over for the last three days, each time he came up with different parting words, and each time I hated them but dared not say so for fear of crippling his confidence. When at long last he could not come up with an impressive finish, I spoon fed him exactly what I wanted him to say.

"And I would just like to add"—a tear dropped from his right eye; his voice was weary and hoarse—"I have never been arrested or in trouble before in my whole life. And I am completely innocent of these charges. But no matter what you decide here today, I lose. No matter what the result, after this case is over, I will never be able to work with children again. And this I have loved more than anything in the whole world."

Ryan never interrupted and asked no questions.

Although I wasn't supposed to, I whispered in Guevara's ear, reminding him of Mrs. Hirsch and the two school mothers in the hall willing to testify if asked.

Every juror's eye was fixed on him, calmly studying him as if the truth would ooze from some hidden place to affirm the testimony he'd given so convincingly.

After Guevara mentioned the witnesses in waiting, Ryan, seemingly impressed but unmoved, asked us both to step outside. I nodded to Guevara, and thanked the grand jurors before we left.

Mrs. Hirsch was waiting in the hall. "Do I go in now?" she asked with girlish excitement.

The grand jury room door swung open. "The jurors would like to hear from Mrs. Hirsch," Ryan said morosely.

"I'm here," Mrs. Hirsch said, her hands gripping the plastic handles of her walker, her leg braces barely visible below her dress. The jurors would see more of them once she sat down.

Ryan held the door open, and then looked down at his watch like an impatient schoolboy. Mrs. Hirsch would enter alone. The law only permits a defendant to be accompanied by a lawyer. Ryan, if he dared, would be no match for her anyway.

I waited outside with Guevara, who was leaning against the wall, head tilted down, eyes closed.

"I think it went well," I said.

"I hope so." He was without emotion, without expression, without movement.

I wanted to say something more, but all I could manage was: "This is only the grand jury. We've still got a trial to win if they indict."

He said nothing, as if he hadn't heard a word.

I started to pace in front of the door, hoping to hear something, anything. Time seemed to stand still, until the door jarred open and Mrs. Hirsch ambled out with her walker scraping the floor.

"Do they want to hear from the other two women?" I asked Ryan.

"No," he said definitively, then closed the door.

Mrs. Hirsch took a seat in the waiting room near the two mothers from P.S. 92, who were chatting about the exorbitant prices of food in The Bronx as compared to the other boroughs. Guevara followed me with his eyes as I took a seat beside Mrs. Hirsch.

"How'd it go?" I asked.

"They were attentive. I was a little nervous. More than I thought I'd be. I tried to keep out of my mind what was at stake for Peter, though it seemed impossible. But don't worry. I told them everything we talked about."

I needed to explain away the anal laceration found on Jose at Lincoln Hospital right after Guevara's arrest. So I had asked Mrs. Hirsch to be sure to mention the many times she discovered bruises on Jose at school, and how she hadn't thought to check his private areas for injury also, or tell the school nurse to.

"Then you did great," I said.

She patted my hand with hers.

Deja vu. I immediately flashed back to Jones Beach and Eleanor and the moon and a distant ship's call.

I wondered whether there was some master planner pulling all the strings, then and now, and I, one of an infinite number of different game pieces with predetermined limits on mobility, strength, and power. Maybe that was the grand adventure—seeking one's own limits.

A few minutes later, Ryan emerged from the grand jury room and stood like a centurion on the opposite wall from where Guevara was frozen in place. The jury was deliberating. Ryan stared at Guevara in disgust. When he turned his attention to me seated in the waiting room, his expression did not change.

Three loud hollow thumps sounded on the jury room door—a signal that voting had ended. Ryan went inside. Seconds later he came out, bolted passed Guevara, and opened the waiting room door.

Like some involuntary defecation, he blurted sourly, "Dismissed."

A sensory high immediately enveloped me. Shula Hirsch hugged and kissed me, then looked at me like I had just won an Olympic gold medal.

I turned to Guevara. He took my hand and squeezed it until my knuckles cracked. Though I had expected him to jump with jubilation and smother me with thanks and praise, he did neither.

"You were the perfect lawyer," is all he said.

Perfect lawyer. That sounded good enough for me.

Chapter 54

S everal attorneys from Complex C, including Tom Miller and Rick Edelstein, who were present the night Guevara was arraigned before Judge Benton, met me for lunch in the Fun City Diner on Sheridan, across the street from Criminal Court. Tom handed over a case of mine I still had to cover in Supreme—a sentence before Judge Graham—Raymond Jackson, my Charlie Farkas predicate felon.

I decided not to tell Jackson that Farkas Sr. had died since the plea date. Ecstatic over the win in the grand jury, I bought lunch for everyone.

Jackson didn't show until 4:00 P.M. And who could blame him? Graham didn't. He sentenced him to the mandatory—two-to-four years, with a recommendation for the earliest parole possible.

While the mandatory sentence was expected, my heart sank anyway. I felt sadder still when Jackson took one of my hands in both of his and thanked me for caring.

Dead or alive, Charlie Farkas Sr. was one lousy son-of-a-bitch for advising him to plead guilty to that bogus felony nine years ago that had saddled Jackson with predicate felony status.

Raymond Jackson should not have gone to jail.

At the office, congratulations came from every corner of Legal Aid. Tom and Rick, true friends and comrades-in-arms, spread the word of the Guevara dismissal as if it were their victory as well as mine. Sheila and Peter gave me a victorious handshake and each, in their own way, winked at me in approbation. This win was special.

Brenda had returned to work and been back a mere week since Jasmine's passing. Before she left, she blew me a kiss and reminded me to check my phone messages. One, she said, sounded important. She put it on top. It was from Arthur Cantwell.

"Is this Nick Mannino, famous criminal defense attorney?" Arthur spoke with familiar affection, probably because I'd given him more defendants to polygraph in the previous six months than all of Bronx Legal Aid combined.

"I may be on the rise but I ain't there yet," I responded. "What can I do for you, Arthur?"

"Well Nick, it's more like what I can or can't do for you."

"Arthur buddy, I'm sorry on this one. We won't need that polygraph on Guevara after all. The grand jury dismissed all charges this morning. He testified like a champ."

There was momentary silence on the other end of the line. "We're talking about Peter Guevara, the teacher's aide charged with molesting three boys?" Arthur sounded like something was about to cut off his air supply. His voice was shaking.

"Yeah, Arthur. What's the matter?"

"He was in here this morning. He asked me to meet him at 8:00 A.M. Said you've been asking him about the test, and that you'd be out all morning and I should wait until after lunch to call you with the results."

"OK. Well, he passed, didn't he?"

"Nick, he didn't take the test. Or rather, he couldn't."

"Arthur, what the hell happened?"

Cantwell answered in a low groaning staccato. "Nick, Guevara confessed to everything," and then in a barely audible voice added, "and more."

Chapter 55

What made the confession to Cantwell even more bizarre was Guevara's insistence that he be allowed to write it down and put his signature to it. The "more" Cantwell had spoken of was Guevara's horrifying revelation that prior to molesting Jose Chavez, Carlos and Rafael Rodriguez, he had, in the last eight or nine years, fondled, sexually abused and sodomized over one hundred other children, mostly little boys and mostly orphaned. This included the mentally handicapped and even the disabled.

I called Peter Guevara and demanded to see him immediately. Apparently awoken from a deep sleep, he spoke irritably. He told me he would come by some time tomorrow.

"The hell you will," I snapped.

In a hollow baritone he replied, "I'll be right there."

I slammed down the phone. A surge of foul liquid rushed up my throat. I thrust back my chair and grabbed the small plastic wastebasket at my feet. After knocking my forehead into the edge of the desktop, I vomited into the container.

Since my heaving had not drawn anyone's attention, it soon became apparent to me that everyone within earshot had gone home. The fourth floor was graveyard quiet.

I rushed to the men's room.

In less than fifteen minutes I returned to my office. Wearing jordache jeans, black boots and a tight red polo shirt, Guevara sat dutifully in front of my desk, his back to the door.

"What can I do for you, counselor?" His lips pursed in annoyance, and I could sense him gauging the necessary limits of his tolerance, his eyes darting like lasers up at the ceiling. They were fixed on the movement of a rodent's tiny clawed feet above the suspended tiles. A sinister smile appeared and disappeared so quickly I wasn't sure if it was real or imagined.

I spoke between clenched teeth. "What the hell is going on? How do you confess to a life of child rape and sodomy, then an hour later lie your ass off in the grand jury?"

"Let me help you through this," he said, like a crooked undertaker calculating a bereaved widow's net worth. "My communications with Mr. Cantwell, orally and in writing, are privileged." He glanced up at the ceiling, and then down at me again. "As are all my conversations with you."

"Your privileged conversations with me did not give you the right to perjure yourself in the grand jury this morning."

"If I committed perjury, Mr. Nickel-Ass Mannino, then you suborned it. That's the right word, isn't it, counselor? Because suborning perjury is a felony too, isn't it?"

My heart was pounding and I could feel my chest constrict.

"When I told you in private this morning about my confession, you should have told me not to testify, instead of telling me to put it all out of my mind and recite the script you'd been pounding into my head all week."

What came over me next upon hearing this inimitable fabrication, I would never be able to explain. Whether the product of truculent irrationality or an explosive flash of insanity, I lunged at Guevara, visions of my fingers and thumbs ripping his throat open.

With the agility of a gymnast he jumped up, turned, and forcefully shoved me away.

I crashed into the side of a metal filing cabinet and dropped to the floor.

Pain shot through my ribs. With my right arm wrapped around my abdomen, I looked up. He was towering over me.

"I always knew you had it in you, counselor." An exaggerated smile grew on his face like some horrific cartoon.

I sat up and leaned against the filing cabinet. Though the pain heightened my senses, it was all the movement I could muster for the moment.

"You're a fucking lowlife pig," I gasped.

His eyes drew down on me like a viper deciphering when and how to strike. Then his smile returned, only this one had a brash charm and hint of malevolence. He mimed a picture frame by joining his thumbs and index fingers. Pressing an index finger down, he pretended to snap a picture.

"Gotcha." He chuckled. "You did a picture perfect job counselor. As I knew you would."

He smugly turned, then walked down the hallway, out of sight. I heard the stairwell door spring open then slam shut.

I managed to pull myself up onto a chair. The pain in my left side had gone from sharp to a dull throb. I phoned Eleanor saying nothing but "come get me"—my Rolodex already open to her name and number.

I limped outside into The Bronx night and leaned against a short chain link fence that ran the corner of 165th Street. I tried desperately to find Eleanor's BMW behind the hundreds of blinding headlights that raced up the Concourse.

I have no idea how long I waited, but at some point a horn blared from a double-parked car. I eased myself inside and Eleanor gave me a kiss.

Sinking back into soft leather, I refused to look her way. Intermittently, she asked if I was all right. With head down, I refused to answer, and then told her everything.

When we got to the FDR Drive and the East River and the area inside the car brightened, I looked over to see her reaction. Her face looked as if she too had been victimized. She calculated all too quickly the powerless position I was in.

As Guevara's attorney, revealing knowledge of his guilt or past crimes was in strict violation of attorney-client privilege. Nothing I could say would ever be used against him in a court of law. And I would probably be disbarred if I tried.

But what had Guevara said or done to get Carlos and Rafael to recant with such childish denials? *That's what a faggot does…I don't want to see Peter go to jail.* Did he start by convincing Carlos that a guilty verdict would brand him a *faggot* by court order, in the eyes of the law? Was Carlos so fond of Guevara and at such a loss for affection that he wanted Guevara back, even at the cost of further sexual abuse?

A stabbing pain in my head blinded me for an instant. I turned away from Eleanor and shut my eyes.

Like the sole passenger on a runaway train, it was only a matter of time before I soared off the mountainside. And there was nothing I could do about it.

Chapter 56

E leanor stayed close and held my hand as we sat on her living room couch. My ribs throbbed like I'd been hit by a bat and my head swam with a jumble of disconnected thoughts.

"I should have been suspicious when Guevara kept missing his appointments with Cantwell," I said.

"But why confess to Cantwell at all?" Eleanor asked. "What did he have to gain?"

"Control," I said with self-centered annoyance.

"Over what?"

"Over me. He could easily say I knew about the confession to Cantwell and had him testify anyway. And just so I could win my first big case! I get tried for suborning perjury, and Guevara's the prosecution's star witness. Jesus Christ! The bastard cried in the grand jury! He confesses before breakfast to molesting a hundred kids, then cries to twenty-three people about how he'll miss working with children."

"And now he holds a felony charge and loss of your license to practice law over your head." Eleanor hesitated. "So that when he does it again, you won't rat on him."

I groaned as I adjusted my sitting position. "It's got to be more than that. If he hadn't confessed, I would still think he was innocent. Besides, I've got a houseful of clients' guilty secrets. He wouldn't be the first to come back through the system. He knows that. There's got to be something else he's afraid of. Some other way I could hurt him."

"Like what? Like how?" Eleanor's face was full of concern—and fear.

I spent the night crumpled on Eleanor's couch, sleeping on my stomach and right side mostly. Eleanor tended to me into the wee hours, the heating pad she gave me never leaving my side.

When I awoke at 6:00 A.M., she was sleeping on the end of an area rug at the foot of the couch, wearing only socks, panties and a Brown University sweatshirt. The bruise on my side looked like a storm cloud and was still sore, but my mobility seemed less hampered. Eleanor woke at seven and we had breakfast by the window overlooking the East River. It was a damp gray morning, but the sun in the east was cracking through a cloud cluster that hovered somewhere over Queens, giving the river a golden sparkling overlay.

I had missed dinner the night before and ate my eggs and toast ravenously. I could tell that Eleanor was still tired. My good night's sleep had been at her expense. She patted her cheeks in a renewed wake up call, but to no avail. Her face still had that puffy sleepy look, and her beautiful eyes had yet to completely open.

"Where are you rushing to?" she asked.

"Nowhere. I'm just hungry."

Her weary eyes fixed on mine. "I want you to walk away, Nick. Please. I want you to walk away now."

"What?"

"I've been up half the night thinking watching you, remembering how we met, remembering Atlanta. You're so relaxed and at ease away from your work. Maybe now is the time to resign, take a position with a private firm. It doesn't have to be criminal defense work."

I stood up and stared out the window, angry that the sunlight shimmering off the river's surface hadn't the magical power it appeared to. I peered down at Eleanor still seated by the window.

"So I should just step aside as if there've been no children abused, no serial rapes or murders, no baby girls killed, no innocent defendants murdered in prison. Oh, and here's a new one for you. No more dead blondes hurled kicking and screaming off apartment buildings!"

"What? She was murdered? Why didn't you tell me?"

"The moment never seemed right. Would you have told me to walk away from that too?"

She took a deep breath in an attempt to fight back tears. "You're being cruel."

I felt sick and half-crazed, and reigned down on her, wanting to hurt her, to hurt myself.

"How convenient. I just throw everyone and everything up there in The Bronx to the dogs, just to run away and marry"—I paused, but not long enough to save myself, to save us—"just to run away and marry some rich girl!"

She crumbled onto the couch, buried her head in her hands, and began to cry.

"El, I'm so sorry. I didn't mean it. I swear."

"So I'm just some insensitive rich girl who doesn't give a shit about anybody. Well I gave a shit about you. And now you can get the hell out of here! I'm going back home. You're the only damn reason I've been staying in New York anyway."

"El. C'mon. Just like that? I say one stupid thing and you're gone?"

"One very stupid thing."

She then gave me the thread that, for better or worse, I could weave into the rope to hold onto. "I'll be in Atlanta. At home. My home. If you really give a damn."

I stepped closer. "El?"

"Don't. Just get out! Take the heating pad with you."

I gathered my things and stopped by the front door. The sunlight behind her made her face and figure a haze. I waited a moment for the light to grow dim again so I could see more of her one last time.

But that heralding sun only shined brighter.

Chapter 57

"It's Saturday. I figured you'd be on Jones Beach celebrating, not mulling around the South Bronx." Father Kerres' tone was caustic. He was chewing on a bread stick, the remainder of which was in his right hand. Without my having to ask, he opened the rectory's screen door.

I stepped inside. "Kingsbridge is not exactly the South Bronx," I said.

"It's all the South Bronx, counselor, when you get right down to it."

I followed Kerres to a small private room with a French desk and two small chairs. A crucifix hung on one wall opposite a framed photograph of the Pope.

"And what would I be celebrating, Father?"

"Oh, I don't know. You're getting the Guevara case dismissed? You tell me. In this room we also hear confessions."

I sat down across from Kerres, who suddenly took on the air of a parochial school principal.

"I tell you what," I said. "You can hear my confession, if I can hear yours."

Kerres leaned back and crossed his legs. "You're not a priest. And it's sacrilegious to suggest otherwise."

"Sacrilegious. That's a big word. Sounds like one a lawyer would use."

"A very good lawyer maybe," he shot back.

"I used to think I was a very good lawyer. I also used to think I had very good instincts. I was wrong on both counts. But it didn't have to be that way—if good men had done something."

"Are you referring to me—or to you?"

"To both of us."

"Speak for yourself, counselor."

"Father, you've known Peter Guevara since he was a boy, since you rescued him from being raped in that orphanage bathroom—"

"What? I didn't rescue him from anything. When I found him, he was lying under the urinals naked from the waist down and writhing in pain. Four boys, older and much bigger, had held him in that bathroom for over an hour. After they all sodomized him, some more than once, they then took turns pissing on him. He was in the infirmary for almost a month, and didn't speak a word for almost two."

I had been staring at my shoelaces, wearing the same rumpled clothes from the day before, straining to make sense of Guevara and Kerres and why Guevara lied to me the day of his arraignment. But in my mind's eye, I kept seeing visions of the Yankee Stadium parking lot—Vinny announcing that the dead blonde's blouse had been traced to a boutique in Danbury, and Kerres fleeing the scene.

"Now, why *did* you come see me?" he asked abruptly.

"Let's just say I found something out yesterday; something you probably knew already."

"You mean that your client Peter, or should I say Pedro Guevara, is less than innocent?"

"Maybe I just don't want to see another little boy molested in The Bronx or anywhere else."

"You mean it has nothing to do with the fact that you feel guilty as hell?"

"I was doing my job, Father."

"Like the Nazis did in World War II? Is that your defense? It wasn't one at Nuremberg. Why should it be for you?"

"Now wait a goddamn minute. Whatever I came to know, I came to know *after* the fact. I'm not a cop, and I've got a professional ethic that swears me to secrecy. What's *your* excuse? You knew about Guevara. You knew full well a little boy was abused yet you sat there, said nothing, and let him recant!" I stood up and a massive throb cratered into my left side. I moaned and dropped back into my chair.

"Are you all right?" Kerres asked.

"No, I'm not fuckin' all right!"

Kerres handed me a couple of tissues, then fetched me a cup of water.

"I'll make a deal with you," he said. "You stop swearing, promise me you'll never reveal the source, and I'll tell you what I know about your client, Peter Guevara."

I looked him square in the eyes. "Former client. Deal."

Kerres grabbed the half-full cup of ice water I had placed on the end of the desktop and tossed it back like it was a shot of his favorite whiskey.

He started slowly, painstakingly, as if struggling with every word to quell the infection of silence that had been eating at his insides.

He began with a warning. "I'm sure you've met some bad characters in the course of your work. Forget them. They've taught you nothing about dealing with Peter Guevara."

"Maybe he's just crazy," I said unconvincingly.

"Does he appear to you, in any way, to be someone *not* in control of every single nerve in his body?"

I remembered Guevara walking into detention after his arraignment and how quickly his tears stopped at the turn of his head, when he had no audience but me. But I had only to think back to yesterday, to his confession to Cantwell and his teary-eyed plea of innocence in the grand jury room, to draw the same conclusion.

"Peter Guevara is a very dangerous man," Kerres said. "In appearance, he is cordial, generous, and responsible. But make no mistake, he has urges—wicked and insatiable."

"You think he's capable of murder?" I asked incredulously.

"Not only capable, but in fact guilty."

I slumped back in my chair and wiped away the perspiration that beaded my forehead.

"Guevara is brilliant," Kerres continued. "I have never beaten him at chess, even when he was thirteen and I twenty-three. At fifteen, he mastered college calculus and learned to speed-read with phenomenal comprehension." Kerres winced and looked away. "After Peter left the orphanage infirmary, word got out about the attack. As a result, he was taunted by practically every juvenile delinquent there. This went on for months. Of the four boys that attacked him, two got released, one ran away, and the other was found hanging from an oak tree. The official report declared it a suicide. Peter was questioned along with many other boys but never formally charged with any wrongdoing."

According to Kerres, by the age of fifteen, Guevara had bulked up to over a hundred and seventy pounds, which is also when administration officials began to suspect he too might have been guilty of victimizing several of the younger boys. Conclusive proof of forcible sodomy was evident from medical examinations, but each time the injured boy would deny he was attacked, and nothing could be proven. When Guevara turned eighteen, he left Saint John's and took a job as a custodian in an elementary school about fifty miles away. Kerres would periodically call the school to inquire. Since there was no solid proof that Guevara had molested any children, Kerres kept his suspicions to himself. Although he had urged Guevara to go to college, Guevara wanted to get out on his own first and work then consider other options. Considering Guevara had been an orphan practically his whole life, Kerres figured this may just be the positive step of a mature and responsible young adult. And each time Kerres called the school, the principal responded glowingly about Guevara. The school never looked better or cleaner.

"But appearances were deceiving," Kerres said. Shortly after Guevara started his third year as custodian, a second grader in Special Ed accused him of sexual abuse. Seems an aroused Guevara rubbed up against the boy while both were fully clothed in a coat closet after school. The boy's mother, who had been dating a local Assistant District Attorney, pressed charges. Guevara was suspended as custodian pending the outcome of the case. He was represented by a public defender. The case got media attention, enough to prevent Guevara from getting any other local job. So he lived off his savings for three months, until the case against him fell apart. The little boy disappeared.

Kerres described Guevara's attorney as a "young, eager beaver," somewhat like me. Come the adjourn date following the boy's disappearance, the courtroom was packed. But instead of moving for dismissal of all charges due to the inability of the District Attorney to make a case without a witness, Guevara's attorney asked the court for permission to withdraw as his counsel. The crowd roared with approbation.

All the local papers ran stories and editorials insinuating Guevara's responsibility for the missing boy. Newspaper accounts continually carried photos of the grieving mother along with her two daughters. The oldest, a teenager, was especially distraught over her brother's disappearance. At a press conference held one week after the public defender withdrew from the case, she lashed out at Guevara and criticized law enforcement for their failure to bring him to justice. The press headlined her outburst. One front page warned in huge red letters: *Sister Vows Revenge.*

"The young boy was never found," Kerres continued. "After the public defender was removed from the case, another lawyer stepped in and, a month later, the charges were dismissed. A week later, the public defender who withdrew from the case was found floating in East Lake, a mile from the elementary school where Guevara worked. An autopsy revealed the cause of death was not drowning, but strangulation. The case went unsolved. Guevara sued for back pay, won, then moved to The Bronx."

Feeling as though something had been eating at my insides, I asked, "You mean Guevara hasn't lived in The Bronx since he left the orphanage?"

"No. In fact, he's the reason I'm in this church. It's my way, you might say, of monitoring his actions."

Kerres unbuttoned his collar and fingered a two-inch scar across his neck. "You see this mark here? I threatened to go to the police once and told this to our friend. I was standing on the altar of Saint Nicholas at the time. I thought that before God he would listen, maybe even get some help. Instead he took a knife to my throat. If I even thought again of going to the police, he said, he would kill me. I was petrified. I can't tell you what that experience has done to me. I thought I was a strong man." His voice cracked and his head dropped. "But, I am not."

"I didn't know. I—"

"There's no way you could have." His expression was gaunt and weary. It was the face of a man who had suffered, and suffered still.

"Father," I said, "I don't remember hearing or reading anything about the two murders you mentioned."

"You wouldn't have," he answered, "unless you were living around Danbury, Connecticut."

A photonegative of the dead blonde encrusted in the lawn of the Riverdale Towers flashed in my head.

Chapter 58

Soft tree-topped mountains of spring green lined the Hutchinson River Parkway North and Route 684. When the highway curved along a wall of jagged rocks of silver and gray, I pressed down harder on the accelerator and found Route 84. I got off at Exit 5 and drove through a business district with a red brick firehouse, church steeple, one-story police station, and newly paved streets until I entered suburban Danbury.

Forty-two East Gate Road was the home of Rita Gillis and the Gillis family, minus Bobby Gillis—missing since two months after his eighth birthday. Determined as I was to identify the dead blonde, when I passed through town and saw Bailey's Women's Wear, I was deeply saddened by the thought that somehow she was connected to this family.

The panoramic quarter-mile of East Gate Road cut through a hill where large homes were spaced hundreds of feet apart, and acres of lawn separated them from the narrow asphalt roadway.

Parking halfway over the grass line, I walked down a tarred three-car driveway to the front door of a sprawling one-story house built into the side of the hill.

A comfortable sun had brought the temperature to almost seventy degrees, and the neighborhood was rife with springtime activity: open garages, bicycles on the lawn, distant music coming from an open car window, two teenage boys playing basketball on a hilltop driveway, a middle-aged man jogging in tennis shorts, leash in hand, with a frisky collie running alongside.

If not for a late model Cadillac in the open garage, and several front windows cracked open, the Gillis home would have appeared unoccupied. I pressed the doorbell.

A slim, freckled, red-haired girl in her teens answered the door.

She eyed me from head to toe. I was unshaven and my suit was rumpled from the long drive. A screen door separated us.

"My name is Nick Mannino. I'm a lawyer from New York."

Announcing my profession, although necessary, did nothing to alleviate the teenager's look of suspicion. She bit down on the side of her lip.

An older, feminine voice with a New York accent called out, "Jess! Who is it?"

"It's a lawyer in a wrinkly suit from New York!" Her eyes stood guard over me through the screen.

An attractive, dark-haired woman in a robe came to the door. She pushed shoulder-length hair behind her ears. The years had not done justice to her milky complexion.

"What can I do for you, mister?" She was giving me seconds to state my business or the solid white door would shut in my face.

As I stared up at her from the landing, I realized that the only connection between the dead blonde and the Gillises was a blouse bought in Danbury, and a beautiful woman asking for me the very day after Guevara's arraignment. A sickening feeling enveloped me.

When I didn't answer, she unlocked the screen, swung it wide and stepped forward, leaning brazenly against the doorframe. "If you came here to gawk at us, you can get in your car and get the hell out of here. I can have the police here in ten seconds."

"Are you Mrs. Gillis?" I asked.

"Yes I am. Now what do you want?"

"I believe I have news about your daughter."

Her face tightened. She nodded for me to enter.

I followed her through a sparsely furnished living room, and then into a dining room where I sat down next to a row of double-hung windows. At the bottom of a sloping hill was a partly covered in-ground pool. The water was murky green, the chain link fence around it bellied and broken, the concrete perimeter tattered and cracked. This pool hadn't been used for years. Five years, I guessed.

I showed Rita Gillis my Legal Aid photo ID, and she grew pale.

"A public defender," she said, "from The Bronx." She looked at her daughter seated beside her.

"You know Peter Guevara?" she asked.

"I was his lawyer."

"For molesting a child?" Her voice was as coarse as sandpaper.

"Yes," I said gently.

Her strength and resiliency was hanging by tender threads. She was in no hurry to get to her last question.

"Donna, my other daughter, has been obsessed, you might say, with this Mr. Guevara. She could not reconcile what happened to her brother and that this—this man was never punished."

"I can understand that."

"She started to use cocaine. Her boyfriends supplied her. There's no excuse for that, mind you. But she suffered so after…" Her voice trailed off. She lifted her head higher. "We all suffered."

My stomach knotted and although I could only imagine the depth of this woman's pain, I was not sure I could bear to be so close to it for much longer.

"Do you have a picture of Donna I could see?"

Rita Gillis gave her daughter a frightened nod, and the teenager went into a den off the kitchen. She promptly returned with a picture frame, and handed it to her mother. Rita Gillis placed it on her lap face down.

"Donna said she was going to stay with some friends who were vacationing in Spain. She said she needed to get away. She left us no address or telephone number." There was a pathetic plea in Rita Gillis' voice. "She was dying here. I was happy for anything that would bring about some change." Her eyes searched around the room. "So she dyed her hair blond and in February took a shuttle bus to LaGuardia. We haven't seen her since. She said she would contact us on her birthday." Her face turned a ghastly pale. "Today is her birthday."

She handed me the framed photograph.

It was definitely the same woman who I'd run into outside AP-3. She was slightly younger in the picture, and brunette. But the face in the photograph was without a doubt, Donna Gillis.

"I met your daughter in Bronx Criminal Court. She wanted to talk to me, but didn't know who I was at the time."

Rita Gillis grabbed a doily off the dining room server and began wringing it in her hands. "She must have known you were Peter Guevara's lawyer. He killed his last lawyer you know, although it can't be proven."

"Yes. I understand." My voice wavered as I pondered how I was going to break the awful news to her.

"What happened to the case? You said you were Peter Guevara's lawyer. Did you withdraw from the case too?" Her thin limbs looked like dangling steel cables.

"No, uh. I didn't. The case…it concerned three boys."

"In Special Ed like my son."

"Two of the boys were, yes."

She nodded once then looked out the rear windows.

I spoke quickly. "Two of the boys changed their stories. The third boy's case was dismissed in the grand jury."

She nodded again as her legs frantically bobbled up and down, and the doily that was now in her hand, disappeared in her tightened fist. She turned away, her eyes fixed on something out the rear windows.

I wrote a name and number down. The number was for the 50th Precinct. The name was Detective Phil Krebs, Vinny Repolla's friend and police hook in The Bronx. I gave it to her younger daughter, along with my card and a *Daily News* clipping of Donna Gillis in her Bailey blouse and white pearls at the bottom of the Riverdale Towers.

Rita Gillis could barely catch her breath. I whispered in the young girl's ear not to show her mother the photo, and to call someone close to them to come over to the house right away.

"I only wish I could change what happened," were my lame last words to the mother and daughter who had now lost almost everything.

The daughter was holding her mother round the neck and shoulders as the older woman sobbed.

I backed out of the room, feeling like a criminal who had violated what little remained of the peace and sanctity of their lives.

Chapter 59

I used the time alone on the open road to analyze everything I had learned in the last day-and-a-half. The shock to my system that came with the knowledge of Guevara's guilt was still firmly in place. My own guilt seemed to be alive and well inside me like some errant antibody out to either destroy every cell and organ, or inoculate and cleanse me with new life and fresh breath. Only the warm sun above life-affirming treetops and ridges of cut gray and brown assured me I was not losing my sense of civilization and going completely mad.

Mom was washing the kitchen floor when I got home. I had been out all night without calling. I always called. I expected there'd be hell to pay. I yelled out to her with exaggerated enthusiasm as if the last twelve hours were just a bad dream and had never really happened. She asked me if I wanted something to eat, and then told me that Eleanor had called. I threw my briefcase onto the couch, walked briskly into the dining room and grabbed the wall phone in the kitchen without stepping on the wet floor.

"She called last night to tell me you were staying over. Said she picked you up at work, and when you got to her apartment, you were so tired you fell right to sleep." Mom's nonchalance annoyed me, as did the sound of the sponge mop running back and forth across the linoleum. "She's such a sweet girl. Said you won your big case."

She left the mop hanging in the sink and turned toward me.

"Nick, you look terrible!" She walked over and ran her hand across my forehead, as if by touch she would know where I had been in this rumpled condition and whom I had been with. "And you smell!"

I resisted the urge to phone Eleanor. I wasn't sure why. Maybe I wanted to give her time to cool off. Maybe I wanted to show her I respected her enough not to chase after her when she was hurt and angry.

Later that evening, my friend, Joey, called. No mention of how I had ignored him of late except to say I was not my old self—an understatement of untold proportions.

I thanked him for noticing and promised, unconvincingly, that we'd get together soon.

"I know you twenty years, Nick. You need me—I'm there. Don't forget that."

"I won't. Thanks, Joe."

I hung up and called Vinny Repolla at home. I asked him to set up a meeting with his cop buddy, Phil Krebs. When he asked why, I filled him in on the Danbury trip.

He called back ten minutes later.

The meeting with Krebs was set for Monday morning at the 50th Precinct in The Bronx. A friend of the Gillis family had already contacted Krebs. On Sunday, Mrs. Gillis was going to the precinct to view photographs of Donna's body. After spending two months in Potters' Field, there would be no point in viewing the corpse for identification. Vinny agreed not to print a word about Donna Gillis without first obtaining my consent.

Then in a quirky voice, Vinny added: "Oh, by the way, after Jose Chavez testified in the grand jury, his mother, believe it or not, dropped him off at school. That's the last she saw of him. At 6:00 P.M., she reported him missing."

"How do you know all this?"

"I got a copy of the missing person's report. Considering the boy was a grand jury witness the same day, the cops acted on it right away."

"They say a grocer saw a boy fitting Jose's description walking off with a black man in the vicinity of that junkyard behind the school. This was around 5:00 P.M. Friday. Your boy Guevara was even taken in for questioning, then released. I got that from Krebs. I've talked to him so much about you—the dead blonde and your hotshot cases—I guess I sparked his interest. Since he works out of Kingsbridge he arranged to be the detective assigned to the case. He was the one who called Guevara in. He said Guevara came right over, spoke freely, showed no malice toward the boy for bringing the charges, and told Krebs he believed it was the boy's mother who was behind it all. Guevara also said he was home sleeping at 5:00 P.M. Friday and that you, of all people, could verify it."

"I did call him about five. And he did sound like he was sleeping." My side was beginning to throb again, along with my head.

"He even offered to take a lie detector test."

"Did they give him one?" I asked incredulously.

"Nah. If he was black, like the grocer described, I guess they would have. But he's not black."

"No," I answered pensively. "He isn't, is he?"

I was overtired and all the bits of horrifying information I had learned were scattered in my mind like the residue of an explosion. I went to bed at midnight and tossed and turned for over an hour before slipping into a deep sleep.

When I awoke at 11:00 A.M., I called Sheila at home. I needed the week off. I claimed burnout. Tom and Rick could cover my cases for me. She told me it would probably be OK and to call her at the office first thing Monday morning.

Monday. 3:00 A.M. I lay in bed, not even trying to close my eyes, not even close to sleep. With stark clarity, I envisioned that junkyard behind P.S. 92 at night—a darkened Kodachrome and as opaque as a blackened celestial sky. I could see the remains of decades of abandonment: the dilapidated fences, piles of metal and rubber garbage, and pockets of vile undergrowth slowly compacted over time, festering, fenced, contaminated. A street-level nightmare in a forgotten borough—where children played. A little boy on a bicycle was racing around on the sidewalk, innocent, unafraid, in danger. Straining to see his face as if some secret lie there, I prayed silently to myself as I fell off to sleep, that that little boy was not me.

227

Newsday. Monday. May 3, 1982. A 10-year old Special Ed student at P.S. 92 was found dead late Sunday night. His body had been stuffed into the corner of a wooden shed in a junkyard behind the school. The side of his skull had been crushed. His mother identified him by the New York Yankee jersey he wore. His name was Jose Chavez.

Chapter 60

It was well into the day shift at the 50th. The desk sergeant, a man in his fifties with gray bushy sideburns half-way down his ears, pointed to a set of caged metal steps leading to the Detective Squad on the second floor.

At the top of the staircase, a stenciled sign that read *Detective Squad* with an arrow pointing down the hall was taped to a wall. I passed several interview rooms cloaked with mini-blinds until the smell of burnt coffee, jelly donuts and stale cigarette smoke told me I was in the right place.

The guts of haphazardly strewn file folders littered the many desktops in the squad room. A white oval clock hung on a wall of peeling paint and chipped plaster sores. I was fifteen minutes early.

A pot-bellied detective in a button down shirt showed me to Detective Krebs' desk. Except for a ballpoint pen lying obliquely on the middle of a brown blotter, Krebs' work area was meticulous.

From behind me, a deep baritone voice called out: "Sir? Excuse me, sir."

A tall, clean-shaven black man of about forty, with tightly cropped hair, waved me over. When I got to the doorway Vinny Repolla was standing there. He was wearing jeans and a short black leather jacket.

The detective directed us into one of the interview rooms down the hall. Vinny went in first, turned and put his index finger to his lips. After the door shut behind us Vinny gave me a hearty handshake and introduced Detective Phil Krebs.

Krebs shook my hand with one fast and firm pump then gestured for us to sit down.

"Did the desk sergeant take your name?"

"No."

"Detective Krebs doesn't get too many defense attorneys coming in to talk to him about pending investigations," Vinny said.

"Vinny here tells me you're a straight shooter." Krebs voice and expression showed none of the tentativeness I suspected he was feeling about this meeting. "So I'll be straight with you. I'm concerned as to why you've come. Vinny told me about your trip to Danbury. I met with the Gillis family." He blinked long and hard. "If your client Guevara is connected in some way to the death of Donna Gillis, I'm not sure we should be talking at all. You're his attorney, after all. If some judge down the line figures you breached some rule of lawyer etiquette, the whole investigation could get flushed. And the Gillis family has suffered enough."

Krebs leaned over the desk—the only piece of furniture in the room other than three short metal chairs. Even seated, he was an intimidating figure.

"First of all," I said, "I am no longer Peter Guevara's attorney. I represented him in three cases, all of which have been concluded. Whatever he said to me or anyone working on his defense about those cases or any prior crimes or bad acts is privileged. But what someone else told me most certainly is not."

"And someone else told you about the Gillis family in Danbury," Krebs interjected.

"Yes. But I can't tell you who it was. I made a solemn promise I wouldn't. So don't ask."

Krebs closed his eyes and jerked his head back in resigned frustration.

"So what the hell *can* you tell me, counselor?"

"I can tell you that a lot of people believe Guevara is responsible for the disappearance of the Gillis boy five years ago."

"I know that." Krebs was hanging on to what little cop patience he had left.

Vinny was sitting close by but keeping his distance, leaving Krebs and me to find our common ground.

"A lot of people also believe he's responsible for the murder of his public defender," I added.

"I know that too, counselor, and I would appreciate it if you would tell me something I do not know."

"Listen," I barked. "If I hadn't gone to Danbury, that blonde would be ashes and you'd still not have a clue as to what really happened to her."

"Fine," Krebs remarked without inflection. "If you want to give me information now, or in the future, fine." A big finger pointed down at me. "I'll keep your confidence, and you damn well better keep mine." Krebs slapped his hand down on his knee, and then spoke to the ceiling. "I'm in cahoots with a newspaper reporter and a Legal Aid lawyer. Boy, am I fucked."

When he stuck out his hand to conclude the meeting, I shook it dispassionately, but didn't let go. "Now you tell *me* something, Detective; something I don't know—about the Chavez murder."

He spoke in a hollow whisper. "The Chavez boy—and we're fairly certain it was him—was last seen walking with a black man about thirty years old who was wearing a cap and sneakers."

"I know that too, Krebs," I said impatiently.

"Yeah, but what you don't know is, when the Gillis boy disappeared five years ago in Danbury, he was last seen walking with a man who had the same goddamn description. What are the odds on that?"

Before I left the 50th, I telephoned Brenda at the office, pretending to be concerned about how my cases were being handled in my absence. I had successfully suppressed the urge to call Eleanor since my Saturday morning banishment—an urge, a need I could suppress no longer, despite the Gillis family tragedies, past and present, and the death of Jose Chavez running interference with my emotions. I was relieved to hear Brenda's voice had some life to it. Maybe the healing for her had begun.

"Are you all right, Nick? You sound more like you're on trial than on vacation."

"I guess I still haven't unwound yet. By the way, I had a little argument with Eleanor over the weekend and was wondering if she called."

"Couldn't be little if she doesn't know where to find you."

"It wasn't."

"No. She didn't call." But you might want to call Charlie Farkas Jr. He got really annoyed when I told him you were out for the week. He demanded I track you down."

"Did he say what he wanted?"

"No. Just that you've got to call him right away. He said it's in your interest. Something like that."

I wrote down his number. Farkas could wait. I wondered how many more times we would run into each other and not come to blows.

I telephoned Eleanor at work.

I got Jo. "Eleanor's gone. She made me type a letter of resignation, effective immediately." Jo's usual Minnie Mouse voice was gone. "Said she didn't want to stay in New York another minute."

With the last twang of Jo's voice a stinging pain arced across my eyes.

I slammed down the phone.

Chapter 61

I emptied my pockets on to my night table. Charlie Junior's name and number was where I'd written it, appropriately, on a twenty-dollar bill. I imagined him hounding and harassing Brenda until I returned his call.

I punched in his number.

"Mr. Mannino, so glad you called." I could tell he had his carpetbagger's face on. Tara was on the auction block.

"What the hell do you want?"

"You won't believe it. A client of yours, whom you no longer represent, is now *my* client." His voice had a wicked singsong quality, like the neighborhood bully who had cornered a kid half his size by a back alley fence.

"And who might this sorry-ass son-of-a-bitch be?"

"Why none other than Peter Guevara. Or should I say Pedro Guevara, out of respect for his Puerto Rican heritage?"

His sarcasm was reaching an unbearable level, and I was a short second from hanging up.

"This Mr. Guevara has one hell of a story. And you know what he told me?" He paused just long enough to turn the knife. "He said I was the perfect lawyer to tell it."

"Get to the fucking point."

Junior faked a laugh. "Well it seems that Mr. Guevara is concerned about the ethics of his former attorney. Go figure. Says after he confessed to you and the polygraph examiner, you put him in the grand jury to testify, and told him verbatim what to say. Bright guy this Guevara—concerned about the ramifications of a perjury charge should he face one—wonders if you'd be sharing a cell with him for subordination. He made me get a certified Supreme Court stenographer in here to make an official record of the lies you made him tell the grand jury over his strenuous objection. He sounded pretty convincing too. Said there were witnesses to your giving him a few pointers, like two mothers and a handicapped schoolteacher. Said you told him to cry if he could. Did you really do that?"

"How the hell did Guevara find his way to you?"

"I'll answer the question you should have asked first, buddy boy. Like, 'where is Mr. Guevara going with all this?' The answer is nowhere, if you behave yourself. Seems he thinks you'll cooperate with the authorities to pin some bum rap on him. Says you got a D.A. girlfriend who's been fucking with your head."

"How does he—?" I thought of my tussle with Guevara—my call to Eleanor—the Rolodex on my desk that was open to her name.

"He seems to know an awful lot. Now to answer your own stupid question, I don't know how he came to me. Maybe he heard about my sterling reputation as defender of the poor and unfortunate."

"Fuck you, Farkas."

"No, fuck you, Mannino." His sarcasm was long gone. Only rage remained. "And fuck you I will if given half the chance, you pompous Legal Aid piece of shit. Some send-off you gave my father just before he died."

"I had no idea—"

"He was carrying on for three fuckin' days over the Jackson case you came in here screaming about. My father had been practicing law here over thirty-five fuckin' years. That client of yours wanted that felony plea. Nine years later, that skell regrets it 'cause he got caught with a loaded gun. Well fuck him, and fuck you!"

There were seconds of silence on the other end as Farkas caught his breath. "Oh, one more thing Mannino. Guevara made me promise I'd tell you something, some quote from a Shakespeare play. *Othello* he said. *Et tu, Brute* is what he told me to tell you. That's it, *Et tu Brute*."

"That's from *Julius Caesar*, you moron."

That afternoon, I called Eleanor's New York number over a dozen times. There was no answer.

After a dinner of Coca-Cola and lukewarm pizza, I called Atlanta.

Charles the butler answered, and with a cool edge told me that Eleanor's plane would be landing at Hartsfield Airport in about thirty-five minutes. I left her a message: *Please call me at home right away.*

No call came. That evening, I phoned again. Again Charles answered. Eleanor was asleep and did not wish to be disturbed.

At 1:00 A.M. I went to bed. Fifteen minutes, later Mom woke me. I had been screaming in my sleep.

I lay awake for the next hour, then turned over a sweat-soaked pillow and felt cool fresh fabric against my face. My head cleared.

I saw Guevara standing over me in my office. He had probably just killed Jose an hour earlier, maybe two—the child brought to him by the same black man in cap and sneakers who had abducted the Gillis boy five years earlier.

Et tu Brute. Othello? Guevara was taunting me, prodding me. And how did he know about Eleanor?

Donna Gillis, obsessed with her brother's disappearance and Guevara going free, had been trying to warn me about Guevara. She had come to the office to look for me that afternoon. Eleanor had come by also, and at the same time, according to Legal Aid's day clerk, Jose Torres.

Could Guevara have come by then too, spotted Donna Gillis, and then followed her? Was he the one who dragged her up to the roof of the Riverdale Towers only to throw her off kicking and screaming?

Mrs. Hirsch said she had posted P.S. 92's bail money that afternoon. Court records stated that Guevara had gotten out of jail that same day. The Bronx House of Detention is only a ten-block walk from Legal Aid's offices on the Grand Concourse and 165th Street.

Mentally exhausted, I drifted off into a restless sleep; a sleep made possible by the fact that Eleanor was home and safe, hundreds of miles away.

I only wished I had confirmed it for myself—if only she had taken my call.

Tuesday morning. 9:00 A.M. sharp. I telephoned the office and spoke to Frances, the receptionist, who was working the afternoon Donna Gillis had come by. She remembered her. Eleanor had stopped by the office so many times that Frances couldn't put a fix on whether or not she'd been there at the same time as Donna Gillis. But Jose Torres had confirmed that for me already.

Frances put me on hold for several minutes while she went to a storage closet to check her message log for that day. Pink copies of all messages remained in their spiral notebooks after the originals were torn out and distributed.

Frances returned to the phone. She told me that at 2:10 P.M., a message was written by her to yours truly, and then crossed out—*Peter Guevara stopped by to see you*. The only reason this or any message would be crossed out, she said, was if the person who left it in the first place, asked her to.

I hung up with Frances, and called Detective Phil Krebs.

Chapter 62

S tanding in front of a one-way mirror in a darkened room the size of a walk-in closet, Vinny at my side, I watched Krebs question Guevara at the same metal desk we had sat around the day before.

An obese detective named Guy Raptakis stood with us. He had a dark pock-marked complexion and sweat stains the size of footballs in the armpits of his white shirt. Krebs had introduced him as "the Greek partner I never let sit in the back seat," and had we been out in the open air, I would have appreciated Raptakis' kind and easy manner more. But in this tiny viewing room, his body odor accosted me like a smelling salt.

After forty-five minutes of questioning, all Guevara had divulged was that which was already public record. He said he knew who Donna Gillis was and had read about her pledge of revenge, but hadn't taken it seriously; she was just upset over her brother's disappearance. It was a time he'd prefer to forget.

Then with coy boyishness he asked: "Was the Gillis boy ever found?"

Krebs didn't answer.

Guevara looked over at the one-way mirror. For a second his eyes seemed to lock on mine. Then he turned back to Krebs.

The Q and A session touched on the topic of Jose Chavez, but only briefly. When Guevara began to repeat answers, Krebs told him he could go.

As Guevara stood to leave, he turned to face the mirror, and smiled slyly. Then, just as he had done in my office, he framed a camera with his fingers and pretended to click a picture.

He left as he arrived—unrattled by Krebs' questions, never having asked to speak to a lawyer, never even mentioning he had one.

"And why should he ask for a lawyer?" Krebs said after he'd gone. "We've got dick on him anyway."

"But what do you think?" Vinny asked.

"What do I think about what?" Krebs responded.

"Is he guilty? Did he kill Donna Gillis, the Chavez boy, little Jamie Gillis, his Danbury lawyer? You've got to have some gut feeling on this."

Krebs sighed, looked at Raptakis, then at me, then back at Vinny. "I think he's guilty as hell. I think he killed every one of them."

Chapter 63

I left the 50th as I came—wearing an oversized ski jacket and a cap pulled down to my eyebrows. I had driven Mom's '79 Corolla to ensure I would travel unnoticed. After crossing over Sedgwick Avenue, I drove alongside the Jerome Park Reservoir until I turned and headed toward P.S. 92.

Shula Hirsch sat alone in her classroom in one of the undersized desks. She was bent over a pile of papers. Her forehead was cupped in her right hand, her left arm dangled down the side of the chair. She looked up as I entered.

"Hello, Nick." She spoke as if we were meeting at a funeral or wake.

"I was very sorry to hear about Jose," I said.

"Poor boy," Hirsch said. "He never had a chance." She gave me a pleading look. "Did I do something bad by testifying the other day?" This expert teacher of the most troubled and difficult children was asking a criminal defense lawyer in the South Bronx the grand moral question.

And as she asked it of me, I asked it of me too.

"No you didn't, Mrs. Hirsch. Don't ever think that, ever. You told the truth. That's all."

"But I really don't know what the truth is. Do I, Nick?"

"No you don't; and at the time, neither did I."

She clutched my right hand in both of hers, brought it to her eyes, and wept quietly.

I knelt down beside her.

"I could tell right after the dismissal," she said in a voice straining to speak, "that Peter was different." She took a few deep breaths and gained some composure. "After Jose's death, Carlos came to see me. He was petrified. He said Peter had approached him many times to change his story;

said Carlos could go to jail too for being a homosexual, only he used the word 'faggot.' When Carlos still turned him away, Peter told him some sick parable about a little boy who ratted on a grown-up and refused to take it back, only to wake up the next morning with his penis cut off."

"A Mr. Farkas called me also," she said. "He told me he was Peter's lawyer and was making a claim for all of the back pay Peter lost since his suspension. He asked if I'd sign a letter of character reference. I told him to submit it to the school principal and I'd see what I could do."

"Did he accept that answer?"

"Actually, he became quite belligerent. So I hung up."

"You did the right thing."

She looked like a child sitting in the tiny school desk. "Could he really have killed Jose? Could he really have done it?"

I squeezed her aged hands and followed her eyes to the upper right hand corner of the desktop, where amid a blend of haphazardly etched graffiti, lay the brash childish carvings of one little boy no more—**JOSE CHAVEZ.**

Chapter 64

The phone rang as I walked in the door. It was Eleanor's friend, Carolyn. "Nick, where the hell are you? I've driven up and down Central Parkway five times. There is no number 104, and I haven't seen any '66 Malibu either."

"Mom's out with it. I've been driving *her* car lately."

"I'm at McDonald's on Merrick Road. I'm lost and frustrated as hell. Come get me? I'm sitting in a blue MG convertible."

The tiny two-seater, a dark sparkling blue, was parked at the foot of an elliptical yellow arch that sailed up, over and down the side of the McDonald's restaurant. The smell of French fries and car exhaust permeated the air. Carolyn was leaning against the passenger door of her car.

Dressed in a tan suit with a white shirt and brown college-knotted tie, all she needed was a wide brim hat to be the complete Annie Hall. Her resemblance to Eleanor, especially at a distance, was uncanny. I fantasized for a brief moment that it was really her; that she'd flown in on a whim to take me in her arms—all forgiven, all forgotten, I missed you.

"I'm hungry, slick," Carolyn said. "Let's get a burger."

We took our orders outdoors and ate at a white table under an open umbrella. Afterward, at Carolyn's insistence, we took a walk. I asked how Eleanor was.

"Resilient," Carolyn said tersely. "That's why you'd better get your ass on a plane and fast."

"Is there an 'or else' in this?" I asked.

"I don't know. I'll tell you this much, though. You're immersing yourself in your work at Legal Aid, your cockamamie marriage conditions—it's enough to give a girl a question or two, I'll tell you that." She turned toward me. "And why? Why are you still here while she's down there?" Her lips tightened, her eyes piercing slits. "Maybe you don't really love her. Ever think about that?"

"I love her. She has to know that." We were almost at the corner. I turned away. Beyond a grassy knoll on the other side of Merrick Road was Cammon's Pond. Lakeside Elementary School was behind it. A young woman with two toddlers in tow was feeding a small army of ducks. "I just can't leave right now. I've got to see something through. It's important. I don't have a choice in the matter."

"More important than her, I guess." She began walking back toward McDonald's with a heartbreaking finality in every step.

I ran to catch up. "Why I have to stay is more important than Eleanor and me put together. Lives are at stake here, Carolyn. And I'm not talking about my clients.' I mean children's lives."

She gave me a long, hard look, then walked off, muttering, "You're either nuts, or the biggest ass I've ever met." She stopped and turned back around. Then, with obvious reluctance, she said, "If you want to talk, I suppose you can call me. I'll be staying at Eleanor's. I have some meetings this week in the city."

She turned and walked away, then turned back. "I asked Eleanor to fly back up and keep me company. Maybe you'll get lucky and she will."

I was in over my head.

I set up a dinner meeting with Rocco and Sallie for 7:00 P.M.

At 5:10, Sheila Schoenfeld called.

She wanted to know why, after dumping all my cases for the week on my fellow Complex C attorneys, I had the time to represent real estate brokers. Evidently, Vincent Tedeschi had called the office.

"He's a former employer of Guevara who posted bail in Guevara's name," I said.

"I don't remember anything about Guevara working in a real estate office."

"He never mentioned it to me either. Seems he was working there without a license." This explanation seemed stranger each time I thought about it.

"You'd think with the guy facing twenty-five years in jail he'd tell you anything that might make him look good," she said, "especially when he's got a boss who has enough faith in him to post bail."

I thought about telling Sheila the truth, but didn't know where to begin, or where to end. I could never admit to her I was working with the police to try and nail one of my own clients. She obviously hadn't heard about the murder of Jose Chavez, or she would have mentioned it. Sheila lived in Manhattan and only read the *Times*; she never read the crime stories. The *Times* hadn't even reported the murder.

"Who can explain why people say and do things," I said.

Sheila recited the broker's telephone number, and then repeated, "I still don't understand why Guevara didn't tell you about his job there."

"It was off the books?" My excuses were getting flimsier.

"This isn't Indiana," Sheila shot back. "It's The Bronx. Everything here is, more or less, off the books."

Sheila also said Charlie Farkas Jr. had contacted her for a copy of Guevara's file. He sent over a notice of appearance as counsel on a suit for back pay plus interest, costs and expenses against the Board of Education.

"I couldn't find the file," Sheila said.

"That's because I have it."

"I told him that you probably did, and then he goes nuts over the phone. Says you'd better not pull any fast ones. I reminded him that you were the one who got his client off, and told him to put all requests in writing. I said you'd get to it when you return next week."

"Thanks."

"Don't thank me. He also said Guevara wants to speak to you immediately. He demanded I give him your home number. That's when I hung up."

My relief was almost palpable.

Chapter 65

The Merrick Marlin, a family seafood restaurant, was a short walk from home. Last time I was in the place, it was a bar called Roaring Hams, where teenagers with phony IDs drank beer and hung out over tabletop candles on worn, second-hand couches and torn vinyl chairs.

The change inside struck me hard—another reminder of the youth I'd left behind.

The bar had been moved closer to the corner entrance. Off to the left, against the wall, was a large flat tank, filled with lobsters. While I waited to be seated, a middle aged couple passed the death sentence on the largest one in the tank. The woman called it "the cute one," and in my mind's eye, I likened the helpless lobsters to little children.

Rocco and Sallie were seated at a table in a rear corner of the restaurant, away from a long picture window that faced Merrick Road. Rocco was wearing his usual white silk shirt and dark blazer. Sallie wore a brown pullover with an emblem of a golfer in swing on the left breast. It fit him well despite his huge belly.

I gave Uncle Rocco and Sallie a kiss on the cheek, then sat down next to Rocco with my back to the wall and a view of the entire restaurant.

Between the waiter's interruptions, I told them everything I knew about Peter Guevara. This was a clear breach of attorney-client privilege, but I didn't care.

The poker faces of the two men changed only in appreciation of the food they ate. When I finished I poked with a tiny fork at my baked clams gone cold.

"This *desgraciato*," Rocco whispered. "You sure he's going to stay in New York?"

"Probably not. But what's the difference? New York, Connecticut, Atlanta." I shuddered when I included Eleanor's home state, and couldn't imagine why I had. "He's going to savage children wherever he goes," I added.

"Why'd you represent this mole anyway?" Sallie asked harshly.

"I thought—" I caught myself. "I hoped he was innocent. I didn't know what a monster he really was until it was too late."

Sallie pushed aside his dish of calamari as if he'd suddenly lost his appetite.

"Nickie," Rocco whispered. "Are you asking me to kill this guy?"

I answered without hesitation: "Yes."

Sallie muttered in discontent, then let out a "damn" as he noticed a small stain on the belly of his shirt.

"Nick, we don't just do that," Rocco said softly. "You want money, a job, a house, fine. But this—we have to have a reason—a good reason to even consider it."

"You never had a better one," I said emphatically.

Rocco patted his mouth with a napkin.

Sallie looked wearily at his lifelong friend and boss, then at me. "What about the cops? Isn't this their job?"

"He could sodomize and kill a dozen more times before getting caught. Five years ago in Connecticut, everyone knew he was responsible for two murders, but the police couldn't prove a thing. Then he moved to The Bronx. The police here are fairly certain he's involved in two more killings, but again, can't prove it. Soon he'll leave The Bronx and go someplace else, then someplace else, then someplace else after that. He may have a partner also—a bald black guy."

When Sallie said he was going to the men's room, he had the look of someone making a quick exit and pleased as hell to be doing so.

Rocco didn't utter another word inside the restaurant, even when he crumpled the bill in his hand and paid it. When we left, Sallie was still in the men's room. I followed Rocco across the street and into the parking lot.

Rocco leaned against his Cadillac. "You got this crumb's address?" His voice was so moribund, it was frightening.

I handed him an arrest photo and a copy of an arrest report with Peter Guevara's vital information on it.

Rocco slipped the papers inside his jacket pocket. "I thought you asked me out here to talk about that Spiderman guy's murder."

"So much has happened since," I answered.

"I'm still glad you came to me," he said. "I'm glad you didn't do something stupid on your own."

"Stupid seems to be a character trait I have plenty of."

"You ain't stupid, Nickie. You never were." His tone was considerate and caring. "But something else is bothering you."

"I may have lost the one woman, the only woman other than Mom, who's ever loved me."

Rocco looked truly pained. "Sorry to hear that."

"She wanted me to leave Legal Aid."

"Smart girl," Rocco said, slowly looking around, as if returning from a far-off dream. "There's something I have to tell you about that other client of yours, the guy who was killed at Rikers."

I could barely see Rocco's face in the glare of the parking lot lights above and behind him.

"Seems there's another guy in The Bronx who likes boys too. Not little ones though. Teenage boys. Male prostitutes. He's an older guy—fifty, sixty, who's been paying ridiculous money to Aldo Leone for a steady flow. Leone's The Bronx *capo* I told you about."

I moved closer to him so I could see his face. We were both leaning on his Cadillac.

Rocco continued. "Aldo Leone does not traffic in young boys. He's got about a dozen houses of prostitution and a half-dozen call girl services— two in The Bronx and four in Manhattan. They have nothing but women there. But this guy, this homo in The Bronx, he's willing to pay two-thousand bucks a visit. So Leone makes a few calls, and through some Mexican friends of his, he gets this guy a steady diet of young fags."

"What does this have to do with Oscar Jefferson?"

"*Ashpete*, I'm getting to that."

"This rich guy, he gets that crazy fuckin' disease the homos have been gettin'."

"AIDS?"

"Yeah, that's right. And when Leone finds out from his Mexican connection why the boys want to get paid double to keep seeing this guy, he panics and cuts the guy off. And it's not because he gives a damn about his stable of tricks."

"The guy's all heart."

"Business is business, kid. Anyway, Leone's now pissed 'cause this rich guy was a steady source of dough. Not that Leone's wantin' for anything. But it's easy to get greedy in this business. So when this guy calls Leone to his house, asks him to whack your client and offers him twenty-five thousand, Leone can't resist. Thought he was actually doing a public service. That your client was in prison, made it all the easier to pull off."

"What's the guy's name?" I clenched my teeth. "The gay guy in The Bronx?"

Rocco pulled a small piece of paper from his pants pocket.

I took it, and held it up to the parking lot light. Scribbled in pencil along the margin of a torn page of newspaper was the name *Norris Terkel*.

Chapter 66

I sped along the Meadowbrook Parkway headed south—to the ocean. Field Six was just beyond the Jones Beach Tower.

I left my car and walked beyond the boardwalk toward the shoreline and into a haze of blackness.

It was early May. The sand under my feet was as hard as asphalt and the beach had a misbegotten feel to it—a by-product of man and nature's indifference and ultimate abandon. I made the mistake of looking too long and too hard, and was confronted with irrepressible visions rising from the night's black sand—dancing ghosts of burnt out apartment buildings.

As a warm wind tore through my hair and a half-moon lit the shoreline, I could have been in another place and era; nothing around me had the mark of time on it.

I sat down, just inches from the spill of the ocean. Blown sand started to curl around the tips of my shoes and with the heartbeat of each rolling wave and gust of wind, I felt myself shrinking.

My hands grew cold. I drew them to my mouth and exhaled long, hard breaths. I stood up and faced east…and ran as fast as I could, my shoes pounding the hard wet earth until the spray of sand rose in a fountain so high I was nearly blinded by it.

Chapter 67

I waited for two hours outside Bronx Supreme Court for ADA Paul Ventura. He was 'on trial' and expected to be in court all day.

I was in Mom's '79 Corolla again: not only to hide from Guevara but also not to be noticed, period. I was supposed to be on vacation. As I stared aimlessly at the Supreme Court building, I was reminded that one final appearance was necessary for Three-Gun Graham to close out the court file and get Guevara's record sealed.

I hoped for the camouflage of rain while I waited. When the beautiful weather did not break, I tilted the seat back, pulled my black cap low over my eyes, and peered over the steering wheel while parked at a meter facing the 165th Street entrance to the court building.

I spied Paul Ventura. I waited until he crossed the Grand Concourse, headed toward Criminal Court. I jogged until I was within earshot, then slowed to a walk, and called his name. I was wearing a leather jacket and dungarees.

He turned and examined me from head-to-toe for several seconds before my identity registered and he smiled.

"Looking to make a new and different impression on the judges today?" he said.

I walked with him toward Sheridan Avenue. Having left my cap in the car I was worried about being recognized by someone from the office. "No," I answered hoarsely. "No cases on; not today."

"I should hope not. You look like shit, Nick." He spoke offhandedly, as if at one time or another we all looked like shit, and now it was my turn.

I stroked two days of facial stubble with the back of my fingers. "I'm actually on vacation."

Ventura was staring straight ahead and appeared lost in thought—natural for a lawyer 'on trial.' I didn't think he had heard a word I said, and since indifferent and unsuspecting is where I wanted him, it seemed the right moment to bring up Oscar Jefferson again.

"Hey Paul, since my boy Jefferson is long gone, and I'm both happy and sorry to say there have been no more Spiderman-type rapes, maybe you can tell me what it is you've been holding back from me." I now had his full attention. "There was something that didn't add up, something that troubled you. And I don't mean when the first victim saw Jefferson on TV, and told you he wasn't the one. Appearances get cockeyed on television, and she never did see Jefferson in person."

"Him passing that lie detector bothered me, I'll tell you that." He was hedging, and we both knew it.

We crossed 165th Street, and headed toward the Sheridan Avenue entrance to Criminal Court. I veered off to the right so we'd stay near the corner. The Farkas' family law office was a few storefronts away. Now was not the time for another run-in with Charlie Jr., but Ventura wasn't taking my lead. When traffic cleared, I grabbed him by the elbow. Once across the narrow street, he'd make a quick getaway through the revolving doors, leaving me with a smile, a sly remark, and no new information. I would have waited two hours for nothing.

"Paul, for cryin' out loud, Jefferson's dead. Talk to me. What have you got to lose?"

Behind him, just a few feet away, was the storefront entrance to the law office of Charlie Farkas. Junior had wasted no time putting up a new tin sign with just his name on it in big black letters. A wilted wreath sat inside the front window, leaning against the glass—a pathetic but fitting remembrance to the shyster king, Charles Farkas The Last.

"Why do you care, Nick?" Ventura asked. "It's over."

"I was his lawyer. He had no family and no close friends. Somebody should know the truth."

Ventura leaned toward me and spoke in a coarse whisper.

"The baby that was killed—" He pulled back. "She had a black substance under two of her fingernails. Since we know the killer wore gloves, we figured the black came from his face. Fact is, we were fairly certain of this, which means, considering this was a four- month old baby, he got very close to the child's face when he killed her."

"OK. So where's the puzzle?"

"The lab couldn't place the substance right away so they began a process of elimination. They immediately determined it wasn't food."

"Black food," I blurted in astonishment. Then thought again. "It could have been chocolate."

"Chocolate is brown, and the baby was four months old, a little young for chocolate."

I nodded in acknowledgment. He went on.

"Like I said, we never determined what it really was."

"C'mon Paul, what else wasn't it?"

He looked away and rolled his shoulders uncomfortably. "It wasn't anything!" he snapped, then shook his head in disgust, and darted into the building.

A black substance found under the baby's fingernails, not positively identified, eliminated Jefferson. Ventura remains a loyal son-of-a-bitch. Case closed. No embarrassment to the Bronx D.A.'s office for driving an innocent man to kill himself—who in actuality, didn't kill himself at all.

Chapter 68

I drove north, deeper into The Bronx.

Kingsbridge Road Realty was well-lit, even in the dim twilight. Guevara lived just around the corner. I circled the block and drove past his building. Shrunk down in my seat with my cap just above my eyebrows, I eyed the entrance and the dimly lit lobby as I coasted past. Then I made a right at Kingsbridge Road and University Avenue and parked on Grand Street, two blocks from the realty office.

I tugged my jacket sleeve down to cover my Rolex as I walked. When I left Long Island, I had planned to track down Ventura and then pay a visit to my alleged broker friend, Vincent Tedeschi. His cryptic call notwithstanding, the Rolex was part of the plan.

Tedeschi was alone. He scrutinized me through the glass storefront. When I took off my cap, he buzzed me in.

"Aren't we dressed casually?" he asked, as he limply shook my hand.

"Just working late," I answered. "So I thought I'd change out of my monkey suit."

"Change back," he moaned with a smile.

Though the place was empty, I asked if we could talk privately anyway. The overhead fluorescent lights made the office bright as day. Concerned Guevara might pass by and spot us, I kept my back to the street as we stepped to the rear and into Tedeschi's private office.

He flopped down in a chair behind his desk. I sat like a customer in front of it.

"Have you got the bail money Guevara stole from me? I'm considering pressing charges." He shot me a wise guy grin.

"No, because you said forget it. Remember? But you can have this." I placed my Rolex in the center of his desk. It sparkled like an expensive toy. "This will cover it, and much more."

Tedeschi picked it up carefully. "Is it real?" His voice quivered as if he feared I'd snatch it back before he legitimized his claim to it.

"Of course it's real, and it's worth a hell of a lot more than what Guevara owes you."

He placed it back on the desktop, a little farther away from him than where I'd first laid it. "What's this all about?" he asked warily. "And how does a Legal Aid lawyer come to afford a Rolex?"

"It was a gift." I paused. "From my fiancée—which brings me to the more of it."

Tedeschi slouched back in his chair and with hands folded on his lap, listened skeptically.

"Since you and Guevara are obviously on the outs, and I suspect will stay that way, I trust I can speak to you in confidence." I paused for some reassuring word or look, but received only a blank stare. I realized then, offering him the Rolex was a mistake. Fences went up between us so high I needed a pole vault to scale them. I backpedaled. "The Rolex is a loaner, a showing of good faith until I return with every cent Guevara took from you, plus a two-hundred-fifty dollar bonus."

Tedeschi sighed.

"Frankly," I continued, "the police are a bit pissed off Guevara walked and may be trying to pin some burglaries on him." I pulled a list of five addresses on folded loose-leaf out of my pants pocket. They were the locations of all five Spiderman rapes, right down to the apartment numbers. I unfolded the paper and flattened it on the desktop as best I could, face up, next to the watch. "If I could check your records for apartments he showed to prospective tenants, say within the last six months, I would know whether he's got a problem here or not."

"And this means so much to you," Tedeschi uttered sarcastically, "that you came here in the dead of night?" He glanced at his own wristwatch, then at the Rolex. "And you offer me a Rolex to hold like I'm some pawnbroker, claiming it's a gift from your fiancée no less." He pushed the

Rolex away. "I don't suppose your fiancée shops off the street vendors on Fordham Road." He spoke with an air of nerdy pomposity that irritated the hell out of me. "So I give you the information you need and maybe, just maybe, these addresses match up with some or all of the apartments he showed." Tedeschi studied the list in front of him, then looked up, wallowing in cynicism, and with a trace of fear. "Then I get sued by each and every tenant for all kinds of bogus amounts that coincide with their inflated stolen property claims."

I was quickly convinced that I had lost all sense of the order and balance of things; so much so, I was actually going to let Tedeschi keep the watch Eleanor had bought me.

I stood and screamed down at him. "Just look at the list! The Spiderman rapist struck at every one of these fucking places!" I slammed my hand on the desk and papers scattered everywhere.

Tedeschi rocked back in his chair. I grabbed the front of his shirt and yanked him forward.

He yelled for me to stop, but offered little resistance. I clutched the back of his neck and pushed his head down into the desk, his face flattening against the hard wood surface, his eyes shut. His right arm was pinned under his chest and his left hand was grasping at my wrist.

I grabbed the list and shoved it in his face. "Open your eyes, goddamn it!"

He did, and with the look of a wounded deer, begged me to release him.

"Look at these fuckin' addresses and tell me if Guevara showed these apartments!" I was howling like a demon.

Tedeschi strained to see them, but the pressure of my hand on his neck made it impossible. I threw him back in his chair and in one arcing movement, was around the desk with my knee in his chest and my hand on his throat.

"1705 Montgomery. 1435 Townsend. 2170 Walton Avenue. These sound familiar? You knew to the penny what he owed you. You knew what he rented. You knew what he showed."

I released Tedeschi but stood inches away, hovering over him.

He flattened his shirt with his fingers and pushed himself back in his chair in an attempt to regain his composure. He looked past me at the wall. What I had done to him was criminal, but I didn't care. I needed answers.

"2045 Webster Avenue. 1500 Southern Boulevard. Now tell me before I stick my fist down your throat and rip your fuckin' lungs out. Did Guevara show apartments in these buildings or not?"

Tedeschi was sweating through his shirt above a washboard stomach. He was in excellent physical condition, but hadn't the psychological or emotional makeup to fight back.

"Yes," he said in a choked whisper, then coughed several times. "I'm— I'm not sure of the Webster Avenue address, but I can look it up, and call you. The others he definitely showed. I recall the addresses from the newspapers." He spoke like a child begging for forgiveness. "The Webster Avenue address was one of them too. I'm sorry, I remember."

I stepped back and patted his shoulder. "I'm sorry too. I'm not sure what came over me."

He chuckled pathetically. "Justice probably."

Chapter 69

The only stone left unturned was Terkel. Doctor Norris Terkel.

I said I'd visit, and as much as it ravaged my psyche each time I ventured back into The Bronx, I could not stay away.

It was Friday, and unlike the week that passed, the weather forecast was rain, and lots of it.

Country Club Estates was in the Throgs Neck section, in the southeastern portion of the borough—where there were no subways, no large four-to-eight lane boulevards or concourses, no apartment buildings, and no blacks or minorities of color, except for maybe an Asian family or two—where large one-family homes with lawns to the sidewalk lined the streets, all well-kept, many right on the water.

The water was the East River and part of Long Island Sound. The Throgs Neck Bridge spanned the two, connecting Queens with the Bronx. I didn't have to travel more than two minutes off its first exit to get to Country Club Estates.

I killed a man. I killed a man. Terkel's ramblings over the telephone the last time we'd spoken no longer seemed the product of a sick tortured soul, but a haunting epitaph, delivered by the murderer himself.

I would not go there alone.

My best friend Joey agreed to drive me in his new white Olds '98. I told him that once I went into Terkel's house, if I wasn't out in twenty minutes, to come get me. AIDS or no AIDS, dying or not, I figured Terkel for one crazy fucker.

I rang the doorbell and was greeted by the same Jamaican attendant who'd been taking my calls. Her voice was unmistakable. She was wearing a white smock over a housedress.

I told her who I was. She remembered speaking to me on the telephone and seemed thoroughly pleased that I had come. As she grabbed her coat, I realized why: she couldn't have been more pleased to get out of the house.

"I should be back in about fifteen minutes," she said. "I have to get somethin' to eat."

"Are you sure it's OK?" I asked.

"Just tell him to keep the mask on 'til I get back."

"The mask?"

"The oxygen mask." She giggled at my confusion. "Listen, if you've not seen anybody like this, dyin' and all, prepare yourself. He's an awful sight." She patted my forearm. "And he's in a nasty mood too. You may want to keep the visit short."

"Has anyone else come to visit him lately?"

"Just Peter. Six months I'm here and he's the only one come visit. You'd think he was losing his father the way he dotes over the doctor." She pointed aimlessly at the house as she hurried out the door and down the marble stoop. "He's in the bedroom in the back."

I stepped in and closed the door behind me. The hardwood floor creaked under my feet. I found myself in a small, dimly lit center hall decorated only with a cherry wood grandfather clock that made me jump as it bonged nine definitive times.

It was dark inside the house and beyond the silhouettes of cluttered furniture in adjoining rooms, I heard a faint repetitive beep.

Surmising it was the digital pulses of a heart monitor, I followed the sound to a darkened hallway that turned to the right, then to the left. A weakly lit candlestick wall sconce glowed in the darkness. At the end of the hall, a bright light spilled from under a closed door.

The pinging blips of the heart monitor pierced through the darkness like a messenger. I could smell rot and decay in the air. I reached for the doorknob but at first could not bring myself to touch it, as if it too bore the seeds of a deadly infection and was going to bite back.

I turned a pearl handle that felt like a cat's head, and pushed the door open.

Bright light cascaded under and over me and blinded me for an instant. From across the room, a coarse rant bellowed out at me. "I told that black bitch I don't want no fucking priest!"

"I'm no priest," I said flatly.

Terkel lay with his upper body, what was left of it, propped up in a hospital bed. Several white sheets outlined an emaciated torso and legs that stretched ghoulishly to his skeletal feet.

The room was a solarium with a ceiling that curved down into a far wall and glass panels so clear, one could not tell where the room ended and the bulkhead and blackened East River began. The heart monitor was behind the bed. Hanging from a metal rack were three plastic bags of yellow and clear liquid that dripped with melancholy regularity into a tube that fed intravenously into Terkel's right arm. An entertainment center on wheels was but a few feet from the foot of the bed. A Beethoven symphony that I'd heard repeated over and over in the movie, *A Clockwork Orange*, was set at a faint volume. Terkel was biting down with brown rotting teeth on the bottom of an oxygen mask that fogged up with each shallow breath he took.

I stepped closer.

His neck twisted toward me as his face contorted in a feeble attempt to focus. His head was completely bald, and on it, three blackened velvety spots stood in stark contrast to its ashen pallor.

The lights on the Bronx-Whitestone Bridge, miles in the distance, marked the outline of his bed before me. The air outside was quickly growing misty as the stars and the moon disappeared beyond an overcast sky. Rain fell, and the outer walls of the solarium filled with crystalline beads of water.

"I know you," he said with a voice that grated like sandpaper. "You're Mannino, aren't you?"

I drew closer to him, within several short feet. If I had not known all that I did about him, I suppose I would have felt pity at this shell of a man scratching a last hold onto life. But all that swelled within me was disgust.

"You're exactly as I suspected, exactly as described," he muttered, as he arched his back slightly.

"As described by whom?" I asked.

"By Peter, of course." He displayed a smile that reminded me of the dilapidated gates to the junkyard behind P.S. 92.

As rain drummed onto the solarium roof like hailstones, the Bronx-Whitestone Bridge all but disappeared. I thought of Oscar Jefferson for the first time since the drive over, as if before that moment I was there for some other reason I did not know. But Terkel knew why I was there.

"It was murder," I said. "Why?"

"I know it was murder," he answered callously. "I was the fucking murderer." His right arm twitched as he spoke, not from the horrible disease but as a limited way of giving emphasis to his words. "And if you have to ask why, you are as stupid as you think you are smart. Asswipe lawyer."

"It was an innocent life. You knew that."

"If the life wasn't innocent, it wouldn't be murder now would it?" And he was right. I was stupid—for trying to reason with a beast.

"You know, you deserve to lie there like the sick bastard you are. You deserve to suffer."

"Fuck you," he growled, then pulled his head up off a yellowed pillow and screamed: "Why, I did the bitch myself!"

"If Oscar Jefferson was killed for being gay, you should burn in the electric chair."

Terkel laughed so hard I thought he would suffocate. His bony fingers tugged at the oxygen mask until the clear plastic cup fell over his mouth. I wanted him to die right there so I could watch, but in a quick swipe he pulled the mask off again and resumed laughing.

I had been walking backward and found myself just inches from the bedroom door. I had heard and seen enough.

Under the roar of pouring rain and inside a crack of violent thunder, Terkel cackled: "And give your Uncle Rocco my best."

His words coursed through me like the jagged-edged knife this maniac had once used. And I knew then that the "bitch" he referred to was Rocco's young and beautiful Dorothy.

"Tell him," he howled, "I especially enjoyed the last sweet taste of her bloody pussy."

A lightening bolt of fear shot through me. Terkel was sitting up, arms in the air, head high, mouth open to the heavens and roaring wildly at the elements around him.

As if on cue, the fluorescent lights dimmed and dimmed again, and then failed completely. I turned and ran, smacking into a hall table and sending a porcelain vase crashing to the floor. I stumbled and fell in the darkness as Terkel filled the house with wretched laughter.

I flung open the front door and leapt down the marble steps, crashing into the wrought iron fence bordering the sidewalk. I fumbled for the latch and swung the gate open with such force, it slammed against the post and bounced back only to slam shut on the cuff of my pants leg, which tore as I raced to Joey's car.

The Olds' lights were off but the engine was running and the wipers were swatting at the vicious rain. Joey's eyes were closed, his head leaning back. The doors were locked and the radio was blasting. I slammed on the side window with my palm. Startled, he quickly opened the door and I jumped in.

"What the fuck happened to you?" he asked.

"Just take off," I demanded.

As we drove away and Joey looked at me in silent amazement and awe, waiting for me to explain, I knew why Terkel despite his well-deserved pain and agony fought so hard to hold onto dear life.

Because as awful as it was, it was far better than where he was going.

Chapter 70

Joey stopped at a liquor store on East Tremont Avenue. He bought two pints of Seagrams, and then ran into a deli and came out with a can of 7-UP. The soda remained unopened on the seat as we drank from separate bottles of rye and soared over the Throgs Neck Bridge.

In minutes, I was lightheaded and pouring my heart out like a lost little schoolboy. By the time we got to Queens, I had finished half the bottle and was sufficiently drunk. Joey listened and asked no questions. I only stopped talking to bring the bottle to my lips for another sip. Thoughts of Guevara and Terkel—spurred me on.

I passed out on the Oldsmobile's front seat, dreaming I was in another one of my nightmares, until the rye churned in my stomach and I vomited onto a grassy shoulder of the Meadowbrook Parkway. When I was done, Joey yanked me back into the Olds, and I passed out again.

When I opened my eyes, it was 1:45 A.M. I was alone in the car outside White Castle Hamburgers in Levittown, Long Island. The two bottles of rye were on the seat next to me. Mine was three-quarters empty. Joey's was nearly full. He approached the car, wiping his mouth with a napkin. When he got in, he smelled of greasy hamburgers and onions. I thought I was going to be sick again.

"I couldn't take you home like this. Your mom would have a fit. With all this driving around I built up an appetite. Since you left your dinner on the Parkway, I didn't think you cared much to join me."

"Just take me home, Joe."

My mouth was as dry as clay and my tongue felt like cardboard. The liquor was well-settled in my system and I had the sensation, even while seated, that I was losing my balance. I held onto the armrest as I caught, in a glimmer, the familiar sight of Hempstead Turnpike in East Meadow.

The car did a tailspin each time I closed my eyes—so I kept my head back and lids open, conscious of every blink, until Joey pulled into my driveway, where red and pink azaleas in full bloom were swallowed by the darkness.

Joey helped me up the stoop where the glare of the living room lights made me squint. Mom appeared at the front door looking like she had been shaken out of a deep sleep. She was holding her hair down with one hand and her robe closed with the other. Under the porch light, she looked much older than her fifty-nine years.

"Hi, Mary," Joey said politely.

Mom's expression of discomfort and weariness didn't change. "Hi ya, Joe," she said weakly. Her concerned eyes fell upon me. "A friend of yours just called. Vinny Repolla. Something like that. He sounded awful. Said you'd better get over to 25 Sutton Place right away. Isn't that where Eleanor lives?"

I sobered in an instant, grabbed Joey's keys, and ran toward the '98. Joey jumped into the front passenger seat as I pulled away. Mom remained on the porch looking like I felt—helpless and frightened.

Twenty minutes later, I was approaching the Midtown Tunnel toll, which I ran without hesitation. Joey held onto the dashboard and back seat, shouting a string of obscenities as I raced through the narrow two-lane tunnel, cutting past cars and mowing down a succession of rubber lane dividers.

Minutes later, we were at Eleanor's building. Two blue and white police cars were angled out front with their doors wide open. Two others were double-parked inches away. Roof sirens on all four silently spun red and yellow warning lights.

But there were no cops in sight.

I slammed the '98 into "Park" and jumped out. The brightly lit lobby was empty and there was no doorman to be found.

I ran for the stairs, spitting up bilious rye as I scaled steps, three and four at a time.

When I opened the door to the seventh floor hallway, I saw two police officers and a paramedic conversing like businessmen outside Eleanor's apartment. An elderly woman peeked out her apartment door, then pulled in her head and slammed it shut. One of the officers had his hand resting on the butt of his holstered pistol; resting, not readied, I thought to myself.

I walked down the hallway toward Eleanor's apartment while letting my fingertips run along the wallpaper, as if feebly searching for something to hold onto. I had yet to be noticed by anyone.

The officers and the paramedic entered the apartment with slow-motion reluctance. When I got to the door, I noticed three nickel-size drops of dried blood on the welcome mat. They were scattered like fallen points on a triangle.

The murmuring of indecipherable baritone voices came from inside as footsteps moved about faintly, creaking on the bare wood floor.

I clutched the doorframe, held my breath, and stepped inside.

Four cops were standing with their backs to me, facing the sofa. In front of them, two paramedics struggled with the zippered flaps of a black body bag. The figure inside was female. The hair, shoulder length and light brown. The frame slight.

I stepped closer.

Clear plastic had already been wrapped around the corpse. A puddle of blood had accumulated inside the plastic wrap under the body.

When the zipper closed over her face, I could see that Carolyn's eyes were wide open. I felt a hand on my shoulder. It was Joey.

"It's not Eleanor, Joe," I said, instantly recalling Carolyn's last words to me: *If you want to talk, I'll be staying at Eleanor's.*

"What the hell are you doing here?" A dark haired man of fifty flashed a gold detective's shield at me. "Do you know this girl?" He was over six feet tall and hunched slightly. He had a Roman nose, but his skin was light, and his eyes were Donna Gillis blue. Though he didn't have all the obvious traits, I knew he was Italian-American. He also reminded me of John Mannino, with his tall, thin build, sloping shoulders and stern manner.

"This is my girlfriend's apartment. That's not her, though. It's—It's our friend, Carolyn. She's a writer."

The blue uniforms backed away while the paramedics placed Carolyn on a gurney. The body bag lifted to reveal a sofa soaked with blood. I had slept there just days earlier, a heating pad on my side, Eleanor looking after me.

"Does your girlfriend have any enemies?" the detective asked while twisting a paperback book wrapped in plastic in his hands.

"No. Not at all." I thought again, and though I knew it might send him in the wrong direction, I added: "She's an Assistant District Attorney in Manhattan."

"And you don't think she had any enemies?" he asked incredulously.

"No enemy from her work did this," I said.

"And how can you be so sure?"

"Because they would have seen her in court, and would know what she looks like." I withheld how much Carolyn looked like Eleanor. It would again lead him in the wrong direction. For reasons I was not ready to disclose, I didn't want him going in the right one.

My eyes fell back on the bloodstained couch.

"Where is your girlfriend, if I may ask?" The detective lit up a cigarette with a silver lighter that had F. Spina inscribed on it.

"Atlanta. With her family."

"Then what brought you here at two in the morning?" Unlike *Columbo,* subtlety was not Detective Spina's forte.

"I did," Vinny Repolla said from the hallway. A press ID was clasped to the lapel of his brown blazer. When he started into the apartment, the detective shouted at him to stop.

"Isn't anyone concerned about securing this crime scene? Everybody out! Forensics still has to go over the place."

When we all left the apartment, the oldest of the plainclothes detectives told Spina they would meet him downstairs. Spina grumbled an acknowledgment and locked the front door with a set of keys that must have been Carolyn's. He then took two yellow strips of crime scene tape and crisscrossed them over the doorframe.

"So tell me now how you"—Spina pointed at Vinny—"know him?" Spina pointed at me.

"I'm a friend of Nick's and I'm also a crime reporter for *Newsday*."

Spina huffed as if everything Vinny would say from that point on was tainted.

"When I got wind of the police response to a homicide and heard the address, I called Nick. I knew his girlfriend lived here." Vinny was un-ruffled by Spina's manner. I suspected he had become quite used to dealing with cranky detectives.

"I'm a Legal Aid lawyer in the Bronx," I added. "That's how I know Vinny."

"That how you met your girlfriend?" Spina sounded suspicious, like he was being jostled.

"No. We met a long time ago." Lifetimes it seemed. "When I was in law school."

"Wonderful," Spina grumbled. He looked at Joey. "And I suppose you're a sitting Supreme Court Judge?"

Joey didn't absorb or appreciate Spina's humor and sarcasm. I gave Joey a good long look for the first time since we left Long Island. He was ashen-faced, no doubt from the sight of Carolyn in the body bag.

"I'm just a friend of Nick's," Joey said. "I've been with him all night, since about 8:30."

"Well, that answers my next question. Thank you."

The elevator arrived, and we all stepped in. Vinny introduced himself to Joey, who was still badly shaken. They pumped hands like old friends at a funeral.

Vinny turned to Spina. "What the hell happened here anyway?"

"Maybe we can help," I said.

Spina rolled his eyes. "Sure you can." He then answered Vinny's question as if accepting a challenge. "The killer, it seems, got in the apartment by breaking the doorframe and double-bolt lock with a crowbar of some sort. I figure he caught her sleeping. She may have awoken from the intrusion, but I guess he got to her while she was still dazed."

The elevator was dropping, and nauseatingly fast. I looked at Joey. He had heard enough. So had I. But I had to listen on.

"And?" I said loudly.

Spina turned to face me, and blurted: "And he gutted her like a fish from her crotch to her sternum."

Joey vomited his White Castle hamburgers into the corner of the elevator. Vinny casually handed him a handkerchief.

I again noticed the paperback, folded this time in Spina's left hand.

I pointed to it. "What is that?"

"Seems your writer friend was also a reader," Spina answered indifferently. "One of the officers found this on the end table next to her body. Figured I'd look it over. Maybe it will tell me something I don't know. And I don't know much." Spina held it up. "Stupid book, probably doesn't count for shit."

It was a paperback edition of William Shakespeare's *Othello*.

Outside 25 Sutton Place, I hugged Vinny and thanked him for calling. I then offered silent thanks that Eleanor had gone to Atlanta, whatever the reason, and prayed she wouldn't return. Not yet. Though none of my prayers of late were being answered.

Thoughts of Carolyn caused my eyes to well up. I gave Detective Spina my office and home numbers. In his best *Naked City* voice he told me not to leave town. He'd be in touch.

Joey remained stupefied during the entire drive back to Merrick, where I dropped myself off and gave him the wheel. I hugged him too, and thanked him for sticking out the awful night with me.

Once in the house, I shut off the living room lights, got a blanket, and covered Mom, who was asleep on the living room sectional. It was 4:00 A.M.

Miraculously, and probably from an irrepressible exhaustion, when my head hit the pillow, my mind was cleared of all thoughts of Terkel, Guevara, and Carolyn's murder, and in seconds I fell asleep. But what was even more miraculous was that I did so with the realization that somewhere there was a bald muscular black man in his twenties, who had an insatiable hunger for human suffering, and whom Guevara and Terkel knew all too well.

Chapter 71

I woke up in the early afternoon. After picking at Mom's ill-conceived breakfast of eggs, pancakes and toast, I left for the beach again and spent the balance of the day walking slowly along the boardwalk of Field Four. When the sun set low in the sky and the beach was nearly deserted (except for a few young lovers braving the elements), I telephoned Mom from a booth near the concession stand.

She said that Eleanor had called earlier, crying, said a friend of hers had died, and that she was planning to catch the next flight to New York. I said I would call back, but had no intention of doing so.

I told Mom I would be home late. She reminded me, as she often did when she sensed something was wrong, that she loved me and that I was all she had in the world. I told her not to worry.

Minutes after leaving the beach, I was on the Southern State Parkway, headed west toward Brooklyn.

I was driving my Malibu this time.

The Carroll Avenue Hunt and Fish Club appeared closed. But then it always did. Fat Julee let me in.

The bar area was full and aside from a few retirees in attendance, I knew practically no one. Sallie was in a corner, talking intently to three younger men. He turned slightly as I entered. Uncle Rocco was standing at the end of the bar. I parted cigarette smoke to kiss him on the cheek before we stepped into the dining room. Rocco and I sat down at the same table where we had eaten macaroni and meatballs and discussed Oscar Jefferson's murder a month before. Rocco spoke first. His tone was businesslike.

"Nickie, I can't help you right now with that Bronx thing."

I had read that Carmine Capezzi was sick, drifting in and out of consciousness, having suffered his second stroke at the age of eighty. It was in times like these, with the boss of bosses out of commission and fading fast, that rival capos looked to jump the chain of command and wars broke out. Rocco's loyalty to Capezzi was legendary, which meant his life was in danger. Sallie's too.

"It's OK, Uncle Roc. I've read the paper. That's not why I'm here."

His eyes widened. "Tell me anything else I can do for you. Anything." He spoke softly, caringly.

"I would really appreciate it if you could get me a gun, a pistol, for my own protection."

His face filled with disapproval. "That's a mandatory year in jail if you get caught. It's a new law."

"I know all about it. With mitigating circumstances, it's a misdemeanor plea and probation." He looked unconvinced.

"Protection from what?" he asked.

I told him about Carolyn's death and how I was convinced Guevara had something to do with it.

"This is New York City. Women get killed, raped. Stuff happens all the time with no rhyme or reason."

"The same night I go see this Doctor Terkel?" I dropped my voice to a whisper. "The same guy who had Oscar Jefferson killed and posted nine thousand dollars of Guevara's bail?"

"Why the hell did you go see him anyway? You want to get *yourself* killed?" He poked the table with a stiffened index finger. "If so, I'll give you a job right here, right now."

"Uncle Roc, this guy Terkel, he's not who he says he is. He's a fucking monster."

"A monster? Would you really know a monster if you met one?"

"They never found Ernest Leskey, alive or dead, did they Uncle Roc?"

His eyes dropped to the table, then turned up at me. "No, they didn't," he said icily.

"He was on the swim team in college wasn't he?"

269

"Yes, but that's not how I know he survived."

All warmth and charm had left Rocco Alonzo. I was talking now to a cold-blooded criminal, the Brooklyn *capo,* who in his younger days carried out orders to kill with calculating ease. I leaned forward slightly, encouraging him to continue.

"Soon after…all the prints found in the apartment somehow got lost along with all the other evidence." His voice cracked. "I should have killed him when I had the chance."

I remained silent for a few seconds, regretting what I would say next, but knowing I must say it anyway.

"Ernest Leskey…is Dr. Terkel, dying of AIDS and living in a house on the water. Yesterday, he admitted to me that he killed her." And with cautious restraint, I whispered: "And he told me to tell you he did it, too."

Rocco bit his fist until he almost broke the skin. "You sure about this, Nickie?"

"Confirm it for yourself, Uncle Roc. Are there are no records at all on him?"

"There's nothing, except the gun."

"The gun?" I asked, not at all understanding.

"I kept the gun, my gun, the one he threw at me once, before he jumped into the East River. I still have it, along with two prints of his fingers on the barrel. When the records disappeared, I had the gun dusted and the prints magnified and photographed. If he's still got his fingertips, I'll be able to prove it's him."

Sallie poked his head in the door. Rocco called him over. Sallie gave me a sweaty kiss on the cheek and apologized for not saying hello earlier. Head down, Rocco told him to take me downstairs and get me "suited up." Whatever I wanted. Sallie squinted his eyes warily at Rocco, whose head remained down and face out of sight.

I followed Sallie through the kitchen and down a rickety stairway to the cellar. He took me to a room in the back that was nothing more than an old walk-in icebox. Sallie opened its heavy door and turned on a light. The smell of pine and a lingering mustiness rushed out at us. We stepped inside. A fan hummed in a far corner above three bags of sand set against a wall.

"I'll be just a minute," Sallie said. He returned with a black .38 caliber pistol in one hand, and a silencer in the other. He pulled the door tightly shut behind him. "Use this only if you have to," Sallie said sternly. "The butt is taped to ward off prints."

"What about the trigger?"

He looked at me curiously. "Can't get a decent print off a trigger." He stiffened his arm and shot twice into the bags. The noise inside the walk-in box was deafening. "Now you try."

"Can you put that silencer on it?" I asked matter-of-factly, while sticking my finger in my ear pretending the gunshot bothered me more than it did.

Sallie took the gun, screwed on the silencer, then handed it back to me. I emptied the pistol into the bags in seconds.

"Keep your prints off it, okay? Hold it by the taped butt only. I don't expect you're gonna need this, Nickie." Sallie reloaded the gun. "You know, there might be some trouble in the next few weeks. So don't go comin' around. We'll let you know when it's safe to get together."

"Is everything going to be all right?"

"Your uncle is going to be passed over when Capezzi dies. Capezzi says *La Cosa Nostra's* now a business and needs a businessman, not a gangster, to run it. So Capezzi's cousin, the boss from Staten Island, will be his successor. Rocco's hurt, but won't admit it. Capezzi's been like a father to him, so he'll respect the decision. Regardless, whenever there's a change of command, precautions have to be taken. And that's all you have to know, which is too much already. Now turn around." He knelt down, picked up my right pants leg and strapped a holstered knife to the back of my calf. "I'm probably nuts for giving you this, but it saved my life once."

I thanked him.

He wiped the gun clean again, placed it in the inside pocket of my jacket, and told me to leave out the back.

I walked down a poorly lit back alley, a half-moon brightening my way to the street.

Chapter 72

W hat surprised me most was how calm I was.

The air in the driver's side window, opened just an inch, drowned out the traffic on the Major Deagan Expressway—along with the rest of the outside world.

When I exited at Fordham Road, I rolled the window tightly shut.

People walked along the sidewalk. Traffic moved up the avenue. But in silence.

I was in a vacuum—locked inside my own shell. And all I could hear was the faint breath of the ocean.

I drove slowly past Devoe Park and watched two teenage boys shake hands and pass a vial of cocaine. A baby cried nearby in the arms of a pretty young Hispanic girl with streaming black hair. The young girl had just exited a liquor store and held in her free hand a pint size paper bag. The *Q* and *U* in the illuminated sign over the storefront was out, leaving only *LI OR* in a weak blood-red fluorescent glow.

I continued up University Avenue. Though I had driven up this street when I last paid a visit to Vincent Tedeschi, I didn't recall its steepness or how much I had to gas the engine to climb it. I was sleep-deprived then and in a state of panic and confusion. Tonight, I was rested, and unnaturally calm.

I passed the four-story red brick apartment building where the monster, Peter Guevara, lived.

A weather-beaten fire escape, two windows wide, ran up the center of the building. A streetlight flickered over the front entrance.

I drove around the block and inspected the rear of the building. Another fire escape ran up the back. A rusted chain link fence about twenty feet high, topped with tangled strings of barbed wire enclosed a small backyard. The fence, though aged and beaten, was intact.

I circled back around and made my second and last pass in front of the building, my black cap pulled down low, the collar of my jacket raised.

A short Latino male, about fifty years old, was walking down the block with a bag of groceries in his arms. He had a dark complexion that, under the pale glow of the streetlight, seemed reddish. His sculptured face had deep-set lines I had seen once before—at the rape trial in December, on the face of Dina Rios' father.

Five months had passed since that verdict, and I wondered if Angelo Bonegura had raped any other girls since.

I passed Tedeschi's closed office on Kingsbridge Road, made a right, and then another onto a block of single-family homes. I parked facing Guevara's building, but far enough to be out of its line of sight.

Looming over the abutting two- and three-family houses alongside it, the building was crowned with a castle rail of concrete arches emblazoned with crests of potted vines and portals that funneled through the moonlight. It housed twenty families in all.

When I shut the ignition, the engine puttered off with an exhausted finality. I felt for the .38 tucked in the breast pocket of my jacket, and then tapped at the silencer.

Guevara lived in #D-5 on the top floor—the fourth floor. I hoped to get in and out unseen. A visitor coming or going on a Saturday night shouldn't attract attention, even into the wee hours. I would abort only if Guevara was not alone.

I walked with hands tucked into my jacket pockets, chin in my chest, and cap lowered. The holster strapped to my calf painfully tugged at a few leg hairs—a pinching reminder of Sallie's cryptic generosity.

I paused at the corner of 192nd, leaned against a tree and looked across the street for any signs of life. There were none. Only half of all the front windows were lit.

I crossed the street and stepped under the flickering streetlight over the building's entrance.

The heavy iron doors that bordered the sidewalk needed a two-handed push. Once inside the vestibule, the interior entrance door was but a few feet away. Black bell buttons lined the wall to the left in two vertical rows of ten. Each tenant's last name was engraved in a plastic strip next to each button. D-5's inhabitant was no secret. It read: GUEVARA.

I was tempted to ring the bell. Pretend to be casually paying a visit. Sit across from him in his living room. Calmly pull out the pistol. Blow him away quietly. Leave without touching a thing.

That I shuddered at how ill-conceived this notion was provided one of few assurances that I had not gone completely mad.

I pulled out a Sears credit card to jimmy the entrance doorjamb, only to discover it was stuffed with toilet paper. With the sole of my shoe, I pushed open the door, then plucked out the toilet paper; careful not to touch the frame and leave even the faintest trace of a print. Tossing aside the paper, I eased the door shut with my knee.

Down a long tiled hallway, I came to a set of marble steps with wrought iron balusters and handrails. Under the stairwell, inlaid into the wall, were twenty shiny silver mailboxes. Guevara's was locked. I tapped it and heard a tinny hollow sound.

I slowly walked up the steps, lifting my shoes to avoid making the harsh scuffing sounds that would echo inside the stairwell. Midway between the second and third floors, I heard the scratchy sound of a television searching for its signal. A man was talking in Spanish and an audience was laughing loudly in response. I reached the fourth floor landing. Apartment D-5 was to my left. My eyes followed another short set of stairs to a landing that led up to the roof. I went over to Guevara's apartment door and listened. It was quiet inside. I stepped to the middle of the narrow hallway and bent my head in the direction of the three other apartment doors. Again, I heard nothing. I walked up the short flight of stairs, turned and went up another short flight until I came to a large metal door. Unhooking a clasp, I pushed the door open.

Moonlight smacked me in the face and a gust of wind blew my cap back. There was no exit from the rooftop. A rear fire escape would only take me to a backyard enclosed by the barbed wire fence.

I would have to leave the building as I had come—through the front entrance doors, and hope that no one would see me.

I pulled the roof door shut.

I went back down to the landing, turned, and peered down the second short connecting flight of steps. Guevara's apartment door was at the bottom, off to the left. Unzipping my jacket, I reached for the gun. Setting my index finger on the trigger, I secured my hand firmly around the butt. I then took a breath and—pausing just enough to gain poise before movement, and not enough to think more than I had to—I descended the stairs.

Facing Guevara's door, I pulled out the pistol and held it down behind my right leg. I pressed the doorbell with my knuckle. A muffled buzz came from deep inside the apartment.

I listened for footsteps. None came.

I buzzed again, and waited.

Nothing.

I sucked in a long, deep breath and expelled it slowly. I could feel my heart pounding. I went back up the stairs toward the roof door and sat down out of sight of the floor below. I returned the pistol to my inside jacket pocket.

I would wait. All night if need be.

The roof door was at my back, just a few short stairs away. I felt a draft through gaps in the door seal and huddled tightly against the wall. It was only a matter of time before the temperature dropped and my breath became visible. I rolled my shoulders to prevent stiffening, and opened and closed my hands to better the blood flow.

I tried not to think about what I was about to do, but just listen for a footstep, a creak in the floor, a ruffle of clothing, a breath.

I waited.

More than an hour, maybe two passed and the cold on my back was starting to affect the circulation in my lower body. I blew warm air onto my hands then stuffed them back in my pockets. No sooner had I leaned my head against the side wall and closed my eyes, than I heard the front door to the building open and the sound of slow heavy footsteps…in the hallway… on the stairs…getting louder.

I stood up and pulled out the .38.

The footsteps smacked the steps with boorish insolence.

Matching their rhythm, I descended the stairs to the landing, turned and aimed downward. When Guevara appeared before his front door, I would fire.

From the third floor, I heard the rattle of keys. The footsteps ceased. A door creaked open, then slammed shut. I returned to my perch just below the roof door and the stiffening cold draft.

Twice more, I heard the front door open. The first preceded the quick steps of a teenage boy. The second accompanied a man and woman, walking clumsily and talking flirtatiously. In neither instance did they reach the fourth floor, the cooing couple dissolving into whispers behind a closed door.

And I thought about Eleanor. Our first dance at Cardozo Law. Our first kiss. The first time we made love. A walk along the beach. Her sweet sexy smile.

An hour passed, maybe two. I drifted off.

In the semi-consciousness before sleep, I saw a little boy riding a red tricycle along the sidewalk of a tree-lined street. He was racing toward his parents' waiting arms. It was my little boy. Eleanor's and mine.

I opened my eyes to the light of the half-moon shining through a filth-laden window high above the landing.

I'm no killer.

I tucked the .38 deep into the breast pocket of my jacket until the silencer scraped against my ribs. I stood up and walked down the stairs. When I got to the landing, the moonlight struck me square in the face. It had to be well past midnight, I thought to myself.

I'm going home.

Casually and quietly, I stepped down the second short flight; still careful not to make much noise, but not concealing my movement either. I stopped at the bottom of the steps. Guevara's apartment door was to my left, looming like an impenetrable wall. I stood there for an indecipherable moment, as if subconsciously wanting to make one last fearless gesture—pausing at the mouth of the beast.

A swishing sound came from inside the apartment. In an instant, the door swung open.

There, before a darkened apartment, stood a man inside an outline of blackness. The whites of cobra eyes bore through the haze of the hallway light that swelled over the doorway. The eyes were still. The figure filled the doorframe.

It crossed my mind to run, except I believed, as with any wild animal, that this would draw a quicker and more immediate response—a leap and a pouncing from which I could not escape. I pulled out the .38 and pointed it at my darkened nemesis.

In a jolt and a flicker of light, the .38 went crashing to the floor.

I was on my back, straddling the doorway—my legs inside the apartment, my arms and torso in the hallway, a muscular black man on top of me.

I let go a precarious barrage of punches, twisting with each one in attempt to escape as the figure pressed down upon me. But it drew only hacking grunts from my attacker, who seemed intent on pinning me to the floor.

A large bicep forged itself against my chest. I turned to reach for the pistol. It was lying against the far wall several feet from my outstretched fingertips.

I felt myself being inched into the apartment. The face of the man was a dark blur as I writhed on the floor, digging in my heels to stop the darkness from swallowing me whole.

My fingers clutched the doorframe. My attacker's hands, which seemed too small for his thick arms and chest, attempted to pry them loose, while I kept landing ineffectual punches into a rock hard side and back.

The bicep moved closer to my windpipe. This man, this killer, was winning. I only hoped death would come painlessly; that I would ease into some eternal peace, a bright light guiding my way.

His head pressed into my chest. I felt a cap fall on my face and reflexively shook it off.

I looked up, aghast.

My attacker was bald.

Amid the fear and the panic and the fight for my life, it registered: the Spiderman—Guevara's evil accomplice—one of Terkel's schoolboys turned rapist and murderer—was murdering me!

The bicep had found my throat.

My strength was near gone. What little I had left was mere frightful adrenaline.

My hand slipped from the doorframe and I was pulled into the apartment.

For a second, my right arm was free.

I pulled Sallie's knife from its leather calf holster. The body on top of me, with the apparent instincts of a wrestler, reached for my free hand.

He gripped my wrist, but not before I cut deep into his leg.

A massive blow thundered down on my chest; his fist, in turn, smacked the side of my head.

Everything went dark. But I could hear. Hear my own death. Like prison doors slowly slamming shut in my head.

Chapter 73

I was standing on straw legs, my vision a translucent glaze, a blur slowly morphing into clarity. I expected to see my stepfather-father, John Mannino, reaching out to me, guiding me through the mist.

My face was being slapped, and hard. I was still in the hallway. Every part of my body ached, my head worst of all.

Rocco was holding me up.

In the doorway, lying on his belly, a bullet hole in his temple and a gleaming puddle of blood under his head, was the Spiderman—a white man with a black face I now easily recognized.

Sallie was on his knees wiping down the doorframe, wall and floor of my prints, careful not to touch the puddle of blood or the body. The gun and the knife he gave me were in his left hand. My cap was in his pants pocket.

"That man's white," I said hoarsely.

"He's delirious," Sallie muttered, while examining the gaping face of the dead man.

"Look behind his ears," I blurted.

Sallie huffed and bent back the dead man's ear lobe.

"Son of a bitch. He's right."

The man on the floor, dead as the devil's messenger should remain— was Peter Guevara.

Shuffling of feet came from behind the adjoining apartment door. Murmuring could be heard on the floor below.

Sallie was the first to rush down the stairs. Moving with amazing quickness for his size, he yelled out from the third floor for the whole building to hear. "Anyone talks to the police, they're fuckin' dead! Your kids won't be safe playing in the street!"

Rocco and I were behind him. Rocco was still holding me up, though I was walking, even running, fairly well on my own. Outside, two cars were double-parked with drivers alert and ready. I recognized the wheelmen as two of the young soldiers from the club. The lead car was Rocco's Caddy, no doubt used at great risk to the Brooklyn *capo*. The second car was mine. The license plates of both had been changed.

Sallie jumped in the front seat of the Caddy. Rocco and I got in the back. In minutes, we were on the Major Deagan Expressway.

Even against the soft leather interior my body was racked with pain.

Midway over the Triborough Bridge, the car slowed. Sallie opened his window. Like backhanding a discus, he flung a small metal object out the car and off the bridge. It was the .22 that Rocco had used to shoot Guevara.

The car accelerated and we headed into Queens.

"You guys must be really pissed at me," I said sheepishly.

The young driver's attention did not waver from the road as he stayed just under the speed limit, but I thought I saw him smile ever so slightly. Sallie turned and looked at Rocco.

"Let's just leave it that we're happy you're still alive," Rocco said.

Sallie handed me a paper bag full of clothes. "Put these on and put everything you're wearing in the bag, even the knife holster. Especially the knife holster."

I did as Sallie commanded. When I was done, we were in Astoria heading down Ditmars Avenue. Looming overhead was a rusted black iron bridge that looked as if it should have been junked years ago.

Rocco nudged me. "That's the Hell Gate Bridge."

We drove along the East River until we came to a desolate area just past the underbelly of the bridge. A large black sign read: NEW YORK CONNECTING RAILROAD and under it, in smaller letters: 'East River Arch Bridge.'

The car pulled over to the curb. A piped railing ran alongside the East River, separating the sidewalk from the rocks and the water. The cuffs on the pants Sallie had given me were dragging below loose fitting sneakers.

The pullover sweatshirt fit fine, as did the socks. There was no underwear in the bag. The three of us stood alone by the railing. The Hell Gate Bridge, a blackened monstrosity, was high above us to the right. The Triborough Bridge was about a half-mile to the left.

"This railing wasn't here in 1955," Rocco said pensively as he grasped the piped rail with both hands and stared out onto the water in the direction of Randall's Island.

"See those currents," Sallie said. "See them spinning. They're fuckin' vicious."

Sure enough, I could see three connecting whirlpools of water, the closest about thirty feet away, each about fifty feet in diameter.

Sallie had the bag in his hand filled with my blood-splattered clothes. After carefully eyeballing the street, the sidewalk, the area along the riverbank and Astoria Park behind us, he flung the knife into the center of the nearest whirlpool.

Rocco pulled the gun Sallie had given me out of the bag and showed it to him. They each let out a short chuckle. Then, like an outfielder throwing home, Rocco hurled the gun into the outer rim of the farthest whirlpool I could see.

Rocco was breathing hard as we walked back to the car.

He directed the driver to take us home—to my home—to Long Island. The Malibu, as if in tow, was directly behind us.

We drove along the Belt Parkway and past Howard Beach. Long Island and the Southern State Parkway were ten minutes away. The emotional numbness had worn off and I welcomed the ache in my left arm and neck— a reminder that I was the one still alive.

I passed my fingers over the left side of my head. A lump was there the size of a walnut from Guevara's last blow.

"What made you guys come after me?" I asked.

Sallie turned and hung his heavy arm over the back of the front seat. "When I mentioned to your uncle that you had taken the silencer, it tipped him off. And when you weren't home when he called at a quarter-to-two in the morning, he suddenly got this urge to run up to The Bronx. I thought he was crazy." Sallie looked apologetically at Rocco, then smiled as he said to me poignantly: "He's been walking around with that bum's pedigree since you gave it him. Rocco Alonzo may be many things, but crazy he's not."

Without turning around, Sallie added, "And Nickie? Next time you go to shoot somebody, make sure you take the safety off the gun first."

11:00 A.M. Sunday morning. I awoke achy and bruised, but rested. After a light breakfast and a hot shower, I joined Mom for 12:45 mass.

She was happy I did. I was happy I did also.

Receiving Holy Communion felt like a cleansing. Absolution though wouldn't come until years later—until chapter and verse of my very own *confession.*

When I got home, I packed one small fat suitcase to capacity and called a taxi to take me to JFK Airport, where I bought a first-class round-trip ticket with an open return.

Flight 125 was scheduled to arrive at Hartsfield Airport, Atlanta, out of warm clear skies at 5:00 P.M. sharp.

And it did. And on time.

EPILOGUE

E leanor and I spoke about Guevara's murder only once, on a day when it seemed nothing could go wrong—a beautiful day—the day I arrived in Atlanta.

We walked where I had walked with Carolyn, by a fountain in the rear yard along a cobblestone path.

Eleanor listened and I told her everything.

At first she was angry, then afraid. Finally she understood, and forgave.

I told her all about Uncle Rocco. But I had underestimated her. She had been suspicious long before. And what she hadn't pieced together from the files at the Manhattan D.A.'s Office, her father told her. He must have paid an investigative firm handsomely because he knew more about Rocco and me than either one of us could possibly remember or know about the other. Surprisingly, I wasn't offended. It meant he took me seriously. He also did me a valuable service—he discovered there was nothing more between my uncle and me than the commingling of blood and an affection, he candidly told Eleanor, he could not measure.

And although our fates had entwined for one dark moment, Rocco had his life, and I had mine. But Eleanor had that all figured out already.

Upon my return from Atlanta, I submitted my resignation to Sheila with every intention of leaving the practice of criminal law forever behind me.

Eleanor never returned to her apartment. Her clothes and personal effects were packed and shipped to Atlanta. Everything else, furniture and the like, were thrown away or given to charity. She never quite got over the loss of her good friend.

Rocco told Sallie all about Carolyn's murder, omitting none of the details. Sallie listened, flashed back to 1955, and was sickened. When he heard that Ernest Leskey had finally surfaced after twenty-seven years, he insisted that he be allowed to "handle the matter."

Two weeks after Guevara's death, a conflagration occurred at 6 Daisy Place in the Country Club Estates section of The Bronx. The house was leveled by a raging fire after one prodigious explosion that completely engulfed it in a cone of flames. Miraculously, the Jamaican nurse escaped unharmed.

Terkel was found the next day, face down, his charred and blackened body floating in the bay behind his house. Dead. Finally dead.

The fire marshal ruled the incident an arson of unknown origin, design and motive. *Case closed.* The following winter, this same fire marshal, along with his entire family, vacationed in Costa Del Sol for a month—his wife having become the benefactor of a small inheritance from a gone, but not to be forgotten, distant Family member.

The body of Peter Guevara, in blackface, belly down in a puddle of blood, was discovered by police from the 50th Precinct just fifteen minutes after Rocco, Sallie and I left the building on University Avenue. Detectives arrived minutes after two uniformed patrol officers responded to an anonymous 911 call. Krebs was one of the detectives. He identified Guevara immediately, pulled off the black skullcap, and made the Spiderman connection. Aside, however, from black camouflage cream found in a dresser drawer inside the apartment, there was no other proof linking Guevara to the serial rapes, and murder of the Brooklyn cop's ex-wife and baby.

Three-and-a-half weeks later, a team of New York City sewer workers responded to a complaint of a blockage in the main line leading from the street to the apartment building on University Avenue. When the line was determined to be clear, a city employee went into the basement of the building and found under the main sewer cap a stone-laden plastic bag held in place by a wrap of white twine, the end of which dangled outside the screwed on cover. Inside the bag were seven pairs of women's underwear. Five were later identified as belonging to Spiderman victims. The other two were of unknown origin, no doubt owned by women who, for whatever reason, failed to report the crimes (or worse, whose bodies were never found).

That the Spiderman had taken the panties of each victim was intentionally kept secret from the press and the public by The Bronx detectives working the case. It was a secret they shared only with the serial rapist. When they found the undergarments, or got a confession that included their mention, they'd know they had their man.

Soon after the grim discovery The Bronx D.A.'s Office was forced to reopen the case and provide a sample from the dead baby's fingernail of the black unknown substance Paul Ventura had told me about. The cream found in Guevara's dresser drawer proved a perfect match.

The case of the Spiderman rapist and murderer was then, finally, and rightfully, closed.

Every newspaper, news and TV talk show ran the story. But only Vinny Repolla, in the magazine section of *Newsday's Sunday Edition*, wrote of the tragedy of Oscar Jefferson.

Toward finding the killer(s) of the Spiderman, a/k/a Peter Guevara, there was but one solid lead: an elderly cantankerous black woman, who said she got a good look at "three white guys" leaving the building shortly after a shot rang out. This lead quickly fizzled, however, with the memory of the lone witness.

So ended the less-than-enthusiastic investigation into the shooting death of the killer of a city cop's ex-wife and infant baby girl.

War never broke out amid the reigning *capos* in New York after Capezzi's death. Rocco, as expected, was passed over at Capezzi's dying command in favor of the Staten Island mafioso businessman and cousin of Capezzi. This new leader, though, would not last long. A younger faction of the mob led by a protégé of Rocco's would see to that—soon after Rocco was gone.

One month before Eleanor and I were to be married, Rocco Alonzo suffered a massive heart attack and died in the emergency room of Brooklyn's Kings County Hospital. I arrived just in time to look him in the eyes, squeeze his hand gently and kiss him goodbye. Sallie was there too, and cried when Rocco died like I had never seen another man do before or since. I stayed close to Mom at the wake as she too wept profusely at the beginning and end of each service.

Brooklyn's infamous underboss—my loving uncle, was finally laid to rest in a mausoleum at Saint John's Cemetery in Middle Village, Queens. Eleanor was in Atlanta at the time and wanted to attend the funeral. Fearing media coverage that never came, she reluctantly complied when I asked her not to.

In a will that professed a love for me as he would have only for a son, I was bequeathed eighteen mortgage-free apartment buildings. All owned by Rocco. All scattered throughout Brooklyn. And so, in the final break of a heartbeat, I was laden with an annual net income of over $1.2 million and a net worth in excess of nine.

On a Saturday in mid-December 1982, Eleanor and I were married at Curé of Ars Church in Merrick. My mother's choice. Over three hundred people attended a reception held at The Garden City Hotel, two-thirds of whom had flown in from Georgia and every state in the union it seemed. All the guestrooms were filled. Even former President Jimmy Carter, a close personal friend of Eleanor's father, attended with his wife Rosalynn. But despite the presence of the rich, the famous, and the politically connected, the night was ours—Eleanor's and mine.

Joey came with a date, Vinny Repolla with his fiancée, and Mom, who never stopped dancing, was even caught on film doing the *tarantella* with our former President who, without warning, was swept away by Mom's abounding energy.

Joey was my best man and when the time came, offered up a brief but poignant toast. I responded with one of my own, professing my undying love for my bride, tearfully thanking Mom for the wonder of life, and asking for a moment of silence for the late John Mannino.

I closed with a prayer to a chair, left empty at Table Two, in memory of Rocco Alonzo.

* * *

On the morning of my wedding day, alone in my kitchen, I stared out onto the empty baseball fields off in the distance, behind the backyard, the cold, hardened grass glistening with frost and the pretense of new life in the December sun.

I thought long and hard—about Rocco's life, my mother's and mine; about the infinite possibilities and how the succession of real events brought me to that day.

And I could make no sense of it.

But now, after so many years with Eleanor, the message is an easy read.

I just have to look into our own children's wide eyes for that special place where hearts turn, swell joyously, and beat on, long after…

A NOTE OF THANKS: *To all the readers from all over the world who made* The Good Lawyer *a bestseller. I am deeply grateful for your support of this, my first novel. I have read every one of your reviews and Facebook comments. I certainly hope you enjoy my new novel previewed below. Please know that without your support and praise it could not have been written.* T. B.

Please feel free to check out The Good Lawyer Page on Facebook at www.facebook.com/TheGoodLawyer and become a Fan or just post your thoughts. You may also contact the author by emailing to tombenigno@ aol.com for book club talks in-person or via skype or Google video and discover the true story behind The Good Lawyer (in as much as can be revealed without violating attorney/client privilege), or to just to share your thoughts about The Good Lawyer with the author. Twitter @thomasbenigno. All communications are welcome.

ABOUT THE AUTHOR

Thomas Benigno is a practicing attorney on Long Island, N.Y. As an actor, he has appeared in many regional productions. As investor, he was involved in bringing to the Broadway and London stages *Hairspray, Young Frankenstein, American Idiot, Sweeney Todd, Company, Porgy and Bess*, and others. He was producer of the Broadway show, *Burn the Floor*, and its U.S. tour. As a young lawyer with Bronx Legal Aid, Thomas Benigno never lost a trial. *THE GOOD LAWYER* is a novel inspired by real events while working there.

The Criminal Lawyer
A new novel by Thomas Benigno
AVAILABLE NOW ON AMAZON!
AMAZON PAPERBACK LINK http://amzn.to/2c33wbc
AMAZON KINDLE LINK http://amzn.to/2bWqptg
Continue the story of Nick Mannino many years later…

It was the perfect day and the perfect place...

He parked his green sun-bleached van on the shoulder alongside the dune. Standing beside the tall mound of sand speckled with beach grass, he had yet to see or hear another car pass on the road behind him.

Amid a warm and oddly soothing June wind, he turned to face north and the bay—a mirror of tranquillity. The faint hum of a crossing motorboat was testament to the resolute serenity of this beautiful day.

He took a long deep breath, looked up at the sky, and smiled. A resplendent sun shone beside a lone white cloud, and as far as his eyes could see, he was alone, but for the man sitting high on the dune, staring blankly at the ocean.

It was late afternoon. The crowd had thinned. Soaking up what remained of the sun, a few leather-skinned seniors lay face up on their recliners. Two teenagers threw a Frisbee. Others played volleyball. Parents gathered together blankets, towels and chairs while struggling to corral their small children into leaving.

In an hour or two, this quarter mile stretch between the dune and the ocean would be nearly desolate, but come morning, it would begin to populate, as ever, once again.

Because the beach is winsome, and seductive, and therapeutic.

There is no cause for worry and fear in the pure and uncomplicated world of sun, wind, and water.

As he pivoted and stepped back down, only the fleeting movement of a shadow marked his presence to the man who remained sitting on the dune, and seemed to pay him no mind.

Walking quickly past his van he looked both ways before crossing the two-lane roadway aptly named Ocean Parkway. After twenty precise steps, and in the marsh up to his knees, he paused to study the small stretch of wetland where the stalks spread thin then disappeared into the encroaching bay. Turning around again toward the ocean, he looked up and across in an attempt to decipher the precise distance between the parkway lamps and the limits of its cones of light in the dead of night.

This would be his last visit, his only visit, in the bold brightness of day. One last breath, one last taste and smell of the salty air, and he would be gone, never to return in the light, but more certain than he had ever been.

This area so close, yet so secluded was, bar none, the perfect place to leave the bodies.

Chapter 1

T ragedy, like a derailed freight train, did not discriminate on its errant path of ruin.

Desmond Lewis was a fifty-two year old black man.

We had much in common.

Born in the same month and year, July, 1954, we were each happily married for over twenty years (or at least *I* thought I was), with two children to show for it, a boy, and a girl.

We were also hard working to a fault, and much too proud for our own good.

It was a hot summer night in June of 2005, when Desmond's son attended a party in his hometown of Valley Stream, Long Island. The boy was seventeen, and had been dating a girl from his high school. She was white and Italian American. It was his first serious relationship. It wasn't hers. She broke it off a week before the party. They had been the only interracial couple at their school.

On the evening that would forever change the Lewis family's life, and all those involved, Desmond's son and his former girlfriend found themselves at that same party. She had moved on. He hadn't. She was there with her new boyfriend, also white and Italian-American.

A beer keg in the living room and an unknown quantity of secluded hard liquor fuelled the fires of discontent. Words were exchanged, and a fight broke out between the two boys. The new boyfriend got the worst of it. Bruised, beaten, and worse, embarrassed, he left the party.

At 3 AM, there was a pounding on the Lewis' front door. It woke the entire family.

Desmond Lewis was scheduled to be at work at 8 AM. He was a supervisor for the Long Island Power Authority and had just clocked in twenty-five years on the job, while his wife worked nearly as long as an elementary school teacher. They planned to retire after the kids graduated college. They would travel and see the world. They earned it. They deserved it. They raised two good kids, a son and a daughter who attended the Marrionist run parochial High School just fifteen minutes from their home.

The Lewis' were also keenly aware that black families like theirs were still a minority in Valley Stream, though the neighborhood was becoming more racially diverse with each passing year. A proud and God-fearing man, every Sunday morning at 8:45 AM sharp, Desmond would drive his wife and two children to Sunday Mass at the Blessed Sacrament Church nearby. He was a member of the Holy Trinity Society. His wife volunteered at every church function. To all eyes and ears, their family was well liked and respected. So when Desmond peeked out his bedroom window and into the darkness of that hot summer night, and saw four high school boys on his front lawn, he was as surprised as he was frightened. The boys, members of the same lacrosse team, were screaming and shouting racial epithets.

Desmond immediately told his wife to stay put and grabbed his deer rifle. She called the police the second he left the room.

Less than a minute later, the new boyfriend was lying on that same front lawn, shot dead, a baseball bat by his side.

The Nassau County District Attorney's Office charged Desmond with second-degree murder. The incident occurred in 2005. Jury selection began in 2006, a year later.

After a gruelling one-month trial, wherein I lost over fifteen pounds and called twenty-five character witnesses, mostly white neighbors and co-workers, I delivered a two-hour summation to an all-white jury that ended in tears—mine and the jury's.

Five days later, after the foreman complained three times that the panel was deadlocked, and three times the judge sent the jury back to continue deliberating, a verdict was reached. Desmond stood in stoic silence while it was read aloud on another hot June night, only this one was rattled by a thunderstorm that lasted until daybreak.

I collapsed into my chair when the jury convicted him of second-degree manslaughter. As for Desmond, he just nodded to the jurors, and then consoled me with thanks and praise for the "fine defense work" I had done.

In retrospect, it is as clear to me now as it was then that I was not trying a case in the Jim Crow South, and that my client should have never left the house until the police arrived even if he had to barricade himself inside.

When Desmond took the stand, he held up well during cross-examination by the head of the felony division of the Nassau County DAs Office. Evidence corroborated his testimony that his front door had been kicked and punched so hard, the deadbolt broke away part of the doorframe. Desmond also testified that all four boys surrounded him once he went outside, that he feared for his life, and fired his rifle only when the one boy—the new boyfriend, swung a bat at the air between them. The bullet pierced the boy's aorta and killed him instantly. Like Desmond's son, the boy was seventeen.

When I saw several jurors with tears in their eyes just before the verdict was read, I knew what was coming. They just couldn't reconcile my client leaving his home with a rifle in his hands. It also didn't help that the victim was a high school student, screaming drunk or not, but not previously known to act in a threatening or racist manner. The boy's father, like Desmond, had worked one job his whole life. The boy's mother was also a schoolteacher.

It didn't matter that the police took six minutes to arrive, and that in those six minutes, I argued, everyone in the house could've been beaten to death, especially his son, the attackers' prime target.

Desmond was sentenced to three years in state prison. He refused to allow me to ask for bail pending appeal, or to appeal the conviction at all. My primary ground would have been the DA's uniform exclusion of every prospective black juror on the panel, while I used up my peremptory challenges excluding every apparent racist I suspected.

Desmond, who also believed he should never have left the house, was grief stricken over the death of the boy. The appeal would have taken years. He wanted this tragedy behind him and his family as soon as possible. He was released from prison after serving less than twenty-four months.

I took no fee for Desmond's defense. After the conviction and sentence, I paid off the mortgage on his house so his wife and their two children could afford to live there on just her schoolteacher salary.

My client was furious with me for doing so. I told him it was my Uncle Rocco's mob money. He thought I was joking, and laughed. I told him I wasn't, and he stopped laughing.

As for me, the case was over. I had lost, and as a result, was impossible to live with.

The Criminal Lawyer
Available Now!
AMAZON KINDLE LINK: http://amzn.to/2bWqptg

The Criminal Mind
Available Now!
AMAZON KINDLE LINK: https://amzn.to/3kBI65L

Made in the USA
Monee, IL
19 June 2024

43d7c84b-a8b0-4064-826f-fa601eedbd1dR01